Double Cross

Double Cross

A NOVEL

BETSY BRANNON GREEN

Covenant

Covenant Communications, Inc.

Cover image © Photodisc/Getty Images, Inc.

Cover design copyrighted 2006 by Covenant Communications, Inc.

Published by Covenant Communications, Inc.
American Fork, Utah

Printed in the United States of America
First Printing: May 2006

12 11 10 09 08 07 06   10 9 8 7 6 5 4 3 2

ISBN 1-59811-105-1

To Andy—
Slow but sure,
Witty and wise,
One in a million.

ACKNOWLEDGMENTS

Thanks first to Butch. He's *still* my romantic interest, and he gave me the idea for this book. I also appreciate all the love and support I get from my children, extended family, friends, and faithful readers. A special thanks to my brother, James Brannon, who speaks Spanish and provided free editorial services for this manuscript. And as always, I owe a huge debt of gratitude to the wonderful people at Covenant who do so much behind the scenes to help me put my best foot forward.

PROLOGUE

Solana looked across the table at Emilio. His brow was furrowed, and his dark brown eyes were concentrating on the chess board that separated them.

"It doesn't really matter what move you make," she told him with a smile. "I'm going to win."

He didn't look up but nodded slightly in acknowledgment of this fact. "I feel it is my duty to challenge you as much as possible."

She sighed and relaxed against the back of her chair. Emilio had never played a game of chess until he had been assigned to be her bodyguard, but he was a quick learner and she was a good teacher. She still always beat him, but the games were increasingly interesting. And even if they had been dull, she would have continued to insist on a match each evening. He was so adorable that just watching him was a pleasure.

He pursed his soft, sensitive lips then stretched out a hand and picked up his last remaining bishop. Solana loved his hands. They were strong and used to working hard—yet they could be so gentle. Emilio placed his bishop on a square, and Solana surveyed the board quickly. She could have him in checkmate with three moves or she could stretch the game out—the choice was hers.

Leaning forward on her elbows, she whispered, "What would you do if I kissed you right now?"

A blush darkened Emilio's handsome features as he looked over to see if the other occupants of the room had heard her question. "Please, Solana," he begged. "Don't be reckless."

She moved her queen, deciding to go in for the quick kill. "I won't mention kissing again if you'll make me a promise."

He moved a pawn without thought—concentrating on her words rather than strategy. Perhaps he realized that the game was over. "What?" he asked with a trace of desperation in his voice.

"You will meet me at midnight in the garden."

Emilio ran his fingers through his thick, curling hair. Whether he was considering her offer or controlling exasperation, she couldn't tell. Finally he shook his head. "It is too dangerous."

"Very well." She stood and moved around the table. "You leave me no choice." She puckered her own soft, sensitive lips.

"Okay!" he capitulated in a strangled whisper. "Midnight."

She smiled. "Don't be late."

"Is something the matter?" her father asked from across the room where he was consulting with the head of his private army, General Hector Vargas.

Solana hated Vargas as much as she loved Emilio, so she carefully ignored him as she replied to her father. "No, everything's fine. I've just beaten Emilio again."

Her father checked his watch. "It took you longer than usual tonight."

"I was toying with him," Solana replied and smiled at the tortured expression on Emilio's face. "And now I'm tired. I think I'll go to bed early." She yawned exaggeratedly, knowing this too would make Emilio squirm.

Her father looked at Emilio and then at his daughter. Finally he said, "Sleep well."

With a wave, Solana flounced out and climbed the stairs to her room.

The hours seemed to crawl by, but finally midnight arrived. Solana dressed in a pair of black jeans and a dark turtleneck shirt for her rendezvous with Emilio. Then she stood in front of the full-length mirror and studied her reflection. Her straight brown hair was pulled into a ponytail, accentuating her high cheekbones and flawless complexion. Anticipation caused her hazel eyes to shine, and she couldn't keep her full lips from smiling. *I look like a happy cat burglar,* she thought to herself as she turned off the light in her room.

After checking the hallway to be sure the coast was clear, she slipped out and hurried to the service stairway. A few minutes later, she stepped outside into the warm night air.

With Emilio nowhere in sight, she moved along a cobblestone pathway toward their favorite bench in the rose section of her father's garden.

Suddenly a hand shot out and covered her mouth, successfully silencing the scream that came involuntarily to her lips. Solana was hauled roughly off the path and into a copse of fruit trees. Her back was pressed firmly against her captor. Reaching up, she touched the hand that covered her mouth. Then she relaxed. She'd know those strong, hard-working fingers anywhere.

Emilio loosened his grip, and she turned in his embrace. She threw her arms around his neck and pressed her lips to his. After a few heated seconds, he pulled back.

"This is insanity," Emilio whispered. "Your father will find out and will kill me."

Solana laughed as she placed a series of quick kisses along his jawline. "My father won't kill you," she replied. "I won't let him."

"You don't *know* him," Emilio returned. "I'd be dead and thrown out for the vultures to feast on before you even knew what happened. General Vargas would see to that."

Solana sobered. Her father she could manage to a certain extent. Vargas was another matter. "That is why we must leave. If you will let me talk to my father . . ."

Emilio shook his head vigorously. "The risk is too great. I won't put you in danger."

Solana nuzzled the soft skin of his neck. "Let's not waste our time together talking of sad things." She pulled his mouth to meet hers. "Kiss me instead."

With a sigh of resignation, he complied.

CHAPTER 1

Kate Iverson was startled awake from a vivid dream by the ringing of the phone. She blinked once then squinted at the clock. It was 3:30 AM. Her husband, Mark, propped himself up on one elbow and switched on the lamp beside the bed.

"Who could that be at this hour?" Kate murmured as she pushed a strand of dark blonde hair from her eyes.

Mark checked the caller ID and grimaced. "FBI field office in Atlanta," he told her. Then he reached for the phone. "Iverson," he said briefly.

"Mark!" The single word boomed so loudly that Kate could hear it. She recognized the voice of Mark's supervisor, Dan Davis. He was not one of Kate's favorite people, and she frowned. "We've got a situation up here and need your help," Dan continued at a deafening volume. "Leave ASAP, and when you get close, call me on my cell phone for further directions."

"You want me to leave now?" Mark confirmed.

"Immediately, if not sooner," Dan bellowed.

"I'll call you in a couple of hours," Mark replied. Then he hung up the phone without saying good-bye.

"Dan wants you to go to Atlanta now?" Kate asked, hoping she had misunderstood.

"Yes." Mark swung his legs over the side of the bed and stood.

A knot of anxiety began to form in her stomach. "Is it something bad?"

"Dan didn't explain, just said there was a 'situation' and that they needed me right away." He leaned down and kissed her forehead. "I'm going to take a quick shower. You try and go back to sleep."

Kate knew that sleep was no longer an option. For the next three hours, she would be awake worrying while Mark was driving the dark roads to Atlanta. Once she knew he had arrived safely, she would worry about the trouble he found when he got there. With a sigh, she made the bed and then laid out clean clothes for Mark.

When he emerged from the bathroom, he smiled and said, "You're getting up a little early today, aren't you?"

She nodded. "It looks that way." She sat on the edge of the bed while he dressed, combed his hair, and double-checked his briefcase. When he was ready to go, she followed him downstairs. "Do you have time for me to make you some pancakes?"

He shook his head. "No, Dan said to hurry."

"How about a granola bar?" she offered in a pitiful attempt to delay his departure.

Mark shrugged into his suit coat. "I'm not hungry, Kate. But thanks anyway."

She accepted defeat. "Well, don't speed," she instructed, reaching up to straighten his tie. "Whatever problem Dan has, it will wait long enough for you to get there safely."

He gave her a sweet, lingering kiss before picking up his briefcase and moving toward the back door. "I'll call you as soon as I know what's going on."

* * *

When Mark reached the outskirts of Atlanta, he called Dan's cell phone. His supervisor sounded pleased when he answered.

"You made good time," Dan commended him. Then he gave Mark directions to a warehouse on Market Street. "You can't miss it," Dan assured him.

Mark was annoyed that his supervisor was still being so close-mouthed about the reason for this middle-of-the-night trip to Atlanta. "Can you give me a little hint as to what this is all about?" he asked.

"Nope," Dan replied cheerfully. "You've got to see it to believe it."

Mark followed Dan's directions and arrived at the warehouse a few minutes past six thirty. As Dan had predicted, it was easy to identify the particular warehouse in question. Police cars with lights flashing were positioned around the building, spectators were huddled behind yellow crime tape, and FBI vans were backed up to the loading docks. Mark drove in as close as possible then double parked his Bureau car. He was required to show his badge several times before he was finally permitted to enter the warehouse. All around him pandemonium prevailed.

"Mark!"

He turned toward the voice and saw Dan talking to a man wearing an FBI T-shirt. "This is Agent Faust," Dan introduced as Mark joined them.

Mark shook hands with the other agent. "What's going on here?"

"Yesterday afternoon we got a call from the district attorney's office," Dan explained. "They had a repeat offender trying to plead out who claimed to know the location of a huge child pornography operation. We told them to take the deal and got a search warrant for this old warehouse. Our guys came in around midnight, and it turned out to be a gold mine. It's kind of a one-stop shop."

Mark surveyed his surroundings. The construction of the building itself looked unsound, and the posters on the walls were extremely offensive. There was an unpleasant smell, and the dim lighting gave the whole place a feeling of doom.

"We've confiscated truckloads of videos and DVDs, arrested their actors, and seized their books. We even got mailing lists."

"It's funny how it works that way sometimes," Agent Faust mused. "You can work for months and never get anything. Then something like this falls into your lap."

Mark wanted to get out of the warehouse. It felt like the evil that had been perpetrated in the place was staining him permanently. "What am *I* doing here?" Mark asked. "And when can I leave?"

Dan smiled. "You've been brought in for your accounting abilities."

"Great," Mark said without enthusiasm.

"Follow me," Agent Faust instructed.

Mark obeyed reluctantly. Near the back of the warehouse they reached a small office, and Agent Faust led them through it to a wall vault. The heavy door was propped open, and inside, Mark could see four large suitcases stacked in a neat row. Faust unzipped one of the cases to reveal stacks of hundred dollar bills. "All four of them are jam-packed full of cash. We haven't had time to do an exact count, but our preliminary estimate is about twelve million dollars."

Mark was surprised. "That's an incredible amount of money to keep in a place like this."

"Based on a quick look at the books, we figure it's probably six months' worth of sales," Agent Faust told them. "The bookkeeper says they were told a few days ago to prepare the cash for pickup. So it looks like we got here just in time." Faust rezipped the suitcase and addressed Mark. "You're supposed to take the money to the field office where you can count it, compare it to the books, and catalog it all so it can be presented as evidence in various trials."

Mark sighed. His degree in accounting had doomed him once again to a job of boredom and drudgery.

Dan walked over and hefted two of the cases. "Man, these weigh a ton."

Faust laughed. "Whoever said crime doesn't pay was a liar." He handed Mark an account ledger, then pulled out a clipboard. "I need to get someone to sign for this."

Dan nodded toward Mark. "I've got my hands full."

Mark signed the form on the line Agent Faust indicated. Then he tucked the ledger under his arm and picked up the two remaining suitcases.

"I've arranged for a couple of police cars to escort you back to the field office," Agent Faust said as he led them back through the warehouse. "We wouldn't want anything to happen to all that money," he added with a smile over his shoulder.

When they stepped out of the warehouse, a newspaper reporter accosted them.

"What's going on here?" he asked. "Is this a drug bust?"

"No comment," Agent Faust replied.

The reporter pulled a small digital camera from his pocket. "Well, can I at least take your picture so when I find out what's happening, I'll have one for my story?"

Agent Faust shrugged. "Sure, why not?" He rested one arm around Dan's shoulder and his other around Mark's. "A little good press won't hurt my career," Agent Faust said as the camera flashed.

Mark and Dan lugged the heavy suitcases filled with money back to Mark's Bureau car and found two Atlanta police officers waiting for them. After they stowed the suitcases in the trunk, Dan said, "You guys follow Agent Iverson to the FBI field office. One squad car in front, the other behind."

Both of the policemen nodded and moved toward their vehicles.

"I'm right over here." Dan pointed to a similar sedan a block down. "I'll catch up." He took off at a trot.

Mark climbed into the front seat, locked all his doors, and waited for the first police car to pull out. Then he eased away from the curb and followed the flashing lights in front of him toward downtown Atlanta.

* * *

When Mark reached the field office, he waved to the policemen and pulled into the parking deck. He was deciding where to park when his cell phone rang. It was Dan.

"Drive around back to the loading dock. I'll park and then come and help you bring the suitcases in. And I don't guess I have to remind you to keep your doors locked," Dan added. "You have a lot of money in your trunk."

"You don't have to remind me," Mark said. He did as he was instructed and only had to wait a few minutes beside the loading dock before Dan emerged from the back of the building. Mark got out of the car and unlocked the trunk. After they each lifted two of the suitcases out, Mark asked, "Do I need to move my car?"

"Just leave it here for now," Dan said. "Once we get this money secured, you can come back and park in one of the visitor spaces."

They carried the suitcases inside, rode a service elevator to the fourth floor, and then Dan led the way through a series of deserted workstations to his office. He got a call on his cell phone as he was unlocking the door that bore his name. After exchanging a few words, he closed the phone.

"Change of plans," he told Mark. "There's a meeting that the special agent in charge wants us to attend. You're to bring one suitcase with you." Dan motioned toward the smaller of the two cases Mark carried. "We'll lock the other three in here."

Mark had only met the special agent in charge of the Atlanta Division once—under unpleasant circumstances—and he wasn't anxious to repeat the experience. "Maybe you could go to the meeting while I stay here and count money."

Dan smiled as he placed the suitcases he was holding inside the office. "No way. The SAC specifically requested your presence."

Mark deposited one of the suitcases he was carrying in Dan's office and watched as his supervisor locked the door. Then he lifted the remaining suitcase and followed Dan down the hall. After several turns, they stopped at the door to a small amphitheater, with rows of chairs descending toward a stage dominated by a podium and wall-mounted movie screen. Milling around the room were about fifteen men. Like Mark, they all had brown hair and brown eyes. *Unlike* Mark, they were all wearing uniforms identifying them as members of the armed forces. Mark expected Dan to say he had mistakenly chosen the wrong room. Instead Dan stepped inside and gestured for Mark to do the same.

Dan moved to a group of men gathered against the far wall. He pointed at the SAC and said to Mark, "You remember Mr. Mitchell?"

During their last encounter, Frank Mitchell had accused Mark of everything from incompetence to criminal misconduct. It was unlikely that Mark would ever forget him. Mark shifted the heavy suitcase into his left hand and held his right out to Mr. Mitchell. "Of course."

The SAC gave Mark's palm one firm shake before releasing it. "Thanks for coming," he said as if Mark had been given a choice in the matter. Then he turned to the men standing beside him. "We're all here. Let's get the preliminaries over with."

The men moved down the aisle and formed a little semicircle behind Mr. Mitchell as he stepped up to the podium and addressed the occupants of the room. "We're ready to start now. Take your seats, please."

This assemblage was in the habit of following orders. All conversation ceased, and the empty chairs were quickly filled by the uniformed men. Dan and Mark took seats on the back row. While waiting for Mr. Mitchell to begin the meeting, Mark saw the SAC signal to a marine who seemed to be guarding a door on the far side of the room. The marine nodded and then disappeared through the door.

"Before I get to the purpose for your presence here today, I'd like to make some introductions." Mr. Mitchell pointed to one of the men standing behind him. "This is Captain Steven Croyle of the 22nd Marine Expeditionary Unit." The captain had the severe flattop and rigid bearing particular to people who choose the military as their career. He was wearing a camouflage flight suit as if he'd been plucked off of an aircraft carrier minutes earlier. Captain Croyle inclined his head toward the group in acknowledgment, and Mr. Mitchell moved down the line.

"This is Howard Bowen, assistant special agent in charge of this field office with responsibility for South American ops." Mark had never met Bowen but knew he had a reputation for being hard-nosed and uncompromising.

Bowen nodded briefly as the SAC pointed to the last man in their group. "And this is Mr. Bowen's right-hand man, Agent Angelo Perez. He is an expert on South America, particularly Colombia."

Agent Perez gave a friendly wave, drawing a few chuckles from the group. Perez looked like a nice guy who didn't take himself too seriously, but the fact that he was Howard Bowen's right-hand man made Mark a little wary.

The SAC reclaimed everyone's attention by announcing, "A situation has arisen that requires creating a special task force. You have all been handpicked because of your unique abilities. Mr. Bowen will supervise the operation. Agent Perez will accompany you and physically run the operation. Captain Croyle and the 22nd Marine Expeditionary Unit will transport you and will provide support for the duration of your mission."

Mark looked at Dan. "I thought this meeting was about the pornography ring," he whispered.

Dan pointed at the SAC. "Listen."

"The creation of this task force falls under the heading of covert operations," the SAC continued. "Secrecy is vital, and each of you will be given information on a need-to-know basis only. You are forbidden to confer with each other regarding your individual assignments. This is necessary for your own safety and for the overall success of the operation."

The door on the far side of the room reopened, and the marine who had left a few minutes before stepped back inside. He was followed by a very attractive woman wearing a conservative gray suit. Her startlingly blue eyes were downcast, and her light blonde hair was pulled demurely back into a neat bun. But these apparent attempts to minimize her beauty were unsuccessful. Mark heard murmurings of approval from the men around him as the woman crossed the room to stand beside Mr. Mitchell.

"This is Britta Andersen," Mitchell told them. "She is the daughter of the former Swedish ambassador to Colombia."

The woman nodded to the room in general. "Hello," she said in slightly accented English.

"Twenty years ago, while living with her parents in Bogotá, Ms. Andersen had a brief romantic relationship with Rodrigo Salazar. For those of you who are unfamiliar with Salazar, I'll give you a quick lesson on the Colombian drug trade."

Mr. Mitchell pressed a button on a laptop arranged on the podium, and a man's image filled the screen on the wall. The man was handsome, in his forties, and dressed in a business suit. "When Ms. Andersen met Salazar, he was just a spoiled rich kid fresh out of college. Shortly thereafter he inherited his father's drug empire, forcing Ms. Andersen to sever ties with him."

A new picture, of a younger Salazar wearing military fatigues, flashed onto the screen. "Salazar was a reservist in the Colombian military for several years, which is where he met Hector Vargas, the psychopath who runs his paid army.

"Salazar used what he learned in college and the military to make some changes in the way his father's business was operated. He also created a few legitimate companies, which gave his government the excuse they needed to overlook his illegal activities. He brought in computers, so his organization could monitor inventory, track sales, and schedule shipments very efficiently. And, with the help of Vargas and a well-trained, well-disciplined army of mercenaries, he eliminated the competition and expanded his territory. He now controls all the drug traffic in the entire northern half of Colombia."

A picture of Salazar wearing a tuxedo at a social gathering filled the screen. "Despite his charming exterior, Rodrigo Salazar is personally responsible for dumping tons of illegal drugs into the United States. He has been on the FBI's Most Wanted List for many years, but since he rarely leaves his home in La Rosa, Colombia, we have very little opportunity to capture him.

"Rodrigo Salazar is a murderer," Mr. Mitchell summed up. "He's greedy, and he's a thief. But he's also the father of Ms. Andersen's only daughter, Solana."

There were more murmurings from the soldiers as the SAC continued. "Two months ago Ms. Andersen received an e-mail from her daughter saying that she was leaving college and going to visit her father."

Britta Andersen took up the dialogue. "She had never met him. I told her about him, of course, but as he never made any attempt to contact us or to interfere with our lives, I naively assumed he had forgotten, or at least had lost interest. Solana would ask me about him occasionally, and sometimes I would see her looking for information about him on the Internet. I guess it is only natural that she would be curious."

Ms. Andersen bit her lower lip. "But apparently Rodrigo was just biding his time. Somehow he made contact with Solana and convinced her to come to La Rosa for a 'visit.'"

Mr. Mitchell pushed a button on the laptop again, and the picture of Salazar in formal wear was replaced by a state-of-the-art compound with a series of outer walls, guard towers, and satellite equipment. In the center was a beautiful house built in traditional Spanish style with stucco walls and a red tile roof. Behind the house, and surrounded by yet another wall, was a garden, a swimming pool, two tennis courts, and what looked like a driving range.

"This is a satellite surveillance photograph of Salazar's home near the city of La Rosa," Mitchell told them. "It's private, luxurious, and—short of using the nuclear option—completely impenetrable. We have reason to believe that Solana is being held here against her will."

In the next picture, Salazar was dressed casually. He was standing in front of a huge stone fireplace, and he had his arm draped around the shoulders of a beautiful teenage girl. Solana was an exotic blend of her attractive parents. She was taller than her mother, thin with sun-streaked light brown hair and large hazel eyes.

"This picture was delivered to Ms. Andersen shortly after her disappearance. She believes that Salazar lured the girl to him and now refuses to let her leave. She assumes he intends this picture as an invitation for her to join them—or perhaps it's a challenge for her to try and retrieve the girl."

"I wanted to go immediately," Ms. Andersen told them. "But my father advised against it. He is afraid that if I go into Rodrigo's compound, I will become his prisoner as well. I have had several e-mail communications from Solana. They are all carefully worded, and I am sure that she is supervised when she is allowed to send them. But last week, I received a postcard. It said that Solana was in danger and must leave La Rosa immediately. It also said that her father could not protect her." Ms. Andersen looked over at Frank Mitchell, and he took up the dialogue.

"The postcard was mailed at great personal risk—so we know that the danger to Solana Andersen is serious and imminent. Ms. Andersen's father has requested help from the United States on his granddaughter's behalf. As a matter of diplomatic courtesy, the president has decided to oblige." Mitchell turned to his assistant. "Is there anything you'd like to add, Howard?" The assistant SAC shook his head. Mr. Mitchell looked at his Latin America specialist. "Angelo?"

Agent Perez stepped forward. "I have spent many years studying the South American drug trade in general and Rodrigo Salazar in particular. Salazar is brilliant and dangerous, so outsmarting him will not be easy. In order to retrieve Solana, I have developed a plan that is multifaceted and flexible—which is why I believe it will work. Each of you will be performing an essential part of that plan, and we must be able to count on you completely. If you don't feel you are up to the challenge, tell Captain Croyle privately, so we can find someone else."

Britta Andersen spoke up, "What Agent Perez says is correct. Rodrigo is a dangerous man, and if you choose to help me, you will be risking your life. I think it is important for you to know this before you agree to be a part of this task force."

Mark felt his stomach muscles tighten as images of Kate and the children flashed through his mind. He knew how terrible it was to have a child kidnapped, so he sympathized with Ms. Andersen. But he wasn't sure he was willing to risk his life for her and her daughter.

Mr. Mitchell interrupted his thoughts by saying, "Let me make one thing clear—if you choose to be a part of this task force, you *will* be putting your life at risk. But you won't be doing it as a personal favor to Ms. Andersen. You will be doing it in response to a specific request from the president of the United States, serving your country and fulfilling your duties."

Mark relaxed a little. That did make a difference.

"At this point Captain Croyle is going to assume responsibility for the task force," Mitchell continued. "You will be transported by helicopter to an aircraft carrier, where you will receive the additional training you need for your individual missions."

Captain Croyle moved to the center of the room. "As I call your name, step into the hallway," he instructed the men. Then he referred to a clipboard and read names off a list. Mark's wasn't one of them. "I'll report to you later," Captain Croyle said to Mr. Mitchell.

Mitchell nodded, and Captain Croyle walked out into the hall. Dan stood and moved to a position behind Mark's chair, leaving Mark the only man still sitting in the large room. Mark felt conspicuous. Apparently he was the only non-hero, the only man *not* chosen to serve his country.

"Why didn't I go with Captain Croyle?" Mark whispered over his shoulder to Dan.

"Mr. Mitchell will explain," Dan replied.

"We'll continue this discussion in my office," the SAC said. Since it was more of an instruction than a suggestion, everyone followed him out the door on the far side of the stage and down the long hallway to the executive offices.

With weary resignation, Mark stood, lifted the suitcase full of money, and trudged behind Dan. He saw the lovely Ms. Andersen walking at the head of the group beside Mr. Mitchell. Maybe she needed her checkbook balanced before she returned to Sweden, and Mark had been chosen for the task.

* * *

Solana paced in front of the door of her father's office, her mind searching for the best way to confront him. Finally Salazar eliminated the need for a clever approach by opening the door.

"Come in, Solana," he invited, "before you wear out the carpet."

She gave him a brilliant smile. "I was afraid I'd be interrupting your work."

"I always have time for you," he said pleasantly while returning to his computer.

She resumed her pacing, this time in a semicircle around his desk.

"You seem restless," he commented after several partial rotations.

She came to a stop in front of him. "Yes, that is it exactly. I'm restless. I guess I miss my home and friends and . . . my mother."

"That is natural, I think."

"I was wondering if, well—would it be possible for me to go to Stockholm for a visit?"

"Solana," her father's tone was mildly reproachful. "When you agreed to come, you understood that it would be for six months. You have been here only two, and already you wish to leave me?"

"I don't want to leave you," she said truthfully. Over the past few weeks she had developed quite a fondness for the father she had never known. She smiled and continued with extreme caution. "But I would like to take a holiday. You could come, too. We'd go some place neutral, and maybe Mother could meet us."

The mention of Britta sparked a little interest in Salazar's eyes. "Where?"

She clasped her hands in front of her to keep from fidgeting nervously. "How about Paris or Athens?"

Her father smiled. "You know I can't travel abroad openly."

"Well, Bogotá then," Solana amended. "We could stay in a grand hotel and eat at fine restaurants."

"You have grand accommodations here, and La Rosa has several nice restaurants."

"There's no adventure in going to La Rosa!" she exclaimed. "I've been there many times. I'm anxious to be in a big city again."

When her father said nothing, Solana pressed on.

"If I write Mother and tell her our plans, maybe she'll come." It seemed that her father was not totally opposed to the idea, and Solana was encouraged. "Emilio could drive us and follow me around every-where, just like he does here . . ."

"You are including Emilio in our grand adventure?" her father interrupted. The wistful look was gone, and his eyes had narrowed shrewdly.

Solana lifted her shoulder in what she hoped appeared to be a casual Colombian shrug. "I assumed Emilio would accompany us since you have assigned him to be my bodyguard."

Her father was studying her much too closely. "Is that what he is to you, then? Just a bodyguard?"

"Oh, I suppose he's the closest thing I have to a friend here," Solana admitted. "You don't mind that I have a friend, do you?"

"You must remember yourself, Solana," her father said with rare firmness. "You are my daughter—Emilio is an employee. If you treat him like something more, you risk his position."

Solana tried to ignore the pounding of her heart and abruptly abandoned her attempt at getting away from the compound in La Rosa. Now was the best chance she might ever have to ask for her father's help.

"That is something else I've been meaning to talk to you about," she said boldly. "General Vargas seems to resent the amount of time Emilio spends with me. Perhaps you could speak to him."

Her father shook his head. "I cannot interfere with the general and his men. He must maintain discipline."

Solana stepped closer and lowered her voice. "General Vargas is a cruel man, and I hate him. Why can't you just fire him?"

Her father laughed. "The general is a necessary evil in my world."

Solana crossed her arms over her chest. "Well, if General Vargas must stay, at least remove Emilio from his supervision. Emilio could report to me." She looked up and saw her father's eyebrows rise in astonishment. "Or to you," she amended quickly.

"Impossible," her father said. "To elevate Emilio's position would insult General Vargas and undermine his authority. He would lose the respect of his men."

Solana didn't understand her father or his archaic ways. "It is as if you work for General Vargas instead of the other way around!" she cried recklessly and was immediately contrite. "I'm sorry."

"You are forgiven," Salazar said. "And I will ask for the general's continued patience with Emilio. I will explain that you are lonely, and since Emilio is close to your age, his company helps to pass the time. I expect that General Vargas will honor my request."

Solana realized that this was the best she was likely to get, so she nodded. "Thank you."

"Now, if there is nothing more you need to discuss, perhaps you could go somewhere else. All that walking in circles is making me dizzy."

Solana moved toward the door. "I'm sorry," she said again. As she left the office, her mind was racing again. Emilio was right. Her father would be no protection against Vargas if the truth about their relationship was discovered. They had no choice but to leave her father's compound as soon as possible.

* * *

Kate was awakened at 7:00 AM on Tuesday morning by a particularly loud television commercial. Apparently she had managed to doze off in spite of her concern for Mark and his strange emergency mission to Atlanta.

She pushed herself off the couch and ignored her stiff muscles as she climbed the stairs to rouse the children. While Emily and Charles changed from pajamas into play clothes, Kate brushed her teeth and ran a comb through her hair. Then they all walked together to the kitchen. Before beginning breakfast preparations, Kate checked both the regular phone and her cell phone. There were no messages from Mark on either one.

"Oatmeal or pancakes?" Kate gave her children the option.

"Pancakes," they chorused.

"Where's Daddy?" Emily asked as Kate got down a bowl for mixing the pancake batter.

"He had to go to work early this morning." Kate understated the situation on purpose. One family member worrying herself sick was enough.

Emily accepted Kate's response without question and immediately changed to another subject. "Can we have hot chocolate with our pancakes?"

Kate considered this. It was only a week before Halloween, and back home in Utah, it would be cold enough for coats by now. Here in Georgia, they were still wearing shorts. But she decided the temperature didn't really matter. "Sure." She removed three mugs from the cupboard along with the can of instant hot chocolate mix.

Kate had the pancake mix poised over the edge of her bowl, ready to pour, when their next-door neighbor, Miss Eugenia Atkins, walked in carrying her little dog, Lady. Miss Eugenia's sister, Annabelle, was trailing a few steps behind with a Marsh's Bakery bag in her hand.

"Good morning!" Miss Eugenia called out in greeting. "No need to make pancakes, Kate. Annabelle brought pastries for us." She noticed the hot chocolate mix on the counter. "Which will go perfectly with hot chocolate on a cold October morning."

"It's 85 degrees outside," Annabelle pointed out.

"It's still October," Miss Eugenia replied. Then she beamed at the children. "I declare if you two aren't a sight for my tired, old eyes!"

Miss Eugenia kissed each of the children in turn and allowed them to pet Lady. Then she put the dog back in the laundry room, instructing the small canine to take a nap, and returned to the kitchen, where she collapsed in a chair by the table.

"You're up early this morning," Kate remarked as she peered into the bakery bag. "Even for *you*."

"Cornelia Blackwood is gone to a prayer retreat," Miss Eugenia explained. "Although if she gets any better at praying, she'll probably send the whole world straight into the rapture."

"I swear, Eugenia," Annabelle said with a frown, "you are so irreverent."

"Listen to who's talking about being irreverent and swearing at the same time," Miss Eugenia shot back.

"So Mrs. Blackwood has gone to a prayer retreat?" Kate tried to return the conversation to safer ground. She pulled two muffins that didn't look completely unhealthy from the bakery bag and handed them to her children.

Miss Eugenia sent her sister one last cross look, then nodded. "Yes, and Cornelia knew I was the only person in Haggerty responsible enough to handle the morning prayer service at the retirement home while she's away."

"And unfortunately I'm the sister of this very responsible person who is afraid to drive in the dark," Annabelle interjected. "So I had to come all the way from Albany to take her two miles down the road to the retirement home."

"I'm not afraid to drive in the dark." Miss Eugenia was quick to set everyone straight. "I just don't see well at night."

Mrs. Eugenia caught Kate looking at the sun shining through her kitchen window. "It may not be dark now, but it was at five thirty when I left for the retirement home!"

Kate wasn't about to argue the point. "You didn't have to call Annabelle to come in from Albany. I would have been glad to take you to the retirement home."

Miss Eugenia seemed pleased by the offer. "I appreciate that, dear, but I hate to bother you since you have the children and Mark to take care of." Miss Eugenia's eyes narrowed. "And speaking of Mark, Polly said he left in the middle of the night. FBI business, I presume?"

Kate didn't even bother to ask how Miss Polly, their neighbor on the other side, knew that Mark left home during the middle of the night. An elderly woman who had never married, Miss Polly had very little going on in her own life. She filled her time watching everything that went on in the lives of her neighbors.

"Mark was called in to Atlanta by the FBI," Kate confirmed. "Some new case—I don't know anything about it." Her eyes strayed to the phone—willing it to ring.

Miss Eugenia followed her gaze. "Well, I hope it was a matter of national security, since it required him to leave his family in the middle of the night."

Kate bit into a bear claw. "I hope it's something small and easily resolved so that he'll be home soon and safe."

"So, what are you two going to be for Halloween?" Annabelle asked Emily and Charles.

"I'm going to be Princess Leia. I have a white dress, and Mama's going to fix my hair in circles around my ears," Emily supplied in detail. "Charles is going to be Luke Skywalker."

"I have a lightsaber," Charles said simply.

Annabelle smiled. "Oh, that sounds wonderful."

"If we had a baby it could be Yoda, but we don't," Emily added with a frown.

"Maybe Lady could be Yoda," Annabelle suggested. "She certainly looks like something from another planet." Annabelle pulled on Lady's ears to make them look like Yoda's. Lady growled, and the children laughed.

Annabelle was used to the little dog's animosity. "I couldn't tell if that was a yes or a no."

"Yoda—the very idea," Miss Eugenia said as Miss Polly called out from the back door, "Knock, knock, anybody home?"

"As if she wouldn't know the second you set your foot outside," Miss Eugenia whispered loudly.

Kate gave Miss Eugenia a disapproving look. "Come on in, Miss Polly," she invited. "Annabelle brought us pastries from Marsh's Bakery."

"She can probably tell you what kind of doughnuts Annabelle bought and how many," Miss Eugenia predicted.

"I heard that," Miss Polly said as she glided into the kitchen. For a large woman, Miss Polly was amazingly light on her feet. "And you are overestimating my skills of observation. I have no idea how many pastries are in that bag, and I wasn't even sure if Annabelle had gotten them from Marsh's. Slocum's Bakery uses white bags too, and their script is similar."

Miss Eugenia rolled her eyes. "I hope you didn't come over here so early just to discuss bakery bags. I would have thought you'd be sleeping in after staying up so late last night looking out your window at Kate and Mark's house."

"I wasn't looking out my window," Miss Polly denied. "When Mark started his car, it woke me up. I glanced out my window in time to see him pass by my house headed down Maple Street. I just assumed he was going to Albany."

"He was called in to work," Kate explained, knowing that Miss Polly would be curious.

"Atlanta," Annabelle provided. "We figure it's something big."

"Oh, my." Miss Polly pulled the lace handkerchief from the neckline of her floral print dress and pressed it daintily to her lips. "I hope it's nothing dangerous."

Kate was forcefully reminded of her fears, and the smile left her lips. Then she glanced at her children, who had both finished their muffins. "Why don't you two go into the family room and watch *It's the Great Pumpkin, Charlie Brown?*" she suggested.

"We've already seen it," Emily reminded her.

"You can never see it too many times," Kate assured her firmly.

Emily took Charles by the hand and led him away. As they left, Kate saw Miss Eugenia give Miss Polly an irritated look.

"I'm sure Mark's new assignment doesn't involve anything more dangerous than adding and subtracting," Miss Eugenia said. "After all, accounting is his specialty."

Annabelle offered Miss Polly a pastry. "I don't mind if I do." Miss Polly chose a gooey cinnamon bun and settled in a chair beside Kate. "And I'm sure you're right about Mark."

"Did you have a reason for stopping by, Polly," Miss Eugenia asked. "Other than to scare Kate and her children?"

The sarcasm was lost on Miss Polly. "Actually I do have an important reason for my early morning visit." She paused long enough to lick some glaze off her pudgy fingers. "We got word yesterday that the Baptist Church's fundraising cookbook, *Dishes from Sea to Shining Sea*, will be available next month, and I'm taking advance orders. How many do you want, Kate?"

"How many could she possibly need?" Miss Eugenia asked.

"Well, I realize she'd only need one for herself, but it's a good cause so I thought she might want to get one for her mother and her sisters and maybe Mark's mother. It would be a wonderful Christmas gift. And remember, part of the proceeds from each book goes to buy Bibles for the people of India."

"How much are they?" Kate asked around a mouthful of bear claw.

"They are twelve dollars," Miss Polly said. "A very reasonable price."

"I'll take five," Kate said, partly because she really wanted that many and partly to forestall any more comments on the subject by Miss Eugenia.

"I'll take ten," Annabelle added, gaining a big smile from Miss Polly.

"In which case I won't need to buy any," Miss Eugenia said. "Since Annabelle always has to be such a big-spending showoff, I'll just let her give me one."

"I'm not showing off," Annabelle objected. "I'm trying to help people in India get Bibles!"

"It would probably be cheaper to buy some and mail them to India instead of buying ten cookbooks from Polly," Miss Eugenia predicted.

Before this could develop into a full-blown argument, Kate clasped one of Miss Polly's chubby hands in hers and said, "Miss Eugenia was just telling us that she has been conducting the morning prayer service at the retirement home for Cornelia Blackwood while she's out of town. Isn't that nice?"

A small frown formed on Miss Polly's chubby forehead. "I heard that, although I have to admit I was a little surprised."

Miss Eugenia lifted both eyebrows. "Surprised? Why?"

"Well, I guess I just figured . . ." Miss Polly's voice trailed off, and the others stared at her.

"You figured what?" Miss Eugenia prompted. "That I don't know how to pray?"

Miss Polly giggled. "No, it's just that I'm surprised Cornelia asked you, since any day now everyone expects that you'll be moving your letter to the Mormon Church."

Now it was Kate's turn to be surprised. She looked from Miss Polly to Miss Eugenia in total mystification. "Your *letter?*" she repeated.

Miss Eugenia threw her head back and laughed. Then she addressed Kate. "Unlike you Mormons who go to a particular congregation based on where you live, here in Haggerty, Baptists and Methodists go to whichever church they please. It might be the one closest to their home, or it might be the church across town with a preacher who is more entertaining."

Miss Eugenia paused, and Kate nodded to let her know she was following the conversation. "Or a Methodist with social aspirations might choose to go to a fancy church in Albany where they irreverently project the scriptures up onto a huge screen on the wall above the preacher's head."

Kate cut her eyes at Annabelle nervously then nodded again. "I get the idea."

"So everyone attends the church of their choice, and their membership letter is hypothetical until someone wants to worship with a different congregation. At which point they request that their letter, or their membership, be moved."

Miss Polly took up the dialogue. "And since Eugenia has been attending with you and the Mormons for so many years, people have begun to talk, wondering if she's going to move her letter permanently."

"You can tell any of the old biddies you've been talking to that I'm leaving my letter right where it is," Miss Eugenia told Miss Polly. "I enjoy going to church with Kate and Mark, but I still enjoy my weekly Bible study classes at the Methodist church and religiously attend the Christmas cantata at the Baptist church. I guess you could say I'm trying to keep all the bases covered."

"The bases?" Miss Polly asked, obviously perplexed.

"Yes, see, Kate and I have a deal worked out," Miss Eugenia explained with a wink at Kate. "While I'm alive, I'll be a Methodist, but when I die, she's going to have me baptized a Mormon."

Miss Polly's eyes grew to the size of saucers. "Oh my."

"Charles, too. She's even going to marry us together in the Mormon temple."

"And that doesn't bother you at all?"

Eugenia waved her hand in a dismissive gesture. "Why should it bother me? I figure if the Mormons are wrong then it will have just been a silly waste of their time. But if the Mormons are right—I get Charles for eternity. The way I see it—I can't lose."

"Heaven help us," Annabelle remarked as she reached into the bakery bag.

CHAPTER 2

When the small delegation reached the reception area outside Mr. Mitchell's office, Mitchell turned Britta Andersen over to his secretary. "She has just arrived from Sweden after a long and exhausting flight," he explained to the kind-looking woman. "Please find her a place to rest, and get her something to eat."

"I don't want to be any trouble," Britta said.

"No trouble," Mitchell assured her. "I'll send for you in a little while."

Then he walked to his office door and held it open for the others to pass. When Dan and Mark reached the door, the SAC reached a hand out to stop them. "You already know everything you need to about this operation, Dan."

Dan was obviously surprised, but he didn't argue. "Yes, sir."

Mark watched Dan walk away with a feeling of desolation. He didn't like Dan much and trusted him less, but at least Dan was a familiar face. Now he was all alone with strangers.

Mr. Mitchell waved for Mark to enter the office. "Have a seat, Agent Iverson."

Mark obeyed reluctantly and settled into one of the chairs arranged in front of Mitchell's desk. He placed the suitcase with the money on the floor directly in front of his feet. Howard Bowen and Agent Perez took chairs on either side of him.

"Well," Mitchell said as he sat down. "I guess you're wondering what your role will be in this operation."

Mark considered that quite an understatement. "I thought I was here to catalog the money seized at the warehouse this morning."

Mr. Mitchell gestured toward Agent Perez. "Angelo is the architect of this operation. I'll let him explain."

Mark turned his attention to the other agent. Perez handed Mark a black and white copy of the surveillance photograph of Rodrigo Salazar's compound in La Rosa, Colombia. "As Mr. Mitchell pointed out during the previous meeting, a frontal attack against Salazar would be impossible without an air strike."

"And the president has approved a covert operation," Mr. Mitchell reminded them. "We can't go in openly. We're trying to gain *friends* in Europe—not more bad feelings among our allies."

"Besides, we don't want to risk Solana's life," Perez said. "That is why we will use stealth and cunning to get her away from Salazar."

"The simplest way to remove Ms. Andersen's daughter from La Rosa is to send in a helicopter," Mr. Mitchell told Mark. "However, helicopters are large and loud—obvious for many miles before they actually land. So before we could commit one to pick up Solana, we would have to ensure that Rodrigo Salazar wouldn't be waiting to shoot it down."

"And how will you guarantee that?" Mark asked.

Perez smiled. "A date has been supplied to us when Salazar will be away from the compound attending a meeting. Many of his soldiers, including his most dangerous employee, General Vargas, will go with him."

"The drug trade in South America has become almost civilized in recent years," Mr. Mitchell elaborated. "The major drug lords meet once a year to discuss boundary disputes and other problems that used to cause bloody battles."

"They've learned that war is bad for business," Howard Bowen contributed to the conversation for the first time.

"For security reasons, few people have advanced knowledge regarding the location of the annual meeting," Mr. Mitchell said, "which makes it difficult for us to get the information."

Perez smiled. "But this year's host is in a tight spot. His son was arrested a few weeks ago in Los Angeles on, ironically, a drug charge. The boy is coming up for trial soon, so the father has offered us a deal."

"The charges against the son will be dropped if the father tells you the location of the meeting," Mark guessed.

Perez nodded. "Since Salazar controls the bulk of the drug trade in Colombia, no major decisions can be made without him, and we feel reasonably sure that he'll attend."

Mark frowned. "So you will wait until Salazar leaves for his meeting. Then you'll hope that Solana leaves the compound during this small window of opportunity when your men can whisk her away."

Perez looked mildly offended. "I have been working on this plan for almost a year, and I can assure you that it is not that haphazard. I have many contacts in the city of La Rosa and two within Salazar's compound itself. I will make sure that Solana is at the pickup point when the helicopter arrives. I will also have my task force hidden in the hills surrounding La Rosa—protecting the helicopter during its approach. My concern is that Salazar will discover the task force—since it must be sent in several days in advance of the helicopter—and will cancel the meeting. That is where you come in."

Mark was surprised. "I will be a part of the extraction team?"

Agent Perez and Mr. Mitchell exchanged a glance, while Howard Bowen made a noise that sounded suspiciously like a snicker.

Agent Perez shook his head. "No. You are my excuse for having American troops in the hills of Colombia."

Now Mark was confused. "I don't understand."

"Our task force is made up of experts, and I expect them to be able to avoid detection. But Salazar's private army combs the hills around his compound continuously. If he finds them, I need to disguise them as something other than a rescue squad for Solana."

"What you need is a miracle," Howard Bowen muttered.

Perez ignored this. "For the past several weeks, I have been looking for a suitable scenario. I had reluctantly settled on something else, but when I got word about the pornography bust, I realized that the perfect opportunity had finally materialized."

Mark didn't see how the two situations could possibly be related and listened closely.

"You will go to La Rosa," Perez told him. "But not as a part of the extraction team. Your sudden appearance will require Salazar to do some investigating. If he buys the story we feed him, then you will be in a position to help us monitor his movements and perhaps even facilitate Solana's escape. If Salazar doesn't believe you are what you seem to be," Perez shrugged, "he will still spend his time trying to determine your purpose for being in La Rosa instead of worrying that his trip might be an opportunity for us to get to Solana."

"Your assignment won't involve use of firearms or heroics of any kind," Mr. Mitchell emphasized.

"Will I be posing as a drug dealer?" Mark asked.

This time Howard Bowen didn't even try to hide his amusement. Mr. Mitchell frowned at his assistant before he said, "No. Agent Perez has planned something more subtle."

"It is unlikely that you would ever be able to convince anyone that you were a drug dealer," Agent Perez told him kindly. "You were chosen for this operation because we want you to be yourself." The other agent paused and glanced at the SAC. "Well, sort of."

With growing anxiety, Mark turned to Frank Mitchell. "*What* is my assignment?"

"This morning our agents arrested forty people at that warehouse on Market Street," Mr. Mitchell began. "They also seized a huge amount of media products and twelve million dollars in cash."

"Which proves that these guys were not only perverts—they were stupid, too," Howard Bowen said.

"I know about all that," Mark reminded them. "I was at the warehouse this morning. I *signed* for the money."

Mr. Mitchell nodded. "Exactly."

Agent Perez regained Mark's attention by saying, "This morning's bust was a huge success, but there is one thing our agents were not able to do."

Mark raised an eyebrow in question.

"They weren't able to find out names for or arrest the people who *own* the porn factory. Aren't you curious about the people who were coming to pick up all that money packed neatly in those suitcases?"

Mark was frustrated by his inability to get a straight answer. "No, not really." At the moment, all he wanted was to find out what his job in Colombia would be.

"Don't you see?" Perez asked impatiently. "If we don't get the people at the top—they will just set up shop in another warehouse and continue abusing children."

Mark spread his hands in supplication. "I don't see what that has to do with me."

Instead of responding, Agent Perez reached into a box beside his chair and extracted a stack of photographs, slapping them on Mitchell's desk. "Do you really want the people responsible for this to be allowed to continue?"

Mark thrust the pictures back at the other agent. "Of course not."

"I want the people responsible for this," Perez picked up the photographs and shook them for emphasis, "stopped. I want them put in jail, where justice in its purest form will take its course—at the hands of the other inmates."

"I thought you wanted to rescue Solana Andersen," Mark said, his voice barely a whisper.

"I want to do both." Perez ripped the pictures in half and dropped them back into the box. "And you're going to help me."

"How?"

"We've altered the FBI records to indicate that you have been involved in the pornography case for the past several weeks." Mr. Mitchell picked up the dialogue. "We made sure you were there when the press showed up at the warehouse. If you get a chance to read the article about the bust in this evening's *Atlanta Constitution,* you'll see your name prominently mentioned."

"By getting my picture taken for the newspaper and having me sign for the money, you've firmly established that I was a part of the investigation," Mark acknowledged. "The question is why?"

"To give you an emotional investment in the outcome," Perez said.

Then Mr. Mitchell resumed his explanation. "After leaving the warehouse early this morning, Dan Davis left you in his office while he went to handle a situation in Cedartown. Your assignment was to analyze the porn company's books and count the twelve million dollars. When Dan returns this evening, he will find you and the money gone. No one on his office staff will remember seeing you, so it will be assumed that you left right after Dan and before the others arrived this morning."

Mark's mouth went dry. If the records had already been altered, that meant that only the people in this room knew the actual facts. If he refused to cooperate—how would he prove his innocence?

"Dan knows we locked most of the money in his office," Mark said. "He knows that I was in the meeting about the task force and that this suitcase has been in plain sight the whole time."

The SAC raised an eyebrow. "Dan will say whatever I tell him to say."

Mark knew by sad experience that this was true.

"We will immediately begin a desperate search for you," the SAC continued. "But it will be too late."

Mark swallowed around the lump of fear that had formed in his throat. "You're going to make it look like I *stole* the money?"

"Some people will think so," Mr. Mitchell agreed.

"No one who knows me," Mark returned with confidence.

Perez smiled. "Officially the FBI will say that you're on vacation. However, unofficial rumors will persist that you have taken the money to South America and set yourself up as bait, trying to smoke out the owners of the child pornography ring."

Mark couldn't control a slight shudder as the images Agent Perez had shown him flashed across his mind.

"I think most people who *know* you would believe that you would sacrifice your career to stop people from exploiting innocent children like this." Agent Perez held up one of the ripped photographs for emphasis.

Mr. Mitchell smiled grimly. "You tried to convince me to keep digging until the owners of the pornography warehouse were found. I felt that the FBI had invested all the resources we could and decided to be satisfied with today's results. Unfortunately, you didn't feel the same."

The pieces of this complex puzzle started to fall into place for Mark. "Do you think the owners of the company will come after me?"

Mr. Mitchell shook his head. "We will do everything in our power to prevent that."

"But from a press standpoint, it will seem that you're holding the FBI hostage," Howard Bowen said.

"It is more like blackmail," Perez corrected.

"Or extortion without any intent for personal gain," Mr. Mitchell added as his legal opinion.

Mark nodded as the picture became clearer to him. "The Bureau would rather complete the investigation to my satisfaction—so I'll return the money, which will soon be needed as evidence in court—than try to explain an embarrassing scandal to both Congress and the press." Then he frowned. "But why would I choose Colombia? Why not Mexico or Europe?"

"You would choose a country that is fairly close," Perez explained, "but not on particularly good terms with the U.S. government so that extradition would not be an immediate concern. In Colombia, government officials can be bribed, and criminals thrive. You will be welcome there."

"If you thought more like a criminal, it would seem like the natural place to you," Howard Bowen informed him.

"No one will be surprised by your choice of countries," Mr. Mitchell added in an obvious attempt to soften the comment by his assistant.

"And if the owners of the money do come after me?" Mark asked. "What will I do when they arrive?"

"You won't have to do anything. I'll handle them," Perez promised.

"With the task force hidden in the hills?" Mark guessed.

"Those punks are the least of your worries," Howard Bowen told Mark. "You'll be camped out in Salazar's backyard. Him you should worry about. He's likely to shoot you just for the fun of it."

Mark looked at Perez for reassurance.

"Salazar won't kill you." The other agent seemed certain. "He'll be too intrigued by you."

Mr. Mitchell leaned forward and claimed Mark's attention. "Salazar has no peer in La Rosa, no equal. He needs a friend. That's what we hope you'll become."

"A friend?" Mark repeated in disbelief. "You expect a supercriminal like Rodrigo Salazar to befriend *me*?"

Howard Bowen waved his hands in exasperation. "Exactly what I said."

Mark regretted that he had unintentionally aligned himself with the assistant SAC, even on a minor point.

"Developing a friendship with Salazar would be helpful, but it is not essential to the plan," Perez said. "If it happens, it happens." He angled his chair away from the assistant SAC, and Mark knew the other agent was angry. "The important thing is that Salazar won't kill you. He'll be interested in you at first—which will provide the distraction we need. Your presence gives us an excuse for the troops in the hills if he discovers them. And if a friendship develops—good." Perez shrugged. "My plan will work either way."

"If Salazar discovers the task force, how will he know that it's there to protect me from the pornography people?"

"We have ways of feeding information to him," Perez said. "And if he asks you—tell him."

"You don't seem to think I'll have any problem making contact with Rodrigo Salazar."

Perez smiled. "You won't have to make contact with Salazar. He will contact you."

After allowing this to sink in for a few seconds, Mr. Mitchell told Mark, "You'll be given a state-of-the-art PDA unit. It will be your means of communication with Agent Perez and will also allow him to monitor you through special precise positioning signals—one of the PDA's features. Since it uses a satellite to transmit, it's very secure, but it looks like the models anyone can buy for $99 at RadioShack."

"We can't risk losing track of you," Perez said. "So you'll also have a secondary, more permanent device as well. One of the stops you'll make this afternoon will be to a dentist. He's going to crown one of your back molars."

In spite of his concerns about his reputation and his safety, Mark had to admit that he was beginning to feel like a real FBI agent instead of a glorified bookkeeper. "What else have I supposedly been doing all morning—besides taking twelve million dollars that doesn't belong to me?"

"If anyone checks, they will find that after leaving Dan's office, you went to a cheap motel on the outskirts of Roswell." Perez held up Mark's cell phone. Mark patted his coat pocket. He hadn't even realized the phone was missing. "I have a talent for picking pockets," Perez admitted with a smile. "Once you were comfortably set up in your hotel room, you began sending text messages from your cell phone. Several were to your secretary in Albany. You had her look through the FBI files for information on Colombian banks and lawyers. You wanted her to find some that had been used by the FBI in the past and that were considered honest."

"Or what passes for honest in Colombia," Howard Bowen interjected.

Perez ignored this. "We made sure that a man named Cristobal Morales showed up on the list of possible lawyers."

Mark still hadn't fully recovered from the fact that Perez had stolen his phone and then impersonated him by messaging Marla. "Cristobal Morales works for the FBI?" he managed finally.

"He has handled several things for us over the years," Perez confirmed. "But the important thing about Morales is that he lives in La Rosa. He knows you have twelve million dollars and has agreed to a retainer of two hundred grand, which you will wire to him, along with enough money for him to rent you a house and buy you a car. It stands to reason that he would rent you a house near him—so that he can stay close to you and all that money."

"That's my excuse for being in La Rosa," Mark realized. "Because Morales is my lawyer and he chose my house."

Perez nodded. "Salazar will check. There can be no unexplained coincidence."

"Obviously it would be unwise for you to enter a lawless country like Colombia carrying suitcases full of American currency. So you will take the money remaining in this suitcase after the wire transfers are complete with you." Mr. Mitchell pointed at the suitcase on the floor in front of Mark. "Dan Davis has already taken the bulk of the money to another bank to be wired to accounts in Switzerland."

"In my name, of course."

Mr. Mitchell nodded. "Of course."

"And how was Dan able to do that?"

Perez rubbed his fingers together. "By showing them your FBI credentials, of course."

Mark patted his pocket where he kept his FBI badge. It, too, was missing. "Sorry," Perez said, although he didn't look repentant. "You'll have your badge back in time to do your own money wiring at two."

Mark wasn't happy, but he controlled his facial expressions. "How will I get to Colombia?"

"At five o'clock this afternoon, you have an appointment to meet the owner of a car advertised for sale in the newspaper." Perez pushed a map of Georgia toward Mark. "You'll pay cash for the car and drive it to Brunswick. From there, you'll be flown out by a navy pilot in a plane confiscated by the Coast Guard yesterday from a drug smuggler."

"I presume that no one knows that the plane is now Coast Guard property?"

Perez shook his head. "Even Morales will think you paid the pilot to drop you off while on his regular illegal rounds. The pilot will take you to an airstrip outside of Cartagena. Morales will meet you there."

"And in the meantime, back here in the United States, the FBI will be searching for me and the missing porn money?"

Perez nodded. "Unfortunately we will always be just one step behind you."

"We will search desperately but quietly," Mr. Mitchell added. "It would be very bad press to admit that the FBI had lost twelve million dollars to one of their own agents."

"However, we will make sure that the rumors persist," Perez said. "And hopefully when Salazar checks, he will believe them."

"What about my family?" Mark asked, clasping his hands together to keep them from shaking. "I have to be sure they're safe while I'm gone."

Perez nodded. "Before you leave Atlanta, we will have a team of agents watching your house. They will claim to be looking for you, but they will actually be providing protection."

Mark felt some of the tension ease from his shoulders. "That's fine for a temporary precaution, but what about the long term?"

"Since the official line is that you are on vacation, it would be best if they go to your parents' house. There's no need for them to pack up in the dead of night and disappear in a suspicious manner. Your wife can tell the neighbors that you've just completed an assignment and that they're going to meet you in Texas for a much-needed vacation. Our agents will follow them to your parents' home, and then we'll have the field office in Dallas provide round-the-clock surveillance until the operation is over."

"I'll need to explain it to my wife and say good-bye."

Mr. Mitchell stood and waved for Howard Bowen and Agent Perez to join him in a far corner of the room. After a quick whispered conference, they rejoined Mark at the desk. Then Mr. Mitchell delivered the verdict. "You can stop by and see her on the way to Brunswick tonight, as long as you do it discreetly. But you can't tell her anything about the operation. It would be dangerous for you and for her."

Mark nodded. "I understand." He hoped that Kate would.

"Once you reach your rental house in La Rosa, you can use your cell phone to call your wife occasionally, but remember that cell calls are easy to intercept. You'll want to warn your wife of that as well," Mr. Mitchell said.

"You know that I'm a bishop in the LDS Church?"

The SAC nodded impatiently. "We're very well aware of that."

"I can't allow the reputation of the Church to be affected by the rumors you plan to spread about me. I need to contact my Church supervisor and explain the situation to him. He may want to release me from my position in advance."

Mr. Mitchell frowned. "You won't be able to give him any details."

Mark nodded. "I understand."

"And we will be listening to the conversation."

Mark didn't bother to respond. This was a given. "I also want something in writing signed by all of you explaining my innocence— just in case."

"That is unnecessary," Agent Perez began.

"We'll sanitize your file," Howard Bowen promised.

"I'd have to get approval for that," the SAC hedged, "which would take too long."

"It's necessary to me," Mark countered with a firm look at Agent Perez. "I won't be here to see how 'sanitized' my files become," he added toward Howard Bowen. "And *you* can do whatever you want," he told the SAC.

The SAC's lips formed a hard line. "Very well. I'll type the memo up myself."

"You need to hurry," Mark encouraged with a hint of sarcasm. "A busy day has been planned for me."

"Go ahead and call your church leader," Mr. Mitchell said, pushing his phone toward Mark.

Mark referred to his stake calendar and dialed the stake president's office number. President Tanner answered personally on the fourth ring. Mark explained the situation in very general terms, and after he was finished, there was silence on the other end of the line.

"I'm not sure how to handle this, Bishop," President Tanner said finally. "I'll have to call Salt Lake and let you know what they say."

Mark gave the stake president Mr. Mitchell's office number and said good-bye as a knock sounded on the door. It swung open to expose Mr. Mitchell's secretary and Britta Andersen.

"Would it be possible for me to speak to Agent Iverson alone?" Ms. Andersen requested.

Mitchell didn't look particularly happy about the request, but he stood up and said, "Of course. And Agent Iverson, I'll type the memo you requested at my secretary's desk."

Agent Perez and Howard Bowen followed the SAC. "We'll be right outside the door." Mark wasn't sure if this remark was for his benefit or Ms. Andersen's.

Once they were alone, the Swedish woman took one of the empty chairs beside him. "I don't know everything that they are subjecting you to, but I do know that over the next few days you will have to work closely with Rodrigo. I felt that it was important to warn you."

Mark sighed. "It's impossible for you to scare me into caution. I'm already terrified of the man."

Ms. Andersen smiled. "But I want you to understand why he is so dangerous. I am not afraid to go to La Rosa because I think Rodrigo will tie me up or lock me in a room. I'm afraid that if I go, I won't *want* to leave."

This unexpected remark caused Mark to frown. "You'll have to explain further."

"I loved Rodrigo when I was a girl," Ms. Andersen admitted. "Perhaps I still do. Leaving him was the hardest thing I've ever done, and I'm not sure I have the strength to do it again. Rodrigo tried to convince me that I could be happy with him. He said he could isolate me from the ugliness of the drug trade yet give me everything money could buy."

"You didn't believe him?"

She raised tortured eyes to meet his. "I did believe him. I was afraid that eventually I would forget that our happiness was built on the misery of others. Then right and wrong would cease to exist. From a distance I understand that you can't do bad things and remain a good person, but when Rodrigo is near, it is hard for me to think clearly. I knew that given enough time, he would convince me, and then I would be lost forever." She brought a hand up to smooth her hair, and Mark noticed that her hand was trembling. "I named Solana after his mother, so you see, even now, he is a part of me."

Before Mark could respond, the door opened, and Perez walked back in. "Your church president is on line four," he said to Mark.

Mark picked up the phone. "This is Mark Iverson."

"Bishop, President Tanner. I've spoken with the Office of the First Presidency. They said as long as what you're doing is a sanctioned FBI operation, there is no need to release you. A little bad press is acceptable as long as your innocence is eventually proven."

Mark didn't realize how important it was to him until the words were said. Then he had to blink back tears. "Thank you, President."

"They also said to tell you they will be praying for you," President Tanner replied. "I will be too."

Mark hung up the phone feeling much stronger than he had before. He wasn't really alone after all.

The SAC returned, followed closely by his assistant, Howard Bowen. Mr. Mitchell handed Mark a piece of paper. Mark quickly read the memo then nodded. "I'd like everyone to sign it, please."

The paper was circulated around the table, and each man signed it in turn. Finally the memo was returned to Mark. He folded it and put it into the inside pocket of his jacket.

Angelo Perez stood. "We're finished here. Agent Iverson, if you'll follow me, we have a lot of work to do."

Mark joined him near the door. Mr. Mitchell met them there. Mark expected some form of gratitude from the man. Instead the SAC said, "We have gone to great trouble and expense setting up this operation. It's imperative that you follow Angelo's instructions exactly.

We can't have you blowing the whole operation over some minor detail."

"If we fail this time, we might not get a second chance," Howard Bowen added with an equal amount of ingratitude.

Mark nodded. "I'll do my best."

It was obvious from their expressions that they questioned whether or not his best would be good enough.

Mr. Mitchell rubbed his hands together. "Well, I'll let Angelo take things from here."

As Agent Perez reached for the doorknob, Howard Bowen spoke again. "For the record, I want to state that I'm not happy about this assignment."

"Come on, Howard," the SAC said with a trace of impatience. "We've been over this already."

"You don't think I can do it?" Mark asked the assistant SAC.

"I think you're a good man and even a good agent," Mr. Bowen replied, "as long as the assignment is tax evasion or embezzlement. But you haven't been adequately trained for undercover work, and you have essentially no field experience. And that aside, field work requires a level of natural aptitude that I don't believe you possess." Mr. Bowen paused for a deep breath. "So, I guess the answer to your question is no. I don't think you have a chance of successfully completing this mission."

Mark waited for someone to refute Bowen's harsh words, but the room resounded with silence. "Then I guess I'll just have to prove you wrong," Mark said softly. Without waiting for a reply, Mark followed Agent Perez out into the reception area.

He paused by the secretary's desk and asked for an envelope and a stamp. Mr. Mitchell's secretary provided both. Mark didn't have much time to decide whom to entrust his memo to and didn't have many choices. Finally he scrawled Jack Gamble's name and, after looking up the senator's office address in the Atlanta phonebook, wrote it on the envelope. He was about to ask the secretary to mail it for him when Britta Andersen took it from his hand and slipped it into her purse.

"I will make sure it gets mailed," she whispered. "You must be careful who you trust, Agent Iverson. People are not always what they seem."

That was a statement he was to remember often during the next few days.

CHAPTER 3

Solana agonized over her situation all afternoon, but she didn't dare make contact with Emilio before their regularly scheduled tennis match for fear that she would alert General Vargas.

Tennis was another game that Solana had introduced Emilio to only a few weeks before. Because Emilio was a natural athlete, he soon became proficient at the game and now beat her often. That afternoon, since she was distracted throughout the session, Emilio finished her off quickly. When the match ended, Solana wiped the perspiration from her face with a towel and met him at the net.

"Congratulations," she said, extending her hand.

"You seemed a little off your game," he returned as his fingers closed briefly around hers. "Is something bothering you?"

"Come," she whispered, glancing up at the house. She couldn't see anyone looking down from the many windows that faced the tennis courts, but that didn't mean that they weren't being observed. She led Emilio to a shady corner of the court where several tables and chairs were arranged. On one table was an ice chest filled with bottled water that the housekeeping staff had provided.

After opening a bottle and taking a long sip of water, Solana said, "I spoke to my father this morning. I asked him to have you removed from the general's army and assigned to me full-time."

Emilio winced. "Oh, Solana."

"He refused," she continued. "He said it would undermine the authority Vargas has over the other men."

"I tried to tell you," Emilio said softly.

She nodded. "I should have listened, but at least now we know for sure. It is not safe here for you. We must leave."

"Solana . . ." he began in his long-suffering tone.

She was not in the mood to be placated. "My feeling is that we should leave tomorrow."

Emilio's hand shook slightly as he reached for a bottle of water. "That is too soon. We will need time to plan."

"There *is* no time," she told him in exasperation. "Vargas is suspicious already. If he decides you have overstepped the bounds of propriety, he will act quickly to prevent interference from me." She looked at him. "I can't live like this. Every time a servant approaches me, I wonder if they bring me news of your accidental death."

Emilio turned his back to the house and any curious eyes that might be watching them. "What is your plan?"

"All we have to do is make it to Cartagena." Solana couldn't keep the excitement from her voice. "Once there, we will contact my mother. She will help us get to Stockholm."

"You act as though getting to Cartagena will be easy."

"Not easy," she admitted, "but possible. How long will it take to drive there?"

Emilio considered the question. "Between two and three hours, depending on traffic."

"Tomorrow evening I will wait until Vargas is handling the changing of his guards. Then I will ask my father if you can drive me to see a movie in La Rosa."

"You hope that Vargas will be too busy to assign additional men to escort us?"

Solana was pleased that he understood. "That would be perfect for our purposes. But even if he does assign some men to follow us, they will be tired from their long day of pacing the hills around my father's compound. Hopefully their fatigue will cause them to be less vigilant."

"That is good," Emilio approved.

"You will drop me off in front of the theater then drive around back and park. If we have an escort, they'll settle down and watch the entrance of the theater until the movie ends. I'll slip out the side door and sneak into the car. By the time they realize we are gone, we should be almost to Cartagena."

"It might work," Emilio said. "I will agree on one condition." Then he leaned down and whispered his requirement in her ear.

"Please, Emilio, not tomorrow. There isn't time!"

"I'm afraid I will have to insist," he told her calmly. "I am willing to risk my life for you, Solana, but do this one thing for me first."

"Very well," she agreed reluctantly. "Now hurry back to the barracks before Señor Vargas comes looking for you."

He gave her a quick smile before hurrying off at a trot.

* * *

As Mark left the Georgia Bank of Commerce with the wire-transfer receipts, he was amazed by how easily it had all been accomplished. He had walked into the bank with a suitcase full of cash, flashed his FBI badge, and immediately had everyone falling all over themselves in anxious attempts to assist him.

The retainer had been sent to Mr. Morales, and large amounts of the money had been deposited into accounts in three separate banks in La Rosa at the lawyer's suggestion. Once the money transfers were complete, the president of the bank had offered his own personal briefcase to house the remaining cash so that Mark could leave with something less cumbersome than the large, now mostly empty, suitcase.

As he exited the bank, a security guard escorted him to the taxi he had left waiting at the curb. He gave the driver directions to the dentist's office and asked him to wait once they arrived.

"Hey buddy, it's your nickel," the driver said as he lowered his cap and hunkered down in the seat in preparation for a nap.

Mark picked up the bank president's leather briefcase and walked into the dental office. The smell of mouthwash mixed with industrial-strength antiseptic was overpowering, and Mark immediately started breathing through his mouth. Angelo Perez was the only person waiting in the small lobby. He stood to greet Mark as a drill whirred in the other room.

"So, how have things been going?" Perez asked.

"No complaints," Mark replied.

"That is good." Perez didn't sound surprised. "Follow me." He led the way through a door and down the hall to a small treatment room. The unpleasant smell was stronger here and the sound of the drill so close that Mark's own teeth started to ache. With a wave toward a dental chair, Perez instructed Mark to have a seat.

Mark sat down, leaned against the headrest, and wondered grimly what would be involved in crowning a tooth.

After a few minutes of uncomfortable silence, the dentist hurried in, followed closely by a nervous-looking hygienist. No introductions were made, and no small talk was exchanged. The crown was quickly glued in place, and Mark was told to bite down several times until the dentist was satisfied with the fit. The dentist nodded to Perez and led his hygienist from the room.

Perez checked his watch. "We'd better hurry if we're going to make your appointment with the owner of the car we've picked out for you."

Mark waited until they were outside to ask, "How did the dentist get a crown that would fit my tooth perfectly?"

Perez smiled. "We got your dental records from your family dentist and did what's called a reverse impression."

Mark made a mental note to change dentists as soon as this was over. Maybe no dentist was any match for the FBI, but he wouldn't feel comfortable taking the kids in to have their teeth cleaned by someone who had surrendered his records.

"Once you have the car, meet me at the Wendy's on Buford Highway. I'll give you your final instructions and send you on your way."

Mark nodded then climbed into the waiting cab and gave the driver the address of the used-car owner—which was all the way across town. While they drove through Atlanta, Mark stared out the window at the traffic without interest. He was tired and worried about Kate and afraid that Howard Bowen was right—maybe he wasn't man enough for this job.

Finally the cab driver pulled up in front of a modest home and leaned over the front seat. "This is the place, buddy. If you want me to wait, that briefcase of yours better be full of cash, cause you're running up a huge tab."

Mark almost laughed but managed to control the stress-induced hysteria. "Thanks for your help today, but this is the end of the line. How much do I owe you?"

The cab driver pointed to the meter, and Mark was astounded. He hadn't realized that cab fares could be that high. He pulled out his wallet and removed the necessary bills—thankful that he'd had the foresight to transfer operating money from the briefcase while at the bank. If the cab driver had gotten a close look at the contents of the briefcase, there was a good chance that the transaction could have turned into a robbery.

Mark waited until the cab pulled away before walking up the sidewalk and knocking on the door of the house. The car owner answered Mark's knock and introduced himself as Clifford Perry. If he thought it strange that Mark didn't provide reciprocating information, he didn't say so. Cliff was a recent college graduate with a new job and a desire to climb the corporate ladder. In an effort to impress potential clients, he had purchased a pricey BMW sedan and was anxious to unload the little Honda Civic that had transported him faithfully since he'd gotten his driver's license ten years earlier.

The car was nothing special, but Mark was sure Perez had checked it out thoroughly before arranging the purchase. So he handed Cliff $2,000 in cash and in return received the title and a do-it-yourself bill of sale. Mark climbed in the Honda and drove down Buford Highway to the Wendy's. He found Perez in a corner booth eating a chicken club combo meal—Biggie-sized.

"Want something to eat?" Perez asked around a mouthful of chicken mush.

Mark averted his eyes as he sat down across from Perez. He put the briefcase on the seat beside him. "No thanks. I'm not hungry."

"You've got a long drive ahead of you," Perez reminded him. "You need to keep up your strength."

"There are plenty of fast food places between here and Brunswick. I can stop and get something later."

"You bought the car?"

Mark pointed through the tinted glass window at the Honda parked a few yards away. "Yes."

"I had a master mechanic scrutinize every inch of that car. You shouldn't have any problems with it."

Mark acknowledged this with a slight inclination of his head.

Perez stuffed the last of his sandwich into his mouth. Then he sucked from his huge soft drink container until air gurgled at the bottom. "Ah, that was delicious. You really should have tried it."

"Maybe later," Mark said.

Perez rose to his feet. "I guess we should get you on your way."

Mark followed Perez out to the blue Honda. Mark climbed in behind the wheel, and Perez slipped into the front passenger seat. They were both quiet for a few minutes. Then Perez said, "I'm not sure you understand. Part of what makes Rodrigo Salazar so dangerous is his charm. When you meet him, you will think, 'This is a nice man—how could he have killed so many people, ruined so many lives?' Yet he has, and he will destroy you too if you let him."

"Your point is taken."

"Another thing that makes him dangerous is his head henchman, the general of his private army, Hector Vargas. The people of La Rosa call him El Diablo." He glanced over at Mark. "It means 'the devil.'"

"I know what it means," Mark returned.

"General Vargas maintains discipline through sheer terror," Perez explained. "He executes people the way you or I would swat a fly. It means nothing to him. Never underestimate his ruthlessness."

Mark didn't foresee this as a problem. "I won't."

"Salazar is a civilized man in many ways, but he knows there is great power in fear, so he makes no effort to restrain Vargas," Perez continued earnestly.

Mark nodded. "I understand."

"I hope you do." Agent Perez looked away, and Mark could tell he was worried. Finally he said, "You know that what Bowen said is true. You are unprepared and unqualified for this assignment. But Salazar has been surrounded by spies his entire life. I felt that the only way to take him by surprise was to send in someone completely unexpected."

"You sound like you regret choosing me."

Perez shook his head. "No, I only regret the necessity. Be constantly on guard. Trust no one. Even the walls have eyes. And as soon as your mission is completed, leave La Rosa. It will try to seduce you—but never forget that it is home to the devil."

"I will leave La Rosa as soon as possible," Mark assured Perez.

Perez opened the passenger door and stepped out of the car. Then he leaned back in and said quietly, "Be careful not to put too much confidence in Morales. If the time comes when he has to choose between you and Salazar, he'll choose the one he fears the most. And that won't be you."

Before Mark could respond, Perez backed out of the car, slammed the door shut, and walked away.

* * *

Kate and the children spent the afternoon at the park. When they returned home, Kate entered the house first, turning on lights as she went.

"It's already dark outside," Emily commented.

"It's getting dark earlier now," Kate agreed. "And we stayed at the park a little longer than I wanted to. We need to get dinner made so we can eat and take baths. It'll be time for bed soon."

"I'm not ready for bed!" Charles informed them.

Kate ruffled his hair. "You're never ready for bed."

Kate picked up the cordless phone and checked to see if there were any messages. There weren't. She had kept her cell phone with her the whole time they were at the park, but it didn't ring once. She stared at the phone in confusion. This lack of communication made no sense. Mark usually called several times every day—even when she had no reason to worry.

Finally she decided she'd been patient long enough. She lifted the phone again and called Mark's cell phone number. It rang four times, and then she heard his voice, asking that she leave a message. She disconnected and called Marla at the FBI resident agency office in Albany.

"Yes, I've heard from Mark several times today," his secretary reported cheerfully. Kate didn't know whether to be relieved or irritated. If he'd found time to contact Marla 'several times,' it seemed like he could have called her at least *once*.

"He's working on some big new case," Marla continued. "It must have something to do with South America, because he's had me checking on lawyers and banks in Colombia." There was a brief pause, and then Marla said, "Oops, I probably shouldn't have said that. It might be confidential."

"Colombia," Kate repeated as she struggled to breathe.

Mark had received a memo a couple of months before informing him that all Spanish-speaking agents were being put on alert because of increased drug activity in South America. Mark had served a Spanish-speaking mission and was fluent in the language. Now it seemed that her worst fears had been realized.

"If you hear from him again, please ask him to call me," she requested weakly. Then she hung up and let the tears fall silently down her cheeks.

"Is something wrong, Mama?" Emily asked as she ran up to Kate.

Kate shook her head. "Just something in my eye."

Charles put a comforting hand on her cheek. "I love you, Mama," he said.

She smiled as bravely as she could. "Let's get dinner made."

"Will Daddy be home soon?" Emily asked, her forehead lined with concern.

"I don't know," Kate replied honestly. "Now you two get cleaned up while I start on dinner."

The phone never rang during the process of cooking the meal, feeding the children, or cleaning up afterward. Finally Kate sent the children to the family room to play so she didn't have to pretend she wasn't worried. She walked over and looked out the window at the driveway where Mark's car should have been parked beside her van.

She felt a shudder start deep inside and rubbed her hands up her arms in an effort to reassure herself. The FBI had always been annoyingly secretive, and it was entirely possible that Mark's emergency trip to Atlanta was routine. If only Mark would call, she'd be okay. She couldn't shake the feeling that the only kind of news he would want to deliver in person was the bad kind.

Her mini-trance was interrupted by the front doorbell. Kate started in surprise. Very few people in Haggerty came to the front door.

"Can I open it, Mama?" Emily called from the family room.

"I'll get it," Kate replied as she walked quickly down the hall, past Mark's empty office, and into the entryway. She glanced through the peephole on the front door and saw two grim-faced men wearing dark, conservative suits standing on the porch. The ground under her feet seemed to shift, and she grasped the doorknob for support. The doorbell rang again.

"Who is it, Mama?" Emily wanted to know.

My worst nightmare, Kate thought to herself. Then, mustering all the courage she possessed, she opened the door.

"Mrs. Iverson," one man said. "My name is Special Agent Lott, and this is Special Agent Applegate. We're from the FBI field office in Atlanta." They both held up their badges for her to see.

Kate managed a nod of acknowledgment and waited for one of them to tell her that Mark had been killed in the line of duty—that she was now a widow responsible for raising her children alone.

Instead he asked, "May we speak to your husband?"

Kate sagged against the door in relief. Mark wasn't dead. "He's not here," she told them. "He left early this morning to meet Dan Davis in Atlanta. You should be able to reach him there."

Agent Lott shook his head. "We've called and left several messages for him. He isn't there."

This was even better news as far as Kate was concerned. "Well, I guess he's on the way home, then."

Agent Lott glanced at his partner before saying, "We'll wait in front of the house and speak to him when he gets here."

"You're welcome to wait inside," Kate offered.

"Oh, no—we wouldn't want to disturb your family," Agent Lott replied.

Kate shrugged. "Suit yourself."

Kate closed the door after the two men turned and walked toward their nondescript government sedan parked at the curb. If Mark wasn't in Atlanta, where was he? And why hadn't he called? The news he had must be very bad indeed. Maybe he'd been fired. Kate's hands began to tremble, and she clutched them together impatiently. There was no sense borrowing trouble. She'd wait for Mark's explanation rather than jumping to dire conclusions.

Unable to help herself, Kate called Mark's cell phone again but still got no answer. Refusing to give up, she dialed the number for the field office in Atlanta and asked for Mark's supervisor, Dan Davis. A few seconds later, a female voice came on the line. She identified herself as the switchboard operator and said that Mr. Davis was gone for the day but offered to take Kate's number and have him call her tomorrow.

Kate disconnected the call and was trying to decide on the best course of action when the phone in her hand rang. Kate answered automatically, "Hello."

"Kate?" It was Miss Polly from next door. The woman was sweet but long-winded, and Kate wasn't in the mood for a lengthy chat. "Who are those men sitting in front of your house?"

"They're FBI agents waiting to talk to Mark," Kate answered succinctly, hoping to bring the conversation to a quick conclusion.

"Why don't they talk to him at his office?"

"They missed him at the office," Kate replied with flagging patience. "I'm sorry, Miss Polly, but I've got to go." Without waiting for a response, Kate hung up the phone.

Kate had just enough time to check on the children, who were playing happily, and to walk back to the kitchen before Miss Eugenia walked in through the back door. "Have you seen the Atlanta paper?" she asked, putting a copy of the evening edition on the Iversons' kitchen table. "Whit brought it back from Albany, and I thought you'd want to read this article."

She pointed an age-spotted finger at a picture on the front page. Kate stared in fascination as she separated Mark's face from the others in the photograph. "It says that the FBI found a warehouse full of dirty pictures and movies this morning. They arrested a lot of folks and confiscated millions of dollars in cash."

Kate would have preferred to read the article herself, but at least Miss Eugenia's synopsis eliminated many of her fears. Mark had been involved in a major case that had ended successfully this morning. He had probably been wrapping up loose ends all day and was now on his way home. Why he had been asking Marla to check on lawyers and banks in Colombia was a nagging question she would try to ignore.

"Those FBI agents sitting in the car in front of your house seem like nice young men," Miss Eugenia continued.

"You've met them?" Kate asked in surprise.

Miss Eugenia nodded. "I introduced myself on my way over. Polly had brought them glasses of iced tea and a plate of tea cakes fresh from the oven."

Kate shook her head in amazement. If Mark didn't make it home soon, Miss Polly would be serving the agents a full-course dinner.

"As long as I'm here, would you like me to help you get the children ready for bed?" Miss Eugenia offered.

Kate checked the clock. She hated to put the kids to bed before Mark got home, but it was getting late. "I could use an extra pair of hands. Thanks."

Kate took charge of Emily and let Miss Eugenia handle Charles. Once the kids were ready for bed, Kate left Miss Eugenia reading them a story and went back downstairs. She glanced out the living room window and saw the FBI agents still sitting patiently in their car. *How long could it possibly take Mark to drive from Atlanta?* she thought to herself. *And why hasn't he called?*

"Well, the children are asleep," Miss Eugenia said as she came up behind Kate. "I'll head home and check on Lady." She looked over Kate's shoulder at the FBI agents. "And I guess I'll make those poor men a sandwich for dinner since Mark still hasn't gotten home."

Kate just nodded. "See you in the morning."

After Miss Eugenia was gone, Kate walked into the kitchen and reread the article in the *Atlanta Constitution*. She had no idea that Mark had been involved in busting a pornography ring, but according to the article, he had been investigating the case for several weeks. She scrutinized it for some connection to Colombia or at least South America, but there wasn't one—at least not one that was printed.

Finally, in desperation she called Marla at home. "Have you heard from Mark lately?" she asked when Marla answered the phone.

"Not since early this afternoon," Marla responded.

"I have a couple of FBI agents from Atlanta sitting in a car in front of my house," Kate said. "They want to talk to Mark, and they claim that he left Atlanta hours ago. Where in the world could he be, and why hasn't he called?"

"I can't answer your questions, Kate," Marla said calmly. "But I'm sure Mark will be home soon and will explain everything. Just try to stay calm. Worrying never helps anything."

Kate knew that Marla was right, but it was easier to say when your husband wasn't the one missing. "I'm sorry to bother you at home," she apologized.

"You're no bother. And if I hear from Mark, I'll call you right away."

Kate apologized again, then thanked the woman and ended the call. Feeling a little foolish, Kate walked to the sink and picked up a sponge. She absently washed the counters, straightened the dish towels in the drawer, and was actually considering a reorganization of the cans in her cupboard when she realized she had to get a grip on herself.

She went upstairs to check on the children, almost hoping one of them would be awake so she wouldn't have to wait alone. But both were sleeping soundly, so she made her way back downstairs.

Finally, as close to despair as she had been in a long time, Kate angled a kitchen chair toward the window that overlooked the dark driveway and sat down. Then, after clasping her hands together, she began to pray. Several minutes later she heard a sound at the back door, and her eyes flew open.

Kate stood with unreasonable terror causing her heart to pound. Mark always encouraged her to keep the doors locked, but after Miss Eugenia had left earlier, Kate hadn't thought to check. Haggerty was a safe place—she'd never felt afraid here. But today Mark hadn't come home, and there were two FBI agents she'd never seen before sitting in front of her house. She put her hand into the pocket of her jeans and let her fingers close around her cell phone. If the intruder intended them harm, she would at least be able to call 911.

The door eased open, and in the dim light she saw Mark's face. Relief washed over her as a cry escaped her lips. "Oh, Mark," she said as she closed the distance that separated them and flung herself into his arms. "I've been so worried about you."

He caught her to his chest in a tight embrace without saying a word. His silence confirmed her dire suspicions. Something was wrong. Slowly she pulled back and led him to the kitchen.

"Where's your car?"

"I left my government vehicle at the field office in Atlanta. I'm driving a little Honda that I parked on Oak Street so Miss Polly wouldn't see me."

She let this sink in for a few seconds and then said, "There are two agents waiting for you in front of the house."

"I know," Mark told her with a quick glance at his watch. "I didn't want them to see me either."

"Can I get you some dinner?" she asked.

He shook his head. "No thanks."

She gestured toward the paper on the table. "Your picture is on the front page of the *Atlanta Constitution*."

He grimaced. "I heard."

She braced herself. "Okay, go ahead and tell me."

Mark took her hand in his, and Kate drew what comfort she could from the contact. "They won't let me say much."

Kate was quite familiar with FBI procedure. "Just what I *need-to-know*."

"I've been given an undercover assignment."

Kate nodded. "In Colombia."

Mark paled. "Why do you say that?"

"I talked to Marla, and she said you'd had her looking up lawyers and banks there. I just assumed . . ."

"Forget about that," Mark said a little harshly. Then he immediately apologized. "I'm sorry. It's just that, well, you're going to have to trust me, Kate."

She frowned. "You know I do."

"Thank you."

"So you're not going to South America?" Anywhere inside the United States would be preferable. Maybe he would be assigned someplace close enough for her and the kids to visit on weekends. She was about to voice these thoughts when she looked into his weary eyes. Then she closed her mouth and swallowed a sob. "What's going on, Mark?"

"There may be some rumors about me, Kate. Nasty rumors. You have to ignore them."

"What kind of rumors?" she demanded, already angry at the thought.

"That's not important," he assured her.

"It's important to me."

"Tomorrow I want you to pack up the van and tell the neighbors we've decided to spend some time with my parents in Texas. Let them assume that I'm already there and that you're meeting me. The agents out front will follow you there to be sure you make it safely."

"But really you'll be working undercover?"

"Yes."

She sighed. "When do you have to go?"

He grasped her hand a little tighter. "Tonight—as soon as I can pack some clothes."

Kate swiped at the tears leaking out of her eyes. "Oh, Mark."

He stroked her cheek. "It will be okay."

Kate pressed Mark's hand to her lips, feeling like her whole world had crashed down around her.

* * *

When Eugenia Atkins took Lady, her miniature wire-haired dachshund, out for a final bathroom break before bed on Tuesday night, she noticed that the lights were still on in the Iversons' kitchen. Eugenia glanced at her watch and saw that it was after nine o'clock—which according to Southern etiquette was too late to make social calls. But Mark's car still wasn't parked in the driveway, and Eugenia was concerned. She decided that a late visit from a well-intentioned neighbor wouldn't be an unforgivable breach of good manners.

After putting Lady back in the house, Eugenia crossed the small strip of lawn that separated the two houses and knocked on the Iversons' back door. As was her custom, she then stepped inside without waiting for a response.

"Helloooo!" she called out in greeting while walking into the kitchen. She found Kate and Mark sitting at the table. Eugenia was surprised to see Mark, since his car wasn't parked in the driveway. She thought Kate looked a little pale, but then that was no surprise. Who wouldn't be pale if they had to wait up night after night for their husband to come home from either his job or his church assignments?

"I'm glad you're finally home," she said to Mark as she took a seat beside Kate. "But where is your car? And why are those two agents from Atlanta still parked at the curb?"

"Mark's using a different car, and he's going to be working out of town for a while," Kate supplied in a dazed tone. "He's leaving tonight and doesn't have time to waste talking to those agents out front."

Eugenia studied them, belatedly taking in the tearstains on Kate's cheeks and the hollow look around Mark's eyes. "What's really going on? Have you been fired?"

"No, ma'am," Mark responded promptly. "Like Kate said, I'm going to be working out of town for a while."

"Are Kate and the children going with you?"

Mark shook his head. "No, Kate and the kids will be staying with my parents."

Eugenia didn't like the idea of Kate and the children leaving, and she definitely smelled a rat—the government agency kind. "I assume this out-of-town work has something to do with the memo you got telling you to grow out your hair and make regular visits to a tanning salon in Tifton?"

Mark didn't look pleased by the question. "This is an unrelated assignment," Mark replied, but he wasn't very convincing.

Eugenia really wanted to press the issue, but Kate was already upset enough. So instead of trying to satisfy her curiosity, she asked, "What can I do to help?"

Mark rewarded her with a grateful smile. Then he stood. "I'm about to call my parents and tell them to expect a visit from Kate and the kids. Maybe you could help Kate pack me a suitcase."

Eugenia fixed Mark with a penetrating gaze and said, "Humph," just to be sure he knew she wasn't buying any of this. "Well, go ahead and make your phone call." She turned to Kate. "I'd offer to pack the bag myself, but you know how funny Mark is about anyone touching his underwear."

Kate gave her a ghost of a smile. "I'm coming." With one last longing glance at Mark, Kate followed Eugenia upstairs to the master bedroom.

Kate didn't seem to be in the mood for conversation, which was good since Eugenia couldn't think of anything comforting to say. She just stood by the bed while Kate packed Mark's bag. As Kate zipped it closed, Mark came in. "My parents are anxious for you to come. Hopefully I'll be able to join you in a couple of weeks."

Eugenia saw the color drain from Kate's face and knew that it was the possibility that Mark's assignment might last weeks—not the prospect of staying with his parents—that upset her.

"I'm sure Mark will be in Texas before you know it," Eugenia said with all the confidence she could muster.

"Mama?" a little voice asked from the doorway. Eugenia turned and saw Emily watching them in confusion. Her brother, Charles, was right beside her. "Why is everyone up in the middle of the night?"

Both Kate and Mark seemed at a loss for words, so Eugenia stepped forward. "Your daddy is going on a little trip for the FBI, and your mama is helping him get ready. We'll go to Emily's room, and I'll read a story until you both fall back asleep."

Eugenia took each child by the hand, intending to lead them from the room. But Mark's voice stopped her. "I need to tell them good-bye."

Eugenia's mother always said the most pitiful thing in the world was watching a strong man cry. When Mark pulled his children into his arms, Eugenia thought her heart would break. The scene was too much for Kate, and she had to walk into the nursery.

"Why are you sad, Daddy?" Emily asked as she touched a teardrop on his cheek.

Mark wiped away his tears with the sleeve of his dress shirt. "I'm sad because I have to leave for a while, and I'm going to miss you," he said softly. "I want you to promise that while I'm gone you'll be good and mind your mother."

Charles was staring at his father with wide, frightened eyes, so Emily spoke for them both. "We promise. Will you come back soon?"

Mark nodded. "I'm going to try." He pressed a kiss to each brow. "I love you so much."

Afraid that none of them could take much more, Eugenia beckoned to the children. "Let's get started on that story."

Mark released Emily and Charles, then stood alone in the middle of the room and watched them leave with Eugenia.

* * *

Kate's entire body was wracked with sobs, and the only thing that kept her from total collapse was the certain knowledge that the Lord would not try her beyond what she could bear. When she felt Mark's arms encircle her, she turned and clung to him.

"It's going to be okay, Kate," he whispered. "You'll be fine."

"I won't!" she wailed. "I know when you married me you thought I was brave, but really I'm just a big wimp!"

Mark made a noise that was something between a moan and a laugh. "You *are* brave."

She shook her head emphatically. "I can't stand the thought of being separated from you for one day—much less weeks." She grabbed fistfuls of his shirt fabric. "We're a team! We depend on each other. I can't do it alone."

Mark covered her clenched hands with his. "You won't have to, Kate. You'll have my parents and the FBI and the Lord."

"I need *you*."

"It will just be for a couple of weeks. You can handle things without me for that long."

She rested her head against his chest and listened to the steady pounding of his heart. "Maybe," she acknowledged. "But how will I be able to stand not knowing where you are or if you're okay? You could be sick or hurt or hungry, and I wouldn't even know."

"Don't worry about me, Kate."

She wanted to tell him that he might as well instruct her not to breathe while he was gone, but the words stuck in her throat, forcing out a burst of fresh tears instead.

"Oh, Kate," he said, his voice thick with emotion. "We'll still be a team—we just won't be in the same game for a little while."

Realizing that she was making it harder for him, Kate sniffled and nodded. "I guess that's true."

He put a finger under her chin and tried to lift her face, but she resisted. "Why won't you look at me?" he asked.

"Because I don't want you to remember me like this—with swollen eyes and red, blotchy skin."

"I think you look beautiful."

"Then love *is* blind," she muttered in a pitiful attempt to lighten the mood.

Mark didn't even smile. "Remember that we can't really be separated—no matter what happens. You're mine for eternity, Kate. Swollen eyes and all."

She looked into his face, so full of honor and sincerity, and thought of the scripture from the Doctrine and Covenants that said to whom much is given, much is expected. Surely no one could ask for more in a husband than Mark Iverson. "Enough talking," she said. "Now kiss me."

* * *

Eugenia read three stories out of the Mother Goose book she had given to the children last Christmas before they finally fell back asleep. She was sitting in the rocking chair trying to decide whether to move Charles to his own bed when she heard a movement by the door. She looked up to see Kate standing there. Kate seemed calmer and more resigned.

"Mark's downstairs," she said. "He'd like to talk to you before he leaves. I'll stay here with the children."

Eugenia hurried down as quickly as her arthritic bones would carry her and found Mark waiting in the kitchen. Eugenia pulled out a chair from the table and sat down.

Mark took a seat opposite her. "Will you help Kate pack and get the kids ready for the trip to Texas?"

Eugenia reached over and patted his hand. "You know I will."

"And will you look after the house while we're gone?"

"I'll even fertilize your garden so you might actually be able to grow something next spring."

He gave her a wan smile.

"What you need to keep in mind is that your precious children need a father. You take care of yourself, you hear?"

Mark stood and picked up his suitcase. "I'll do my best."

Eugenia followed him to the back door and watched him walk across the yard and down the alley to the dark blue car that was parked on Oak Street. Then she walked slowly back upstairs and found Kate lying on Emily's bed between the children.

"He's gone then?" Kate asked, her voice hoarse from crying.

"Yes," Eugenia told her. "But he'll be back."

"I don't know if I can stand this," Kate whispered.

"You can," Eugenia said firmly, "because you have to." Eugenia took a step closer to the bed. "But no one can see you now. Go right ahead and cry yourself out."

With a nod, Kate buried her face in a pillow.

Eugenia used Emily's quilt to cover them all. Then she settled into the rocking chair and began her watch.

* * *

Kate was awakened at midnight by the sound of someone pounding on the front door. She sat up and tried to get her bearings. She was in Emily's room. The children were asleep on either side of her. Miss Eugenia was in the rocking chair. Then memory returned. Mark was gone, and someone was about to beat down the front door.

"I declare, I think we should call Winston and have him come arrest whoever that is," Miss Eugenia suggested. "They are at least disturbing the peace and probably defacing private property!"

Kate climbed over Charles and put her feet on the hardwood floor. "Go ahead and call the police station and ask them to send someone over just in case," she requested. "But in the meantime, I'm going down to see if I can put an end to that racket before the entire neighborhood wakes up."

Kate ran out into the hall and down the stairs. Once she reached the foyer, she could see two large, male shapes looming in the front porch light. She peered through the peephole and wasn't a bit surprised to see Agents Lott and Applegate, looking even grimmer than they had the previous afternoon.

"What can I do for you gentlemen?" Kate demanded through the thick wooden door.

"You can let us speak to your husband immediately," Agent Lott returned without a trace of good humor.

"My husband isn't here," Kate replied, wiping the last vestiges of sleep from her eyes.

"He's been here, but he left without speaking to us," Agent Lott accused. "In fact, he purposely avoided us."

"Where was he headed?" Agent Applegate demanded.

"I don't know," Kate replied honestly.

"If you don't cooperate, you could be considered an accomplice." Agent Applegate's tone was mildly threatening now.

"An accomplice to what?" she scoffed. "Failure to return phone calls?"

Agent Lott sneered at the peephole. "Yesterday morning your husband signed for twelve million dollars that was confiscated during a raid. Immediately thereafter he disappeared, and all that money is unaccounted for. It looks like he's taken the money and run."

"Ridiculous," Kate said. But then she thought about the worried look in Mark's eyes and his plea for her to trust him. He had said that there might be nasty rumors about him. Before she had a chance to say more, a Haggerty police car turned the corner onto Maple Street with blue lights flashing. Kate watched gratefully as Winston Jones himself climbed out of the vehicle and loped up to the front porch.

"Evening, fellows," he said to the disruptive FBI agents in his best good-old-boy tone. "I heard you were causing a little ruckus."

Kate watched the agents display their badges.

Winston seemed unimpressed. "Do you have a warrant for Mrs. Iverson's arrest?" he asked.

"Of course not!" Agent Lott replied.

"A search warrant for these premises?" Winston further inquired.

"No." Agent Lott's response was a little more subdued this time. "We don't want to arrest anyone or search anything. We just want to speak to Agent Iverson."

"Is Mark home, Kate?" Winston called through the door.

"No," she replied. "He's not."

Winston returned his attention to the FBI agents. "Well, fellows, if Mark's not home, you're wasting your time banging on his front door and scaring his old lady neighbors, his wife, and his children."

"We have official business with Agent Iverson," Agent Applegate reiterated. "Very important business."

Winston removed his hat and scratched his head. "I don't know how you boys ever got into the FBI. Seems to me like you're both slow learners." He distorted his lips to exaggerate his words as he said, "Mark Iverson ain't home." He returned his hat to his head. "And this is private property. You can't stay here unless Mrs. Iverson invites you." Winston turned and addressed the door again. "Did you invite them to stay, Kate?"

"No," she assured him.

Winston shrugged. "Then unless *you* want to be arrested, you'd better get back in your car and stay there."

"You're going to regret this," Agent Lott promised Winston. "And see if you're still talking so smart when your husband is on trial for grand larceny," he yelled at the door.

Winston pulled out his pocketknife and started trimming his fingernails. "I'm trembling in my boots." Once the FBI agents were retreating toward their car, Winston lowered his voice and asked, "You okay, Kate?"

She pressed her face against the cool wood. "Physically, yes. Emotionally, I'm not sure."

"Did Mark really steal a lot of money from the FBI?"

"What do you think?" she asked.

He considered the question for a second. Then he laughed. "Not a chance."

"Of course not," she agreed.

"Well, you go on back to bed. I'll sit here and keep an eye on these yo-yos."

"Thank you, Winston," she whispered.

He saluted the door with the pocketknife. "Hey, what are friends for?" Then he walked slowly toward his squad car.

* * *

Kate had just started up the stairs when the phone rang. She grabbed it without checking the caller ID—hoping it was Mark. It wasn't.

"Mrs. Iverson, this is Fred Pressnell from the *Atlanta Constitution.* I wrote an article in yesterday's paper about your husband helping to crack a pornography ring. I guess you saw it."

"Yes," Kate replied absently.

"Well, I'm preparing my article for today's paper, and I'm hoping you can help me clear things up."

"I don't see how I can be of any help," Kate told him.

"Where is your husband, Mrs. Iverson?"

"He's on assignment with the FBI," Kate replied. "I don't know where."

"What about the twelve million dollars?"

"I don't know anything about that."

"But you're sure your husband is still actively working for the FBI?"

"Yes."

"Even if the FBI claims otherwise?"

Kate considered this briefly before saying, "Yes."

"If you hear from your husband, please tell him to contact me. I like to be fair in my stories, print both sides and all that."

"I'll tell him," Kate promised. Then Mr. Pressnell disconnected the call.

Miss Eugenia was waiting for Kate at the top of the stairs. "That was the reporter from the *Atlanta Constitution* who printed the story about the pornography ring yesterday. He says he's running a new article today claiming that Mark has disappeared with the twelve million dollars."

"What do you think?" Miss Eugenia asked.

"I know Mark didn't steal anything," Kate said firmly.

"I agree, but the news reporter is just doing his job by trying to find out all the facts. Maybe the FBI is even doing their job by saying Mark is on vacation."

Kate looked at the old woman whom over the years she had learned to trust. "So what's my job?"

"Your job is to defend your husband."

Kate nodded wearily. "You're right."

"Of course I am. But you can't do anything tonight except go back to bed and try to get some rest."

CHAPTER 4

On Wednesday morning, Eugenia was awakened by a gentle shake. She opened her eyes to see Emily standing beside the rocking chair. Charles was still asleep on the double bed, but Kate's spot was empty.

"Did we have a spend-the-night party?" Emily whispered, careful not to wake up her brother.

"No." Eugenia started moving her limbs one at a time to be sure they still worked. "After I said good-bye to your daddy last night, I just decided to stay."

Emily frowned. "Daddy had to go away. Why?"

Having confirmed that she could move, Eugenia pushed herself into a semistanding position, causing every muscle to scream. "Your father has an important job that helps our country to be free," she told Emily through clenched dentures. "He had to go away so he could do his job."

"Then why is Mama sad?"

Eugenia answered carefully. "Because she's going to miss your father very much. We all will. And you're going to have to be especially good and brave to help your mother."

"I will," Emily promised. Then she asked, "Why are you standing funny?"

"Because seventy-seven-year-old bones were never intended to sit all night in a wooden rocking chair," Eugenia replied. "Now why don't we walk over and feed Lady? Then we can make breakfast."

"Pancakes?"

Eugenia shook her head. "No, that's your mother's specialty. I'm partial to scrambled eggs and crisp bacon and creamy grits and buttermilk biscuits."

Emily giggled. "Me too!"

Eugenia smiled. "Let's find your mother and tell her where we're going."

* * *

Kate was standing at the living room windows, looking out at the FBI car that was still parked in front of the house, when Miss Eugenia and Emily joined her.

Miss Eugenia glanced outside and then said, "I see our friends haven't given up yet."

Kate shook her head. "No. Winston went home a little while ago, and Miss Polly's already brought them breakfast."

Miss Eugenia seemed pleased to hear this. "It's good that we're being neighborly even if those agents don't have good manners."

"We're going over to feed Lady," Emily told her mother. "Then we're going to make breakfast."

"We'll be back in a few minutes," Miss Eugenia promised.

Kate watched them leave. Then she climbed the stairs to rouse Charles. She walked into Emily's room and sat on the edge of the bed. Charles was curled on his side, breathing evenly. She reached out and brushed the dark hair from his forehead. He opened his eyes and blinked up at her.

"Mama?"

She looked into his eyes. They were big and brown—just like his father's. "Good morning," she managed.

"Daddy's gone?"

She nodded.

"But he'll come back?"

She nodded again.

"Where's Emily?" he asked.

"She's next door with Miss Eugenia. They'll be back in a few minutes to make breakfast for us."

Charles smiled. "Can I help?"

She held her son close and pressed a kiss on his forehead. "I'm just sure you can."

Kate and Charles combined to make Emily's bed. Once that chore was accomplished, Kate supervised as Charles got dressed. Since she was still wearing her clothes from the day before, dressing wasn't a necessity for Kate. She ran a toothbrush across her teeth, pulled her hair into a sloppy ponytail, and then led the way downstairs.

They walked into the kitchen just as Miss Eugenia and Emily were returning from next door. Emily was carrying Lady, and the little dog barked in greeting when she saw Charles.

"Lady!" he cried.

Emily handed the dog to Charles, then told Kate, "We're not making just pancakes. We're cooking a bunch of stuff."

"I want to help too!" Charles lifted his face away from Lady's enthusiastic licking.

Miss Eugenia put a grocery sack on the counter and fixed Emily with a stern look. "You're not helping me make anything until you wash your hands and change out of your pajamas."

"I'll be right back!" Emily called as she hurried to obey.

Miss Eugenia turned her attention to Charles. "And I was counting on you to watch Lady."

Charles giggled as the little dog licked his neck. "Okay."

"Why don't you take Lady into the den to watch PBS until breakfast is ready." As Charles made his exit, Miss Eugenia turned to Kate. "I brought everything we need for breakfast except for eggs," Miss Eugenia continued. "Mine have expired. Do you have fresh ones?"

Kate opened the refrigerator door and checked the expiration date on her carton of eggs. "They still have a week to go."

"Good," Miss Eugenia said. "Now instead of standing around, maybe you could make yourself useful by frying some bacon?"

Kate knew that Miss Eugenia was being extra bossy in an effort to distract her from feeling sad—so she tried not to give in to irritation as she removed a skillet from the cabinet and put it on the stove.

"Here's the bacon." Miss Eugenia put a package on the counter beside the stove.

Kate spread several strips of bacon out in the skillet and watched as they slowly started to cook.

Emily returned wearing an outfit Kate bought her a few weeks ago for their trip to Hawaii. Kate's mind wandered to those glorious days spent on the white sand beaches of Oahu—the kids building sand castles and playing in the waves with Mark . . .

Miss Eugenia's voice snapped Kate out of her reverie. "If you don't watch that bacon closely, you'll burn it."

Kate blinked back her tears and muttered, "I won't burn it."

Once the bacon was cooked, blotted, and neatly arranged on a small platter, Miss Eugenia had Kate reconstitute the orange juice and scramble the eggs. When they finally settled around the kitchen table, Miss Polly called from the back door, "Good morning!"

"Come in," Kate invited.

Miss Polly emerged from the laundry room wearing one of the many floral print dresses she preferred, a freshly pressed lace handkerchief tucked in the neckline.

"There are two new FBI men sitting in front of your house now, Kate. I just took them breakfast."

"I guess the others had to go somewhere and sleep for a while."

"I was so shocked by the behavior of Agents Applegate and Lott last night," Miss Polly said. "Banging on your door in the middle of the night like that! If they don't watch their manners, I won't be so quick to feed them again." She pressed her lips together in a firm look of disapproval. "Besides, Mark had been gone for hours by the time they came knocking."

Kate had to smile. The FBI really should hire Miss Polly. Nobody escaped her natural radar.

Miss Polly studied Kate. "You look tired."

"I've had two nights in a row with little or no sleep," Kate admitted.

Miss Polly frowned. "Sleep deprivation can be a serious thing. I saw a special a few years ago about a radio announcer who went without sleep for twenty-seven days. He finally went completely crazy."

Kate glanced at Miss Eugenia, who was regarding her with raised eyebrows. "Well," Kate responded finally. "Thank goodness I have another twenty-five days to spare before I turn into a raving lunatic."

"Me and Miss Eugenia made this great breakfast," Emily informed their other neighbor.

"Miss Eugenia and I," Miss Eugenia corrected.

Emphasis on the I, Kate thought to herself since she had done almost everything. But instead of pointing this out, she smiled at Miss Polly. "Won't you join us for our breakfast?"

"I don't mind if I do," Miss Polly said, her eyes widening with pleasure as she saw the array of breakfast foods. "I taste tested what I made for the FBI men but didn't really *eat.*"

Kate stood to get Miss Polly a plate, and when she returned, she saw the morning edition of the *Atlanta Constitution* on the table. "Where did this come from?" she asked.

"Oh, I almost forgot!" Miss Polly said. "Whit dropped this off a while back. He stopped at Eugenia's house, but she wasn't home. I just happened to be looking out my front window, so I walked out and asked him if there was anything I could do."

"You just happened to be looking out your front window?" Miss Eugenia repeated.

"Wasn't that a blessed coincidence?" Miss Polly affirmed as she piled strips of crispy bacon onto her plate. "Anyway, Whit said he thought Eugenia might like to see the article about Mark, so I was headed over here when I noticed the new FBI agents. By the time I fixed them breakfast, I had completely forgotten about the paper."

Kate and Miss Eugenia both reached for the paper at the same time. Kate saw Mr. Pressnell's article in the bottom right-hand corner of the front page of the *Atlanta Constitution*. The headline, in medium bold letters declared: "Rogue Agent Steals Millions." From that point on, there was really no contest—Kate was determined to win at any cost. Finally Miss Eugenia gave up. Kate carried it over to the kitchen counter where she could read in relative privacy.

FBI Agent Mark Iverson usually mans the resident agency in Albany, but for the past several weeks, he has been working with the Atlanta field office. Yesterday Iverson was instrumental in cracking the child pornography ring on Market Street (exclusive photographs and interviews can be accessed on our website). However, according to sources inside the FBI, shortly after the history-making arrests at the warehouse, Special Agent Mark Iverson went AWOL. Also missing is the twelve million dollars in cash that was confiscated during the bust. Officially, the FBI isn't admitting that anyone or any money is unaccounted for. Assistant special agent in charge at the field office in Atlanta, Howard Bowen, would only say that Mark Iverson is currently on an extended leave of absence and that the FBI had no further comment.

All attempts to reach Agent Iverson at his home, his office in Albany, and the field office in Atlanta have proven futile. However, a bank clerk at the Atlanta Bank of Commerce said that yesterday the agent spent an hour at the branch where she works, in the department that specializes in international money wiring. And a man in the Roswell section of Atlanta claims to have sold the agent a used car late yesterday afternoon. Police and the FBI are checking into these reports. At this point, all indications are that Agent Mark Iverson found himself in possession of a substantial amount of money and decided to take it. The FBI, not wanting to admit such gross negligence on their part or the part of one of their agents, is covering up the theft while they scramble to recover the money and their rogue agent.

By the time Kate finished reading the article, her breath was coming in quick, angry gasps. Mr. Pressnell made Mark look like a common criminal. And whoever Mr. Bowen at the FBI was, he had done nothing to protect Mark's reputation or stand up for him in any way.

"What does the article say?" Miss Eugenia asked.

Kate squared her shoulders and turned to face the others. "To put it mildly, the reporter and the FBI seem to be doing their jobs much better than I am."

Miss Polly frowned. "What job do you have, Kate?"

"The job of defending Mark." She crossed her arms over her chest. "And based on what is printed here, if I take the children and go to Texas as planned, I will confirm in everyone's mind that Mark is a criminal and we're running away."

"Texas?" Miss Polly and Emily repeated in confused unison.

Miss Eugenia ignored everyone except Kate. "But what else can you do?"

"I think I'll start by making some phone calls." Kate took a few steps toward the hall before Miss Eugenia stopped her.

"You haven't eaten breakfast."

"I'm too upset to eat," Kate assured her.

She marched into Mark's office and turned on his computer. She already had the number for Mark's supervisor, Dan Davis. With the help of Google, she was able to find numbers for the special agent in charge of the Atlanta field office, Frank Mitchell, on the Internet. Encouraged by her success, she looked up Capitol Hill and got numbers for the senators from Georgia and several that claimed to be direct lines to the White House. Then she reached for the phone.

Thirty minutes later, she had been politely snubbed by a secretary at the FBI field office in Atlanta, two secretaries in senate offices on Capitol Hill, and five switchboard operators at the White House. When Miss Eugenia came to check on her, Kate admitted, "No one took me seriously."

"They might find it harder to ignore you in person," Miss Eugenia suggested.

"You think I should go to Washington?"

Miss Eugenia smiled. "Well, maybe you could start with Atlanta. And if you don't get results at the FBI field office there, I'll bet you could find some newspaper and television reporters who would be happy to hear what you have to say."

Kate considered this for a few seconds and then nodded. "I think you're right. Can you watch the kids for me?"

"It will be my pleasure," Miss Eugenia agreed.

* * *

Kate stood before her closet and surveyed her wardrobe options. Her eyes passed over the skirts and blouses she wore to church on Sunday and zeroed in on the bright red Christmas dress, still covered with dry cleaner plastic from last year. She smiled grimly as she removed the dress from its hanger. She had once used the dress to alert Mark that she was in extreme danger. It seemed only fitting that she wear it for her meeting with the special agent in charge of the

Atlanta field office. Then, at least, he would never be able to say that she hadn't given him fair warning.

She slipped the dress over her head and studied her reflection in the mirror. She had inherited the dress from a New York socialite several years before. It was now a little tight through the hips. *That's what two kids and four years of happiness will do for you,* Kate thought as she continued her self-scrutiny. It might be tight and no longer be the latest style, but she would certainly be difficult to ignore.

Kate fixed her hair and applied more makeup than usual—hoping to bolster her confidence. Then after one last quick inspection, she hurried downstairs.

"Oh, Mama!" Emily cried when she walked into the family room. "You look beautiful!"

Kate smiled. "Thank you, Emily."

"Very smart," Miss Eugenia agreed. If she saw any significance in Kate's choice of dress, she didn't say so.

"Pretty smart." Charles combined the two compliments and earned himself a maternal kiss.

Kate paused to wipe the lipstick from her son's forehead. Then she picked up her purse and extracted the van keys. "I'll call you when I know what time I'll be home."

Miss Eugenia nodded. "I've already called Whit and told him to bring pizza for dinner. We'll take care of the children for however long you need us to."

Kate wanted to go over and hug them all but knew that if she did that, she'd start crying. Then she'd have to repair her makeup, and it would be late by the time she reached Atlanta. So instead she gave them a quick wave and hurried outside.

Kate climbed into her van and drove up beside the FBI car. She rolled down her window, and the agent sitting in the passenger side did the same. Then both agents regarded her with surprise and caution.

"Kate Iverson," she introduced herself. "I don't believe we've met. Give Applegate and Lott my regards. I'm headed to Atlanta. Maybe I'll see you when I get back."

Now confusion joined the assortment of facial expressions. "But we thought you were going to Texas," the one closest to Kate said.

"We're supposed to follow you. All the way," he added as if the trip were to the moon.

"Well, it looks like you're off the hook. I'm not sure what Miss Polly's planning for lunch, but she's a wonderful cook, so at least you've got something to look forward to."

"If you're going to Atlanta, I guess we should go too," the agent behind the wheel said.

"But what if my husband comes home while I'm gone?" Kate asked. "Isn't that the whole reason you're here in the first place? To speak to him?"

"Well, at first, yes, but then they said we were supposed to follow you to Texas . . ."

"But now I'm not going to Texas," Kate reminded them. "So either you'll have to go to Atlanta, or you'll have to stay here. I don't really care which. The only thing to consider is that if you stay here, Miss Polly will provide you with meals."

Kate pressed the button that automatically rolled up her window. Then she stepped on the gas and drove away. She meandered through town for a few minutes to see if they had decided to follow her—but apparently they had decided to stay and take advantage of Miss Polly's cooking.

* * *

Mark peered through the thick cloud cover and tried to see the ground below.

"We'll be arriving at the airstrip near Cartagena in about fifteen minutes," the navy pilot told him.

"Thank you," Mark said automatically. They had been flying for almost five hours, and Mark was anxious for the chance to stretch his legs. But while landing would bring great relief to his cramped muscles, he knew that once he stepped off the plane, he would be completely alone.

The plane made an amazingly smooth landing considering that the landing strip was little more than a swath of hard-packed earth in the middle of a field. Once they rolled to a stop, the pilot held out his hand, and Mark shook it firmly. "Good luck," the pilot said.

"Be careful flying back home," Mark replied.

Mark opened the door and stepped out of the plane. A wall of humid heat greeted him and made him wish he'd had the foresight to remove his suit coat before leaving the relatively comfortable confines of the plane. He stepped back and watched as the plane turned around and took off again. Feeling conspicuous, Mark stood alone on the sun-scorched dirt for several minutes. Finally he saw a white Jeep approaching in the distance.

The Jeep was at least ten years old and was covered with a solid layer of road dust. The windows were open, which presumably meant that the air conditioner didn't work. But Mark was too grateful to care when the vehicle rolled to a stop in front of him. A Hispanic man with longish gray hair and wise brown eyes sat behind the wheel.

"Mr. Morales?" Mark guessed.

"Yes," the lawyer confirmed. "And I presume you are Mark Iverson."

"I am."

Mr. Morales leaned over and pushed open the passenger door. "I have taken the liberty of purchasing this all-terrain vehicle for you. It was a great bargain—cheap price."

Mark climbed in and slammed the door shut. "Thank you, Mr. Morales."

The other man smiled. "Please, call me Cristobal. And don't thank me. I will charge you obscenely for my services."

Mark smiled back. "I don't mind—just as long as I get my money's worth."

Cristobal's smile dimmed slightly. "I will do my best."

During the drive from the landing strip to La Rosa, Cristobal Morales filled Mark in on things that Angelo Perez hadn't had time for—like what he could expect from the weather in La Rosa. "The main thing you need to be aware of this time of year is heat." Cristobal paused to wipe the perspiration from his forehead, emphasizing his point. "Here along the coast it is humid, and the temperatures exceed ninety most days. It cools off some at night and gives us relief."

Cristobal switched from English to Spanish smoothly in a natural bilingual speech pattern. Unsure which language to use, Mark decided to reply in whatever language Cristobal was using at the time of his last comment or question. "It feels a lot like Georgia in the summertime," he said.

Cristobal smiled. "Ah, then you are acclimated already."

Mark noticed that the roads became progressively steeper as they got closer to the town of La Rosa. Finally they climbed a hill that would have been impossible without the four-wheel drive feature of their Jeep and turned a steep curve. At that point, La Rosa came into view. It was a beautiful little city, and Mark found it hard to believe that it was, as Angelo had warned him, the home of the devil.

"I hope you like the little villa I have purchased for you," Cristobal said while negotiating the Jeep through a series of hairpin turns. "The rent is expensive, but you said that you were willing to pay for privacy and comfort. This property has both."

"Then I'm sure I'll be very pleased," Mark replied.

"And I can personally vouch for Pilar, your new housekeeper, since she worked for me until I gave her to you."

Again, Mark wasn't sure if this was a kindness or a way to keep tabs on the new arrival. "Thank you. I hope your own household won't suffer because of your generosity."

Cristobal laughed. "My household suffers because of my six rowdy daughters. An army of Pilars couldn't keep them all under control. So I figure she will be put to better use at your house."

Cristobal slowed the Jeep and eased off the gravel road and onto a dirt one, branches hitting the Jeep on both sides. Mark peered through the windshield, watching for his rental house.

The term *villa* conjured certain expectations in Mark's mind. He assumed that the house would be made of white stucco with a red tile roof—a miniature of Rodrigo Salazar's home. The house would be surrounded by a tall, impenetrable security fence, and once inside the gate, Mark could picture a charming little courtyard—with a small fountain in the middle.

So when Cristobal stopped in front of a dilapidated cabin made of weathered wood and surrounded by a lawn of overgrown weeds, Mark was both astounded and disappointed.

"This is my *villa?*" he asked in Spanish.

Cristobal laughed. "Just wait until you see the inside."

The lawyer waited while Mark retrieved his luggage. Then he led the way to the front door. Mark's eyes moved from the peeling paint to a shutter hanging on by one rusty nail and finally came to rest on the very modern keypad that Cristobal revealed by moving a loose shingle.

"If you'll place your palm here, please," Cristobal requested, and Mark complied. "I have programmed the security system to recognize you. The only other people who are currently entered in are myself and Pilar."

"All I have to do is put my palm on the screen?" Mark asked.

Cristobal nodded. "The system reads your prints and body temperature."

Mark frowned. "Body temperature?"

"To be sure that the palm pressed against the screen is still attached to a *body*."

Mark swallowed hard. "Oh, very clever."

"I gave you overriding control," Cristobal continued. "So you can remove our access if you would prefer to be the only person who can gain access."

Mark wasn't sure yet how limited he wanted the access to his hovel to be, so he said, "I'll decide that later. Now let's get inside. I'm melting out here." He knew the interior of the house would at least provide shade, and if he were extremely lucky, there would be a fan to blow the hot, humid air around. But when Cristobal swung open the door, Mark was surprised by a blast of cool air. Encouraged, he crossed the threshold into a small entryway with a terra-cotta tile floor. The walls were the white stucco he had expected for the exterior with the room's dim lighting provided by a lamp on an old-style Spanish table.

"The best part about this house is that it doesn't look impressive from the road," Cristobal explained. "Crime is a problem in Colombia. It comes hand-in-hand with few jobs and much poverty."

Mark nodded. "I understand. Understated is better."

"Much better," Cristobal agreed. Then he led Mark through a formal living room that he called a salon, into a large kitchen. Pilar was there waiting for them. She was younger than Mark had expected, probably close to his own age of thirty-three. She was wearing jeans and a T-shirt—which also didn't fit into his house-keeper stereotype.

After Cristobal made introductions, Pilar offered, "I will make any changes to the household routine that you prefer."

"For now, just keep everything the way you have it," Mark told her.

"How should I handle meals?"

"Keep them simple," Mark replied.

She nodded. "I hope the house will meet your approval."

"I'm sure it will."

"If you will excuse us," Cristobal said to Pilar, "we will continue our tour of the house."

Pilar stepped back, and Cristobal showed Mark the rest of the ground floor, which consisted of a laundry area and a huge glassed-in porch with an incredible view of La Rosa.

"The glass is tinted so that it can't be seen from below," Cristobal informed him. "It is also thick and imbedded with lead to make it difficult for listening devices to penetrate."

Mark looked around. "This is wonderful," he said enthusiastically. Casual, comfortable furniture was neatly arranged, and fans hung from the high ceilings, humming softly.

"I'm glad you approve," Cristobal returned. "Now let me show you the upstairs."

The lawyer took him to the master bedroom suite where Mark left his luggage. There were also two smaller guest rooms separated by a bathroom. Then Cristobal led him back downstairs and through the kitchen, where Pilar was busily chopping vegetables. They descended another set of stairs into the basement.

"This is where you will store the Jeep," Cristobal pointed to an empty parking space beside a battered blue Escort that Mark assumed belonged to Pilar.

"You people don't believe in buying nice cars, do you?"

Cristobal smiled. "Nice cars attract thieves. A wise person in La Rosa finds a dependable vehicle that no one else wishes to call their own."

Mark acknowledged the wisdom of this. "I think you have much to teach me, Cristobal."

The lawyer laughed. "I am sure that is true!"

The rest of the basement consisted of a small workout room and a spartan bedroom. "For servants if you ever choose to have someone live-in," Cristobal explained from the doorway.

Mark was favorably impressed. "This place is perfect. There is nothing I might need that you have not anticipated."

Cristobal accepted the praise with humility. "I have tried to assure your comfort," he said as he led the way back to the kitchen. "It is good for me that you and your money remain in La Rosa."

Pilar had breakfast set out on the table for them. "I was not sure which foods you prefer," she told Mark.

"I'll eat most anything." He picked up a corn tortilla, rolled it, and took a bite. "This is very good."

"You will eat too, Señor Morales?" Pilar invited the lawyer.

"Thank you, but no. I must get back to my office." He turned to Mark. "I arranged for one of my employees to come and pick me up. I suggest that you rest now, and then this evening when the sun goes down and it is cooler, you can meet me at one of La Rosa's fine restaurants. Perhaps you can even buy me dinner."

Mark smiled. "I'd be glad to."

Cristobal handed Mark a piece of paper as they walked to the entryway. "Here are the directions to La Cocina, my favorite restaurant in La Rosa. We will meet there at seven o'clock if this is fine with you."

Mark nodded. "That's fine."

They had reached the door, and Cristobal looked to be sure Pilar wasn't nearby. Then he lowered his voice and said, "I consider it my duty to make your stay here comfortable in every way. If you need female companionship—there are many beautiful women in La Rosa, and I could arrange something."

Mark tried to hide his distaste. "I'm a married man."

"That is not a problem," Cristobal assured him. "I could find you a woman who would understand that the relationship would be temporary."

Mark shook his head. "No thank you."

Cristobal shrugged. "Let me know if you change your mind."

"Thanks for your help," Mark said, instead of responding to the subject at hand.

Cristobal waved good-bye, then opened the door and walked to the Volkswagen Beetle parked behind the dusty Jeep on the dirt road in front of Mark's rental house.

Once Cristobal was gone, Mark returned to the kitchen and sat down in one of the wooden kitchen chairs. He filled a plate with food that Pilar had prepared and started to eat.

* * *

Once Kate was driving down I-75, she got out her cell phone and dialed the number for her in-laws. It was the only part of her plan she dreaded. She knew that Mark's parents were going to be disappointed when she told them that their visit was at least postponed and maybe permanently cancelled.

She was thankful when Mark's father answered. She had always found him easier to deal with than Mark's mother. She briefly explained about the change in plans. Mark's father listened closely, and when she finished, he said, "Kate, is there anything I can do to help you?"

Kate felt tears sting the back of her eyes. She didn't know what Mark had told his parents or what would be appropriate for her to say, but it was comforting to know that they were there to help if she needed them. "Not right now, but thanks for offering. I'll be in touch."

Then she closed the phone and forced back the tears. *Oh, Mark,* she whispered to herself. *Where are you and what are you doing?*

* * *

After eating a delicious breakfast, Mark went up to the master bedroom and used the PDA to contact Perez. Mark typed in a brief message notifying the other agent that he had made it to La Rosa in one piece. Perez replied briefly with congratulations and a reminder to use caution.

Mark stretched out on the huge bed and reveled in his success thus far. He had traveled to a foreign country in a confiscated drug transport plane and was still alive to tell about it. Surely that meant that Howard Bowen hadn't been completely right about him.

* * *

Kate arrived in Atlanta a little after two o'clock in the afternoon. Traffic was snarled in the perpetual construction, but she finally made it to the FBI office at two forty-five. She parked in a space reserved for visitors and used the rearview mirror to touch up her makeup. After saying a quick but fervent prayer, she grabbed the copy of the *Atlanta Constitution* Miss Polly had brought over that morning and climbed out of the van. Then she walked purposefully into the building.

Kate passed through the metal detector and showed her identification at the security counter. She was escorted by a uniformed guard to the information desk.

"I'd like to speak with Frank Mitchell, please," she said, using her best impression of Miss Eugenia in no-nonsense mode.

The woman at the information desk had obviously never dealt with anyone like Miss Eugenia and apparently didn't understand that in some FBI circles the color red was code for "extreme danger." She raised a perfectly waxed eyebrow and said, "You're here to see Mr. Mitchell, the special agent in charge of this facility?"

If this statement was intended to intimidate Kate, it didn't. She had just driven three and a half hours in a tight Christmas dress and was completely out of patience. "Your hearing is accurate."

This remark earned Kate a bland stare. "I presume you have an appointment," the woman said.

"I do not," Kate replied. "But I'm sure Mr. Mitchell will see me anyway."

Now both perfectly formed eyebrows lifted almost to the woman's professionally colored hairline. "I doubt that very seriously. Mr. Mitchell is a busy man."

Kate leaned between two smiling Halloween pumpkins decorating the information desk and resisted the urge to grab the woman by her neat little linen collar. In what she hoped was a menacing voice, she hissed, "You call and tell him that Kate Iverson is here to see him. He'll either meet with me right now, or I'll have an impromptu press conference on the front steps of the office. I'll tell the cameras everything I know about his little undercover operation in Colombia, and I'll make up some things I don't know just for good measure."

The woman scooted her chair back a few inches. Then, after a quick glance at the security guard standing beside Kate, she reached for the phone. She held a brief, whispered conversation and replaced the receiver. She cleared her throat and addressed Kate. "Mr. Mitchell will see you."

Kate gave the woman a victorious smile and pushed her sleeves up in preparation for the next battle. She followed the security guard to the elevators. They rode up to the fourth floor and walked down a series of hallways to the executive wing. With adrenaline still pumping, Kate sailed into the reception area outside Mr. Mitchell's office.

His secretary was a nice, grandmotherly woman. She gave Kate a pleasant smile, but Kate was not about to be distracted. "Mr. Mitchell is expecting me," she said.

"Yes, so I understand," the secretary said soothingly as she stood and came around her desk. "He'll be with you soon. If you'll just have a seat, I'd be happy to get you some coffee and maybe a doughnut . . ."

"I don't want anything to eat, and I'm not sitting down," Kate said, cutting through the friendly babble. "I need to speak to Mr. Mitchell *now*."

The secretary's plump little hands fluttered in agitation, but before she could reply, a male voice spoke from behind them. "I'll take things from here, Lurleen."

Kate turned to see a tall, thin man standing in the doorway to the office. His suit had an expensive sheen and fit him well. His hair was salt-and-pepper gray and neatly trimmed, his eyes shrewd and regarding her with open hostility.

"Won't you come in, Mrs. Iverson?" He pointed toward the office.

Kate felt a wave of misgiving. She was really just a housewife, a mother of two small children, the organist for her church. This man was a government official. She wasn't sure that she was up to battling him. Then her eyes fell to the newspaper she clutched in her hands, and the words *Rogue Agent* came into focus. Her resolve returned. She could do this for Mark.

She squared her shoulders and walked past Mr. Mitchell into the office. Another man was already there, seated in a chair in front of the large wooden desk. Unlike Mr. Mitchell, he was not perfectly groomed. His suit was a size too small and needed to be dry-cleaned. His expression was sullen, and he didn't stand or introduce himself when she entered.

"Mrs. Iverson, this is Howard Bowen." Mitchell corrected Mr. Bowen's breach of etiquette as he circled his desk and took a seat in the large, leather chair behind it. "He's one of my assistants."

Kate slapped the copy of the *Atlanta Constitution* on the polished surface of the desk. "He's also a liar," she said and was pleased to see both men register various degrees of surprise. "My husband is *not* on vacation."

Howard Bowen cleared his throat and leaned forward. "Officially . . ."

"I don't care what your official line is," Kate interrupted him. "We all know that Mark is on an undercover assignment. And we all know that he wouldn't steal a paperclip! He won't even use FBI ball-point pens for personal correspondence! And yet you are allowing, actually *encouraging,* this newspaper reporter to print lies about him. You're making him look like a common criminal, and I won't have it."

"Mrs. Iverson," Howard Bowen tried again.

"I want my husband's name cleared," she said. "I realize you may not be able to give the details of the operation he's working on, but I want you to state categorically that he is not suspected of any wrong-doing."

"And if we don't?" Mr. Mitchell asked quietly.

She stabbed her finger at the article from the morning paper. "Two can play this game. Since facts are apparently extraneous, I'll work the television cameras and legitimate newspapers until they get tired of the story. Then I'll go to the tabloids and talk shows. It shouldn't take long for your superiors in Washington to get concerned about the way you handle your office."

"That can backfire on you," Mr. Mitchell warned.

"You've already attacked Mark's character. If mud's going to be slung around, I'll make sure you get your share."

Mr. Mitchell laced his fingers together in what appeared to be a casual gesture, but Kate could see that his knuckles were white with tension. "Give me until eight o'clock in the morning. By then, we will have worked out a plan and a statement for the press."

Kate laughed out loud. "By then you could have me committed to an asylum and my children in foster care."

Mr. Mitchell had the good grace to blush. Apparently her guess was not too far off. "Until five o'clock this evening, then."

Kate checked her watch. "You have one hour. I'll be calling the press during that time. When your hour is up if I don't like what you have to say, I'll go with my plan."

Kate retrieved her newspaper, turned on her heels, and walked out of the office, closing the door behind her with a satisfying slam.

* * *

After the door stopped reverberating, Frank Mitchell and Howard Bowen faced each other. Both men wore grim expressions.

Finally Bowen voiced the obvious. "If she takes it to the press, she's going to blow this whole operation wide open."

Frank Mitchell nodded.

"I warned you about dealing with these Christian types. They have a problem with deceit, and their good name *means* something to them."

Frank Mitchell ignored this remark. "We might actually be able to use this situation to our advantage. We'll tell her that Iverson has set himself up as bait—trying to smoke out the owners of the pornography ring. We'll tell her that we've been trying to keep a lid on that until we could get men in place to protect him. And we'll agree to make a public statement."

"What kind of statement?"

"That we have complete confidence in Agent Iverson—that he is not rogue and is not suspected of any wrongdoing."

"Do you think she'll go for that?"

"She will if she thinks that saying any more publicly will endanger his life."

"What's to keep her from digging deeper after the press conference?"

Mitchell frowned. Then he reached across his desk and picked up the phone. "Lurleen," he said into the receiver. "Connect me with

William Evans, the SAC in Chicago. Tell him I only need a few minutes of his time, but it's urgent. Buzz me when you have him on the line."

Mitchell returned the receiver to the phone console.

"We're asking Chicago for help?" Bowen clarified.

Mitchell nodded. "Evans had dealings with Iverson and his wife a few years ago. Maybe he'll know the best way to neutralize her."

CHAPTER 5

Solana and Emilio slipped into the truck and faced each other breathlessly. Solana pushed her hair back from her face and said, "That little detour you insisted on just cost us almost an hour that we could have used driving to Cartagena. I hope you're satisfied."

He leaned over and kissed her softly. "I am."

She rolled her eyes in exasperation. "You are about to be a satisfied dead man. Now let's get going. The movie will be over much too soon, and then they will begin looking for us."

Emilio started the truck and drove toward the outskirts of the city. Solana leaned against the warm vinyl seat and willed herself to relax. They were on their way, and with each passing minute, she began to feel more confident. Soon they would be in Cartagena. Then she would call her mother so passage could be arranged for herself and Emilio to Stockholm. She knew her father would be angry. She knew it was possible that Vargas would still seek revenge against Emilio. But from Sweden they could defend themselves. Here in La Rosa—they were helpless.

"What are you thinking of?" Emilio asked.

She smiled across at him. "I was thinking how glad I will be when we get off these open roads and onto the crowded streets of Cartagena."

"I look forward to just the opposite thing," he countered, his voice low and husky. "The chance to have you all to myself."

She reached over and caressed his cheek. "I look forward to that too—once we have put Colombia and General Vargas far behind us."

He caught her hand in his and pressed her fingers to his lips. She closed her eyes, enjoying the sensation. Solana was torn from her pleasant thoughts by the sound of a muted explosion. Emilio dropped her fingers abruptly and grasped the steering wheel hard with both hands. He fought the swerving truck for several yards before finally bringing it to a sudden stop.

"What happened?" Solana demanded, expecting the worst. "Did someone *shoot* at us?"

Emilio shook his head. "No, it is just a flat tire."

She felt an overwhelming sense of relief. All was not lost. "So you will change it, and we can go on to Cartagena?"

He nodded, but she saw the worry in his dark eyes. "As long as it doesn't take too long."

Solana understood. If they were still here on the outskirts of La Rosa when the movie ended, they would never make it to the safety of Cartagena before a search was initiated. They would be caught, and Emilio would be punished, possibly even killed.

"Hurry," she whispered.

* * *

Mark awakened suddenly and looked around the strange room, feeling disoriented. Then he remembered where he was and why. He sat up slowly and swung his feet over the edge of the large bed. He checked his watch and saw that it was almost five thirty on Wednesday evening. He needed to move quickly if he planned to shower before meeting Cristobal for dinner in La Rosa.

He walked to the window and looked out at the lush forest that came within a few feet of the house. The villa was very private, he had to admit. But the same trees that protected him from prying eyes would also keep him from being able to see anyone who was watching his movements—all the more reason to follow the advice of Angelo Perez and be very cautious.

After a shower, Mark changed into a clean shirt and a pair of black dress pants. He was going to shave but at the last minute decided the two-day stubble was more in keeping with his new renegade lifestyle. He brushed his damp, longish hair back from his face and stared at the reflection in the mirror. He barely recognized himself.

Slightly unnerved by the changes in his life reflected in his face, Mark turned and walked downstairs for his date with Cristobal Morales.

* * *

Solana wasn't sure when exactly she realized that their escape plan was doomed. She didn't give up hope when they discovered that there was no jack in the back of the truck. Emilio was a smart, resourceful young man. He could compensate for this. And he had. Using a crowbar and an abandoned cinderblock, he had lifted the truck up high enough to maneuver the wheel off.

The beginnings of panic set in when he broke a lug nut, but Emilio assured Solana that the wheel could function properly without one, so she tried not to worry as he mounted the spare. It was when they saw that it was also flat that she started to tremble with terror. Her fear was beyond tears. Emilio was going to die because of her. Later, when she explained everything, her father would probably regret the events that would surely follow, but by then, it would be much too late.

She looked at Emilio, who still knelt beside the truck. His hair was damp with sweat, his face was streaked with road dust, and his hands were covered with dirt from the faulty wheels. But his eyes were full of acceptance and courage.

"I am so sorry," she managed, although her teeth were chattering. "This is all my fault."

"No." He stood and, after wiping as much dirt as he could from his hands onto the sides of his pants, took her into his arms. He pressed her face against his chest and soothed her. "I knew the risks of every choice I made. I would do it all again, give up everything, just for the chance to call you mine."

At these words, tears did come. "Oh, Emilio." She wept.

"Shhh," he said, stroking her hair. "We will enjoy these last moments together."

* * *

Kate closed her cell phone and leaned her head against the van's steering wheel. She had called Mr. Pressnell first and asked him to come to the FBI office for the press conference. Then she had contacted each of the four local television stations, and all had promised to have a camera crew in attendance.

The righteous indignation that had fueled her fury earlier was gone, leaving her tired and a little afraid. She didn't want to face cameras and reporters. She didn't want to force the FBI to bend to her will. She just wanted to go home.

Someone knocked on her window, and Kate jerked her head up. The security guard from the main lobby was standing beside the van.

"Mrs. Iverson?" His voice was muffled by the window glass.

Kate lowered the window. "Yes?"

"Mr. Mitchell would like to talk to you if you're available."

Several sarcastic comments jumped to Kate's lips, but she bit them back. "I'm quite available." She closed the window, switched off the car, and climbed out. Then she followed the guard back into the building.

* * *

"We've worked out something that we hope will be acceptable to you," Mr. Mitchell said when Kate was seated in his office.

"You know my terms," Kate returned firmly. She had come too far to back down now.

"Yes. Mr. Bowen will make an official statement at your . . ." his expression became pained, "street-side press conference. However, there are aspects of the operation Agent Iverson is involved in that we cannot make public—for his own safety."

Kate's mouth went dry.

"You know that your husband was involved in cracking a child pornography ring here in Atlanta yesterday?"

Kate nodded.

"We arrested almost forty people and confiscated thousands of DVDs and photographs. We also found mailing lists and, of course, a large amount of cash. However, we did not find the people who owned the company.

"They managed it through a middleman who never met them personally. Naturally we would have been pleased to get all of them, but we have to be satisfied sometimes. We are restrained by time and money and personnel issues."

Kate finally shook her head. "I don't understand what you're telling me."

"Your husband couldn't accept our decision to end the investigation without uncovering the names of the top people. He decided that if he took the money and set himself up as bait, he might smoke them out."

Kate hoped that all the horror she felt didn't show on her face. "So Mark isn't on a sanctioned FBI operation?"

"Well, as I said, we were satisfied with the arrests made yesterday, so no, trapping the owners of the warehouse is not something the FBI considers a priority. But, as you have so clearly pointed out, your husband is an excellent agent—honest and a great asset to the Bureau," Mr. Mitchell said.

"Plus, we need that money back," Mr. Bowen added.

"So we've pulled some strings and arranged for a commando group to go into the jungles near where he's staying to provide protection and backup if necessary. Hopefully it will all be over soon."

Kate had walked into this office a little while ago ready to strangle Mr. Mitchell, and now she was tempted to hug his neck. "Thank you," she managed.

"Of course, for Mark's own safety, none of this can be made public."

"I understand."

"We had hoped to just bluff our way through it and make explanations when Mark was back and the owners of the pornography ring were in jail," Mr. Mitchell said. "But after some consideration, we can see how you feel, having your husband's name sullied and all."

Kate felt all the wind leave her sails. She was at their mercy. Worse—Mark was too.

"There has also been some concern about your safety and that of your children," Mr. Mitchell added.

"If these porn people decide to play rough, the simplest thing for them to do would be to take you as a hostage and to force your husband to give them the money, rather than chase him around the world," Mr. Bowen pointed out. Kate started to feel a little light-headed.

"That's why we've had a set of agents watching your house since yesterday afternoon." Mr. Mitchell's tone seemed so kindly now.

Kate thought about how rude she'd been to the agents this morning and wondered if her humiliation could get any worse.

"That's also why we had suggested that you take your children and go to your in-laws' home in Texas," Mr. Mitchell continued. "However, we can see your point—leaving might look to some like an admission of Mark's guilt. So we agree that you should stay, but we're not sure that one set of agents in front of your house is protection enough. So I'm looking for an available female agent to stay in the house with you. I'll try to have one there in the morning."

"I don't know how to thank you," she said finally.

Mr. Mitchell smiled. "We're all on the same side here, Mrs. Iverson. Once we understand that, I think it will be better for all of us."

The press conference was anticlimactic. Instead of getting an exposé on the FBI, the news crews she'd begged to come heard only a simple statement read in deadpan by Howard Bowen stating that Mark Iverson was an agent in good standing. And Kate, far from breathing fire as she had been earlier, stood docile at his side fighting tears throughout the entire proceedings.

When Mr. Bowen finished his statement, the reporters looked stunned for a few seconds. Then they consulted with each other as if trying to find a scoop in what had been said. Finally one desperate soul called out, "You got anything to add to that, Mrs. Iverson?"

Kate smiled and said, "Just that I agree with everything that has been said. My husband is the best man I know, and I'm grateful to the FBI for making that clear. And I'm thankful to all of you for coming on such short notice."

From the looks on their faces, Kate hoped she never needed to assemble an emergency press conference again because it was unlikely that any of them would attend.

* * *

Mark walked downstairs and found the house immaculate but empty. He stepped out onto the front porch and reset the alarm system, then climbed into the Jeep and turned the vehicle around.

After referring to the directions Cristobal gave him, Mark followed the narrow, winding road down the hill. He turned right then he reached the two-lane paved road that led to La Rosa. He was driving along, almost looking forward to dinner and a chance to visit with Cristobal, when he saw a vehicle pulled off on the side of the road. It was a truck painted military green.

He eased over into the other lane, intending to pass it quickly and safely, when he saw them. Later, when he had time to consider the whole incident, he liked to believe that even if he hadn't recognized Solana, he would have stopped to help them.

The man was young, probably early twenties and in extremely good physical condition. Mark guessed that he worked out vigorously and daily. The young man was wearing a khaki shirt and matching pants, both stained with sweat and dirt. It wasn't exactly a uniform, but close.

Solana was even more beautiful than she had appeared in the photograph Mr. Mitchell had displayed during the slideshow in Atlanta. Mark stopped his Jeep a few feet in front of the truck and walked back. When he reached the couple, he took note of Solana's tear-stained face and the way she clutched Emilio's hands for dear life. His first thought: *They are in love.* His second: *She might not want to be rescued.*

"My name is Mark Iverson," he said in Spanish. "I'm new in town and on my way to have dinner with my lawyer." He gave the truck a quick perusal. "It looks like you've had some trouble." Mark noticed that the young man's name, Emilio Delgado, was stamped above the breast pocket. Mark guessed that Emilio was probably a member of Salazar's private army.

"Yes," Emilio agreed. "One tire and the spare are both flat."

Solana seemed too distressed to speak, which surprised Mark. A flat tire was never a good thing, but for the daughter of Rodrigo Salazar, it was no huge crisis.

"Can I give you a lift back into town?" Mark offered.

He saw a spark of something like hope form in Solana's lovely eyes. She chewed her bottom lip as she considered the offer, and finally she nodded. "Actually, we are in more trouble than it appears," she said with a straightforwardness that he had to admire. "My name is Solana Andersen. I am the daughter of the most powerful man in La Rosa."

Mark raised an eyebrow. "Congratulations."

She ignored his sarcasm. "Emilio is my bodyguard, my father's employee," she clarified. "Our relationship is supposed to be merely professional."

Mark glanced at their intertwined fingers. "But it is something more?"

"We love each other," Emilio said bravely.

"We are supposed to be at the movie, but . . ." Solana looked behind herself at the woods as if they would provide her with a good excuse for being on the side of the road. "We wanted some time alone. If Emilio's commander finds out, he will be shot!"

Mark realized that she wasn't kidding. "You're serious."

"Of course! The movie will end shortly, and if we do not return to my father's compound, he will send men to search for us. Then they will find that we did not go to the movie but instead were out here alone . . ." Solana's voice trailed off. "Please, what can you do to help us?"

Mark studied their truck and then turned and looked at his Jeep. "Emilio, let's check and see if I have a spare that will fit your truck well enough to get you at least back to town."

Emilio followed Mark around to the back of the Jeep. They found a jack, a lug wrench, and a new spare all neatly arranged. Mark reminded himself to commend Cristobal for his thoroughness. With Mark's assistance, Emilio was able to put the spare on the truck quickly. Then he tossed both the flat tires into the back of the truck.

"Thank you, señor," Emilio said.

"Yes, thank you," Solana added, looking at her watch with a frown.

"You will still be late?" Mark guessed.

She nodded.

Anxious to make the most of this opportunity, Mark said, "I am on my way to eat dinner with my lawyer. Why don't you come with me? You will need an explanation about how I provided my spare tire anyway. Your father won't have to know exactly where your flat tire occurred."

"That is true," Solana said thoughtfully.

"I was passing by and saw that you had a flat tire . . . Then being the very nice person that I am, I offered assistance."

"But being the very poor mechanic that you are, it took you a long time to put on the spare," Solana contributed with a smile.

"We did have to deal with two flats," Mark pointed out.

"True," she acknowledged.

"Then if I invited you to dinner at a restaurant after I helped you, it would be rude to say no. Isn't that true?"

"Definitely true," Solana agreed.

"If you use the phone at the restaurant to call your father and explain, do you think he would understand?"

"Maybe." She gave him a grateful smile. "Anyway, it's the best we can do." She turned to Emilio. "Let's follow Mr. Iverson. Quickly," she added with urgency.

Mark climbed into his Jeep and waited for Emilio to turn the truck around. Once Emilio was in position, he proceeded into La Rosa. A few minutes later, the two vehicles were parked side by side in front of La Cocina.

As they walked into the restaurant it began to rain.

"The Holy Saints be praised!" Emilio whispered.

"You've been hoping for rain?" Mark guessed.

The young man blushed. "It will help to hide the fact that we had a flat tire on the road outside of town instead of behind the theater where the truck should have been," Emilio explained.

Mark nodded. "I see." Then he opened the front door of the restaurant and waved the young couple inside. A man holding a stack of menus stepped forward to greet them.

"Welcome to La Cocina!"

"Thank you," Mark replied. "We're here to meet Señor Morales."

"Oh yes. His table is just this way." The man waved toward the large eating area with a handful of menus.

"We would like to clean up a little before we eat," Mark interrupted. "We had to change a flat tire on the way."

The man narrowed his eyes and examined Solana and Emilio with particular care before pointing to the restrooms. "Señor Morales's reservation was for two only."

"I met some friends and asked them to join me," Mark said firmly. "If that is a problem, we can try another restaurant."

The man didn't look happy, but he shook his head. "Of course there is no problem. The restroom is there."

Mark and Emilio went to the men's room and worked with stiff paper towels and watered-down liquid hand soap to remove the dirt from their hands and arms. Mark was able to accomplish this more completely and more quickly than Emilio. When he was finished, he stood by the door and started some small talk.

"So, do you like working for Solana's father?"

"I like being with Solana," Emilio answered carefully.

"Her father wouldn't be happy if he knew his daughter was in love with you?"

Emilio's hands paused in their vigorous scrubbing. "It is a question of suitability. Solana is rich with many advantages and options. I am poor, and my hopes for the future are limited."

"You seem like an intelligent young man."

He resumed his scrubbing. "Solana's father might be willing to overlook our social differences to make her happy. But my commander, General Vargas, will overlook nothing. To him, my love for Solana will be considered a breach of discipline, and he will make an example of me." Emilio pulled a final handful of paper towels from the dispenser, dried his palms and forearms, and then pushed open the restroom door. "After you, señor."

Solana was waiting for them near the entrance. "I should call my father now," she said to Mark, and he realized that she wanted him to ask the man holding the menus for permission.

He relayed the request, and the man reluctantly pulled an old rotary phone from behind his little stand. "Very fast, please," he instructed Solana, and the girl nodded.

"You will bring them to Señor Morales's table when they complete their phone call," Mark requested in an effort to give Solana some privacy. Then he followed the waiter across the room to a table in a far corner near a large window facing the street.

"Mark!" Cristobal stood and extended his hand in greeting. The lawyer still wore the same suit he'd had on earlier that day, and Mark felt sinfully fresh in comparison. "I was beginning to worry about you."

"I stopped to help some young people who had a flat tire," Mark explained. "Thanks to you and the emergency equipment in the Jeep, I was able to get them moving again."

"Ah, well good!" Cristobal replied as the waiter gave them both menus. "This restaurant is, in my opinion, the best in the city."

"I have eaten in many fine restaurants," Mark replied. "The food here will have to be very good to impress me."

"Prepare to be impressed," Cristobal said with confidence. "The wines are also excellent."

Mark shook his head. "You'll have to impress me some other way. I don't drink alcohol."

"You are serious?" Cristobal seemed amazed by this.

"Completely," Mark assured him.

"Personally I can't imagine a day without wine."

Mark smiled. "Look on the bright side. At least one of us will have a clear head in case there's unexpected trouble."

Cristobal frowned. "Giving up fine wine is a big sacrifice for trouble that is not expected." He shrugged. "Even without wine the food here is . . ." He kissed his fingers, apparently finding no word sufficient. Cristobal frowned at the menu. "So hard to choose . . ." His face brightened suddenly. "But since you are paying, I guess we can have one of everything and share."

"That's fine with me," Mark agreed.

Cristobal motioned to the waiter and told the man that they would like to sample each item on the menu. Once the waiter had gone to fulfill this request, Cristobal said to Mark, "I understand that you still have substantial financial holdings in other countries. Perhaps you would like me to arrange for more of your assets to be transferred here, where they will be convenient to you?"

Mark smiled. "Thank you for your kind offer, but I prefer not to keep all my eggs in one basket."

"Eggs in a basket?" Cristobal repeated in obvious confusion.

"It's an American expression that means it's safer to spread your money out in many different places."

The lawyer looked disappointed, but he nodded. "Oh, I see."

"However if I have a legal problem, you will be the first person I call."

At this point Solana and Emilio finally reached the table.

"May I introduce Solana Andersen and Emilio Delgado," Mark said. "Solana and Emilio, this is Señor Morales, my lawyer."

"How do you do, Mr. Morales?" Solana said with perfect manners.

Cristobal opened his mouth but seemed unable to speak.

Emilio held out a chair for her to be seated at the table. "Señor," the young man said to Cristobal as he took the remaining empty chair.

"Solana and Emilio had permission to go to a movie this afternoon, but their truck got a flat tire, and the spare was also flat. I was able to help them by loaning them my spare."

Cristobal still didn't speak, but he looked from Mark to the young couple and then back again.

Thunder crashed outside, causing Solana to say, "It was very fortunate that you found us when you did, Mr. Iverson. Otherwise we might have been caught in this storm."

"Excuse me, please," Cristobal finally managed. He pulled his napkin from his neck and rushed from the table.

Solana frowned as Cristobal disappeared into the men's room. "Your friend is not as courageous as you are."

Mark raised both eyebrows. "You think it is dangerous for me to be seen with you?"

Solana nodded. "Your friend thinks so too. Even the owner of the restaurant is not happy about serving us. Didn't you notice?"

Thinking back, Mark had noticed. "Why?"

"No one wants trouble with my father," Solana told him.

"Or with General Vargas," Emilio added quietly.

"Did you speak to your father?" Mark asked.

"Yes," Solana confirmed. "He gave his permission for us to stay for dinner and said that he would notify General Vargas that we had been located, but apparently a search for us had already begun."

Emilio sighed audibly. "The general will come for us."

The waiter arrived with their food, and after arranging the various dishes, he addressed Mark. "Mr. Morales would like to speak to you in the men's room."

Mark stood. "Please tell Mr. Morales I will be right with him." Then he spoke to Solana and Emilio. "We ordered a sample of everything on the menu, so there is plenty. You two go ahead and start eating while I check on my lawyer. If you'll excuse me?"

"Of course," she answered for them both.

He found Cristobal pacing wildly around the bathroom.

When the lawyer saw Mark, he threw up his hands. "I said there are many beautiful young women in La Rosa who could help to ease your loneliness, but not *that* one."

Mark couldn't resist the opportunity to tease him. "Why not?"

Cristobal slapped his forehead and muttered some Spanish words Mark wasn't familiar with. "She's the daughter of the most wealthy, most powerful, most *deadly* man in Colombia!" he cried. "The girl is running around without an armed escort, which means she has given her father's hired general the slip. When he arrives here, heads will roll, and you'd better make sure one of them isn't your own."

Mark frowned. "So, you're saying that you won't be joining us for dinner?"

"No! And you will be a fool if you go back to that table yourself."

Mark shrugged. "I can't desert them. They are young and afraid. Don't you remember when you were their age, Cristobal?"

"My father was not Rodrigo Salazar," he said simply. "Good night, Mark. If you survive, I will speak to you in the morning." With that dire statement, Cristobal left the restroom.

Mark took a deep breath and walked back to his table. Neither Emilio nor Solana had eaten any of the vast array of dishes that covered the table.

"Cristobal had to leave, so it's going to be up to the two of you to help me eat all this food."

Solana bravely reached for a serving spoon and transferred some guacamole salad onto her plate, but Mark noticed that her hand shook slightly. Following her example, Emilio began putting food onto his plate.

They ate in silence for a few minutes—each waiting for the calamity that they knew would come. Finally their worst fears were realized. The front door was opened with much more force than necessary, and Mark looked up to see three men wearing khaki uniforms similar to Emilio's entering the restaurant. All the men had automatic rifles strapped across their chests, although the one in front was obviously in charge.

"General Vargas, I presume?" Mark said quietly.

Solana only whimpered, but Emilio confirmed with a soft, "Yes."

After a brief discussion with the man holding the menus, Vargas and his associates approached Mark's table with purpose.

Vargas appeared to be in his late fifties, of medium height, a thin frame with gray hair shaved so short it was barely visible. His brown eyes were beady, his posture was stiff, and his attitude was aggressive. Behind Vargas was an angry-looking young man who kept fingering his weapon, as though hoping someone would give him an excuse to use it. The man bringing up the rear had the blank expression and mechanical movements of a robot.

Mark expected Vargas to confront the young couple and was prepared to defend them to the best of his ability. But he was surprised when instead he found three guns pointed in his direction.

"What business do you have with Miss Solana?" Vargas demanded.

"We are just having dinner," Mark said calmly. "Surely there is no harm in that."

"We have spent the last thirty minutes in the pouring rain searching La Rosa and the surrounding woods for her," Vargas replied. "It has been a great inconvenience."

"But you've found her safe and sound," Mark pointed out. "So all's well that ends well."

Vargas kept his stare on Mark just long enough to be sure that his displeasure was felt. When he transferred his gaze to Solana, it became more of a leer. "The clerk at the theater remembers you going in, but he did not see you go out."

Solana shrugged. "A lot of people leave at one time. He can't be expected to see them all."

Vargas obviously didn't believe her, but he didn't accuse her of lying. Instead he turned his intense eyes to Emilio. "It took you three hours to change a tire?"

"There was no jack," Emilio began. "Then the spare was flat."

"Why didn't you just go inside the theater and call for someone to come and bring you another tire?" Vargas asked.

"I would have," Emilio said, "if the movie had gotten over and I still hadn't been able to handle it. But then Mr. Iverson arrived and offered me the use of his spare. I thought it would be better to accept his help than to waste another man's time bringing me a tire."

The general obviously did not agree with this.

"Mr. Iverson is new in town and doesn't know people yet. He wanted company for dinner, and it seemed like such a small thing to repay him for his help," Solana said, drawing the man's attention away from Emilio and back to her. "I called my father and asked his permission."

Vargas gave her a speculative look. She stared back unwaveringly. Finally the general nodded. "Well, I hope you enjoy your meal," he said, although his sincerity was questionable. "I brought a replacement tire with me. My men will put it on the truck, and your spare will be back in your Jeep, Mr. Iverson."

"Thank you," Mark said.

Vargas ignored him and addressed Solana. "We will be waiting outside to escort you home when you're finished eating."

"That is really not necessary," Solana tried. "Emilio is here, and now that the truck tire is fixed . . ."

"Oh, but we want to make sure you arrive safely, without any more car trouble." Vargas cut his menacing gaze toward Emilio. Then he indicated toward the door with his rifle for his men to lead the way outside.

Once they were gone, Mark heard Solana sigh.

"Well," Mark said. "Now that our uninvited guests are gone, let's eat."

Solana ate very little, and Emilio didn't eat much more. Mark enjoyed the food, which was as delicious as Cristobal had promised. He was pleased that he had been able to help the young people and was anxious to report to Perez that he had already made contact with Solana.

Finally Solana pushed away from the table and stood. "We cannot thank you enough for your kindness, Mr. Iverson," she said, "but we really should go."

Emilio stood as well. "Yes, thank you."

"I'm glad our paths crossed," Mark told them. "I would have been very lonely tonight without your company."

Solana gave him a small smile. "I hope that we will have the chance to meet again."

Mark bowed politely. "I hope so too."

* * *

By the time Kate made it home from Atlanta, she was exhausted, mentally and physically. And the Christmas dress felt like it had permanently adhered to her skin. She parked in front of the house behind the FBI men and stopped to apologize before going inside. Agents Lott and Applegate, who were finishing off pieces of Miss Polly's pecan pie, accepted her apology for themselves and in behalf of the other set of agents she had tormented that morning.

Feeling that she had done her duty, and wishing *she* had a piece of Miss Polly's pie, Kate hurried into the house. She found her children, Miss Eugenia and her gentleman friend, Whit Owens, along with Annabelle and her husband Derrick, all in the family room. Emily and Charles met her with enthusiastic hugs. Then Annabelle and Whit complimented Kate on her television appearance, while Miss Eugenia and Derrick rushed to the kitchen to fix her a plate of dinner.

"I made the salad," Derrick informed her. "I found the recipe in this month's *Southern Living*."

"Whit bought the pizza," Miss Eugenia added. "He found it at Domino's."

Annabelle gave Eugenia an annoyed look. "Why do you always have to be such a smart alec?"

Kate laughed. "Actually, it's good to know that some things never change." She accepted a plate of pizza from Miss Eugenia and a bowl of salad from Derrick. "This looks delicious. I was just thinking how hungry I was." She balanced the plate on her knees and put the bowl of salad on the coffee table. "It's almost nine o'clock," she told the children. "Time for bed."

"But we're playing Candyland! Can we finish?" Emily negotiated.

"I guess," Kate agreed, her mouth full of pizza. She settled back on the couch and ate while watching the game come to a conclusion. Whit and Charles were a team opposing the combination of Emily and Derrick. Since Miss Eugenia and Annabelle were providing technical assistance, the game was complicated beyond anything Kate had ever seen, with strategies and alliances and even trick plays. With a sigh, Kate wondered if they might need to have a peace summit when it was all over with.

Kate finished her pizza and went to work on her salad. As she ate, her eyes drifted back to the clock, and she wondered what Mark was doing right now. She hoped he was safe and . . . she shook her head, determined not to cry at least until she was in the privacy of her own bedroom.

She polished off her salad and stood to collect her dinner dishes. Then she carried them into the kitchen. She stacked them in the sink and was trying to get the empty pizza boxes into a garbage bag when Annabelle walked in.

She took the bag and held it wide open. "Looks like you can use a hand."

Kate nodded. "Thanks."

"I'm sorry that Mark has to be away for a while," Annabelle continued. "I know you're going to miss him."

"I am," Kate agreed.

"And Eugenia may kill you with kindness before he gets back."

Kate had to smile. "That's a real possibility."

"What's a possibility?" Miss Eugenia asked as she walked into the kitchen.

"That we're all going to fall asleep on our feet," Annabelle replied. "It's after nine o'clock, and I'm tired."

"It's past the children's bedtime," Kate concurred.

"I know, I just told Whit and Derrick to simultaneously surrender, so the game will be over in a minute. Kate, Annabelle and I will clean up this mess. You go get the children in bed. We've got a big day planned tomorrow, and they need their rest."

"A big day?" Kate repeated.

Miss Eugenia nodded firmly. "Might as well stay busy—no sense moping around."

Annabelle shot Kate a look of commiseration. "Kindness can kill," she whispered.

"What are you mumbling about again?" Miss Eugenia demanded.

"I was just saying that you're right," Annabelle said with a wink at Kate. "Kate should go put the children to bed while we clean up the kitchen."

"Of course I'm right." Miss Eugenia sent her sister an annoyed look. "I declare, Annabelle, I think you're going senile."

Hoping to avert a fight, Kate thanked them again for dinner and for their babysitting services. Then she went into the family room to collect her children. Once Emily and Charles had brushed their teeth and changed into pajamas, Kate read them a story out of the Mother Goose book.

When they kneeled together by the side of Emily's bed, Charles volunteered to say the family prayer. He itemized the things he was grateful for including all the animals at the Ragsdale's mini-farm, his Star Wars action figures, and the pumpkin that they were going to carve for Halloween. Then he prayed that his father would come home soon.

Kate was still fighting tears when she went downstairs to do a load of laundry. As she passed through the entryway, she heard a clap of thunder and the sound of rain pelting the windows. She found Miss Eugenia sitting at the table in the kitchen, reading from the Bible.

"Are the others gone?' she asked.

"They are," Miss Eugenia confirmed.

"Reading anything good?" Kate asked politely.

"As a matter of fact, I am." Miss Eugenia pointed at the words as she read a scripture aloud, "'Be strong and of a good courage, fear not, nor be afraid . . . for the Lord thy God, he it is that doth go with thee, he will not fail thee, nor forsake thee.'" Miss Eugenia looked up. "That's in Deuteronomy."

"And it's very good advice." Sensing a lecture, Kate continued into the laundry room and started a load of towels in the washer. Then she removed the clothes from the dryer and began folding them. She was fine until her fingers closed around the soft, well-worn fabric of Mark's favorite T-shirt. Involuntarily she brought the shirt to her face and gave into the sobs she'd been holding back all day.

Miss Eugenia found her there a few minutes later. "I was reading an article in the September *Ensign* the other day about dealing with grief," she said. "It said that the spirits of the dead are aware of the loved ones left behind, and if the survivors are sad, the spirits are sad too."

"You think Mark is going to die?" Kate forced herself to ask.

"No," Miss Eugenia said. "I think he's going to be just fine. But that article got me to thinking. I wonder, since you and Mark are so close, if on some level he is aware of your feelings even though you're apart. If you are grieving, he'll know it and be distracted. We want him to give his full concentration to his assignment, don't we?"

Kate nodded.

"And we don't want to frighten the children, do we?"

"Of course not."

"Then you're going to have to pull yourself together."

Kate took a deep, shuddering breath. "I know."

"In fact you should be glad you miss Mark so much. There are plenty of women who wouldn't mind a vacation from their husband."

Kate looked up. "Did you ever feel that way?" She'd always been fascinated by the subject of Charles Atkins, Miss Eugenia's late husband. He had died before the Iversons moved to Haggerty, and it was hard for Kate to imagine a male counterpart to the incomparable Miss Eugenia.

"The very idea!" Miss Eugenia dismissed. "Charles was a saint among men. But you are a lucky woman too."

Kate wiped the last of her tears on Mark's T-shirt and tossed it into the dirty clothes basket. "You're right."

"I thought we settled that before Annabelle left," Miss Eugenia reminded her. "Now let's get to bed."

Kate turned to finish folding the clothes. "Are you sleeping here again tonight?"

"Yes, but I'm moving to the first guest room." Miss Eugenia rubbed her back. "Another night in that rocking chair might kill me."

"Where's Lady?"

"She's more comfortable at my house. I asked Whit to stop by and check on her."

"You go on to bed," Kate said with a smile. "I'll be up in a few minutes."

Miss Eugenia nodded and started toward the kitchen. Kate folded the last towel and tested the locks on the back door. She walked into the entryway to check the front door, and just as she reached up to engage the deadbolt, the phone rang. Kate gasped in surprise.

"I declare, who in the world could that be at this hour?" Miss Eugenia asked from her position halfway up the stairs.

Kate moved toward the phone in the living room. "I don't know . . ." she began. Then she saw the number on the caller ID and dove for the phone. "Mark!" she cried.

"Kate!" he answered only a little less desperately.

"You're okay?"

"Yes. I can only talk for a minute, and I can't say much—except that I love you."

"I love you, too."

"How are the kids?"

She clutched the phone tightly to her ear as if that could bring Mark physically closer to her. "They're fine. Asleep."

"Next time I'll try to call earlier."

She could tell that he was wrapping up the conversation, and she dreaded the moment of parting. "Take care of yourself," she pleaded.

"I will."

"Call again soon."

"Good-bye, Kate."

"Good-bye." Slowly she replaced the receiver.

"It was Mark?" Miss Eugenia asked from the doorway of the living room.

Kate nodded. "He said he's fine, and he'll call earlier next time so he can talk to the kids."

"Well, I declare, we might just get some sleep around here tonight after all."

* * *

Mark closed his cell phone and sat for a few minutes in the total silence of his rental house in La Rosa. He stared out the wall of windows in the sunroom, his loneliness so intense it was almost a tangible presence.

He reached into his pocket and removed a family picture from his wallet. It had been taken the previous Christmas at an Olan Mills studio in Albany. He had rushed over after work and was wearing one of his many dark business suits. Kate had brought him a cheerful red tie with little green Christmas trees on it. Then she had insisted that he put it on right there in the studio waiting room. He smiled at the memory. Kate was not often demanding, but when her mind was made up about something, resistance was futile.

His eyes moved to Emily, who was a miniature replica of her mother. She was wearing a white dress with Christmas trees smocked across the bodice. Her light brown hair had been pulled into a pony-tail secured with a red satin bow, and her green eyes reflected the excitement of the season.

Next he studied little Charles, who a year ago had been just a baby. He was wearing what Kate called an Eaton suit. The jacket had a rounded collar—no lapels—the pants were short, and he had a little bow tie covered with Christmas trees to match Mark's. His brown eyes and straight brown hair also matched his father. And he was grinning at the camera for all he was worth.

Mark purposely saved Kate for last. He just had time to take in the red Christmas dress that she wore every year because she claimed it brought them luck, when his PDA started to flash, indicating that he had a message. He replaced the picture in his wallet and picked up the PDA. The message was from Perez. It said simply, *Report.*

Mark began typing on the small keyboard:

Made contact with Solana. She and her bodyguard had a flat tire. Provided assistance, hopefully opened door for further communication.

Mark waited for Perez to respond. Finally a new message appeared.

Good. Do not offer rescue unless specifically instructed to do so.

Mark felt he'd better warn Perez that there could be a hitch in the plan.

Solana is romantically involved with the bodyguard. She may not want to be rescued.

After a short wait the response came.

Rescue will go forward as planned. Girl can return later if she chooses.

Once he was certain that his conversation with Angelo Perez was over, Mark signed off the PDA. He walked through the dark house, checking doors and windows just as he would if he were at home. As far as he could tell, the security system was working. Finally he climbed the stairs and stretched out across the huge bed, hoping sleep would come and erase the loneliness for awhile.

* * *

Solana stared at the ceiling in her bedroom. No one believed them about the movie and the flat tire. Neither Vargas nor her father had openly accused them of lying or asked them for a better explanation, but she could tell that they saw through her story. Her biggest fear was that after separating Emilio from her, Vargas would try and torture the truth from him. Since he would never betray her, this would result in his unspeakable death.

She curled onto her side, pressing her pillow to her stomach in an effort to relieve the nausea that kept coming in waves. For so many years she had wanted to come here—to meet the handsome father that existed only in pictures. And she couldn't regret that she had taken the opportunity when it presented itself, since it was here that she met Emilio. But now it was a dark and dangerous place. She had to get away and take Emilio with her. Otherwise they were both doomed.

Perhaps this American, Mr. Iverson, would help them as he had with the tire. She didn't know his reasons for being in La Rosa or how long he planned to stay. But maybe when he left, he could take them with him. Feeling slightly more hopeful and less sick, she removed the pillow from her stomach and did something she had never done before. She said a prayer.

"Dear God, Emilio says You exist, so if You can hear me, please protect him from General Vargas and others who would harm him.

Help us to know if we can trust Mr. Iverson, and help us find a way out of La Rosa. Please." At this point she faltered because she wasn't sure how to end a prayer. Then, with a smile, she remembered what Emilio always said. "Amen."

* * *

Kate shed a few tears for Mark that night, but her grief was tempered by the happiness she felt from having talked to him. She dozed off with a smile on her face. At first her dreams were pleasant—full of Mark and Emily and Charles, but as she slept they became darker and confusing. She was in her house, but she couldn't find her children or Mark. She had looked everywhere and was starting to panic.

She climbed the stairs, and when she reached the landing, she looked down the dark hallway and saw her deceased first husband, Tony, standing at the far end. He said something, but she couldn't understand him. Then he beckoned to her before he turned and started to walk away. She ran after him, but no matter how fast she ran, she couldn't catch him. In her dream, the hallway seemed endless. Finally she called out, "Tony! Wait!" But he didn't stop. Now he was just a tiny figure in the distance. "Tony!" she tried again, reaching out a hand to him. "Don't leave yet!"

The sound of her own voice awakened her. Feeling frustrated and confused, she sat up and stared at the door that led into the dark hallway. Pushing back the bedcovers, she stood and walked through the door. No one stood at the end of the hallway, and she felt both relieved and disappointed.

Kate walked across the hall and into Emily's room to check on her daughter. The little girl was sleeping peacefully. Kate smiled and then turned to go back to her own room. As she reached the doorway she inhaled deeply and stopped dead in her tracks. She felt the blood drain from her face and grabbed the doorframe for support.

"Tony?" she whispered. Then she took another breath and smelled the unmistakable scent of Tony's special soap. "You *were* here," she whispered. She turned to look back at Emily, who was Tony's daughter.

Then she started to tremble. Why would Tony come to see her, and what had he tried to tell her?

CHAPTER 6

Mark woke up suddenly at five thirty on Thursday morning. Sensing that something was amiss, he swung his legs over the side of the bed and stood. He moved silently into the hallway and then proceeded with caution down the stairs. As he walked into the kitchen, he felt a slight draft, and the hair on the back of his neck stood up.

Before he had a chance to react, he was grabbed from behind. For a few seconds he struggled futilely against an arm that felt like steel covered in flesh pressed against his neck. Knowing that it wouldn't be long before he lost consciousness, Mark decided to try a desperate approach. He went limp, and the arm against his neck relaxed slightly. After mustering all his remaining strength, he twisted and rammed an elbow into his captor's solar plexus. Mark heard a whoosh of air, and the arm dropped away completely.

The lights went on, and as his eyes adjusted, Mark saw that the arm belonged to Hector Vargas—the man who had been sent to collect Solana the night before. Vargas was now holding his abdomen and gasping for breath.

From the far side of the room there was a laugh. Mark glanced over to see Rodrigo Salazar standing by the light switch. "It is not often someone gets the best of Hector," Salazar said. "I commend you."

Mark ignored the look of pure hatred Vargas sent his way and rubbed his neck. "It's not often that someone breaks into my house and tries to strangle me." Mark frowned. "Speaking of which, how did you manage that?"

Salazar smiled. "We convinced your housekeeper to admit us."

Another member of Salazar's private army stepped forward dragging Pilar by the arm.

"I'm sorry, señor," she said with tears shining in her eyes.

"It's certainly not your fault that some people don't know how to knock on the front door when they come to visit," Mark said to the housekeeper. Then he addressed Salazar. "Perhaps you could have your man release my housekeeper. Then, if she's not too upset, she might make us all breakfast."

After a few seconds of consideration, Salazar agreed with a slight nod of his head. "Let her go."

The soldier allowed Pilar to slip from his fingers, and she moved away, rubbing her arm.

"You wish for me to cook, señor?" she asked Mark.

He nodded. "Please fix a nice breakfast for me and my guests."

She kept her eyes averted from the armed men who had forced their way into the house and moved to the refrigerator.

"Won't you gentlemen have a seat?" Mark invited.

"My men will take positions around the outside of your house to be sure that we aren't interrupted," Rodrigo Salazar replied. "But I will be happy to join you for breakfast."

The soldiers left through the back door while Mark and Salazar sat across from each other at the table. Salazar waved his hand to encompass the room. "Nice place."

"Yes," Mark agreed as Pilar placed a pot of coffee and two cups on the table between them. "I was very fortunate that it was available."

Salazar poured himself a cup of coffee. Then he said, "I am Rodrigo Salazar, and you are Mark Iverson." He looked up. "The question is why are you in La Rosa, Agent Iverson?"

"I have a . . ." Mark paused, choosing his words carefully, "a little problem at work. I need a nice, quiet town where I can stay until things can be arranged for my return to the United States."

"Since you are an FBI agent, and I am on your most wanted list, aren't you going to try and arrest me?"

Mark smiled. "Capturing you would probably go a long way toward helping me win my way back into the good graces of my superiors at the FBI, so I guess I should try. Would you be willing to turn yourself in?"

Salazar smiled back as he shook his head. "I'm sorry. I would like to help you, but sacrificing my freedom is too big a price for me to pay."

Mark spread his hands in mock surrender. "Well, at least I can say I tried."

Salazar took a sip of coffee. "This problem at work—tell me about it."

"Earlier this week, we found a warehouse in Atlanta that was full of pornographic material. We arrested forty people and confiscated an incredible amount of product and money. We didn't get the people who own the company, so I wanted to continue the investigation, but my superiors wouldn't approve of it. They said we had already spent enough time and money on the case and had a satisfactory resolution."

"So you took the money? Why?"

"In retrospect, maybe it wasn't such a good plan, but I didn't have long to decide—just a few minutes really. They left me alone with the money and told me to count it and match it to the books they'd found in the warehouse. I thought that if I took the money, the FBI would be forced to complete the investigation so that I'd give them the money back."

"Did you expect to keep your job afterward?"

"Yes, I guess." Mark rubbed the back of his neck. "I don't know. I'm hoping that they won't want anyone to know about the whole mess and will just be willing to let me go back to my old job."

"And what if the people who used to own the money decide to retrieve it?"

"That would speed up the resolution of the case," Mark said.

"Which is good—if they don't kill you," Salazar commented dryly.

"True," Mark admitted.

"And what made you think that you could come into a lawless country like Colombia with twelve million dollars and not be robbed by the first native thug with a switchblade?"

Mark looked up sharply. "You know the exact amount?"

Salazar smiled. "I make it my business to know everything about the people who come to La Rosa. It is how I have lived such a long and healthy life."

"I moved quickly and without fanfare," Mark explained. "And I don't have all the money with me. I have a little cash and some in bank accounts here, but most of it is in Switzerland. Anyone who wants the money will need to keep me alive."

Salazar seemed impressed. "For a poorly planned scheme, that is not bad."

Mark decided this was his chance to explain the presence of the task force. "And as far as the porn guys, I suggested that if the FBI wanted to protect the money, it would be wise to send in some soldiers."

"Well, your request was granted. American troops have been spotted in the hills around La Rosa."

Mark was pleased to know that the task force was in place but alarmed by the amount of information Salazar had been able to collect in such a short time. "Good."

"So now you wait?"

"For a few days anyway. Then I'll see what the FBI offers me."

Pilar placed a platter of fresh fruit in the middle of the table, and Salazar picked up a plump strawberry. "I understand that you met my daughter last night."

"Yes. She's a beautiful and intelligent girl. You must be very proud of her."

"I am," Salazar replied as he bit into the strawberry.

"I hope you weren't too hard on her for the flat tire incident," Mark continued carefully. "We were all young once."

Salazar nodded. "Yes, and she fancies herself in love with her bodyguard. She thinks I don't know, but I would have to be a fool not to notice."

Mark couldn't deny this. "They did seem fond of each other."

"I thought it was something that would pass, but it has been going on for almost two months now, and if anything, it has escalated. So I'm not sure what to do. What would you suggest?"

"Why not let them be young and in love?"

Salazar frowned. "Because it annoys the head of my private army, General Vargas."

"Oh yes, a charming man," Mark said sarcastically. "We've met twice now, and both times he looked like he wanted to kill me."

Salazar laughed. "He probably does. Hector has a mean streak."

"Solana is terrified of the man. She seems to think he might harm Emilio as well."

"The possibility is there," Salazar confirmed.

"And you can't protect the boy?"

"Not without infuriating Hector. Not that I am afraid of my own army commander," Salazar was quick to clarify. "But in my world, Vargas provides the threat of violence I need to live a civilized life. Without him, there would be chaos. Lives lost, property destroyed." Salazar shook his head. "A teenage infatuation is not worth such a cost."

Mark was grateful when Pilar interrupted again by placing a steaming plate of food before each of them, since this gave him time to consider his response. As rich, spicy aromas filled the air, Mark found that he was starving. He took a large bite of what looked like an omelet and spoke to Pilar. "This is delicious," he told her.

She nodded and returned to the counter.

Salazar blew on his food before taking a bite. "I agree. Your house-keeper is a skilled cook. I wish I could say the same for my chef. I hired him from a culinary school in Bogotá—very prestigious and expensive. But the man burns everything. I have come to dread meals."

Mark smiled. "I offer you my sympathies."

"You could offer me your housekeeper."

"I'm not that nice."

Salazar laughed again. "You Americans are so funny."

They ate in silence for a few minutes. Then Mark asked, "What if I could offer a solution that would protect Emilio and appease General Vargas?"

Salazar filled his mouth with food and then waved his empty fork for Mark to continue. "Let me hear this great solution."

"As we discussed, I am in a dangerous position here—vulnerable if you will. It would be wise for me to hire a bodyguard until the situation with the Atlanta pornographers is settled. And who better to ask for help than you?"

"You want me to give Emilio to you?"

Mark nodded. "Yes. Well, I want you to let me hire him. You'll make it clear that I requested someone who has been trained by General Vargas because of his local reputation."

"I can see how that will protect Emilio, but if it separates him from Solana—why will she be pleased?"

"Because you will allow her to visit me often. I could tutor her in English."

"Her English is quite good already."

"Spanish then," Mark proposed.

"Her Spanish is impeccable."

Mark smiled. "There must be something."

Salazar considered the situation for a few seconds. "Do you play chess?"

"I played competitively in college."

"Then it might work. I will tell Hector that in addition to the chess lessons, I hope that if Solana spends time here, you will win her affections away from Emilio. And in fact, if that proves to be true, I will be doubly pleased."

Mark raised an eyebrow. "I'm happily married. Besides, I'm too old for Solana."

Salazar tilted his head and studied Mark. "You are young enough, and your wife is far away. I don't want you to establish a lasting relationship with my daughter, but if you show her that her heart can pound madly for someone other than her young bodyguard, you will do them both a favor. You have already been gallant, and I'm sure Solana will be pleased to visit you regularly. If you encourage her girlish, romantic tendencies, she will soon be dreaming of you instead of poor Emilio." Salazar stuck out his hand. "So, as you Americans say, do we have a deal?"

It was more than Mark had expected. He clasped Salazar's hand in his. "Deal."

Salazar pushed his chair back from the table and stood. "Breakfast was delicious. And if you ever get tired of waiting for the FBI to forgive you, I might be able to find a use for you in my organization."

Mark forced a smile. "I'm a patient man, and I really enjoy being an FBI agent."

Salazar laughed. "I could get used to your American sense of humor. We will have to visit again."

Mark rose to his feet. "I'd like that. But next time you come, maybe you could just knock on the front door instead of terrorizing my housekeeper." He said it in a way that brought a smile to Salazar's face.

Salazar was still laughing as he walked toward the front door. "Funny man."

* * *

After her dream about Tony, Kate spent the remainder of Wednesday night tossing and turning and wondering if her sleep had been interrupted by a weird dream or if she had actually been visited by the dead. When she finally got up at six o'clock, she still hadn't determined what category the previous night's incident fell into. But one thing was certain—after three nights of little sleep, she was tired. And the prospect of having Miss Eugenia boss her around all day was not a pleasant one.

Kate went downstairs and started a load of laundry and took the garbage cans to the road. By the time she returned to the kitchen, Miss Eugenia and the children were there waiting.

"You're all up early," Kate remarked.

"I have to get up early so I can call Whit before he goes into the office," Miss Eugenia explained, holding up her new little cell phone. "That saves me the misery of having to talk to his annoying receptionist, Idella."

Kate nodded. "I can see the wisdom in that."

"And when I heard Miss Eugenia talking on the phone, I woke up too," Emily explained. "Then I woke up Charles."

"Well," Kate said. "I guess since we're all awake, I should fix breakfast."

Miss Eugenia pointed at a pan on the stove. "I made some biscuits and gravy. Then after we eat, I thought you and the children could help me in my garden."

Kate looked up in confusion. "You've already plowed your garden under for the winter. What's left to be done?"

"Several things need to be done now if we expect to have a good harvest next summer," Miss Eugenia told her.

"Like what?" Kate asked, sensing a scam.

"You'll see when we're out in my garden doing them," Miss Eugenia replied vaguely.

Kate seriously doubted that Miss Eugenia needed their help with her garden. More than likely she had made this suggestion to distract Kate and the children from Mark's absence.

"Give me an example," Kate requested.

"For one thing, we have to pre-till the ground before the first frost."

Kate frowned. "Well, since it hasn't even dropped below 70 degrees yet, I think we're in plenty of time. And what exactly is the purpose of this pre-tilling process?"

"Pre-tilling is just like pre-heating," Miss Eugenia claimed. "It's something that's got to be done. Besides, during the pre-tilling phase, we might find a rock or two."

Kate tried not to laugh. "If you didn't have any rocks when you turned your garden under a couple of weeks ago, why would you have any now?"

"Rocks can pop up anywhere and anytime," Miss Eugenia assured her.

"I want to help Miss Eugenia with her garden," Emily contributed. "And even if we don't find any rocks, we might see a worm."

Charles grinned. "A worm."

Kate nodded in surrender. "Now that's something to look forward to."

Before Miss Eugenia could say more, there was a knock on the back door. "Anybody home?" Miss Polly called from the back stoop.

"Don't answer," Miss Eugenia hissed. "This is the second day in a row she's come over right at breakfast time. Feeding Polly is like feeding a stray cat. Once you establish the habit, you can never stop!"

Kate rolled her eyes. "Come on in, Miss Polly. Miss Eugenia made biscuits for breakfast."

"Mark my words," Miss Eugenia muttered under her breath as she walked over to the stove. "Just like a cat."

"Oh, I love cats," Miss Polly said as she entered the kitchen. "And Eugenia makes the best biscuits."

This seemed to mollify Miss Eugenia somewhat.

"Although I couldn't eat a bite," Miss Polly informed them.

"Now I've heard everything," Miss Eugenia muttered and earned a reproachful glare from Kate.

"I fixed those nice FBI men breakfast again, and I made myself a plate at the same time."

"Well, as long as you're here, you might as well have a seat and visit with us while we eat," Miss Eugenia suggested. "Emily, you and Charles set the table while your mother mixes up some frozen orange juice."

Everyone rushed to fulfill their assignments, and once they were all settled around the table eating, Miss Eugenia said, "I guess it's just as well that you came over, Polly. Didn't you volunteer to make pimento cheese sandwiches for the bridge club meeting today?"

Miss Polly nodded, sending her white curls into a flurry of motion.

"Well, we're having it over here instead of at George Ann's, so just bring them about eleven thirty." Miss Eugenia looked at Kate. "You don't mind, do you?"

"Of course not," Kate replied blandly.

Miss Polly, however, was frowning. "George Ann already moved all her furniture and set up the card tables."

Miss Eugenia waved this aside. "I know. I asked Winston to send Arnold over to George Ann's after he gets off his shift at the police station and pick up the card tables. When he drops them off here, we'll get him to help us move Kate's living room furniture against the walls. Then he'll bring all my harvest-colored potted plants over, and we'll scatter them around Kate's house for decoration."

Miss Polly was still frowning. "I can't believe you convinced George Ann to give up her position as hostess on such late notice. You know how she loves showing off all her antiques and her pictures of her father with important people from the past. And she said she had made some kind of pumpkin succotash to serve with the refreshments."

"She was a little grouchy when I called her at six o'clock this morning to tell her about the change," Eugenia admitted. "Of course, part of her bad mood can be attributed to the fact that I woke her up—proving that she's not the early riser she claims to be. And I told her we'd serve that succotash here."

"What is succotash?" Emily asked.

"It's usually a kind of corn and bean soup," Miss Eugenia explained. "But Miss George Ann made it with pumpkin and several different varieties of squash."

"I hate that." Charles was sure.

Kate ignored the culinary discussion. "You're saying Miss George Ann didn't have any objection to the bridge club meeting being moved here?" she clarified. "She just said, 'I'll bring my pumpkin-squash mush and be right over'?"

"Succotash," Miss Eugenia corrected. "And you know George Ann—she always has an objection to everything. But after I agreed to a few conditions, she approved the change."

Kate's eyes narrowed. "What conditions?"

"Well, for one thing, I'm going to be her partner today," Miss Eugenia admitted.

Miss Polly gasped. "Eugenia!"

Kate was shocked as well. The two women were practically enemies and agreeing to partner with Miss George Ann was a huge concession on Miss Eugenia's part.

"It won't be so bad. George Ann is annoying, but she's a decent bridge player. And I also offered to let her take my turns as bridge club hostess for the next ten years."

This didn't seem so bad to Kate. Both women were in their late seventies, and there was a good chance neither would *live* another ten years. "What will we do with the kids during the meeting?" Kate asked. The old ladies were incredibly serious about their cards, and she knew Miss Eugenia didn't intend to have Emily and Charles running through the proceedings.

"Annabelle's going to take them to her house. After the meeting, we'll join them for swimming in their little indoor pool."

Emily's eyes widened. "You're going to swim with us?"

Miss Eugenia laughed. "The very idea! No ma'am, I'm going to be the lifeguard. Then Derrick's going to grill hamburgers and steaks and some kind of vegetable kebabs for dinner. Whit's promised to bring ice cream for dessert."

"It will be another party!" Emily said. "Would you like to come, Miss Polly?"

"Oh, thank you, dear," Miss Polly said. "But I have choir practice this evening."

"Maybe we can play Candyland again," Charles said hopefully.

"Competitive situations get Whit's blood pressure up," Miss Eugenia said. "We'd probably better leave the game at home."

"Maybe we can carve our pumpkin!" Emily proposed. "It's getting close to Halloween."

"It's getting close!" Charles concurred.

Kate smiled. "Maybe so."

Miss Eugenia stood. "Well, right now we've got gardening to do. So Polly, if you'll excuse us." She looked pointedly at their other neighbor.

"Oh, yes," Miss Polly stood. "I've got to start on my pimento cheese sandwiches since I'll need to make extra for the FBI men."

Once Miss Polly was gone, Miss Eugenia sent the children up to change into work clothes and suggested that Kate clean the kitchen. Kate was used to Miss Eugenia's constant involvement in their lives. However, under normal circumstances she would have objected to such total domination. But these were not normal circumstances.

"I wonder how I ever functioned without you planning every minute of my day," Kate mused aloud.

Eugenia ignored her sarcasm. "I declare, I wonder that myself. And this afternoon when we go to Annabelle's, be sure to bring your bathing suit. Annabelle assures me that the glass panels on their pool house don't block out ultraviolet rays, and lately you've been looking mighty pasty."

* * *

After locking the front door securely behind Salazar and his men, Mark found Pilar in the kitchen. The woman's eyes were red and puffy, so he knew she'd been crying. Agent Perez had warned him to trust no one, but Pilar's distress certainly seemed sincere.

"I'm sorry that you were treated roughly," he said. When she didn't respond, he added, "You must have been very afraid."

She wiped a hand across her eyes. "I deal with men like Hector Vargas every day. It is not him I fear."

"Rodrigo Salazar?"

She shook her head again.

Mark was confused. "Who?"

"It is you."

"Me?" Mark asked in surprise.

She lowered her eyes in shame. "I need this job, but I have failed you, and I know you must fire me."

Now Mark understood. Pilar had been raised in an environment where mistakes weren't tolerated. "I think that your experience today will make you more cautious in the future," Mark said. "I would be foolish to fire you right after you have learned such a valuable lesson."

Pilar glanced up, her expression hopeful.

"I am going to call Señor Morales and see if we can arrange for the security system to be altered, so you can use a remote to open the garage. You'll want to stay in your car with the doors locked until the garage doors are closed again and you're sure you're alone. Then you can get out of the car and enter the code into the security system."

"Thank you, señor," she said.

Mark went into the sunroom and called Cristobal Morales. "I have a security issue that I need you to handle for me as soon as possible," he told his lawyer.

"I heard you had a visit from Señor Salazar," Cristobal said. "And I'm glad to see that you survived it."

"News certainly travels fast in La Rosa."

"As the Americans say—like wildfire."

"Yes, Mr. Salazar forced his way in here. It wasn't a pleasant experience for Pilar. His men ambushed her outside the garage and forced her to unlock the house."

"I tried to warn you that getting involved with Solana was a bad idea."

Mark sighed. "Yes, you did. But it's too late for that now." He explained his idea about the remote garage door system. "That way Pilar could open the garage door without having to get out of the car. They aren't expensive or difficult to install. Do you think you could arrange for one to be put in today?"

He heard Cristobal sigh. "It will be more expensive here than in the United States, but I can arrange it."

"Thank you," Mark replied. Then he disconnected the call.

* * *

At eight thirty, Kate and her children were assembled in Miss Eugenia's garden. The little dog, Lady, was running around their feet happily.

Kate pushed at a clump of soft dirt with her foot. "Now what?" she asked.

"We'll rake while the children look for rocks," Miss Eugenia said.

"And worms!" Charles added with a smile.

"If you find a worm, don't touch it," Kate cautioned. "Just observe it from a distance."

After the children and Lady ran off in search of rocks and worms, Miss Eugenia handed Kate a rake. "What am I supposed to do with this?" she asked.

"For heaven sakes, Kate, surely they have rakes in Utah." Miss Eugenia demonstrated vigorously.

Kate pressed her rake to the lumpy soil and dragged it forward listlessly. After several passes, Kate leaned on her rake and yawned.

"Tired?" Miss Eugenia inquired.

Kate nodded. Then her fatigue reminded her of the reason she had been unable to sleep the night before, and she felt a little chill run down her spine.

"Did a rabbit run over your grave?" Miss Eugenia asked.

"No, I was just thinking about a strange dream I had last night. Are your dreams ever so vivid you can actually smell things?"

Miss Eugenia considered this for a few seconds. "I don't think so."

Kate hugged the rake against her chest. "I dreamed that I was searching the house but couldn't find Mark or the kids."

Miss Eugenia nodded knowledgeably. "Probably anxiety over the separation you're experiencing."

"I walked up the stairs, and at the end of the hallway I saw Tony."

"Tony, not Mark?" Miss Eugenia clarified.

"It was Tony," Kate confirmed. "He looked just the way he did that last time I saw him. I think he was trying to tell me something, but I couldn't make out the words. Then he waved for me to follow him."

"Maybe he was going to show you where Mark and the kids were," Miss Eugenia said, completely caught up in the dream.

Kate controlled a smile and continued. "I ran after Tony, but I couldn't catch him no matter how hard I tried. He just kept getting farther and farther away. I kept calling to him and finally woke myself up."

Miss Eugenia was frowning. "So where's the smelly part?"

"When I woke up I went into the hall and looked—just to be sure."
Miss Eugenia nodded as if this was a most sensible reaction.

"There was no one in the hallway, so I went into Emily's room to
check on her."

"Of course you did." Miss Eugenia's head bobbed again.

"Emily was sleeping peacefully, but when I headed back to my
room, I distinctly smelled Tony's soap—the special scent made for
him by a shop in Myrtle Beach." Miss Eugenia didn't respond immediately, so Kate added, "You probably think I'm crazy."

"I don't think that at all," Miss Eugenia assured her. "After my
experiences in Hawaii, I never discount the power of dreams. Mr.
Tony Booth, the Dream Weaver for Channel One in Honolulu, told
me that often we sense danger subconsciously, and that is played out
in our dreams."

"So my dream may be me warning me?"

"At the very least, I think it means you're worried about Mark,
and your anxiety has transmitted itself into your dream."

"What's the very most it could mean?" Kate asked.

"That the Lord allowed you to have a comfort dream."

"A comfort dream?" Kate repeated. This term was unfamiliar to her.

Miss Eugenia nodded. "I had one a few weeks after Charles died."

Kate loved stories about Charles Atkins. "What happened in your
dream?"

"I dreamed about peanut butter."

Kate wrinkled her nose. "You hate peanut butter."

Miss Eugenia waved this aside. "I know, but in my dream, I loved
it. And the dream was so vivid that when I woke up, I still felt a
craving for peanut butter. I went down to the kitchen and opened the
jar I bought just before Charles had his heart attack."

"And?" Kate prompted.

"And, there was one spoonful missing." Miss Eugenia smiled.
"Charles had this habit of eating spoonfuls of peanut butter straight
from the jar. I used to fuss at him about it. I don't know why really. It
just seemed . . . silly. But that night when I saw the missing spoonful,
I felt so close to Charles—almost like he was there giving me a hug."
She paused to wipe her eyes. "I know the Lord sent me the peanut
butter dream to comfort me."

"That's sweet," Kate said. "Weird, but sweet." She pressed the rake into the soft earth and dragged it forward. "But if my dream was supposed to comfort me, why did I dream about Tony instead of Mark?"

"Mark can't watch over you from . . . wherever he is," Miss Eugenia said. "Maybe Tony can."

Kate was unnerved by this thought. Her feelings for Tony were complicated and conflicting. Since his death she had made a point to avoid them as much as possible. Besides, far from leaving her with a feeling of comfort and peace, the dream had left her restless and uneasy. So she decided to change the subject. "What time is Annabelle coming to get the kids?"

"I told her to be here about ten," Miss Eugenia replied. "We'll work here for an hour, then go inside and get the children cleaned up. After they leave, we'll still have two hours to straighten the house before your guests begin arriving."

"*Your* guests," Kate corrected. Then she checked her watch. "I don't know if I can stand another hour of pre-tilling!"

Miss Eugenia gave her a narrow look. "I declare, Kate, sometimes you can be so dramatic."

Before Kate could think of a reply, she saw a nondescript tan sedan pull up to the curb in front of the FBI car already parked there. "It looks like we're going to have another changing of the guard," she said, then lifted a hand up to shield her eyes. She watched as the driver's side door opened and a tall black woman stepped out. Kate's hand flew to her mouth as tears stung the back of her eyes.

"Is that who I think it is?" Miss Eugenia asked.

"Miracle," Kate whispered, and took off at a dead run.

* * *

Kate barely had time to give Miracle a hug in greeting before Miss Eugenia arrived at the curb with the Iverson children in tow.

"Well, Miracle Moore, I declare you're looking mighty good."

"Hey, Miss Eugenia," the FBI agent from Chicago returned. "You're not looking half-bad yourself. Are you going to introduce me to your little friends?" Miracle asked with a twinkle in her eye.

"Why, this is Emily and Charles Iverson," Miss Eugenia played along. "You remember them."

"I remember them, for sure," Miracle confirmed. "But the Emily and Charles I know are tiny babies—not a grown up lady and little gentleman like this."

"I am Emily," Kate's daughter insisted. "And this is Charles too!"

"You both remember Miracle, don't you?" Kate prompted.

Emily frowned. "A little," she said after consideration. "And I've seen her in some pictures."

Kate looped her arm through Miracle's. "Well, she's a very good friend of mine, and I can't believe she's here." Kate turned to Miracle. "Why are you here?"

"Let me get my suitcase, and we'll talk inside," Miracle suggested.

"Suitcase?" Kate said, raising an eyebrow. "That sounds like you're staying for a while."

Miracle nodded. "Until Mark comes home."

This time tears spilled over onto Kate's cheeks before she could stop them. "You're the agent they've sent to stay inside the house with us!"

"Yep." Miracle pulled a suitcase from the backseat of the car, and then they all walked into the house with Lady running circles around them.

"Where did this little dog come from?" Miracle asked as she stepped cautiously to keep from trampling Lady.

"Her name is Lady von Beanie Weenie Atkins, and she's a pure-bred dog," Miss Eugenia informed their guest. "Very expensive. I inherited her from Miss Geneva Mackey when she died last summer."

Miracle stared at the dog for a few seconds but seemed at a loss for words. "Well," she said finally.

Miss Eugenia scooped up the dog, and they all escorted Miracle upstairs. "Emily's in Mark's old room across from the master bedroom," Kate explained as they passed by. "And Miss Eugenia's moved herself into the first guest room, so you'll have to take the last one."

Miss Eugenia gave Kate a reproachful look. "If I'm inconveniencing you, I guess I could move back into the rocking chair in Emily's room."

"The last one is fine with me," Miracle said.

Kate turned into the last guest room and switched on the light. "Nothing's changed much since you were here," she remarked.

Miracle looked around the room and then her eyes settled on the children. "The house is the same, but the children sure have grown."

Kate nodded. "Children have a tendency to do that."

"Have you had breakfast yet?" Miss Eugenia asked.

"Only an oatmeal and yogurt bar on the plane."

Miss Eugenia shuddered. "I'm not sure that qualifies as *food*, let alone breakfast. There are a couple of biscuits left over from our breakfast, and I can whip up some eggs and bacon to go along with them. Before you know it, we'll have you a hearty breakfast ready," Miss Eugenia said. "Emily, Charles, come with me, and we'll fix Miracle something decent to eat."

Kate and Miracle watched the children follow Miss Eugenia out of the room. When they were gone, Miracle said, "I see Miss Eugenia hasn't changed over the years."

"If anything she's gotten bossier."

Miracle studied Kate. "You haven't done too badly for yourself."

Kate smiled. "No, not at all. Life here in Haggerty is good. The kids are great, and Mark, well, he's beyond great. The only thing I'd change if I could is . . ." Kate looked away, blinking back more tears. "I wish I could have another baby."

"Most people would consider two kids, two teenagers, and two college educations plenty to worry about!"

"I know," Kate acknowledged. "But like you said, they grow so fast and . . ." She waved around the room. "This is what I do. I make pancakes and take trips to the park and put Band-Aids on skinned knees and read books and sing songs and give baths. What will I do when I run out of children and still have so much time left?"

"I say there's no sense worrying about that bridge until you're ready to cross it. Right now you just concentrate on being a good mom and thank the good Lord you're in a position to stay home with your children. My mama said those days were the best of her life."

Kate took a deep breath. "I'm lucky, and I know it. Some days I can't help but want more."

Miracle laughed. "We're all that way."

"Now, explain what you're doing here."

"Mark's SAC had some security concerns about you and the children. They wanted someone inside the house since a car parked in front is not foolproof."

Kate laughed. "I don't know if Mark would appreciate that remark. He slipped past them without any problem—does that make him a fool?"

Miracle pulled some clothes from her suitcase and began hanging them in the closet. "No insult intended. Anyway, Mr. Mitchell knew I had been closely associated with your family, so he called my boss and asked if they could borrow me for a week or so."

"I feel awful," Kate murmured.

"Why? I thought you'd be glad to see me!"

"I am glad to see you. I feel awful because I was horrible to Mr. Mitchell yesterday. I threatened to go on television talk shows and make up stuff about the FBI if he didn't stop the rumors about Mark. And now he's gone to all this trouble to protect me—and to do it in the way I'd be most comfortable."

"Don't feel bad," Miracle comforted in a brisk manner. "Mr. Mitchell is looking out for himself and the FBI and his operation as much as he's looking out for you. And I was working a dead-end case on the south side of Chicago so I personally hope you'll need me for a long time."

"And your arrival saved me from another hour of standing around pre-tilling in Miss Eugenia's garden."

"Pre-what?"

"She made it up. She's trying to keep me busy so I won't miss Mark." Kate rolled her eyes. "Like that's possible. So she made up some crazy story about needing us to help her pre-till her garden with a rake and look for rocks before the first frost."

Miracle laughed. "Well you definitely beat the first frost, but did you find any rocks?"

"The kids found two pieces of gravel from the alley, and I'd bet my life that Miss Eugenia put them there herself."

"That Miss Eugenia is quite a character." Miracle stowed the suitcase in the closet.

Kate took a step toward the door and waved for Miracle to follow. "Let's go downstairs so you can eat."

The phone started ringing when Kate and Miracle walked into the kitchen. Kate answered it, her heart pounding. "Hello?"

"Kate?" Miss Polly asked a little louder than absolutely necessary. "Was that Miracle that I just saw getting out of that FBI car?"

"Yes," Kate confirmed. "She's come to stay with us for a few days."

"Well, if that isn't the most exciting thing! I will have to call George Ann and tell her. Maybe that will snap her out of her pout over not getting to host the bridge club meeting."

"I hope so," Kate said. "Good-bye, Miss Polly."

"Well, I see Miss Polly hasn't lost her touch," Miracle said as she took a seat at the table. "She still knows what's happening almost before it happens."

"I'm surprised it took her as long as it did to call," Miss Eugenia replied. "She must have been in the bathtub when you arrived. That's the only time she can't see out of a window or reach her phone."

"Um-um, this looks delicious," Miracle remarked. "I miss a lot of things about my childhood, but the thing I miss most is the biscuits."

"Biscuit making is something of a lost art," Miss Eugenia agreed as she placed a gravy boat on the table beside Miracle's plate.

Miracle broke open two biscuits and poured gravy on top. "My mother used to make a hundred biscuits every morning."

Emily and Charles had been standing by the window, watching Miracle from a distance. But at this comment, Emily stepped forward and asked, "A hundred?"

"Yes, ma'am," Miracle confirmed. "I had eight brothers, and all of them were big eaters. After breakfast was over, she'd put ham inside the leftover biscuits and send them with my brothers for lunch."

Emily took another step toward the table and wrinkled her nose. "Biscuits for lunch?"

"You should try it sometime," Miracle advised. "It's very good."

Emily watched Miracle eat for a few minutes. Finally she walked up to the corner of the table and asked, "Do you like to play Candyland?"

Miracle thought for a second. "It's been a long time since I played, but I think I used to like it pretty well."

"Me and Charles play almost every night," Emily informed their guest. "And if you want, you can play too."

Miracle smiled. "Thank you."

"My daddy used to play with us," Emily continued. "But he had to go away."

"Far away," Charles added dolefully.

Emily took another step closer to Miracle. "We've got a pumpkin, and my mama said tonight we might carve it for Halloween."

"Which means tomorrow it will be molded," Kate said. "In Utah we could carve a pumpkin, and it would last for weeks. Here you carve it one day, and it will be fuzzy the next."

Miracle laughed. "Well then we'll just have us a pumpkin with a beard."

"You're funny," Emily said with a smile.

"Well, enough of this silly pumpkin humor," Miss Eugenia told them firmly. "Kate, will you get Miracle some more orange juice?"

Throughout the meal Miss Eugenia kept small talk going and in the process managed to elicit a few facts about Miracle's personal life. They learned that she had recently bought a house in a suburb of Chicago, and she'd been dating a policeman for several months. The relationship had possibilities but wasn't serious yet.

"Won't your boyfriend miss you while you're visiting us?" Emily was now at Miracle's elbow.

"Well, I sure do hope so." Miracle stood and carried her dirty dishes to the sink.

"Don't worry about those dishes," Kate said.

"The very idea!" Miss Eugenia concurred as she rose slowly to her feet. "You'd better leave those dishes right where they are. We'll go in the family room to finish our visiting so Kate can clean up the kitchen. We've got company coming over in a couple of hours, and I know she wants to tidy up before then."

* * *

When Cristobal Morales arrived, Mark was in the sunroom trying to concentrate on a John Grisham novel.

"Good book?" the lawyer asked.

"Probably," Mark acknowledged. "I'll let you know if I can ever make myself read it."

Cristobal nodded. "Señor Salazar has an unsettling effect on people."

Mark certainly wasn't going to disagree with that. "Did you get an automatic system for the garage door?" he asked instead.

"Yes," Cristobal replied as Pilar walked in with a tray. "I have some men in your garage installing it now."

Pilar placed the tray on a table near Mark. "I made lemonade."

"That was very thoughtful," Mark said. "Thank you."

"If you are hungry, I can bring some food," Pilar offered.

Mark rubbed his stomach. "No thank you. I'm still full from breakfast."

Cristobal waved a hand impatiently. "Nothing for me."

Pilar left, and Mark poured himself a glass of lemonade. "You sure you don't want some?"

Cristobal shook his head as he paced in front of the thick, tinted windows. "It was foolish of you to get involved with Solana last night. Now you have attracted unwanted attention and may not be able to stay in La Rosa."

Mark smiled. "You've gotten very attached to me in such a short time."

Cristobal didn't return his good humor. "I'm attached to your money and the percentage I can earn by working for you. And a dead American, even one in bad standing, could mean trouble for La Rosa."

Mark appreciated the lawyer's concern but felt it was unwarranted. "Actually Salazar and I hit it off pretty well."

"Hit it off?" Cristobal repeated.

"It's an American expression that means our meeting was friendly."

Cristobal stopped pacing and stared at Mark. "Friendly?"

"In a wary sort of way."

Cristobal dismissed this with a wave of his hand and said, "Señor Salazar has no friends."

Mark made a show of examining his fingernails. "Well, he likes me well enough to offer one of his soldiers as my bodyguard and to ask me to teach his daughter to play chess."

Cristobal's expression changed from worried to astonished. "Why would he ask a stranger to teach his daughter a game?"

Mark laughed. "Really he just wants to entertain the girl. He thinks that given time she might find me more attractive than her soldier she's in love with."

Cristobal frowned. "You are more than ten years older than the girl, not to mention married! Why would she choose you over a man her own age?"

"In that case, I guess I'll just teach her to play chess."

Cristobal sat heavily in a chair beside Mark. "This is very unexpected." He didn't sound pleased. "Señor Salazar never takes such a personal interest in strangers."

Mark was mildly irritated with the lawyer's reaction. "You've got to agree that it's better for me to be Salazar's friend than his enemy."

Cristobal tilted his head in a noncommittal gesture. "I think you are lucky that Señor Salazar didn't put a bullet in your head this morning. Whether his *friendship* is a good thing or not remains to be seen. However, I warn you to use great caution in your dealings with him." Cristobal's gaze returned to the window. "Association with him is often fatal."

"I've heard it can also be profitable."

When Cristobal turned to face Mark, he seemed disappointed. "So that is how it is."

Mark shrugged. "If I can't work out a suitable arrangement with the FBI, I may have no choice but to stay here."

"If you want to make more money, Señor Salazar is the one to talk to in La Rosa," Cristobal acknowledged. "I just hope you live long enough to enjoy your ill-gotten gains."

Mark forced a laugh and poured lemonade into the extra glass Pilar had provided. "Don't worry so much. Here, have a glass of lemonade. It's great."

Cristobal accepted the glass and took a long sip. Then he replaced it on the tray and took a step toward the door. "I need to get back to my office. When the workmen are through, they will give Pilar two remote garage door openers. One is for her—one is for you."

Mark nodded. "Thank you."

Cristobal didn't smile when he said, "Take care, my friend."

CHAPTER 7

By the time Annabelle came to pick up Emily and Charles, Kate had them bathed and dressed and looking so cute that Miss Eugenia voiced regret over her decision to send them away.

"Can't you at least wait and let all the ladies see how cute they are?" she asked her sister.

"I most certainly cannot," Annabelle replied. "The ladies know how cute they are, and besides, that would mean hanging around here for two hours taking orders from you." She turned to Kate and Miracle. "Good luck, and may God bless you." Then to the children she said, "Let's get going while the going is good!"

Emily and Charles kissed their mother, waved good-bye to Miss Eugenia and Miracle, and then followed Annabelle outside.

"It's for the best, really," Kate comforted Miss Eugenia after they were gone. "The children would distract us while we're trying to clean, and by the time the ladies got here, they'd probably be all dirty again anyway."

"I guess you're right," Miss Eugenia said, but she didn't look convinced.

Arnold arrived with the card tables and helped move the living room furniture against the walls. "Look at this dust!" Miss Eugenia exclaimed when they were finished. "We'll do what we can, but we might not be able to have this place as clean as I'd like it to be for the bridge club meeting."

"Next time, give me more than a couple of hours notice, and I'll dust," Kate said, trying to hold in her temper.

"From what I remember about those old ladies, it doesn't seem like any of them could see well enough to notice any dust," Miracle said.

"They may not be able to see their hand in front of their face, but believe you me—they can make out a speck of dust a mile away," Miss Eugenia assured them grimly. "Let's get busy."

Miss Eugenia assigned Arnold to vacuum and distributed dust rags to Kate and Miracle.

"What are *you* going to do?" Kate asked as she crawled under an end table.

Miss Eugenia settled into a chair. "Somebody's got to point out the dusty spots."

Once the cleaning was done, Miss Eugenia sent Arnold over to her house to bring a selection of fall-colored plants to use as decorations.

"We'll place them strategically to hide areas we weren't able to clean," she told Miracle and Kate as Arnold walked back in with a huge pot of yellow mums. "Like here on the fireplace."

By the time Miss Polly and the other members of the food committee arrived at eleven thirty, the house was mostly clean and full of beautiful fall flowers. Kate thought the transformation was miraculous, but Miss Eugenia looked around with a critical eye.

"I guess this is the best we can do," the old woman pronounced finally. "You go home and get some sleep," she told Arnold. "Your next shift at the police station will start soon." Then she turned to Kate and Miracle. "And you two go get cleaned up. I need you dressed and standing at the front door to welcome guests in twenty minutes."

Thus dismissed, Kate and Miracle hurried upstairs. They changed clothes, repaired their makeup, and were at the front door with two minutes to spare.

"Kate, you know Eva Nell," Miss Eugenia said when their first guest arrived.

"It's good to see you again," Kate said dutifully. "And let me introduce my friend, Miracle Moore. She's an agent for the FBI and used to work with my husband."

Miss Eva Nell's eyes widened at this announcement. "An FBI agent?" she repeated. Then she shook Miracle's hand politely and moved on into the living room.

The next guest to arrive was Miss George Ann Simmons. "How do you do, Agent Moore," Miss George Ann said, holding her head just a little higher than was necessary or becoming. "I'm sure you remember me. We met the last time you were in Haggerty. I live across the town square in that nice house beside the Baptist church . . ."

"And her father donated the land that the church was built on," Kate interjected to keep Miss Eugenia from doing so. "Wasn't that generous?"

Miracle raised both eyebrows. "Extremely."

"I know Miracle would love to hear more, but we've got to keep this line moving," Miss Eugenia said, propelling Miss George Ann forward.

"Don't forget that you're supposed to be at my house next Tuesday at ten o'clock AM to fold napkins for my neighbor's granddaughter's baby shower," Miss George Ann reminded Miss Eugenia over her shoulder.

"I remember," Miss Eugenia muttered. "Now go on into the living room and get us a good table."

George Ann looked regretfully back at Miracle. "I was hoping we'd get to talk a little more. Donating the land for the Baptist church is just one of many interesting stories in my family history."

Miracle waved. "Maybe we'll get a chance to visit later on."

"Only if you're living your worst nightmare," Kate whispered after Miss George Ann was out of hearing range. Then she turned to Miss Eugenia. "You're helping Miss George Ann fold napkins for a baby shower?"

Miss Eugenia grimaced. "Yes, and the worst part is she wants the napkins to be folded in the shape of baby diapers."

"Sounds kind of disgusting if you ask me," Miracle remarked.

"I tried to tell her that," Miss Eugenia concurred. "But once George Ann has her mind made up, it's hard to make her see reason."

Before Miracle could respond, Miss Agnes Halstead stepped up and said, "Aren't you the Iversons' old maid?"

"I'm going to have to take exception to the word *old*," Miracle said with a smile.

"Miracle posed as our maid when I was in the witness protection program," Kate tried to explain. "But she's actually an agent for the FBI."

The ancient little woman behind Miss Agnes put a hand to her ear and said, "Huh?"

"She used to be their maid, Myrtle, but she's not anymore!" Miss Agnes hollered directly into the other woman's cupped hand.

Miss Myrtle grinned up at Miracle. "Well, if you need work, I could use help on Mondays and Fridays."

Kate gave up trying to explain Miracle's occupation and just yelled, "Sorry, Miss Myrtle. Miracle lives in Chicago now."

After the old ladies had moved on, Kate whispered to Miracle, "We never did fully explain the whole story of Tony's death and my various marriages to Mark. We were afraid it would be too much for the town folks."

Miracle eyed the women who were milling around the card tables in the living room. "They seem like pretty tough old birds to me. I think they could have handled it."

Kate shrugged. "Well, it's too late now. In their minds, you were our maid."

"I guess I can deal with that as long as they don't call me Mammy."

"Oh, what a lovely name," a little lady with light blue hair and a pillbox hat said to Miracle. "It's nice to meet you, Mammy. I'm Hazel McNutt."

Kate opened her mouth to explain, but Miracle just stuck out her hand. "How do you do?"

When all the ladies were seated around the card tables, Miss Eugenia called the meeting to order. She thanked Miss George Ann for graciously allowing them to change the location at the last minute. "Kate's husband went off on a top secret undercover operation for the FBI and gave me responsibility for her safety and that of their children. I just didn't feel that I could leave them even for something as important as our weekly bridge club meeting."

"Oh brother," Kate murmured to Miracle.

"In the newspaper it said that Mark Iverson stole money from the FBI," one of the old ladies said.

"You must not have watched the news last night," Miss Eugenia replied. "The head of the FBI in Atlanta got on television and said that Mark is one of their best agents and never stole a thing. I can't give you any details about the case he's working on, because it's so secret and all, but I can promise you that he is on very important business for our country."

Miracle cleared her throat, and Miss Eugenia glanced back at the agent.

"I've already said too much." She returned her attention to the ladies seated at the card tables. "Deal the first hand!"

"I think we should go to the kitchen and taste test the refreshments," Kate whispered to Miracle.

"It does seem like the thing for a good hostess to do," Miracle agreed, "to make sure that all the food is safe for human consumption."

Kate grabbed Miracle by the arm and dragged her toward the kitchen. "Exactly."

A few minutes later, they were sitting around the table eating pimento cheese sandwiches and sipping fruit punch.

"They don't make pimento cheese in Chicago," Miracle told Kate.

"I'd never heard of it before I came to Haggerty."

"It's a shame for the rest of the country."

"Umm," Kate agreed with her mouth full.

"What's that stuff that looks like throwup?"

Kate made a face. "I think that must be Miss George Ann's pumpkin and squash succotash."

"Excuse me," a voice sounded from the hall. Kate and Miracle looked up to see two of the bridge players standing in the doorway. "We're looking for the powder room."

Kate swallowed a bite of sandwich and said, "First door on the right under the stairway."

As the ladies retreated, one said, "Isn't that the maid?"

"I thought she was the nanny," the other replied.

"No, her name is *Mammy*," the first corrected.

"Oh, well they certainly need a maid. Do you see that dust along the baseboards?"

As the voices faded, Kate shook her head at Miracle. "I don't know which one of us should be more offended."

Miracle reached for another sandwich. "I've got thick skin. I refuse to be offended."

"Okay, Mammy."

Miracle shrugged. "Nobody's accusing me of keeping a dirty house."

Kate laughed as she picked up their punch cups and carried them to the sink. She ran some warm water over the cups and was placing them in the dish drainer to dry when she glanced out the window. A man was walking down the sidewalk, having just turned off of Maple and headed up Oak. His back was to Kate, but something about the length of his stride and the way his dark blond hair curled against the collar of his shirt was so familiar . . .

"Tony," she whispered.

"Did you say something, Kate?" Miracle asked.

Momentarily confused, Kate looked over her shoulder at Miracle and then back out the window. The man was gone. Either he was hidden by one of the houses on Oak Street, or he hadn't ever been there in the first place. Even if he did exist, his resemblance to Tony may have been exaggerated by her overactive imagination. If she hadn't smelled Tony's soap the night before, she would never have associated the fleeting glimpse of a blond man with her first husband. But she had smelled the soap.

"Is something wrong?" Miracle sounded concerned now.

Kate shook her head and tried to smile. "I'm going on three nights without sleep, and it's obviously catching up with me. Miss Polly promised me that it took much longer to go crazy from sleep deprivation, but I'm beginning to wonder."

Miracle walked over to the sink and handed Kate a chocolate-covered strawberry. "See if this helps."

Kate took a big bite. "It can't hurt."

By the time Kate had eaten six strawberries, she had convinced herself that the man she'd seen wasn't Tony. "So," she said as she reached for a seventh, "did Mr. Evans call you personally and tell you to come here?"

Miracle moved the tray of strawberries out of Kate's reach. "Miss Eugenia's going to have my head if she comes in here and all these strawberries are gone. And as far as coming to Haggerty, Mr. Evans's secretary called me yesterday afternoon and said I was being temporarily reassigned. I was instructed to be on the flight that left

O'Hare International at 8:35 PM. I got to Atlanta about eleven eastern time. A crabby man in a tight polyester suit named Bowen picked me up and took me to a hotel."

"I met him," Kate said, eyeing the plate of strawberries. "I didn't like him either."

"Then early this morning, Mr. Bowen brought me a car and sent me on my way to Haggerty."

"They didn't tell you anything about the operation Mark's working on?"

Miracle shook her head. "Not a word. Just said that I was supposed to stick with you like glue until Mark gets home."

"Mr. Mitchell told me that Mark helped the Atlanta agents crack a child pornography ring. They arrested a lot of people and confiscated a bunch of stuff, including millions of dollars, but they didn't get the owners. Mark wanted them to keep investigating, and they wouldn't. So he took the money to South America."

"Why would he do that?"

"To try and smoke out the owners or force the FBI to keep looking for them or something."

Miracle frowned, and Kate continued. "Sounds risky, but I guess it might work. The strange thing about it is that I didn't know that Mark was working with Atlanta agents on anything," she said.

Miracle seemed surprised. "Mark discusses his cases with you?"

Kate laughed. "You know better than that. But it seems like if he'd been working with Atlanta agents, he would have had to make some trips up there over the past few weeks. Or that he would have at least told me he was working on something big that he *couldn't* discuss with me."

"That would be logical."

Kate shrugged. "Oh well. Hopefully it will all be over soon, and in the meantime, I'm grateful to have you here."

Miss Eugenia and Miss Polly found them there a few minutes later.

"We've been wondering where you two were," Miss Eugenia said.

"Well, we've been right here," Miracle replied, "guarding all this food."

"Oh, thank you," Miss Polly gushed as she picked up a tray that was now short several pimento cheese sandwiches.

Miss Eugenia eyed the plate of strawberries and gave them a stern look. "Well, it's time to serve what's left of the refreshments, if you'll give us a hand."

"Sure." Kate pushed herself up and took the tray from Miss Polly. "Where do you want me to put this?"

"In the middle of the dining room table, next to the punch bowl," Miss Polly instructed.

"Then if you'll just help us keep all the trays and plates and bowls refilled as necessary," Miss Eugenia added. "And scoop some of that succotash out every chance you get. I know that nobody is actually going to eat it, but I don't want George Ann to get her feelings hurt."

Once they were out of the kitchen, Kate whispered, "Did she just say she didn't want Miss George Ann to have her feelings hurt?"

"That's what she said," Miracle confirmed.

"Usually upsetting Miss George Ann is her *goal*," Kate said in confusion.

Miracle put the plate of sandwiches on the table as the subject of their discussion walked up. "We were just saying that this is some delicious looking succotash," Miracle lied through her bright, white teeth.

"It's my mother's recipe," Miss George Ann told them.

"Let me dish you up some," Miracle offered.

"Well, aren't you helpful, Mammy," Kate whispered as she hurried back to the kitchen.

Once everyone was served, Miss Eugenia dismissed Kate and Miracle from kitchen duty. They sat down on the living room couch that was pushed against the wall just as Miss Agnes announced that a male exotic dancer had moved into her rental house.

"What's an exotic dancer?" Miss Myrtle, the little deaf woman, inquired with a hand to her ear.

"A stripper," Miss Agnes yelled.

This had to be hollered into Miss Myrtle's ear three times before she finally nodded. "I've been looking for someone to refinish the hardwood floors in my kitchen. Could you ask him to come by and give me an estimate?"

Miss Agnes pointed to the plate of food on the card table in front of Miss Myrtle. "Eat your sandwiches, Myrtle," she instructed. Then she returned her attention to her avid, hearing audience. "I've had to drop by several times to go over terms of his lease."

"What's his name?" Miss Polly asked.

"His legal name is Terrance Sprayberry," Miss Agnes informed them. "But his stage name is Frisky."

Miss Polly pulled her handkerchief from the neckline of her dress and dabbed the perspiration that formed along her upper lip. "Oh my."

"I think this is a highly inappropriate conversation for a group of Christian ladies to be engaged in," Miss George Ann announced. "Besides, I'll bet this Sprayberry person isn't really a stripper at all. I'll bet he's an accountant or a bank teller or something boring like that. Agnes probably made it all up just to get attention."

"George Ann Simmons, you have a lot of nerve accusing *me* of trying to get attention," Miss Agnes began.

Kate nudged Miracle. "This is about to get good."

"Please, ladies!" Miss Polly pleaded with her hands clasped in front of her chest. "Remember that we are all friends here, gathered for a day of pleasant socialization."

"And Agnes, I'm sure you can understand why George Ann would have doubts about such an amazing story," Miss Eugenia added.

"It may be amazing," Miss Agnes said. "But it's completely true." She sent Miss George Ann one more venomous look before saying, "I, for one, enjoy pleasant conversation among friends. But just to make sure that everyone is clear on the facts of the matter, I have *proof* that Frisky makes his living as a male stripper."

"Agnes Halstead, please don't tell me you went to his show!" one of the ladies said with a gasp.

"Of course not," Miss Agnes replied. "Savannah Wilcox, our State Farm Insurance agent, does some seamstress work on the side, and she was hired to make him a costume for his act."

"I wonder what kind of costume he wears before he, well, you know, takes it all off?" Hazel McNutt speculated aloud.

"I guess you would have to go to the club where he works to find *that* out," Miss Agnes said.

"Do you know how much it costs to get into a place like that?" the lady with the blue pillbox hat asked the room in general.

"Heaven help us," Miss Eugenia said, employing her sister Annabelle's favorite phrase. Then she picked up a tray of cheese straws and thrust them at Kate. "Hurry and pass these around. Maybe we can get them interested in eating instead of strippers before George Ann has a stroke."

* * *

Just after Mark finished a delicious lunch prepared by Pilar, his cell phone rang. The caller was listed as unknown, but Mark answered anyway. It was Rodrigo Salazar—confirming Angelo Perez's claim that cell phone calls were easy to intercept and trace.

"Mark!" Salazar said in response to Mark's cautious "Hello."

"Would it be convenient for me to deliver your new bodyguard now?"

Mark was surprised and a little wary that Salazar was asking permission. "Of course."

"Good. We're on our way."

"I'll be watching for you."

Mark was waiting on his front porch ten minutes later when a military-style truck, like the one he had seen Solana and Emilio in the night before, and a late-model SUV pulled up and parked in front of his house. Four armed soldiers climbed out of the truck and quickly secured the premises. Then Salazar and Emilio emerged from the SUV.

Emilio's face was badly bruised, and he walked stiffly, as if in pain. Apparently, he had been punished for the flat tire escapade. Perhaps that was why Salazar was so anxious to get the young man away from Vargas and into Mark's employ.

Mark led the way inside and offered his guests lunch. "I have eaten," Salazar replied. "But I am sure the boy is hungry." He turned and addressed Emilio in rapid Spanish. "Go to the kitchen, and the cook will feed you. She will show you where to sleep, and later Mr. Iverson will outline your new duties."

Emilio nodded and walked to the kitchen, clutching a green duffel bag that probably contained all his earthly possessions.

"Cristobal Morales will know a fair wage for Emilio," Salazar said. "You can give him one day off in seven and allow him use of your

Jeep when you do not need it. More liberties than that would be noticed."

Mark nodded. "I won't pamper the boy too much."

"You must guard against your natural American softness. It could be misinterpreted by others, and Emilio must continue to live here after you leave."

"I understand," Mark reiterated. "Will Solana and I begin our chess matches this evening?"

Salazar sighed. "Yes, although rumors will soon be circulating that I am not a man to be feared."

Mark smiled. "I think it's acceptable to be indulgent with one's daughter."

Salazar shrugged. "It is a risk I am willing to take."

Mark led the way out to the sunroom, and the men sat down. "You have a nice view here," Salazar remarked.

"Yes," Mark said. "When I chose Cristobal to be my lawyer I chose La Rosa by default. I didn't know what to expect when I got here, but I am very pleased."

"La Rosa has a lot to offer a man like you," Salazar said. "One can be anonymous here, and it is quiet yet close to Cartagena when you desire entertainment. If your FBI friends won't forgive you, staying here permanently would not be a bad thing."

Mark frowned. "Unless I'm willing to be involved in the drug trade, I would have no way to make a living in La Rosa."

"You Americans are so self-righteous," Salazar said contemptuously. "You talk about the drug trade and how we make our dirty money. But really we are the same as you. Our economy runs just as yours does—on supply and demand. You point your finger at us and say, 'If you would stop producing these illegal substances, all the problems that exist in our country would go away.' But the truth is that if the demand for what we produce did not *exist* in your country, we could not supply it. You need to concentrate on your own social problems. Solve them, and you do not have to worry about us and our nasty drugs."

Mark could tell that he had to tread carefully. Salazar was passionate about the subject. But he couldn't patronize the man. "Surely you admit that selling illegal drugs is wrong."

"I admit nothing!" Salazar returned. "The drugs we produce are illegal only because your government makes them so. And a question you should ask yourself is why."

"Because they're addictive and unhealthy and kill people," Mark itemized. "They ruin lives."

"Have you ever seen a lung that has been exposed to nicotine?" Salazar asked, and Mark saw he had walked straight into a trap. "Your own surgeon general puts a warning on cigarettes saying that they will kill those who smoke them. They are addictive and unhealthy and ruin lives—and yet cigarettes are not illegal in your country. And why is that?"

Mark shrugged. "I don't have an answer."

"Money, my friend. The American tobacco industry is big business, big tax revenue. The reason heroin is illegal is because it is produced in my country—not yours."

Mark wasn't sure how to respond. Salazar was a convincing advocate for his cause. But his cause was inherently evil. "I wish that we lived in a society where there was no tobacco or heroin," Mark said finally. "We would be healthier and happier if that was the case. But it is foolish to say that just because we have already allowed some detrimental things to affect us that we should welcome more."

"Not welcome, maybe," Salazar was willing to concede. "But allow legally—let people make their own choice." Salazar got a shrewd look in his eyes. "Let me put it another way. Suppose your father built many cigarette factories and became very rich. Then he died and left them to you. Since your religion prohibits the use of tobacco, would you feel that it was morally wrong for you to operate the factories or even to sell them and receive reasonable compensation?"

Again Mark was stunned by the amount of research Salazar had done on him in such a short amount of time. Finally he managed to say, "I don't know. Maybe I could close the factories and just sell the land they were built on."

Salazar smiled, and Mark sensed that this was another trap.

"So you would close the doors to the factories your father built. And how would you feel when you looked into the faces of your employees—many of whom may have worked for your family's company for generations—and tell them that they no longer have jobs?"

"That would be terrible," Mark answered honestly.

"If I close my factories, my employees lose their jobs and their children starve."

"You could change to a legal commodity like flowers. The profits would not be as great, but . . ."

"Do you know the wholesale value of a single *pound* of heroin?" Salazar demanded. "About $100,000. Do you know the wholesale value of a pound of flowers?"

"I'm sure it's not comparable . . ."

"If the people in your country would value flowers as much as they do heroin—then that is what I would produce."

Mark looked across at the man, at a loss for words.

"When I took over my father's drug empire twenty years ago, do you know how many of his employees died on an average day in what passed for our 'factories'?"

Mark shook his head. He had no idea.

"Twenty. Twenty people died on an average day! And that wasn't from violence or the drug wars that you heard about on television. That was from heat exhaustion and malnutrition and illness due to poor sanitary conditions. I took over my father's business and cleaned up the factories, modernized the equipment, and improved the overall standard of living for my employees. And what did I get for my efforts? Does anyone say, 'Rodrigo could have made more money and ignored the suffering of his people, but he chose to do this because he has a heart?' No! Instead they call me a barbarian and put me on their most wanted list along with international terrorists who blow up buildings with airplanes!"

"Do you know how many people die every year in my country of drug-related causes?" Mark asked.

"Does someone put a gun to the head of these people and force them to take the drugs?" Salazar demanded.

"You're breaking the law," Mark insisted.

Salazar sighed. "When my father died, if I had closed his factories, others would have stepped in quickly to fill the void—others who would not have cared about sanitary conditions and the health of their workers. Do you not see? Stopping the flow of drugs into your country is hopeless as long as the demand is so great. Regulation and monitoring is the best we can do."

Mark shook his head. "I can't accept that."

"Then you are a fool," Salazar said, but his voice held no malice. "If men like me ever decide that the effort is too much, you will see a much darker age full of drug wars and human misery beyond what has been before."

"I can't agree with legalizing drugs, but I know that we do have some serious social problems that need more attention in my country," Mark admitted.

Salazar smiled. "In that, at least, we agree." Salazar rose to his feet. "Well, we have discussed the problems of this little corner of the world long enough. I must go home."

"I appreciate you allowing Emilio to come and work for me," Mark said.

"Your solution will, I think, work to everyone's advantage. After dinner this evening, I will send Solana for your first chess match."

"That will be fine."

"Once she finds out that Emilio is here, I suspect that she will want to play chess every night. If she becomes a nuisance, let me know."

"I'll look forward to our matches, and I'll make sure Pilar is always here as a chaperone."

"In that case, instead of chess matches, she should come for cooking lessons. That breakfast we ate this morning was delicious."

Mark walked Salazar out onto the front porch and watched as he motioned for his men to follow him. They climbed into the vehicles, turned around in the small road, and sped away, leaving a trail of dust in their wake.

Mark went back inside, reset the alarm, and found Emilio sitting stiffly in a kitchen chair.

"I told him there is a room downstairs with a bed where he could rest, but he wants to wait for you," Pilar explained.

Mark sat down in front of his new bodyguard. "It looks like you've run into some trouble since I saw you last night."

Emilio nodded. "It is no less than I expected. I am lucky to be alive."

Mark noticed the way the young man kept his arm pressed firmly against his left side. "I would be glad to take you into La Rosa and have a doctor look at those ribs."

Emilio shook his head. "Thank you, but it's just a crack—nothing that won't heal on its own."

Mark watched the young man for a few minutes before saying, "I'm glad to have your services as a bodyguard. It's possible that some men will come and try to kill me. Do you have a gun?"

Emilio nodded again.

"Keep it with you at all times. However, I will only be in La Rosa temporarily. Once I can work out a problem at home, I'll be returning to the United States." Mark paused, but when Emilio didn't respond, he continued. "I'm concerned that when I leave, you will again be in danger from General Vargas."

Emilio raised his eyes to meet Mark's. "I am concerned about that too."

"Well, we'll have to see what we can do."

* * *

Solana hadn't seen her father or Emilio all day. She and Emilio had agreed that they would follow their normal schedule for the next few days—no special requests for shopping trips or movies. They had been fortunate the night before, but at any moment their luck could change.

Solana wanted to talk to her father about the possibility of inviting Mr. Iverson to their home for dinner one evening that week. She thought her father would like the American. Also, if she could learn more about him, he might provide a means of escape from La Rosa.

She had been to her father's office several times, but it was always dark and empty. Now it was almost dinnertime, and she was becoming desperate. She paced around the large living room, hoping he might find her there. Her eyes strayed occasionally to the chessboard, still set up from her last game with Emilio. She walked over and picked up his king, which he had laid down on the board in defeat, and pressed it to her lips. How she hoped that he was safe.

"Solana," a voice whispered into her ear.

She gasped in surprise, and the chess piece fell to the floor.

She turned to see Hector Vargas lean down and retrieve it. "The fallen king." He held the chess piece out to her, and after a brief hesitation she took it. He was still much too close, threatening in a subtle way. "Of course now that Emilio is gone, you'll need someone else to play with."

Solana grabbed the back of a chair for support. "Gone?" she managed.

"Didn't your father tell you?" Vargas asked. "No, I see that he didn't. Well, Emilio is no longer with us—not that he is any great loss to your father's army."

Solana had to know Emilio's fate, so she commanded herself to keep breathing. "I don't understand."

"I'm sure your father will explain when it pleases him," Vargas responded. "But now that Emilio is gone, you can share the favors you gave to him with me."

She controlled a shudder, hating to reward him with the satisfaction of seeing her discomfort. "Emilio was always a perfect gentleman."

Vargas stepped even closer so that now she could feel his hot, sour breath on her face. She backed up until she was pressed firmly against the chess table with no means of retreat. Knowing she was trapped, he smiled. "There are still those unexplained hours yesterday. I cannot prove it, but I know you were not in that movie theater. I believe you were in the woods with Emilio, and if you will allow a lowly foot soldier such liberties, then how can you refuse a general like me?"

"Please," Solana pleaded. If only one of the servants would walk by or if her father would come home and find them . . .

Vargas's arm shot out and grabbed her around the waist. She twisted frantically to extricate herself from his grasp, which only seemed to amuse him. He reached up and traced the neckline of her shirt with his forefinger, and she began to panic.

"So beautiful," he murmured as his fat lips moved with purpose toward hers.

Unable to think of any other defense, Solana threw all her weight back against the chess table. Taken by surprise, Vargas staggered slightly and relaxed his grip just enough for her to slide out from under him.

"Don't you ever touch me again," she hissed at him once she was a safe distance away. "If you do, I will tell my father."

"Don't make your father choose between us, Solana," Vargas advised. "He can live without you, but without me, his world would come to an end." Vargas put his fingers to his lips then waved them at her. "We will meet again in a more . . . private place," he promised. "And then I will finish what I have begun."

She watched him walk away, her mind in turmoil. She had no choice but to talk to her father. She had to find out what had happened to Emilio and to tell him of the general's inappropriate behavior. She put her face in her hands. When had things gotten so out of control?

* * *

Kate rested her head against the back of the chaise lounge and let the waning rays of the sun that penetrated the glass panels of the pool room warm her skin and melt away the tension. The kids were swimming in the pool, with Miss Eugenia and Whit Owens providing vigilant watch. Derrick was outside grilling meat and vegetables on the brick barbecue grill while Annabelle prepared side items in the house. Lady was running laps around the small pool, barking alternately at the children and Miss Eugenia.

"I think she wants to go swimming," Emily said.

"She can share my floaty," Charles offered.

Miss Eugenia shook her head. "I just had her groomed, and I don't want to mess up her coat."

Miracle opened one eye and examined Lady. The little dog closely resembled a moving Brillo pad. "She just had that thing groomed?"

Kate nodded. "You should have seen her before."

Miracle closed her eye. "Praise the Lord that I didn't."

Kate laughed. "Amen."

"Are you girls having fun?" Annabelle asked. "Can I get you anything to drink?"

"We're fine," Kate assured their hostess.

"This place is great," Miracle praised. "I love all the plants and the little paths and that cute wooden bridge."

"We patterned it after a place we visited on Maui," Annabelle confided. "Derrick and I both loved it and decided that when we got home we were going to try to create a space just like it here."

"In case anyone doesn't know it, Annabelle has been to Hawaii numerous times," Miss Eugenia announced. "She works that into every conversation just like George Ann always mentions that her father donated the land the Baptist church is built on, so I thought I'd save us all a lot of time and cut to the chase."

Annabelle shook her head. "And this is how she treats people who have spent the entire day doing her favors. Imagine how she treats people who *aren't* nice to her."

"Who would dare be mean to me?" Miss Eugenia demanded. "And why didn't you ask me if I wanted anything to drink? I'm parched. Bring me some of that fresh-squeezed lemonade Derrick was making earlier."

Miracle laughed as Annabelle walked off to get the lemonade. "Yeah, I love this. All the benefits of sunbathing without the sun."

"You don't like the sun?" Kate asked.

"I sure don't need a tan," Miracle pointed out. "And I never did understand why you white folks want to lie around in the blazing heat and bake yourselves."

"It's relaxing," Kate told her with a smile.

"It's torture," Miracle retorted. "And the best part about this little glass pool house is that the smoke from the grill can't get in here. When I grill at home, no matter what I do, the smoke seems to get in my face."

"You know, they say that smoke follows beauty."

"At least they got that right," Miracle said.

* * *

Solana felt a strange sense of calm as she waited in the dining room for her father. For the past several days she had been racked with anxiety—weighing decisions with their consequences and trying to determine what was best not only for her, but also for Emilio as well. Tonight she knew that all the decisions had been taken from her hands. After her encounter with Hector Vargas in the salon earlier that evening, there was really nothing left to do but tell her father everything and throw herself on his mercy.

The kitchen maid bustled in and out, placing dishes on the table, and Solana hoped this meant that her father's appearance was imminent. She hadn't exactly hidden in her room since being manhandled by Vargas, but she had made a point to stay out of public areas, which had greatly reduced the chance of running into her father as well.

Finally the double doors that led from the salon opened, and Rodrigo Salazar walked through them into the dining room. Solana's relief at seeing him was doused immediately when she saw that Hector Vargas was in his wake. Vargas gave her a sly smile and then let his eyes run the length of her body. Solana shuddered, feeling unclean.

"Solana!" her father called out crossing the room to embrace her. "I have missed you today."

She clung to him a little longer than normal. "I have missed you too, Father," she replied with feeling.

As he patted her cheek, she saw an odd look in his eyes—maybe love, maybe fear. "Have a seat, and I will tell you all about my busy day and how it will affect your life."

Solana swallowed hard. "My life?"

Her father held the chair for her, and after she was seated, he slid it effortlessly under the table. Then he took his regular seat at the head of the table, Vargas seating himself directly across from Solana. She watched as the men enthusiastically filled their plates with food, knowing that she would be too nervous to eat.

After the servants had left them, her father lowered his voice and said, "I ate a particularly good breakfast at the home of the American, Mr. Iverson, this morning. When he leaves La Rosa, I am thinking of hiring his cook."

Solana's hand, which had been stirring her fork in a little pile of salad, froze. "You visited Mr. Iverson this morning?"

"I did," her father replied as he swallowed then gulped a mouthful of wine. "And his housekeeper is a much better cook than this chef I brought in from Bogotá, I can promise you that!"

"Why did you go to see Mr. Iverson?" Solana prompted.

"To thank him for being of assistance to you yesterday," her father replied. "And to check him out," he added. "You know that I have to be careful about strangers in La Rosa."

Solana took a deep breath. "What do you think about him?"

Her father considered this for a few seconds. "I like him. He is idealistic and arrogant—as all Americans are—but he is entertaining. In fact, he offered to tutor you in English."

"Oh?" Solana was stunned.

"Of course, I told him that you didn't need any help with your English."

Solana dropped her eyes to her lap so he wouldn't see her disappointment. "Of course."

"But then he said that he played chess competitively in college, and I knew you would love the chance to learn more about your favorite game. He has offered to play a game with you each evening, and I have agreed. You will begin this tonight."

"This evening?" she confirmed.

Her father turned to look at her. "That is unless you don't want to spend time with the American. If you would prefer to remain here . . ."

"No," Solana interrupted and then regretted the desperate tone of her voice. With an effort she calmed herself and said, "I would like to go to Mr. Iverson's house. Thank you for arranging that, Father."

He smiled at her. "You are welcome."

She knew it was rude to bring up unpleasant subjects during a meal. Besides, she hated to make another demand so soon after her father had given her such a large concession. So for the remainder of dinner, she sat quietly while the men discussed business. Several times she felt Vargas staring at her, but she would not meet his vulgar gaze. But by the time dessert was served, she felt she would go crazy if she didn't know Emilio's fate.

She was formulating the question in her mind when her father said, "Solana, I forgot to tell you that General Vargas has assigned you a new bodyguard."

For a few seconds, Solana was so light-headed she feared she would faint. She grasped her wine glass, and after a few sips, she felt fortified enough to ask, "A new bodyguard? Where is Emilio?"

"Oh," her father seemed surprised. "Did no one tell you? Mr. Iverson needs a bodyguard, so Emilio has gone to work for him."

Now Solana feared she would faint from relief. "He is working for the American?"

Her father nodded. "Yes. He is no longer in my employ."

"I have assigned Lucien Sanchez," Vargas said, forcing her to look at him. His eyes were full of satisfaction. Solana knew that Sanchez was loyal to Vargas. He might protect her from one of her father's enemies, but he would not protect her from the general.

However, Solana would not complain about the choice of bodyguards or report the general's earlier misdeeds to her father. Emilio was safe, and that was the important thing at this point.

"If you are finished with this slop that my expensive chef calls dinner," her father said with a frown at her uneaten food, "then you are welcome to go to Mr. Iverson's house."

Solana smiled at her father. "Thank you."

"If you see Emilio there, remember that he has duties to perform for Mr. Iverson," her father cautioned. "I know that you have grown fond of the young man, but you cannot interfere with his new job, or he might lose it."

Solana stood and kissed her father on the cheek. "I will not bother him." Just as she thought she was about to escape without having to speak to Vargas, she heard his hateful voice.

"I'll have Lucien bring a truck around to the front of the compound for you in thirty minutes if that will be convenient."

Solana turned and forced herself to look into the face she had grown to hate above all others. "That will be fine, thank you." Then she hurried from the room.

* * *

Solana applied her makeup with a trembling hand. It had only been twenty-four hours since she had seen Emilio, but it seemed like an eternity. She had been so worried, and now she was filled with anticipation. She might not be able to touch him, but just to see him, to hear his voice, and to know he was safe would be blissful. After one last glance in the mirror, she hurried from her room and down the stairs. She half-expected her father to be waiting in the salon to tell her good-bye, but the large room was empty.

She walked across entry hall, her heels echoing on the tile floor. She pulled open the front door and stepped out into the cool night air. A green truck was parked in front of the house, and she could see Lucien Sanchez behind the wheel. She did not see Hector Vargas standing in the shadows on the edge of the stairs that led up to the house until he stepped out. And by then he had her in his grasp.

"What do you want?" she demanded, although it was a foolish question.

He laughed, giving her a close view of his coffee-stained teeth. "I just want you to give my regards to Emilio," he said.

Then he pressed his thick, slimy lips against hers. She tore her lips from his, and his mouth trailed along her jawline and down her neck. She cried out for help, but Sanchez didn't even glance their way. Vargas pinned her against the truck, in the shadows where they couldn't be seen from the house, and she was afraid all was lost. Then the general's cell phone started to ring.

He cursed as he pulled it from the clip on his belt. He glanced at the screen and then at her. "It is your father," he said. "I guess I'd better go and see what he wants."

She almost wept with relief.

"But don't worry." He leaned close. "I always finish what I start."

And he was gone, leaving her trembling against the side of the green truck. She straightened her clothing, wiped her mouth with the back of her hand, and climbed into the truck beside Lucien. She knew that he had witnessed her humiliation and had done nothing to help her. Instead of hating him, she tried to look at it as a learning experience. Never would she trust Lucien to help her, and never would she risk herself for him. Staring straight ahead, she buckled her seatbelt. Her new bodyguard started the truck, and they turned toward La Rosa.

Solana fought tears all the way to Mr. Iverson's house. The evening she had been anticipating had been largely ruined by the general's attack. When they arrived, she allowed Lucien to lead the way to the front door and knock. Mr. Iverson's housekeeper answered the door. Their host was right behind her.

"Welcome," Mr. Iverson said. "Please come in."

Solana walked in and tried not to be too obvious as she searched for Emilio. He was nowhere to be seen. She followed the housekeeper into a salon. "Are you hungry?" Mr. Iverson asked. Solana shook her head. He turned to Lucien. "Well, I'm sure this young man is starving. My housekeeper is an excellent cook, and she always makes more food than I can eat. My bodyguard is in the kitchen. Please join him."

Left with no polite response other than to accept, Lucien followed Pilar into the kitchen. Once they were gone, Mr. Iverson led Solana into a large sunroom.

"I hope you don't mind that I took Emilio from you," Mr. Iverson said quietly.

Solana shook her head. "No, I am grateful. He was in danger at my father's compound."

"Don't be shocked when you see him," Mr. Iverson warned. "He, well, there are some bruises."

Solana sat down in the closest chair and closed her eyes. "Did they hurt him badly?"

"He wouldn't let me take him to a doctor—he says it's only bruises and a cracked rib." Mr. Iverson stood. "I'm going to go into the kitchen, and I'll send Emilio in here. I can't promise you much time, but I'll keep your new bodyguard in the kitchen for as long as I can."

Solana tried her best to compose herself, but despite Mr. Iverson's warnings, when she saw Emilio, she wept.

Keeping his eyes on the door that led to the salon, Emilio pulled Solana into his arms. "Don't cry," he begged. "We both know that I am fortunate to be alive."

"I think we can trust Mr. Iverson," Solana said. "You will have to ask him to help us get away from here."

Emilio nodded. "I think we have no choice. To stay here is death—or worse. I know that Vargas is determined to dishonor you."

She had made up her mind not to tell Emilio about her encounters with Vargas, knowing there was nothing he could do except worry. "How?"

"Sanchez was only too happy to tell me about the incident at the truck," Emilio said, his lips forming a hard line. "You must tell your father, Solana."

She nodded, but she knew she couldn't do as he asked. If she took any action against Vargas, the general would retaliate, and Emilio was the most helpless target.

"Mr. Iverson said that your father has agreed for you to come over here every night to play chess. Sanchez will come too, so we will not have time alone together . . ."

"But we will be safe," Solana finished the sentence for him. *And I can look at you,* she thought to herself, *and feel of your goodness instead of the evil that is so often present at my father's house.*

Emilio pressed a quick kiss to her forehead and then moved over to the wall of windows and took a position to one side. Solana obediently turned away from him. She saw a novel on a table near the couch, so she picked it up and began leafing through the pages. A minute later Mr. Iverson and Lucien Sanchez walked in. Lucien moved over and stood near Emilio by the windows. Mr. Iverson waved to the chessboard he had set up in a corner.

"Shall we play?" he invited.

She put down the novel and nodded. "Yes."

* * *

After eating a delicious dinner, Kate made the children wait the requisite thirty minutes before allowing them to swim again. Once it got late, Miss Eugenia declared that it was time for all decent people to be at home.

"Well, since I definitely want to be included in the decent category," Kate said, "I guess we'd better gather the children and go."

"Dinner was delicious," Miracle told Derrick. "And I love your climate-controlled pool house."

"I'm glad you enjoyed yourself," Derrick said graciously. "Come back anytime."

"How about tomorrow?" Miracle asked. Then, in response to their startled expressions, she added, "Just kidding. I imagine Miss Eugenia's got a full day planned for us tomorrow."

Kate nodded, taking her cue. "First we'll probably spend a couple of hours in the garden pre-tilling and looking for more gravel that mysteriously migrated from the alley in the two weeks since Arnold turned it under. After that we'll probably be hosting a meeting of the Baptist Bible study class that Miss George Ann Simmons had her heart set on having at her house."

"But first we'll have to rearrange the furniture and dust the baseboards," Miracle put in.

Kate raised an eyebrow. "That's your job, Mammy."

"Oh hush, both of you," Miss Eugenia insisted. "We won't have time for gardening or moving furniture tomorrow. At ten o'clock Sandy Ragsdale is expecting the children to come over and help her feed her animals. Miracle, you'll go with them while Kate and I go to the Christmas bazaar planning meeting."

"Christmas bazaar?" Miracle repeated.

"It's held on the first of December, and it's Haggerty's largest fundraiser," Miss Eugenia explained. "All the proceeds go to the Phoebe Putney Memorial Hospital Children's fund, and this is the first year that a Mormon has been invited to sit on the committee."

"I guess that would be me," Kate said with a sigh.

Miss Eugenia frowned. "You should be honored."

"I'd be more honored if I didn't know you blackmailed them into putting me on the committee just to keep me busy so I won't miss Mark."

Miss Eugenia got a smug smile on her face. "You think you're so smart. Well, this time you're completely wrong."

Kate raised both eyebrows. "I am?"

"Yes, you are. I asked them to put you on the committee long before all this came up with Mark, and I didn't blackmail them. I just told them that I was bequeathing my seat on the committee to you."

This took Kate by surprise. "You can't bequeath anything yet. You aren't dead."

"No sense waiting until the last minute," Miss Eugenia said. "I figure if we share the committee seat for a few years prior to my demise, by the time I'm six feet under, you ought to have the hang of it."

"Why are you going six feet under?" Emily asked.

"Can I go to too?" Charles wanted to know.

Kate rolled her eyes. "'Six feet under' is nothing like 'Six Flags,'" she assured him. "Trust me."

As they all started toward the vehicles, Miss Eugenia told Miracle, "You go on with Kate. I'll ride with Whit."

Kate stopped, put a hand on her hip, and addressed her nosy neighbor. "You have got to be kidding."

Miss Eugenia, along with all the others, seemed surprised by Kate's reaction. "What?"

"Today you had an entire bridge club meeting moved to our house and risked the wrath of Miss George Ann, which is no small thing, to keep your eye on us because Mark charged you with our safety. And now in the middle of Albany and in pitch black darkness you're going to send us off with only Miracle for protection?"

Miss Eugenia did look a little uncomfortable, but she waved at Miracle. "She's an FBI agent, after all, and I will be in the car right behind you."

But Annabelle shook her head and said, "I thought Eugenia changed the bridge club meeting to your house today to try and stem all the gossip about Mark and show people that regardless of what they say, she is still firmly in your court."

Kate turned back to her neighbor and could tell from the look on the wrinkled old face that what Annabelle had said was true. All day Kate thought she had been putting up with Miss Eugenia, being long-suffering and patient. When in reality Miss Eugenia had been moving heaven and earth to help her. She felt the tears that lately were never far away brimming in her eyes. "Oh, Miss Eugenia."

"Please stop crying," Miss Eugenia instructed. "You'll upset the children. And you can't believe a word Annabelle says. My mother called it a very vivid imagination, but I say she's just a liar."

"Eugenia," Annabelle began.

"Let's get home," Miss Eugenia interrupted. "These children are asleep on their feet."

Before anyone could object, Miss Eugenia collected Lady and herded the children toward the van.

* * *

Solana stayed at Mark's rental house until nine o'clock on Thursday evening, and even when she stood to leave, Mark could tell that she hated to go. But while he felt sorry for the girl, he was anxious to call Kate. So even though she gave him several opportunities to insist that she stay for another game, he didn't take her hints.

Finally she accepted defeat and walked to the front door. "I would like to come again tomorrow if you don't mind," she said as they stood on the porch.

"I don't mind at all," Mark told her. "I get bored just sitting around this house. In fact, there's no reason for you to wait until the evening for our chess match," he said in a burst of kindness. "I'll call your father, and if he doesn't mind, maybe we can take a drive around the area. Lucien and Emilio can show us some of the local landmarks."

"I am from Bogotá originally," Emilio said. "So I'm not very familiar with tourist attractions here. Perhaps Lucien knows some points of interests."

Sanchez shrugged. "There are some ruins not far from here that Americans seem to find interesting. But we would need more men to provide protection if we are going out."

Mark nodded. "I will check with Mr. Salazar and see if he can loan us some extra men. And would it be possible for you to follow Pilar as far as La Rosa?" Mark requested. "I hate for her to be out on the roads alone after dark."

Sanchez considered this for a few seconds before nodding.

Mark followed his guests outside and watched as the green truck and Pilar's Escort pulled off down the dirt path. Then he walked back inside to call Kate.

* * *

As Kate parked in the driveway, she turned and gave her children some last-minute instructions. "When we get out of the van, I want both of you to go straight upstairs and change for bed," she said. "Do not ask Miss Eugenia if you can take Lady for a walk, do not ask Mr. Whit to play Candyland, do not ask for a snack."

"Is it too late to carve our pumpkin?" Emily asked.

"I'm afraid so," Kate told her. "But we'll be sure to do it tomorrow."

The children nodded obediently, and Kate could see that they were both too tired from their busy day to offer much resistance. Whit pulled his car up beside the van, and as Kate was walking around the van to let the children out, she saw a car driving slowly down the street toward them. The driver was wearing a hat, but between the collar of his shirt and the edge of his hat, about an inch of dark blond hair was visible.

She forgot about the children and took a step toward the street. "Tony?" she whispered.

His head turned, and she stared into the gray eyes she remembered so well. And then he was gone.

"Kate!" Miss Eugenia's voice snapped her out of the semi-trance just before she stepped into the street. "What are you doing?"

"Did you see who was driving that car?" Kate asked weakly.

Miss Eugenia turned to study the disappearing taillights. "It looks like that little foreign car that Carolyn Lovell's son drives, but I can't be sure."

"Does he have blond hair?" Kate asked.

Now Miss Eugenia sounded worried. "I think so. Why?"

Before Kate could answer, her cell phone started to ring. She answered it automatically. "Hello."

"Kate?" It was Mark. "How are things?"

"Well," she answered without thinking. "Either I'm going crazy, or I've just seen Tony."

"Tony who?"

"My husband!" Kate cried. "Surely you remember him!"

There was a brief pause, and then Mark said, "Kate, Tony Singleton died four years ago."

Kate couldn't control a little bubble of hysterical laughter. "Yeah, they keep telling me he's dead, but he just keeps turning back up alive!"

Miracle pried the cell phone from Kate's fingers. After giving Kate a look somewhere between pity and exasperation, she spoke into the little receiver. "Mark, this is Miracle Moore. Your SAC arranged with Mr. Evans for me to come and stay with Kate and the kids until all this is over."

Kate couldn't hear Mark's response, but after a brief pause, Miracle continued.

"Kate hasn't gotten any sleep for three days now, and she's not thinking clearly. A blond guy in a sports car drove by, and all of a sudden she started hollering about Tony. You don't need to worry about her. I'm going to get her into bed, and after a good night's rest she'll be fine. Call back tomorrow morning at nine o'clock our time. You can talk to Kate and the kids then." Miracle closed the cell phone with a distinct snap.

Agents Lott and Applegate were walking toward them looking alert. "Is something wrong?" one asked.

"Everything's fine," Miracle told them. Then she motioned to Kate. "Let's get the kids inside."

"I'll head on home," Whit said. "See you tomorrow, Eugenia."

Miss Eugenia nodded, but she looked a little pale. Kate realized she wasn't dismissing the Tony sighting as lightly as Miracle had. Of course Miracle didn't know about the dream, and Miss Eugenia didn't know about the man who had walked by during the bridge club meeting.

With a sigh, Kate opened the van door and smiled at her children. "Why were you yelling, Mama?" Emily asked.

"Are you scared?" Charles added.

"I'm tired and a little nervous," Kate admitted. "So let's hurry inside, okay?"

As soon as the children were settled in bed, Kate walked into the hallway to find Miss Eugenia and Miracle waiting for her. "We need to talk," Miss Eugenia said.

Feeling like a condemned woman being led to her doom, Kate nodded and followed them to the kitchen.

* * *

Mark paced around the sunroom, trying to decide what to do. His first inclination had been to drive to Cartagena immediately and take the next flight to the United States. Only the possibility that he would be arrested when he landed on U.S. soil kept him from this desperate course of action. Once he calmed down, he realized that it would be foolish to abandon his position now. He had made contact with Salazar, and if not friends, they were at least wary associates. He had established the beginnings of a trusting relationship with Solana and was all that stood between Emilio and probable death.

Kate had Miracle and Miss Eugenia to support and protect her. Tony Singleton was dead. Mark felt certain of that fact. But even if he were alive—surely he meant Kate no harm. So patience was called for. As Mark reached this conclusion, his PDA alarm sounded, indicating that Perez was trying to establish contact.

Mark hurried over, signed on, and read the message that appeared.

Report.

Mark sat down and replied:

Contact made with Salazar—no mention of meeting or confirmation of trip next week. Solana is anxious to leave and will welcome news of rescue. Be prepared to take her and young man named Emilio Delgado currently in my employ—she will not leave without him. Will see her daily, can pass details of rescue if necessary.

Mark waited, and finally Perez answered:

Good work. Better and faster than expected. Pickup information will be transmitted to Solana through agent inside compound. You are not need-to-know.

Mark struggled with himself and finally decided to ask Perez for a personal favor.

Speaking of need-to-know—it's possible that Agent Tony Singleton, who officially died of a gunshot wound four years ago, really lived and was given a new identity. If he's alive, it will be classified information—hard to confirm. But I have to be sure. Can you check it out for me?

The screen on the PDA remained blank for so long that Mark had given up hope of a reply when a message finally appeared.

*You realize that I am in the jungles of Colombia. My resources
are extremely limited. Even if I wanted to find the answer to your
question, which I'm not sure I do, I don't know if I can until I
return to the U.S.*

Mark sighed before responding:

At least you have limited resources. I have none.

Mark waited for thirty minutes. When no message popped up on
the screen, he signed off and picked up the John Grisham novel.

* * *

"I think I'm going to make myself some hot chocolate," Miss
Eugenia said when they reached the Iversons' kitchen. "Would either
of you like a cup?"

Kate nodded, and Miracle said, "I guess I'll make it unanimous.
Hot chocolates all the way around."

Miss Eugenia busied herself at the counter, filling mugs with hot
water. Over her shoulder she said to Kate, "Go ahead and tell Miracle
about your dream and the soap smell."

Kate cleared her throat. "Do you remember the special soap Tony
used to buy from that little candle shop in South Carolina?"

Miracle nodded. "I remember he used to smell divine."

Kate smiled. "He said he found the place when he was working
undercover. They allowed him to create his own personal scent. He
mixed lemongrass and lavender and sandalwood and rosemary and
even tobacco flower until he came up with just the right combination. They only made a year's worth of soap at a time because they
said it would lose its fragrance. That's how I know . . ."

"How you know what, Kate?" Miracle asked.

"Tell her," Miss Eugenia encouraged.

"Two nights ago I had a dream. I was in the house looking for
Mark and the kids, but I couldn't find them anywhere. I climbed the
stairs, and when I got to the top, I saw Tony standing at the end of
the hallway. He said something, but I couldn't make out the words.

Then he motioned for me to follow him. I tried, but I couldn't catch up to him—he just kept getting farther and farther away. Finally I lost him completely. I woke myself up calling out to him. So I got up and checked the hall."

"I presume Tony wasn't standing there?" Miracle asked as Miss Eugenia put a mug of hot chocolate in front of her.

"No," Kate said. "But since I was up, I checked on Emily."

"Why Emily and not Charles?" Miracle asked.

Kate shrugged. "I guess because Charles sleeps in the nursery attached to my room. Someone would have to go past me to get to him. But Emily's room opens into the hall."

"Or maybe it's because Emily is Tony's daughter, and you thought he'd want to see Emily if it was him," Miracle suggested.

Miss Eugenia put a mug of hot chocolate in front of Kate. This was something she hadn't thought of and didn't want to delve into.

"Go on with your dream, Kate," Miss Eugenia prompted with a stern look at Miracle.

"Emily was sleeping soundly, so I turned around to go back to my room. That's when I smelled the soap."

"Tony's soap?" Miracle confirmed.

"Yes. The personally designed soap that loses its scent after a year."

Miracle looked unhappy. "Do you think it was his ghost?"

"At first I did, but now I think it was really him."

"Kate," Miracle began.

Kate reached out and grabbed the agent's hand. "I've seen him twice," she said. "This morning during the bridge club meeting I glimpsed him walking up the street that runs perpendicular to Maple and then tonight in the car. Two sightings and one smelling."

"What are you saying?"

"At first I was afraid that I was going crazy," Kate admitted. "Now I'm sure I'm not. I know what I saw and what I smelled. I want you to ask for an investigation."

"Ask who?" Miracle demanded. "Mr. Evans? You just want me to call him up and say, 'I hate to bother you, but did you fake Tony's death the second time too?' And if he did, what makes you think he'll tell me?"

Kate had to admit that Miracle had a very good point. "Well, do you think it's possible they faked Tony's death the second time?"

Miracle was quiet for a few seconds. Then she said, "Anything is possible. You were in the room when he was shot. Do you think he really died?"

Kate closed her eyes and tried to remember what for years she had tried desperately to forget. "Mr. Morris was going to kill Mark and me," she said. "I was so shocked that Tony was still alive and heartbroken that he was romantically involved with the woman seated next to him. The things he said and did . . ." She shook her head, unable to voice all the memories of that night.

Kate cleared her throat and continued. "Anyway, they were going to kill us, and it seemed like Tony didn't even care. Then he moved so quickly that I didn't realize he had grabbed a steak knife until it was buried in Mr. Morris's chest. Gunshots exploded from all around the room, and Mark shoved me under a table."

Kate opened her eyes and faced them.

"So you didn't actually see Tony get shot?"

Kate shook her head. "No."

"Then it's possible that while you were under the table and shots were flying, that Tony could have been made to appear dead," Miss Eugenia said. "Maybe they gave him some kind of shot with a drug that made him almost stop breathing."

Miracle was frowning, which Kate was afraid meant that this was a possibility and not something Miss Eugenia had come up with from watching too much television.

"Tell me the next thing you actually *saw*," Miracle requested.

Kate closed her eyes again. "The room was a mess. Tables were turned over, bullets had made holes in the walls; there were broken dishes everywhere. Mr. Morris was still sitting there with the steak knife in his chest. There wasn't much blood associated with the wound, which surprised me. There were several more bodies lying around the room and lots of men with guns pacing back and forth. The blonde woman who had been Tony's . . . girlfriend was standing by the far wall crying."

"Tell me about Tony," Miracle commanded gently.

"His face was down on the table, like he'd fallen asleep, except there was a large puddle of blood under his cheek."

"That would be easy enough to fake," Miss Eugenia inserted.

Miracle motioned for Kate to ignore the elderly woman and continue.

"His left hand was clutching the tablecloth."

"Clutching?" Miracle asked. "That could be important, Kate, so you need to be sure. Was his hand holding the material firmly, or was the material just wrapped around his fingers?"

Kate tried to remember. Finally she exhaled and opened her eyes. "I'm sorry. I don't know for sure. It seems like he was holding on, but maybe the material was just tangled in his hand."

Miracle shook her head. "It's not enough."

"One thing I know for sure," Kate said. "When I brought his fingers to my lips, they were warm."

"The shots you heard only took place a minute or so before," Miracle pointed out. "His fingers would still have been warm even if he was dead."

They were silent for a few minutes, and finally Miss Eugenia said, "If Tony is alive and here, the question is why?"

"I don't think he means us harm," Kate said slowly.

"If he meant to harm you, he's already had plenty of opportunities," Miracle said.

Kate expressed her biggest fear. "I'm afraid that he might want Emily. But I think if I can talk to him and explain that he doesn't have to be excluded from her life, we can work out an arrangement we can all live with."

"So, how are we going to set up a conversation with him?" Miss Eugenia asked.

Kate shrugged. "I guess we'll have to catch him."

"I'm not completely convinced that this guy is Tony Singleton," Miracle said. "But whoever he is, the next time he shows up, we'll be ready for him."

CHAPTER 8

On Friday morning Mark got up early after a mostly sleepless night. He was tempted to call Kate immediately to reassure himself that all was well at home, but Miracle had said to call at nine Haggerty time, and he knew it would be best to wait until then. He checked his watch. That was still three hours away.

He found Emilio in the small workout room in the basement. The young man was sitting on a bench, curling a twenty-pound dumbbell with the arm that was on the opposite side of his body from the cracked rib.

"How are you feeling this morning?" Mark asked as he stepped onto the treadmill and adjusted it to warm-up speed.

"Sore," Emilio admitted.

Mark settled into a steady pace. "I've never had a cracked rib, but it seems like some soreness is to be expected. You need to take it easy for a few days and let it heal."

Emilio nodded and set the dumbbell aside.

"Tell me a little about yourself," Mark requested.

Emilio didn't look pleased, but he complied. "I lived with my grandmother in Bogotá until she died about a year ago. I was lucky. Many boys without parents don't have such an advantage. I was able to finish high school and even attend a year at the university. My grandmother told me she had savings, but after she died, I found out she had mortgaged her house to pay for my education." He shrugged. "The money was gone, so I had to leave school and find a way to support myself. There are few options for a poor man in Colombia."

Mark nodded, remembering Salazar's discourse from the day before.

"I applied for the Colombian military, but it takes a long time for them to process all the paperwork, and I was afraid I would starve to death before they recruited me. Then someone told me about Señor Salazar's private army. The pay was better and the recruitment process much shorter."

"How long have you worked for Mr. Salazar?"

"Six months," Emilio replied.

"And how did you get the job as Solana's bodyguard?"

Emilio's expression became more guarded, and Mark could tell he didn't like discussing the girl. "She came to visit her father about two months ago. Señor Salazar requested me. I think it was because he knew I had some education and hoped I might be able to amuse her."

Mark laughed at this remark. "From what I've been able to see, her father was right about that."

Emilio blushed. "I love Solana."

"I didn't mean to make light of your feelings," Mark told him. "I met my wife under similar circumstances."

"Really?"

"Really," Mark assured him as he turned up the speed on the treadmill. "Someday I might tell you about it. Now why don't you watch for Pilar while I finish my run?"

* * *

Kate woke up on Friday morning feeling better than she had in days. *That's what a full eight hours of sleep will do for you,* she thought to herself. *And no visits from a dead husband,* she couldn't help but add as she padded to the bathroom.

By the time Kate made it downstairs, Miss Eugenia had the children dressed and fed and watching *Dora the Explorer.*

"Where's Miracle?" Kate asked as she picked up a piece of bacon off the platter on the table.

"In Mark's office," Miss Eugenia replied. "She's been doing some research."

Kate walked down the hall and into the office. This room, more than any other in the house, was uniquely Mark's, and being there made her miss him more. Miracle was sitting at Mark's desk, studying the computer screen. "Have you learned anything new?" Kate asked Miracle.

"Not much yet, but I'm working on it," Miracle said without looking up.

Kate propped herself on the corner of Mark's desk. "Where did you start?"

"With that little store in Myrtle Beach where Tony ordered his special soap," the agent murmured. "I asked for the name of the person who had been buying his soap after he died. They said that they'd never been notified of his death. They've been delivering twelve bars to the same post office box in Chicago every January for almost ten years."

"Who's been paying for the soap for the last four years?" Kate asked.

"A guy named Troy Sorenson in Las Vegas, Nevada."

"Troy Sorenson sounds very similar to Tony Singleton," Kate whispered.

Miracle grimaced. "Yeah, I thought of that, but it's almost too cutesy. A good agent would never be that obvious if he was really trying to hide out."

Tony had been an extremely good agent, but if he was still alive, Kate wasn't sure how hard he was trying to hide. "So now what?"

"I've called in a few favors. A friend of a friend is checking out the address in Vegas for me. I should hear something back soon." Miracle pushed away from the computer and turned the swivel chair around to face Kate. "In the meantime we need to get ready for Mark's call."

Kate glanced at the clock. "He'll be calling in about ten minutes."

"Mark's a long way from home," Miracle reminded Kate unnecessarily. "He's in a hostile country, surrounded by danger, and already under enough stress. I don't see any point in having him worry himself sick that Tony's lurking around here, threatening you and the kids while he's not able to defend you."

Kate stared at Miracle for a few seconds before saying, "I can't lie to him."

"I wouldn't ask you to," Miracle returned quickly. "All I'm asking is that you don't say anything that's unconfirmed."

Kate laughed. "At this point nothing is *confirmed*."

Miracle nodded. "Exactly."

"So you don't want me to say anything at all?"

"You could just tell Mark that after a few hours of sleep, you feel much better and think that you probably overreacted to whatever you saw last night. Both of those statements would be completely true."

Kate considered the request for a few seconds and then nodded. "Okay," she agreed. "But don't think you're tricking me. I'm doing this because it is *not* a lie, and it *is* best if Mark doesn't worry, and mostly because I *don't* believe that Tony is still alive."

Miracle didn't disagree, but she didn't look happy with Kate's final analysis.

* * *

When Mark ended his phone call with Kate on Friday morning, he felt much better than he had since their brief conversation the night before. Kate was calm and even seemed a little embarrassed about her hysterical claims that Tony Singleton was alive and stalking her. The children sounded happy and excited about their plans for the day. The only negative aspect had been at the end when they had to say good-bye. Now the house in the hills behind La Rosa seemed even lonelier than it had before.

Mark was still holding his cell phone when it rang, and he answered quickly with the irrational hope that Kate was calling back. But instead of his wife's voice, he heard Rodrigo Salazar on the other end of the line.

"I understand that you would like to take a tour of La Rosa, get a feel for the area, tromp through some ancient ruins—that sort of thing." Salazar's tone was decidedly sarcastic.

"Actually, that's true," Mark replied. "I'm not used to sitting around inside a house day after day. I'm going stir crazy."

"Well, you are in luck," Salazar told him. "It just so happens that I have some spare time today, and the weather is nice, so I will show you around personally."

Mark was surprised and not completely pleased. If it was Salazar's intention to kill him, this would be a perfect opportunity. "I wouldn't want to impose on your time."

"I would not allow you to do so," Salazar assured him. "We will pick you up in an hour."

"We?" Mark repeated.

"Solana and I. Bring your bodyguard. Otherwise my daughter will be most disappointed." Salazar disconnected the call.

Mark and Emilio were waiting on the front porch when Salazar and his entourage arrived. There were a total of five vehicles—the SUV in which Salazar and Solana were riding and four green trucks containing armed men. Salazar rolled down the window of the SUV and waved to Mark.

"You and your bodyguard can ride in here with us," he said.

Mark noticed that Emilio kept his eyes on the ground as he approached the vehicle. This made him wonder if some of the men in the trucks were the ones who had disciplined Emilio on General Vargas's order after the flat tire incident.

First they drove around La Rosa. With an entertaining man like Salazar and a beautiful landscape, Mark didn't have trouble concentrating on the tour. Then they stopped at some ruins on the outskirts of the city. Everyone climbed out of the vehicles, the guards taking positions along the road while the others walked among the remnants of an ancient civilization.

Salazar allowed Solana and Emilio to get several yards ahead. Then he said to Mark, "I'm afraid that I have some bad news for you."

Mark waited in nervous anticipation for Salazar to continue.

"As I told you, I did some checking into the information you gave me about your situation, and I have found some disturbing developments."

"What are you talking about?" Mark asked, unable to mask his impatience and concern.

"First, and you may actually consider this good news, the owners of the pornography factory in Atlanta have cut a deal with the FBI. So they will not be coming to reclaim their money."

Nothing Salazar could have said would have surprised Mark more. "You must be mistaken," he said finally. "If some kind of arrangement had been reached, I would have been notified."

Salazar shook his head. "I'm sorry, but my source is impeccable. There is no possibility of a mistake. But I don't blame you for doubting me. You would be a fool to accept my word. You will, of course, check for yourself. I am just telling you what I know."

"So you're saying that the owners of the pornography company are willing to just give up twelve million dollars?"

Mark saw something very close to sympathy in Salazar's eyes. "Well, that is another thing. Apparently the two million dollars in the suitcase you brought with you to Colombia, less the retainer and other funds you wired to Señor Morales, was all the money actually confiscated at the warehouse in Atlanta. According to my impeccable source, the other three suitcases were full of shredded paper. There is no money in Swiss accounts in your name. That should be fairly easy for you to check."

Mark felt a little dizzy. He hadn't personally seen any money in the other three suitcases, but Dan had told him that they were full of cash. Or had it been that other agent, Faust? And they hadn't actually given him account numbers for the other money . . .

"Not that two million is an amount to sneeze at," Salazar was continuing, "but it is not worth a big operation by the FBI either."

Mark shook his head in an effort to clear it. "So, what are you saying?"

"There are no longer troops in the hills around La Rosa," Salazar said quietly. "They have been withdrawn. You are completely unprotected—even from local thugs who would gladly kill you for *ten* dollars in American money."

Mark couldn't believe it was true. He had been in the meeting with Colonel Croyle and all those soldiers when the task force was organized. But why would Salazar lie about the soldiers or the pornographers or the suitcases full of money?

"It's good that you have Emilio," Salazar continued. "But I will be leaving a couple of extra men with you when we return to your house. If the locals see that you are under my protection, they will think twice before bothering you."

Mark knew that he had to come to terms with the situation and deal with it. "Why would the FBI tell me there was twelve million dollars in the suitcases if there was only two?" he said as much to himself as Salazar. "And why would they let me come here to draw out the owners of the pornography company if they already knew who the owners were and planned to make a deal with them?"

Salazar shrugged. "Politics often play a role in such things. Maybe your superiors wanted it to seem that their achievement was bigger than it really was—for the cameras and the American public. More money and more arrests would result in more political goodwill for the FBI. But you are an honest man, and they knew that you wouldn't lie. So they tricked you."

Mark frowned. "That's a possible explanation for the discrepancy in the amount of money," he agreed finally. "But it doesn't explain why they didn't tell me they knew who the owners were."

"Maybe the owners are important people, and their names were kept quiet in exchange for other information. Again, they might have hidden this arrangement from you. And they could not anticipate that you would decide to become a maverick agent and take matters into your own hands."

Mark shook his head. "But what if they *could* anticipate exactly that? What if someone actually suggested the whole idea to me?"

Salazar considered this for a minute then nodded. "In that case you have a very powerful enemy, my friend. And two million dollars *is* missing. There is *no* sanctioned FBI operation. If you try to return to the United States, you *will* be arrested."

"But who would do that to me?" Mark ran his fingers through his hair. "Who would want to ruin my life—separate me from my home and family?" But even as he said the words, a name came to his mind. Tony Singleton.

* * *

After distributing Happy Meals to her children and a couple of chicken nuggets to Lady, Kate settled down on the park bench between Miracle and Miss Eugenia and unwrapped her cheeseburger.

"So, how was the bazaar meeting?" Miracle asked around a mouthful of fish sandwich.

"*Bizarre* meeting would be a more apt term," Kate replied. "Miss Agnes Halstead was determined to mention that male stripper at every opportunity."

"She only mentioned him twice," Miss Eugenia corrected. "Once to let everyone know that her rental house is available again. It seems that there are only a couple of clubs in Albany who employ exotic dancers, and none of them use men. So her tenant, Frisky, was unable to find a permanent position near here. Agnes said he's going to wait around until Savannah Wilcox finishes the new costume, but then he'll be moving on to a larger community with more open-minded clubs. She only mentioned him the second time because she could tell it aggravated George Ann so much." Miss Eugenia shrugged. "And who can blame her for that?"

Kate waved her hamburger. "Anyway, they discussed crocheting doilies that went out of style decades ago and making plant holders that require ten miles of yarn and a hundred man-hours. I finally suggested that we just forget the whole thing and go door-to-door asking for donations for the children's hospital."

Miracle smiled. "I take it that suggestion wasn't met with a lot of support."

Kate grimaced. "I may be six feet under before Miss Eugenia is."

"What Kate doesn't understand is that money isn't the only goal of the bazaar," Miss Eugenia explained. "The event keeps a lot of folks busy, and the holidays can be a lonely time for old people."

"Not to mention that any store that sells yarn would go out of business if the bazaar is discontinued," Kate said as she tossed the remnants of her sandwich into the nearby trash can. Then she turned to Miracle. "So, how was your morning?"

"Well, I ruined a new pair of boots by stepping in cow poop, and a chicken that I swear is possessed by the devil chased me. But other than that it was fine."

The children finished their meals and asked permission to take Lady over to the bridge to look for fish.

"It's okay with me as long as you don't get in the water," Kate consented.

"And don't let Lady get wet," Miss Eugenia added. "I just had her groomed."

"And goodness knows we don't want to see her looking worse," Miracle muttered under her breath to Kate.

"What's that?" Miss Eugenia demanded.

Miracle squinted at the clear autumn sky. "I said does it look like rain to you?"

Miss Eugenia frowned. "It looks fine to me, but we probably should head home soon. The children need to take their naps."

Kate yawned. "I could use one too."

Miracle's cell phone rang. She opened it and said, "Agent Moore." Miracle listened for several minutes, contributing only a few grunts to the conversation. Then she said, "I owe you one," and closed the phone.

"Well?" Kate prompted.

"That was my friend with a friend in Las Vegas."

"Did he find the apartment?"

Miracle nodded. "Yeah, and the guy who lives there matches Tony's description. The pants hanging in the closet were thirty-fours and the shirts sixteens."

Kate put a hand on her neck. "Tony's sizes."

"There were lots of jazz CDs—the kind of stuff Tony liked to listen to and . . ." Miracle's voice trailed off, and Kate knew there was more, something worse that Miracle didn't want to say.

"Let's have it all," Kate insisted.

Miracle sighed. "There was a picture—one of you and Tony. It was just a little snapshot," Miracle was quick to point out. "But it was framed," she admitted.

"So it's his apartment," Kate whispered.

"It looks that way. My friend's friend said nobody's been home for a week or so. The milk in the refrigerator's spoiled, and the neighbors haven't seen the guy around. They don't know where he worked—said he kept kind of crazy hours."

Kate waved this aside. "So Tony didn't die in Miami four years ago, and the FBI gave him a life in Las Vegas."

Miracle's eyes drifted over to the children standing on the bridge. "The question that's got to be answered now is what is he doing in Haggerty?"

"Are you going to ask Mr. Evans?" Miss Eugenia wanted to know.

"If Mr. Evans realizes we're onto him, he could hide Tony so that we'll never find him," Miracle said.

"I don't care if Mr. Evans puts Tony on the moon as long as Emily's safe," Miss Eugenia said. "That's all that matters."

Kate shook her head. "Emily is the most important consideration, but it's not all that matters to me. If Mr. Evans hides Tony again, it would deny me the chance to explain things and to get some answers about the past four years. Besides, why would he hide Tony?"

Finally Miracle shrugged. "It's up to you, Kate."

Kate chewed on her bottom lip for a few seconds. Then she said, "As long as it won't compromise Emily's safety, I'd like to try and find Tony without contacting Mr. Evans."

"Okay," Miracle agreed. "But I can't impose on my contact anymore. If you want to pursue this without help from Mr. Evans, you'll have to hire a private investigator in Las Vegas."

Kate nodded. "Can you arrange that?"

"Yes." Miracle pushed herself into a standing position. "Now let's get those babies home for their naps."

* * *

When they left the ruins, Mark stared out the window of Rodrigo Salazar's SUV and tried to remember every word that had been spoken by each person at all the meetings he had attended in Atlanta. His understanding was that he had been sent to La Rosa to distract Salazar and thereby facilitate Solana's escape. The whole stolen porn money scenario had been added at the last minute to give him a reasonable excuse for being there. So why had the FBI removed his excuse? Why had they exaggerated the amount of money involved? Was Solana really going to be rescued or not? Was Tony Singleton alive and using the situation to his advantage?

Mark had a headache by the time Salazar dropped him and Emilio off at the rental house. He went up to the master bedroom and took two Tylenol. Then he sat on the edge of the bed and called Cristobal Morales.

"I need you to check on something for me," he said. Once Cristobal agreed, Mark outlined the questions Salazar had raised about the accounts in Switzerland. "Can you check and see if I really have any money there?"

"The Swiss are known for being very secretive about their accounts," Cristobal replied. "But I can probably check on the other end. American banks are much less secure. I should be able to see if any money was transferred in your name from a bank in Atlanta on Tuesday."

"Thank you," Mark said, feeling better. "Let me know what you find out as quickly as possible."

"You Americans," Cristobal replied. "Always in a hurry."

Mark ignored this. "And I also need your assistance on another matter."

"Quickly, I presume?"

"Yes," Mark confirmed. "I'm sure you've heard that Salazar allowed me to hire Emilio Delgado as my bodyguard?"

"I heard," Cristobal's tone was neutral.

"Salazar said you would know a fair salary for Emilio. Can you handle payment procedures and any other employment arrangements that need to be made just as you do with Pilar?"

"This is wonderful," the lawyer said without enthusiasm. "You have less money and more employees."

Mark had to smile. "Thanks, Cristobal. And let me know as soon as you hear something."

He disconnected the call and signed onto the PDA. He sent an urgent message to Perez:

Need clarification of my mission immediately. Understand that owners of porn warehouse have been arrested. And money involved is considerably less than I was led to believe. Is this true, and if so, why? Also Salazar said that the troops have been withdrawn from La Rosa. Confirm.

Mark sat anxiously in front of the PDA. Fortunately he didn't have to wait long for a response.

Mission unchanged. Adjustments during any operation are common. If any of them affect you, you'll be notified. Remember, you're only a small part of the big picture. Troops have been pulled back until arrival of helicopter is imminent for their own safety.

Mark stared at the words on the PDA. Was he being reprimanded for questioning a huge discrepancy between the actual facts and what he had been told? Forcing himself to remain calm, Mark typed:

Is Solana's removal from La Rosa still scheduled for next week, and will I leave at the same time?

After a brief pause the answer appeared:

No details available yet.

Frowning, Mark typed:

Were you able to find out anything about Tony Singleton?

After another pause there was a one-word response.

No.

Then the screen went blank.

Mark considered his options for a few minutes before picking up his cell phone. He dialed Jack Gamble's cell phone number. Jack was the state senator who represented Haggerty, a member of the LDS Church, and a personal friend of Mark's.

"Hey, Jack," Mark greeted when the senator answered.

"Mark?"

"It's me."

"I've been reading about you in the paper," Jack replied.

"Yeah, well don't believe everything you read."

"I don't," Jack assured him.

"Did you get something from me in the mail?" Mark asked.

"No. Should I be expecting something?"

If Britta Andersen had mailed the memo on Tuesday as she had promised, it should have arrived at Jack's senate office the next day. Mark realized he had been unwise to trust Ms. Andersen. "Yes, but it's not important."

"Is everything okay, Mark?"

"I hope so." Mark tried to convey with his voice some of the doubt he couldn't safely put into words.

"Well, if Kate needs anything while you're gone, tell her to feel free and call me."

That was what you said to someone to be polite—when you really had no intention of getting involved. He had thought that Jack was different. "Thanks," Mark said. "I'll let her know." Then he disconnected the call without saying good-bye.

* * *

After putting the kids down for their naps, Miss Eugenia took Lady next door to spend a little time in her own habitat. Kate stood at the kitchen window and watched them walk across the stretch of grass that separated the two houses. Then she studied the sidewalk up and down Maple Street. She craned her neck and looked as far as she could down Oak Street, too, but there was no sign of a blond man.

"You looking for Tony?" Miracle guessed as she came up beside Kate.

"Yes, but I haven't had so much as a glimpse," Kate said with a frown. "It's like he knows we're on to him."

"If it's Tony we're dealing with, that would be like him—to toy with his prey," Miracle mused. "That would explain the cutesy name and flagrant drive-bys. He would want us to know he's here but wouldn't actually let us catch him."

"So we're assuming it is Tony?" Kate asked.

"I guess." Miracle frowned at the window glass. "But his timing is bothering me. He's had four years to make a move, so why did he wait to contact you until Mark was out of the country on this strange secret mission?"

"It does seem awfully convenient," Kate agreed.

"I sure would like to know more about the operation Mark is on," Miracle continued. "But I can't seem to get a straight answer from anyone in Atlanta. I'm beginning to wonder if they know what's going on themselves."

In spite of her anxiety, Kate had to laugh at this. "You mean the FBI might have finally taken the need-to-know policy too far?!"

Miracle smiled. "It was bound to happen sometime."

* * *

Barely an hour after Salazar dropped Mark off at his house, he called Mark to ask if he could bring Solana back over for a few games of chess. Mark was a little annoyed by the self-invitation. He knew the girl wanted to be with Emilio and understood her feelings, being miserable and lonely himself. However, having company didn't make things better for him.

But even if good manners didn't require that he acquiesce, at the moment Rodrigo Salazar might be the only thing that stood between him and death by Colombian bandits. So wearily he agreed.

"I'm sorry to impose," Salazar said when they arrived, although he didn't look the least bit repentant. "And while Solana is dying to massacre poor Emilio in a few chess matches, what I was really hoping was that your housekeeper would cook us lunch."

Mark smiled. "I'm sure she would be glad to fix lunch for all of us." Mark turned to Solana. "Would you mind going to the kitchen and warning Pilar that she will have additional mouths to feed? I believe Emilio is there too."

Solana nodded and hurried off to fulfill her assignment.

Once they were alone, Salazar's cheerful expression faded. "You probably think me a rude oaf," he told Mark, "but I actually had an important reason for returning and taking advantage of your hospitality—a better reason than being an indulgent father. Earlier when we talked, you wondered who within the FBI could want to keep you out of the country, and I have come up with the name."

Mark's heart was pounding, but he tried not to look too interested.

"The name is Troy Sorenson."

Mark felt his shoulders sag with relief. This name meant nothing to him.

Then Salazar continued, "But I believe that is an alias for a man you knew as Tony Singleton."

Mark tried to hide his shock but was sure he failed.

"He is, I believe, your wife's first husband. Since his presumed death four years ago, Mr. Singleton has been living in Las Vegas."

"How do you know this?" Mark managed.

"I was able to access some information collected by your friend, Miracle Moore."

So Miracle knew about Tony's resurrection and was collecting information on him, but neither she nor Kate had mentioned it to him. Mark rubbed his temple. The news just kept getting worse and worse.

"Today Agent Moore arranged for Mr. Singleton's apartment to be searched. I obtained a copy of the written report." Salazar held out a sheet of paper.

Mark took the report and scanned it quickly. The off-duty police officer who convinced the resident manager to open the apartment had cataloged a long list of personal possessions owned by the tenant, Troy Sorenson. The only ones that jumped out at Mark were a softball signed by an FBI city league team from the Chicago field office and a framed photograph of Tony Singleton and his wife, Kate. The dizziness Mark had experienced earlier returned for a moment, and he sat down in the closest chair.

"Agent Moore must feel that she has reached the limits of her friendship because today she hired a Las Vegas private investigator to continue the search for information about Tony Singleton—in your wife's behalf, of course. At the bottom of the report, you will see a note that the other residents of the apartment complex were questioned. None of them knew Sorenson well, and they haven't seen him for the past week or so."

Mark looked up at Salazar.

"Apparently that is because he has been in Georgia, stalking your wife—or his wife. I'm not really sure about the legalities."

From the beginning of Mark's relationship with Kate, Tony hadn't been much of a rival because he'd always been dead, or at least presumed dead. Now Mark was in Colombia—unable to return to the United States—and Tony was in Haggerty with Kate.

"It makes no sense," Mark said. "If Tony's been alive for all these years and wanted to be a part of Kate's life, why didn't he approach us openly?"

"Maybe he felt he wouldn't have a chance against you on a fair playing field," Salazar suggested. "But if he could discredit you, even arrange for you to lose your position with the FBI and your citizenship, then your wife would be in a vulnerable situation. She would need help and comfort."

Mark clenched his fists but tried to keep the fury he felt from showing in his face.

"At that point Mr. Singleton could move in and save the day—so to speak."

"But why would the FBI help him?" It was hard to even form the words, but Mark forced himself to do it. "Why destroy me and my life?"

Salazar shrugged. "According to my sources, Tony Singleton worked on several sensitive cases when he was an active agent for the FBI. He is sure to know many things that the Bureau would not want to be made public knowledge."

"What are you saying?"

"That to protect their reputation, the Bureau might be willing to sacrifice the happiness of one agent."

Mark thought about Kate and Emily and Charles in the old house on Maple Street. Did Singleton plan to just move in? To sit in his place at the kitchen table? To kick back in his recliner in the evenings and watch his television? To let his children call him Daddy and climb into bed with his wife at night?

"Why didn't he just kill me?" he whispered. "It would have been more humane!"

"That may be his ultimate goal," Salazar said quietly. "Perhaps he thinks your wife will forget you more easily if she is convinced that before your death you went bad."

Mark had never felt such total misery and helplessness. He walked over to the window and looked through the bulletproof glass at the city of La Rosa and tried to force himself to think logically and unselfishly. If what Salazar said was true and if there was nothing he could do to stop the events that had been set in motion, then Singleton had gone to an incredible amount of trouble to get Kate back. So it stood to reason that he would be good to her, and after an initial period of grief, Kate could probably be happy with Singleton.

Although Mark was the only father Emily had ever known, he was not her natural father. He didn't have any concerns about

Singleton's ability to love the little girl. But what about Charles? Mark's heart contracted with pain as he thought about his son, who resembled him so much. When he looked at Emily, he never saw the child of another man—but would Singleton? Would he be able to love the boy as he would a son of his own or would he—

"What can I do?" Mark burst out desperately. "I can't just sit by and let this man steal my life."

Salazar joined Mark by the windows. "I have considered your situation. The way I see it, you have two options. You can continue as you are—trusting that those who have sent you here will bring you home as they promised to do."

Mark remembered Britta Andersen's advice: "Trust no one." Then he remembered that Britta herself had failed to mail the memo to Jack Gamble—the insurance he had wanted for the exact situation he now found himself in. He felt like a tightrope walker working without a net.

"What's the other option?"

"You can come to work for me. I could use a man with your bookkeeping skills, and I can protect you. Your wife and children can join you here. You can all live in my compound until other arrangements can be made."

"If my family leaves the United States, they might never be able to return. How can I commit them to a life of hiding?"

"The life I lead is not so bad," Salazar countered. "Maybe it is time you visit my home and see that it is not a dungeon."

Mark took a deep, shuddering breath. "I appreciate your offer, and while logically it may be the wisest option, I can't accept it. I have moral and religious obligations to consider. I won't willfully break the law, even if it costs me my life and my family."

"Don't be too hasty," Salazar advised. "It would not be necessary for you to become involved with the drug industry. I own several perfectly legitimate companies, and Colombia is a wonderful place to raise children." Salazar paused, his gaze becoming thoughtful. "I have a business meeting near Medellin next week. I hate to leave you unprotected in La Rosa while I'm gone, and a trip through my country might convince you that it would be a good place to live. So, will you come along with me?"

Mark was forcibly reminded of his original mission. This was the first confirmation he had received that Salazar was going to the meeting, which meant that Solana could be removed next week as planned. Mark nodded. "I'd like that. Thank you."

"We will leave early on Monday morning. I will send a vehicle to pick you up."

Mark nodded again.

Salazar patted him on the back. "Don't look so sad. Everything will work out in the end."

Solana came rushing in, her cheeks flushed with pleasure. "Pilar said lunch is ready."

After the meal Solana challenged Mark to a game of chess. They contended with one another for nearly an hour. Finally Salazar, who had spent much of the time on his cell phone, walked over to the chess table and laid both kings down. "Stalemate," he declared.

"Father!" Solana objected. "In just a few more moves I would have defeated him!"

"I'm familiar enough with the game to know that is not true," Salazar contradicted her. "You are just trying to delay the moment of our departure." He gave Emilio a look, and the young man blushed. "But we have imposed on Mr. Iverson's hospitality for too long. We must go."

Mark could tell that Solana was displeased by the prospect of leaving Emilio, but she didn't complain further. Instead she thanked Mark and asked her father for permission to thank Pilar as well. This was a poorly concealed attempt to get Emilio alone for a few minutes, and the young man's blush deepened. But Salazar nodded tolerantly, and the couple hurried into the kitchen.

"I will send fresh men to relieve the guards I have posted in the woods around your house," Salazar said when they had gone. "If you need anything, you have only to call."

Mark felt a strong sense of gratitude toward this man who owed him nothing and yet offered him a great deal. "Thank you."

"You are welcome." Salazar moved through the salon toward the front door. "Solana!" he called. "Time to go!"

The girl emerged from the kitchen with Emilio on her heels.

"Come see me again soon," Mark invited.

"Don't encourage her," Salazar warned. "We might be back in a matter of minutes."

After their guests were gone, Mark waited until he heard Pilar leave. Then he transferred the PDA from the bedroom to the sunroom and signed on again. He typed a short message to Perez confirming that Salazar was going to the meeting near Medellin on Monday morning. He added that he had accepted an invitation to join Salazar. He didn't tell Perez that Salazar had offered him protection and a job. Mark also purposely forgot to mention that there was some question about whether or not the FBI would allow Mark to return to the U.S. when this operation was over or that Tony Singleton might be trying to steal his family.

Mark sent the message then stared at the blank screen. He needed to call Kate, to hear her voice and assure himself that his family was safe. He would also like to hear about her investigation of Tony Singleton. But he didn't want to be interrupted once they began their conversation, so he decided to wait until after Perez responded to make his call. An hour later he was still waiting and had almost given up hope when a message appeared on the small PDA screen.

Confirm Salazar will attend meeting—leaving on Monday. Helicopter will remove Solana and Emilio Delgado while you are gone. Report in when you return, and additional orders will be forwarded.

And then the screen went blank again. With a sigh, Mark signed off and picked up his cell phone. Once he was sure he had his emotions under control, he dialed his home number. Emily answered the phone.

"Daddy?" she said.

He wiped a tear from his cheek and accepted that he might not be *able* to control his emotions where his family was concerned. "Hey, Em," he returned. "How have you been?"

"I've been missing you," she told him. "But I've been having a lot of fun. Miracle is here, and she took us to the Ragsdales' farm to feed the animals. Then we went to the park and ate a Happy Meal. For dinner tonight Mama's going to make spaghetti with little meatballs.

Then we're going to carve our pumpkin, and Miracle says it can have a beard."

Mark could picture them all gathered around the family room. He looked out the window at the quiet desolation that surrounded him. "That does sound like fun. And I don't even have to ask if you're being good."

Emily laughed. "I'm always good."

Mark closed his eyes and thought of her bright green eyes, her long brown hair with the little wispy curls around her face. "Yes you are."

"Do you want to talk to Charles?"

Mark cleared his throat. "Of course."

"Daddy?" Charles came on the line. "I'm good too."

Mark clutched the phone tighter. "I know. Did you have fun at the park?"

"Yes, but we didn't see a fish."

"Maybe next time," Mark comforted.

"I miss you."

"I miss you, too."

"Mama wants to talk to you."

"Good-bye, Charles."

Mark didn't realize he was holding his breath until he expelled it all at once when he heard Kate's voice.

"Mark."

All the longing and misery and fear welled up inside him at once, and it was a few seconds before he could say, "I'm here."

"Are you okay?" she asked, instantly in tune to his emotional turmoil.

"No. I want to be home with you and the kids. I want this all to be over."

"Me too," she assured him. "Will it be soon, do you think?"

"I'm not sure," he told her honestly. "I hope so." He paused to give her a chance to volunteer information about Tony. When she didn't, he decided to prompt her. "What's going on around there?"

"Just the regular stuff, except that we're worried about you," Kate replied. "And missing you, of course."

He decided he'd have to be more specific. "No more Tony sightings?"

"Not a single one." She sounded almost pleased to inform him.

"Well," Mark said, disappointed and more confused than ever. Kate knew there was a good chance that Tony was alive and had even hired a private investigator to find out about him. So why didn't she tell him? "That's good, I guess."

"You're not in danger there, are you?"

"No," he replied absently. "I'm safe. I'll try and call back tomorrow."

"I love you," Kate said softly.

"I love you, too," he echoed. Then he turned off the phone.

* * *

When they reached the compound, Solana followed her father into the house. Hector Vargas was waiting for them in the salon. He and her father began discussing the need to hire some more men if they were going to continue to provide surveillance at Mark Iverson's house.

"Go ahead and begin the search for some new recruits," her father said. "However, I have invited Mr. Iverson to join our organization. If he agrees, he will move to the compound, and we won't need any additional men. But it is probably best to be prepared with extra manpower just in case."

Solana heard this announcement with intense disappointment. If Mr. Iverson joined her father's organization, he wouldn't be leaving La Rosa and therefore wouldn't be able to provide them with a safe means of escape. In fact, the degree to which they had trusted him already might come back to haunt them. She would have to get word to her mother again. Somehow she had to get out of La Rosa . . .

"Solana," her father's voice penetrated her troubled thoughts. "General Vargas asked you a question."

Solana forced herself to look at the general. "Pardon me," she said. "What did you need to know?"

"I just wondered if you would like to join me for some tennis tomorrow afternoon. Now that Emilio is gone, you have no opponent, and I know how much you enjoyed the physical exertion."

Solana didn't want to be on the same planet with Hector Vargas, let alone the same tennis court. But she couldn't think of a polite way to decline. And at least she would be in plain sight of the household staff. "That is very thoughtful. I will meet you at two if that is convenient."

He nodded with an amused expression on his hateful face. "It is quite convenient."

Controlling a shudder with great effort, Solana turned to her father. "I would like to do a little shopping in La Rosa tomorrow morning."

Her father didn't voice any objections. "Just let Lucien know so he can arrange to drive you in."

She was relieved. Hopefully this would be her opportunity to get a message to her mother. "Well, I'm tired, so I think I will go and lie down until dinner."

"What a disappointment," Vargas said. He was still smiling, and she knew he was pleased that he was causing her discomfort. "I was hoping you would like to play a game of chess."

She forced a yawn. "Not now . . . maybe later." It was all she could do to keep herself from running as she left the salon.

CHAPTER 9

The children were so excited by their pumpkin carving that Kate thought she would never get them settled that night. But when she finally had them asleep, she walked back down to the family room. Miracle was standing at the front window.

"Anything exciting going on out there?" Kate asked.

"Not unless you call watching Miss Polly feed your bodyguards exciting," Miracle replied.

Kate moved beside Miracle and pulled back the curtain. The FBI agents charged with watching the Iversons' house were sitting on the hood of their nondescript government sedan with linen napkins spread out on their laps. Miss Polly moved between the two men, distributing pieces of chocolate pie and dainty china cups filled with coffee from a doily-lined silver tray.

"I wonder if she's got any of that pie left," Kate murmured.

"I doubt it. She gave them each a piece at lunch, one for an afternoon snack and one at dinner," Miracle itemized. "So this should finish it up."

Kate shook her head. "What's Miss Polly going to do for entertainment when I don't need protection anymore? Providing round-the-clock meals for these agents has given her life meaning."

"One thing's for sure," Miracle said as Kate dropped the curtain back into place. "Both sets of agents are going to have to join Weight Watchers afterward. Miss Polly has probably quadrupled their daily calorie intake."

Kate crossed the room and picked up some toys. "Where's Miss Eugenia?"

"She said she was going to retire early," Miracle said. "But I think she really wanted to talk to that lawyer boyfriend of hers." Miracle frowned. "Can you call an eighty-year-old man a *boy*friend?"

"He's not eighty," Kate corrected. "He's only seventy-seven—and what about your policeman *boy*friend? Have you talked to him lately?"

"Now that you mention it, he's due for a call. I guess I'll turn in early too."

After Miracle left, Kate finished straightening the den. Then she walked to the kitchen and started the dishwasher. She checked the back door to be sure it was locked and headed down the hallway toward the front door. As she passed Mark's office, she averted her eyes. Somehow seeing it empty was just too sad.

She confirmed that the regular lock and deadbolt were both engaged on the front door and had turned to climb the stairs when she glanced over her shoulder and saw a man silhouetted against the living room windows. Kate wanted to scream but found that terror had strangled all the air from her lungs.

"Kate," the form said. "Don't be afraid."

The only thing that kept Kate from laughing hysterically at this ridiculous command was the fact that she still couldn't breathe. *Calm down,* she told herself. *Try to think. If he was here to kill you, he would have done it already.*

"I mean you no harm." It was a voice she recognized but couldn't place. She put a hand to her neck and massaged her throat in an effort to get some air into her lungs. "Who are you?" she gasped. "And what are you doing in my living room?"

The man moved closer, and a beam of porch light fell across his face. It was William Evans, the special agent in charge of the Chicago field office for the FBI. Kate had never expected to see Mr. Evans again and certainly not under these circumstances.

"I'm sorry if I frightened you," Mr. Evans said in the slightly condescending tone that she had become accustomed to during the weeks following Tony's first "death." He seemed to imply that if she was frightened, it was because of her weakness and no fault of his. "But stealth was necessary."

"If you're trying to convince me that the agents in the car outside and Miracle upstairs are no protection, then you did a good job."

He didn't smile. "That was definitely *not* my intention. Miracle is aware of my presence. In fact, she let me in the back door."

Kate made a mental note to thank her friend for this later.

"And we took advantage of your neighbor's determination to overwhelm the agents from Atlanta with food. I guess we can't really blame them for a few moments of inattention, but no one would be able to gain access to your house without Miracle's cooperation."

Kate thought of Tony and wondered if that statement were entirely true. However, rather than voice her doubts out loud, she asked, "Why are you here, Mr. Evans?"

He waved toward the dark living room and answered her question with another question. "Could we talk in here?"

Kate moved into the room. As she passed a lamp, she leaned to turn it on.

"No light, please," he requested.

She dropped her hand from the lamp switch and sat down on the couch.

He claimed a chair across from her. "This afternoon some information came into my possession," he began. "I, that is to say, well," he stumbled uncharacteristically over his words, and Kate's anxiety level increased.

"What is it?" she demanded. "Did something happen to Mark?"

He shook his head. "No, not yet, but I believe his life is in danger." Mr. Evans took a deep breath and leaned forward. "Apparently his cover in Colombia is more complicated than he has been led to believe. I can't go into detail, but Mark was told that his primary purpose for being there was to facilitate the rescue of a girl named Solana Andersen. Actually the girl's retrieval is secondary. The major focus of the complex operation is to arrest the girl's father, Rodrigo Salazar—a dangerous fellow responsible for the majority of the illegal drugs that come into this country from Colombia. If they can capture him, they can greatly interrupt the Colombian drug trade."

Kate nodded to let him know she understood that ending this man's career would be a reasonable goal for the United States government.

"Salazar is very security conscious," Mr. Evans proceeded. "His home in La Rosa is an impenetrable fortress, and he rarely leaves it.

Next week, however, he's scheduled to attend a meeting near the city of Medellin. During the car ride he will be heavily guarded but still more vulnerable than when he's behind the walls of his home. So that is when the arrest attempt will be made."

Kate shook her head. "I don't understand how this is a danger to Mark."

"Mark was told to establish a friendship with Rodrigo Salazar. In this particular aspect of his assignment, he has been successful beyond expectations. In fact, Salazar has invited Mark to join him on the trip to Medellin. Mark had to accept; otherwise, Salazar might have become suspicious and canceled his plans to attend the meeting."

"Why is Mark's presence at the time of the arrest a problem?"

The nervous behavior Mr. Evans had exhibited earlier returned. "As I mentioned, Salazar's men will be heavily armed. The soldiers who make the arrest attempt will also be armed, and with that much firepower, the likelihood of people getting shot is high."

Kate stared at the man. Mr. Evans had flown all the way from Chicago on very short notice, so she knew he was trying to tell her something important but, for the life of her, she couldn't figure out what or why.

"There would be no way to guarantee anyone's safety in that type of situation," Mr. Evans continued. "In fact, in some ways it would be much easier for all parties concerned if Salazar were to die during the arrest process."

Kate's heart started to pound again. "Are you saying they are going to kill him?"

Mr. Evans shook his head. "I'm not *saying* that, no."

But of course that was exactly what he *meant*. That was what he had flown from Chicago to tell her. Kate's mouth was dry as she carefully formed the words of her next question. "How can we make sure Mark is not a casualty of this arrest attempt?"

"The only way to be sure is to remove Mark from the convoy before the attempt takes place."

"But you said he had to go with Salazar to Medellin."

"He must *leave* with the convoy," Mr. Evans confirmed. "But he doesn't have to *stay* with the convoy. I believe I have found a way to save Mark without sacrificing the operation." He handed Kate a small package. It was prescription chewing gum with Mark's name on it, dispensed by a pharmacy in Albany. "Once they have traveled a calculated distance from La Rosa, if Mark were to get violently ill, Salazar would have him removed from the convoy."

"This gum will make him sick?" Kate guessed.

Mr. Evans nodded. "Just for half an hour or so."

"How will we get it to Mark?"

She was shocked by his reply. "You will take it to him."

"Me?"

"There isn't time to make arrangements through normal channels, and there's no room for error," Mr. Evans told her softly. "And no one can know that I gave you the gum—not even Mark. I am risking my career over this."

"I understand."

"You've already proven yourself to be a difficult, persistent woman. So this afternoon when I told Mr. Mitchell that you were demanding a visit with Mark—to see for yourself that he is mentally and physically healthy—he wasn't surprised. I offered to handle arrangements for your expedited visa and passport, round-trip ticket to Cartagena, and hotel reservations. He was most appreciative."

Kate's hands started to tremble, and she clasped them together impatiently. "In just a few hours I'll see Mark?" she clarified.

Mr. Evans nodded. "Yes."

"Does he know yet?"

"No. You'll call him in the morning and tell him to meet you at the airport in Cartagena. You'll give him the same story—that you've demanded the trip, and the FBI is cooperating reluctantly. You won't tell him about the gum or Salazar's arrest until Monday morning just before you separate. And remember, you won't tell him about my involvement at all. It's really for his benefit as well as mine. It would put him in an awkward position later when he's required to answer questions about the operation."

Kate swallowed hard. "Okay."

"Now let me give you some final details. Nothing can be written down, so you'll need to listen carefully."

Kate scooted closer to the edge of the couch. "I'm ready."

"If anyone asks him, the gum is specially formulated to protect his dental work. You'll notice that the date on the prescription label is prior to his trip to Colombia."

Kate glanced down at the package. It looked completely legitimate.

"There is only one piece of gum left in the package—to avoid anyone else chewing a piece accidentally. When they have been driving for exactly one hour and eighteen minutes Mark should chew it. In a matter of minutes he will begin to vomit."

Kate couldn't control a shudder. "Poor Mark."

Mr. Evans didn't waste time with sympathy. "He'll only be sick for a little while, but the timing is essential. Make sure Mark understands that. At one hour and eighteen minutes they will be far enough from La Rosa that turning back will be impractical. The logical thing for Salazar to do will be to sacrifice one man and one vehicle to take Mark to the closest city with a hospital—which is Cartagena."

"What if Salazar decides to keep Mark with him?"

Mr. Evans shook his head. "That is highly unlikely since he will be vomiting uncontrollably. As I said, Salazar is fond of Mark. I believe he will seek medical help for him. But he won't want to risk catching a virus himself."

The plan seemed a little too haphazard for Kate's comfort. "What if he chooses a different town with a hospital?"

"Then it will be up to Mark to get to you. You must stay safely in the Cartagena airport."

Kate took a deep breath. "Suppose we're lucky and this Salazar person sends Mark to a hospital in Cartagena—what then?"

"Once Mark arrives at the hospital, he will get away from his escort and take a taxi to the airport, where you will be waiting. Then the two of you will fly home, and this whole ordeal will be over."

She couldn't keep a little nervous laugh from escaping her lips. "You make it sound so easy."

"I didn't mean to." His expression was serious. "Nothing about this is easy, and I'm most unhappy about the necessity of using a civilian." He cleared his throat. "You."

She nodded. "I knew who you meant."

"There is no guarantee that Salazar will be successfully arrested or otherwise removed from this situation. If he is still free after the arrest attempt, he may blame Mark and seek revenge. Even if the attempt is successful, one way or another his men may retaliate in his behalf. In any case it will be very dangerous, and I want to be sure you understand that before you agree to the assignment."

"Do you think I should do it?"

Mr. Evans regarded her with a level gaze. "I think there is a very good chance that no one in that convoy will survive the arrest process."

She nodded. "In that case, I'm headed to Cartagena tomorrow."

He placed an envelope on the coffee table. "This contains your passport and visa along with your airline and hotel reservations."

He stood, and Kate did the same. "Thank you," she said.

"We are helping each other."

"And Mark."

"I owe him at least this much."

Kate couldn't disagree with that. She wanted to ask him about Tony, but just as she was about to, something made her change her mind. "I guess you'll be leaving by the back door?"

"Yes. And as far as anyone knows, I was never here." And then he was gone.

Kate opened the envelope and looked through the contents. Once she was sure everything was in order for her trip, she walked upstairs. Miracle was waiting for her on the landing.

Kate stopped on the top step and put a hand on her hip. "I thought you'd be cowering in your room."

Miracle shook her head. "I figured I might as well get what I had coming to me."

Kate wanted to be mad but couldn't quite muster the energy.

"At least you're getting to see Mark," Miracle pointed out.

Kate had to smile. "Yeah."

"That bad attitude of yours finally paid off."

"It's about time." Kate moved on past Miracle into the hallway. "I've got to pack, and I guess I'd better wake up Miss Eugenia. We've got to decide how to arrange for the kids while I'm gone."

"Gone?" Miss Eugenia asked as she stuck her head out of the first guest room. "Where are you going?"

Kate waved toward the kitchen. "Follow me," she requested.

Once they were gathered around the table, they discussed the options.

"We could just keep the children here," Miracle proposed. "In familiar surroundings they might not be as upset about you leaving."

Kate shook her head. "While I'm gone I'd feel better knowing that anyone who wanted to get to the children would have a hard time even finding them."

Miracle raised an eyebrow. "Anyone?"

"The pornographers who might want their money back," Kate clarified, "or Tony, who might want his daughter back."

"So where else could we keep them?" Miss Eugenia asked.

"We could get on a plane and take them to Mark's parents' house in Texas," Miracle suggested.

Kate chewed her bottom lip. "That would be a huge upheaval for the children."

"What about a hotel room in Albany?" was Miracle's next idea.

Kate didn't like this much better. "They'd be stir-crazy in an hour."

"How about Annabelle's house?" Miss Eugenia asked. "The children are comfortable there."

"Plus they have that nice pool house that looks like the island of Maui," Miracle added.

Miss Eugenia smiled. "And Annabelle should know . . ."

"Since she's been to Hawaii numerous times," Miracle finished for her.

Kate sat there feeling more conflicted than she had ever been in her life. She trusted Miss Eugenia and Miracle; however, parental responsibility was not something she was comfortable transferring to anyone else. Especially since there was the possibility that people wanted to harm her children or take them from her. But Mark needed her—in fact, his life might depend on her. So she had to go.

Finally she said, "That's probably the best option. Are you going to call Annabelle and ask her?" she said to Miss Eugenia. "Or should I?"

"I'll call her," Miss Eugenia offered, pulling out her new little cell phone. Miss Eugenia dialed, listened, and then disconnected. "I got her answering machine," she reported. "I'll call again in a few minutes." The elderly woman stood, and while rubbing her back, she told Kate, "I'm going to take some of my arthritis medication, and then Miracle and I will pack the children's clothes while you pack for yourself."

Kate and Miracle were both about to obey when the front doorbell rang.

"Who in the world can that be at this hour?" Miracle wondered aloud.

"After all that's happened over the past few days, I'm afraid to find out," Kate muttered.

But Miss Eugenia was already halfway down the hall. She peeked out the peephole and then opened the front door. "It's our state senator, Mr. Jack Gamble," she announced as the gentleman himself stepped inside.

After a polite nod at Miss Eugenia, Jack addressed Kate directly. "Sorry I'm stopping by so late, but we just got in from Atlanta."

"We?" Miss Eugenia demanded. "You brought Beth and the children back to Haggerty with you for the weekend?"

"At least," Jack confirmed before he turned back to Kate. "I got a strange memo in the mail this afternoon. I should have gotten it yesterday, but it was delivered to the wrong office by mistake. Anyway, once I read it, I thought you might need me. So we packed up and came home."

Kate was still searching for words to thank him when Miss Eugenia said, "Well, that works out perfectly. Kate has to fly to Colombia tomorrow to visit Mark, and we need a safe, convenient place for the children to stay. How would you feel about having some houseguests for a couple of days?"

* * *

Solana woke up early on Saturday morning. She took her shower and dressed, even though she knew she couldn't go into La Rosa until later when the shops opened, since that was her excuse for the trip. It was risky to try and get another message to her mother, both for her and for those who helped her, but she was becoming increasingly desperate. Mr. Iverson had seemed like such a promising link to the outside world. Then he had developed this unexpected friendship with her father, and now she didn't dare trust him.

In frustration she walked over to the window and looked out at the gardens below. The plots of artfully arranged flowers intersected by intricate stone paths made her think of Emilio and the many hours they had spent tucked away on hidden benches, stealing kisses and falling in love. She missed him and was weary of spending every conscious moment worrying about his safety and her own for that matter.

His job with Mr. Iverson seemed like a good thing, but in every new development, Solana saw hidden danger. When her father offered to loan Mr. Iverson additional guards, she thought how easily Vargas could turn this into an opportunity to harm Emilio. An anonymous soldier could approach Emilio under the cover of darkness, put a switchblade in his back, and walk away with no one the wiser.

With a shiver Solana turned away from the window. They had to get out of La Rosa. And yet, in leaving there was sadness too. She loved her father and knew that by escaping, she would wound him deeply. No letter left behind or phone call made after the fact would sufficiently explain or apologize. The relationship that was just beginning to grow would end.

The image of Hector Vargas came to her mind, along with a terrible shiver. She knew if they stayed, she might suffer a fate worse than death. So they would go, hoping her father would understand.

Solana forced herself to wait in her room until eight o'clock. Then she went in search of Lucien. She found him in the kitchen eating breakfast. Trying to appear casual, she sat down at the table and nibbled at a piece of toast until he was finished.

"It's good that you're already eating," she said by way of small talk.

"General Vargas said you'd want to get an early start," Lucien told her, and the toast in her mouth turned to dust. It was almost as if the man knew her very thoughts. And how he loved to torment her with his knowledge.

Determined not to be intimidated, Solana replied, "The early shoppers get the best bargains." She stood and threw away the remnants of her toast. "I'm ready whenever you are."

Lucien pushed back from the table and wiped his mouth on a napkin. Then he led the way out to the truck parked in front of the house. They rode to La Rosa in silence, and once they reached the marketplace, she suggested that he park. "I prefer to walk around."

He complied with her request, but instead of staying with the truck as she had hoped he would, he followed a few steps behind as she shopped. Finally she realized that he wasn't going to give her any privacy, so she decided to take the brazen, I-have-nothing-to-hide approach. She turned down a residential street, and when she reached the house she wanted, she waited for Lucien to catch up with her.

"I have a friend who lives here," she told him. "I'm going to see if she's home. You can wait here."

He seemed unsure of what to do, and she took advantage of his momentary uncertainty to walk quickly up the stone pathway to the home of the lawyer, Cristobal Morales. "Please," she prayed silently to Emilio's God as she walked. "Let help come."

* * *

On Saturday morning Mark woke up early and worked out with Emilio in the small exercise room in the basement for an hour. Then he ate a huge breakfast prepared by Pilar.

"We might have to start working out twice a day," he told the young man seated across the table from him, "if Pilar is going to keep feeding us like this."

"It will be worth two workouts," Emilio replied with his mouth full. Mark was pleased to see that the young man seemed to be in good humor. Hopefully that meant his rib was healing.

After breakfast Pilar left to go grocery shopping, and Emilio went outside to check with Salazar's guards. More alone than usual, Mark walked into the sunroom to stare out the wall of windows. The empty day stretched before him like the endless Colombian landscape, and Mark almost wished that Rodrigo Salazar would call, wanting to walk through ancient ruins or discuss more about FBI betrayal.

Before Mark could get too morose, his cell phone rang. He checked the screen and was pleased to see Kate's cell number. The day was better already. "Hello."

"Mark?"

"Is everything okay?"

"Fine," she assured him. "How about with you?"

"Okay."

"I have kind of a surprise," Kate said. "I've been a real nuisance to the FBI, and they'll probably make you pay for that when you get back, but they're going to let me come down for a short visit."

Mark processed this information. Then he repeated, "You're coming here? To La Rosa?"

"Well, almost. I'm flying into Cartagena this afternoon. Can you meet me at the airport there?"

Mark's vision blurred with tears, and he was glad that no one was in the room to witness his emotion. "I'll be there," he promised. "What time?"

"I'm sitting on the plane in Atlanta now, and it should be taking off in minutes. I fly into Bogotá first and then from there to Cartagena. I'll be on Avianca flight 9540 that arrives in Cartagena at three thirty. The FBI has arranged a hotel room for the weekend and everything."

"I can't believe it," Mark told her. "But I'm so glad."

He heard her laugh. "Me too."

"What about the kids?"

"They will be taken care of while I'm gone."

He understood. He'd told her cell phones were not secure, and she didn't want to broadcast whatever security precautions she had taken. "Well, then I guess I'll see you soon."

"Soon," she agreed. "Good-bye."

He disconnected the call and looked back out the wall of windows. Suddenly the day didn't seem endless or without hope. He had to pack and get to Cartagena and . . . Laughing like a madman, he dialed Cristobal's cell number.

"My wife is coming to visit," he said when the lawyer answered.

"I know," Cristobal replied. "Who do you think the FBI called when they needed a nice hotel room in Cartagena?"

"Poor Cristobal," Mark commiserated. "Always being bothered by Americans in a rush."

"Oh well, I charge extra for short notice."

"Speaking of charges, how much credit do I still have with you?"

"That depends on the type of service you require," Cristobal answered carefully.

"I just need you to find Pilar and tell her not to buy a bunch of groceries. I'm going to be gone all weekend and most of next week."

"I'll send one of my daughters to the market. If she doesn't catch Pilar in time, I'll tell her to bring the food to my house. I have six daughters to feed, you know."

Mark laughed as he moved toward the master bedroom. "Tell Pilar she can have a few paid days off if she wants them."

There was a pause before Cristobal said, "I will tell her."

"Thanks," Mark said. "Now I'd better start packing."

Mark had time to pull his suitcase out of the closet in the master bedroom before his phone rang again. This time it was Rodrigo Salazar.

"So, you're going to Cartagena."

"Do you have my phones tapped or my house bugged?" Mark demanded, mildly annoyed.

"Both!" Salazar teased. "Neither! We routinely monitor Cristobal's calls, and that is how I knew about your trip."

Mark made a mental note to be careful about what he said to Cristobal in the future. "Yes, I'm going to Cartagena."

"Don't leave until I get there," Salazar instructed him. "I'm on my way."

Mark sighed as he closed the phone. Nothing could be simple, it seemed.

Salazar arrived just as Mark walked downstairs carrying his suitcase. Mark opened the front door and led his guest into the sunroom.

"I have some advice for you," Salazar said without preamble. "Remember, you are not in the United States, traveling from your home in Georgia to visit your parents in Texas."

Mark raised an eyebrow, and Salazar laughed.

"Surely you would expect me to be thorough. Anyway, you are in a foreign country—one that has moments of violence. You must be cautious, and Emilio must go with you."

Mark started to object, but Salazar held up a hand. "Hear me out," he requested. "A lone man, especially an American, driving along a highway in Colombia is like an advertisement—*please rob me or kidnap me or kill me!*"

"You must be exaggerating," Mark said. "Yesterday you were telling me what a wonderful place Colombia would be to raise a family."

Salazar laughed. "Okay, so I may have overstated the truth a little when we were talking yesterday. Do you know how many foreigners have been kidnapped or killed here during the past few years?"

Mark shook his head.

"Good. Then you can still enjoy your weekend. In addition to Emilio, I will send a truck with two of my men to follow behind your Jeep."

Mark was going to argue, but Salazar held up his hand again.

"Trust me," Salazar pleaded. "This is minimal security for an American traveling in Colombia. Once you reach Cartagena, you will wait with my men while Emilio goes into the airport to get your wife. If he sees any sign that it is a trap set up by the FBI, he will leave and escort you back to La Rosa."

Disappointment overwhelmed Mark, and he sat down on one of the rattan chairs. "You think that's what this is—a way to ambush me?"

Salazar shrugged. "I think it is a good possibility. Your wife may not ever actually arrive in Cartagena. It is possible that she will be met in Bogotá and sent back to Atlanta. I have sources in Bogotá who will check to see if your wife makes her connection to Cartagena. If she doesn't, you can return to La Rosa."

"And if she does?"

"That still doesn't mean they aren't setting a trap. It just means they are very serious about the bait. But they will be looking for you, not Emilio. He can bring her to you. Then you will find a hotel and pay cash, of course."

"The FBI has already made reservations . . ." Mark began.

"You would be a fool to use reservations made by the FBI if they are trying to trap you," Salazar pointed out. "Pick a hotel at random—no reservations, no credit cards. The more anonymous the better."

"Do you think they will find us?"

Salazar shook his head. "Cartagena is a large, busy city and very full of tourists. I think that for two days you and your wife can blend in and be unnoticed." He studied Mark for a few seconds. "Of course, you will be easy to spot if you dress like that."

Mark looked down at his clothes. "What's wrong with what I'm wearing?"

"Nothing if you want everyone who sees you to know you are an American FBI agent. Even your tourists dress more casually. Did you bring other clothes with you?"

Mark shook his head. "I don't have much in the way of casual clothes, and I had to pack in a hurry."

Salazar waved this aside. "It is no problem. Before you leave La Rosa today have Emilio stop at a clothing store. He will know what to buy."

Mark knew it would be foolish to argue. "Okay."

"And buy enough casual clothes for several days. Even though your stay in Cartagena will be brief, we will leave for Medellin almost immediately upon your return Monday morning. Being appropriately dressed will be equally important there."

Mark frowned for a few seconds. Finally he had to ask, "Why are you helping me?"

"Because you are my friend," Salazar replied. "And because I hope that once your wife sees how beautiful my country is, it will be easier to convince her to move here permanently. I could use a man like you in my company. Someone I can trust."

"I'm not sure what time Kate's plane leaves on Monday."

"Her flight leaves Cartagena at eleven o'clock AM," Salazar informed him. "But she will need to be at the airport no later than eight. Since the FBI will certainly be watching for you to bring her back to the airport, I would recommend that she go alone by taxi. She can call you to confirm that she has arrived safely. Then you can return to La Rosa. We want to get an early start for Medellin, so as soon as you get home, I will send a car for you. Then your next adventure can begin."

Mark wasn't sure what to say. He didn't like the idea that Salazar was so involved in his personal life, but at the same time he realized that Salazar's interference was making the weekend with Kate possible. "Thank you doesn't seem like enough."

Salazar smiled. "I'm glad I could help. I wish that I had a beautiful wife and could spend a romantic weekend with her in Cartagena."

"You have a beautiful daughter," Mark reminded him.

Salazar nodded. "Yes, but only for a while. She misses her mother, and I know that soon the pull of maternal apron strings will be too much. I had hoped that Solana's presence here would be enough to draw her mother back to me as well. But apparently I am so abhorrent that even the lure of her only child is not enough. So I will have to give Solana up." Salazar smiled again, but this time it did not reach his eyes. "I will live with the choices I have made."

Mark nodded. "We all do."

Salazar stepped toward the door. "Good day then, my friend. And give my regards to your lovely wife."

* * *

Solana was so happy that she feared she would burst. After she had arranged for a postcard to be sent to her mother, she had gotten word that plans for a rescue were already underway. On Monday afternoon, once her father and General Vargas were headed to Medellin, she and Emilio would be extracted from La Rosa by helicopter. The feeling of relief was overwhelming.

She had briefly considered trying to cancel the postcard to her mother but finally decided that another contact would be more dangerous than the original request. So she would let the postcard go. She would probably make it home before the postcard did and could explain the whole thing to her mother in person.

She was dying to tell Emilio about their imminent rescue—which meant she had to arrange an evening of chess at Mr. Iverson's house. After taking all the purchases she'd made in town up to her room, Solana rushed to her father's office. He was frowning at his computer screen when she knocked on the open door.

"Am I disturbing you?" she asked.

He sighed and pushed away from his work. "I could use a break. Did you find many bargains at the boutiques in La Rosa?"

"A few," she acknowledged with a smile.

"Lately you've been a little solemn, but this shopping trip seems to have cheered you up," her father commented.

"It was fun," she said.

"Then I guess it was worth making poor Lucien wake up so early."

She laughed and perched herself on the edge of his desk. "I would like an opportunity to wear some of my new purchases for an appreciative audience. So I was hoping I could go to Mr. Iverson's house tonight for some chess."

Her father's pleasant expression faded. "That won't be possible. Mr. Iverson and Emilio are in Cartagena."

Solana was certain that she had misunderstood. "Cartagena?" she repeated.

"Mr. Iverson's wife is visiting from the States, and Emilio went along as protection. That is his job, you know," her father reminded her. "To protect Mr. Iverson."

Solana blushed. "I know. I, just . . . well, I'm surprised. He didn't mention a trip when we were there yesterday."

"Mr. Iverson didn't know about the visit yesterday. His wife wanted it to be a surprise, I think," her father said.

"Oh." Solana knew that her disappointment was apparent. "When will they return?"

"Monday morning. Mr. Iverson is going to Medellin with me, so they will have to be coming back early."

"And Emilio?"

Her father smiled. "I will have plenty of men with me to protect Mr. Iverson. I'm sure he will leave Emilio here to guard his house and Pilar."

"And I will have permission to go over and play chess with Emilio at Mr. Iverson's house while you are gone?"

He frowned. "I will have to consider that one. Now go and let me work. I will see you at dinner."

* * *

Eugenia settled into a chair and faced Jack Gamble in the office that he kept at his home in Haggerty. She had never been in it before and couldn't help but notice that he didn't have any awards or diplomas framed on the walls. Nor were there pictures of him with the many famous people he had represented and associated with over the years. There were, however, lots of pictures of his family and drawings made by his children. Her estimation of Jack went up a notch. He may not have always had his priorities in order—but he seemed to now.

"We can't thank you enough for all you are doing to make the Iverson children both safe and happy," she told him. "How did you manage this little trip home—since the last time I checked, elementary schools and Congress are both in session?"

"The Georgia State Senate started a two-week break on Friday because the floors are being refinished in the capitol," Jack told her. "And I've explained things at Chloe's school and hired a tutor, so she won't get behind in her work. If Kate and Mark need us longer than two weeks, I can commute to Atlanta during the week and take Chloe with me."

Eugenia nodded in approval. "Mark deserves a friend like you."

"He's been there for me a couple of times," Jack responded. "So, since safety was the first concern, we now have the Iverson children inside this house with a state-of-the-art security system and surrounded by a ten-foot fence that some people believe to be electrified."

"Is it?" Eugenia couldn't help but ask.

Jack didn't smile. "Let's just say it would be unwise for anyone to touch it after midnight."

Eugenia swallowed hard. "I'll remember that."

"Additionally, we've got two sets of FBI agents taking turns guarding the gates. I'd say an intruder would have his work cut out for him."

"Yes," Eugenia agreed. "I don't see what else we can do."

"We're all set," Jack said.

* * *

The trip to Cartagena was much more tedious than Mark had expected, partly because he was so anxious to get there and partly because he had underestimated the amount of interference they would run into. They were stopped twice by government soldiers and countless times by traffic problems. There was a stalled car and a bus that ground to a halt regularly to unload various passengers. And once, they sat for thirty minutes while a farmer herded goats from one side of the road to the other.

"This is insane," Mark said finally.

"This is Colombia," Emilio countered. "You Americans seem to always be in a hurry."

"Well, nobody could accuse this farmer of rushing his life away," Mark muttered as another goat meandered across the highway at a pace that redefined *leisurely*.

"While we wait we should talk about what we will do when we get to the airport at Cartagena," Emilio suggested. "Señor Salazar and I discussed it, so I know what to expect."

Since Mark himself wasn't sure what to expect, this came as quite a surprise. "Well, that makes one of us, then."

Emilio smiled. "He said I would need to have a plan, and I have been thinking. I wanted to ask if you think it is a good one. When we near the airport, I think we should park the Jeep. One of the men will stay with you while the other drops me off at the front of the airport. Since you can be recognized, I will go inside and look around."

Mark was familiar with this idea, so he nodded. "What do you expect to see inside the airport?"

"The regular soldiers," Emilio said. "Maybe a few extra police— airport security a little more alert than usual."

That made sense to Mark. Kate wasn't a criminal, and neither was he. If anyone was trying to trap Mark and Kate, they wouldn't need a complex plan.

"Did your wife check any baggage?" Emilio continued.

"I didn't think to ask, but I doubt it. The trip is just for two nights."

"Then she will not need to go to baggage claim. When her plane lands, she will call you?"

"Yes."

"You should tell her to come straight to the street that runs in front of the airport. There are many taxis waiting there. Describe me and say that I will approach her. Once she sees me, she is to take the next available taxi and go to El Centro. It is a shopping area in the old part of the city."

"But surely the people who meet her plane will follow her outside. When they see her get into a taxi, they'll get one too, and soon everybody will be in El Centro."

"Yes." Emilio had thought of that. "I will have to come up with a distraction."

"What kind of distraction?"

"Maybe I will shoot my gun into the air or yell that there is a fire in the airport." Emilio gave a typical Colombian shrug. "Or maybe I will push a pedestrian in front of a bus."

Mark looked sharply over at the young man. "Did you just make a joke, Emilio?"

"I think I did," the young man replied. "Maybe I am turning into an American. Soon I will be rushing everywhere."

Mark laughed as the farmer finally herded the last goat onto one side of the highway and traffic began to move again. "Worse things could happen to you. So, what will you do after you start a riot or kill an innocent bystander?"

"Señor Salazar's man will be parked nearby. I will signal for him to come pick me up. Then we will follow Señora Iverson's taxi. When you see us go by, you will follow as well."

Mark thought for a second and then nodded. "It might work, but there's still the chance that someone from the airport will see through your clever distraction and keep track of my wife."

"Once we get to El Centro, we should be able to lose them."

"I guess that's the best we can do," Mark said. "Salazar also told me to pick a hotel other than the one where the FBI made reservations. Do you have any suggestions?"

"I think it should be one that is not big but not small. A big hotel will have valets and parking attendants—with so many employees the chances are increased that one of them will remember your face. The problem is similar with a small inn—not enough people means it is easier for the management to remember each guest."

"Do you have a particular hotel in mind?"

"I was planning a trip to Cartagena myself not very long ago," Emilio told him. "I was going to stay in the Santa Teresa Monastery.

It has been renovated into a luxury hotel, but it is relatively small—only sixty-nine rooms. It is also right in the middle of the old city, so you would be in walking distance of the beach and the marketplace."

"I was thinking we would stay in a little inn on the outskirts of town."

Emilio nodded. "That is where your FBI friends will look first."

After a few seconds of consideration, Mark knew the young man was right. "Does the hotel take cash?"

"Yes, in fact, they prefer your American dollars. Once you and the señora are in your room, I would suggest that you stay there during the day. You can order room service for your meals. After dark if you want to walk on the beach or go shopping, call me. Señor Salazar's men and I will go with you."

Mark turned and looked out the window at the Colombian terrain that they were now passing at an acceptable speed. "I'm interested in spending time with my wife—not sightseeing."

"That will be much safer." Emilio sounded relieved. "Señor Salazar said that our vehicles will be difficult to hide—perhaps impossible—so I told him we could park them in a public lot. Then on Monday he could send some men into Cartagena. Two will go to collect our vehicles and answer questions for the officials, who will surely be watching them by then. The others will pick us up."

Mark was very impressed. "You *have* been thinking."

"I am your bodyguard," Emilio replied solemnly. "It is my job to keep you alive."

* * *

Solana stared at herself in the mirror, thinking she would almost have preferred an appointment with death than a tennis date with Hector Vargas. But since she would do anything to keep Emilio safe until they could escape next week, she gritted her teeth and hurried from her room and down to the tennis courts.

Vargas beat her handily in five straight sets, but then she wasn't really paying attention to the game. When they met at the net she tried to think of an excuse not to shake hands. Failing, she put her palm in his, intending to keep the contact brief. Vargas, however, had other ideas. He grasped her fingers tightly and drew her against the net. She could feel the heat emanating from his body, and she recoiled automatically.

"Release me, please," she said a little more sharply than she intended. She modified her voice and added, "I'm hot and uncomfortable. I'd like to go upstairs and take a shower."

"By all means." His eyes raked her, and she regretted the reference.

"Tonight at dinner, you should wear some of the new clothes you bought in La Rosa today. Lucien said you did quite a bit of shopping." The general's voice dropped a little lower, a little more menacing. "Then you did some visiting—with *friends,* I believe he said."

It was unnerving to know that he was so interested in every aspect of her life and that Lucien reported to him so faithfully. "After dinner maybe we could play a game of . . . chess." He gave her another leer.

She despised him and his determination to make her relationship with Emilio seem dirty. "I'm tired," she said, pulling as far away from him as his arms would allow. "I don't feel like playing chess tonight. In fact, I may not even eat dinner."

"What a pity," he murmured. When he released her, she rushed into the house and up to her room. As she ran, she dreamed of the day when she would never have to see those reptilian eyes again.

CHAPTER 10

Kate watched as the plane began its descent. The clouds parted, and she glimpsed Cartagena for the first time. The aquamarine waters of the Atlantic were lined with miles of pristine white sand. The beaches yielded to skyscraping hotels and lush jungle foliage, while azure skies provided a backdrop for the whole incredible scene. It was exotic and wild and completely enchanting.

Normally a patient person, Kate found herself chafing at the delays imposed on the passengers once they reached the gates. At least she was able to call Mark and assure him that she was on the ground—just a few yards away from him. He explained the precautions they were going to use in the airport. This dimmed her enthusiasm a little, since she had counted on seeing Mark's face the minute she left the secured gate area of the airport.

Finally they deplaned, and Kate breathed deeply, enjoying the freedom of being more than a few inches away from her fellowmen for the first time in hours. She had researched Colombia on the Internet the night before, but so far, Cartagena had been a pleasant surprise. According to the articles she found, the country had a reputation for violence, cocaine production, poverty, and civil disobedience. But the Rafael Nunez International Airport was modern by anyone's standards, and although there was a definite military presence, it was subtle. Instead of making Kate feel that she had stepped into a war zone, it made her feel safe.

After a brief stop at a currency exchange counter, she walked through the airport and out onto the street as Mark had instructed her to do. From the corner of her eye she noticed a handsome young man who met the description of Emilio Delgado. She stepped up to the curb as if trying to determine which of the fifty taxis would best suit her purposes.

"Señora Iverson," the young man said softly, "I suggest you choose a white one since most of those have air conditioning."

She didn't respond but raised her hand and motioned to the closest white taxi. It lurched forward and screeched to a halt directly in front of her.

The driver leaned across the front seat and pushed open the back passenger door for her. "Welcome to Cartagena!" he boomed as someone screamed a few yards down the sidewalk.

Kate slipped into the backseat and said, "El Centro. Quickly, please."

The driver didn't need any further encouragement. He pressed his foot on the gas and propelled the taxi headlong into the traffic. Kate glanced discreetly in the rearview mirror and saw that pandemonium prevailed behind them.

"You expecting company?" the driver asked.

"Maybe," she admitted honestly.

He smiled. "Nobody follows me! I drive very fast!"

Having been duly warned, Kate clutched the seat for dear life.

The taxi ride to the older part of the city was harrowing but blissfully short. When the taxi driver slammed on his brakes, Kate threw out an arm for support. After the whiplash effect of the sudden stop slung her back against her seat, she breathlessly asked the man how much she owed him.

He smiled and quoted an amount double what Kate had mentally calculated. But he'd gotten her there quickly as requested, and she didn't have time to waste on haggling, so she handed him the number of pesos he requested and stepped from the taxi. She immediately lost herself in a large crowd of tourists and moved with them into the busy shopping area.

She purchased a floppy pink hat, partly to hide her face and partly to shade it from the punishing Colombian sun. She put on her sunglasses and removed her plaid overshirt. Dressed now in a white T-shirt, she had altered her description and lowered her body temperature. Kate moved along the crowded streets, admiring the diversity that was Cartagena.

Rich tourists walking elbow to elbow with the poor vendors; old, crumbling buildings standing beside sleek new restaurants; platforms covered with colorful fresh fruit set up right next to dumpsters filled with rotting fish.

Kate tried not to be obvious when she looked around for Mark, but she desperately wanted to see him. She was close now—she could feel him nearby. And then, suddenly, he was there, just a few feet away. His appearance was so altered from his normal agent-bishop look that she almost gasped in shock. He was wearing loose-fitting khaki pants and a brilliantly white, short-sleeved cotton shirt, open at the neck. No tie, no socks, and just sandals—no shoes. Her eyes flew back up to his face.

She'd forgotten how deeply tanned he was and how long his dark hair had gotten. It was tucked behind his ears and brushing his collar. He hadn't shaved today—or maybe for several days. He had that scruffy look that was so popular among Hollywood actors. He was different—still extremely handsome, but there was an added dimension. Danger maybe . . . almost as if he belonged to Colombia now. Then he smiled, and she knew that no matter how he looked, he was still hers.

He moved his hand, just a slight gesture, like a wave, and she couldn't help but think of all the romantic movies—and the many parodies thereof—where the couple runs toward each other. And for the first time in her life, she understood the inclination. But since they had gone to all this trouble to be inconspicuous, she decided a foot-race reunion wouldn't be wise. So instead of running at him, she continued to examine the jewelry displayed on the tables in front of her. Each step moved her discreetly, and ever so slowly, toward the spot where Mark was standing.

She was just about to look up and check her progress when she felt his arms slide around her waist. His lips touched her neck, and she sagged against him. "Kate." The one whispered word spoke volumes.

She covered his hands with hers and tried to absorb every wonderful sensation of the moment. It was something she never wanted to end or forget. Much too soon he lifted his head and loosened his embrace. He laced the fingers of one hand through hers.

"So," she managed. "No one's following us?"

"Probably not," he replied, continuing to scan the crowd. "Do you see something you like?"

Her eyes moved from his stubbly chin to his soft lips and finally up to his deep brown eyes. "At this moment, I like everything I see," she assured him.

He laughed softly. "I meant the jewelry. I thought you might want to get a souvenir."

She made a face. "The cab driver cheated me out of a good portion of my spending money. So jewelry isn't really an option."

"Maybe he had a wife and ten children to support."

Kate squeezed his fingers. "I'll try to look at it that way."

Mark took her carry-on bag from her shoulder and pulled her gently by the hand. "Well, if you don't want to do any shopping, let's get out of here."

* * *

Emilio met them on the sidewalk in front of the hotel. "Kate, I'd like to introduce you to my friend and bodyguard, Emilio Delgado."

Kate extended her hand, which Emilio shook with near reverence. "It's nice to meet you officially," she said.

"Señora," he replied. Then he turned to Mark. "I registered a small suite for you in my name," he said as he handed Mark a key. "It is on the fifth floor, so you should have a very good view of the ocean. I told them I was going to get *my* wife." Sadness and concern clouded his eyes. "I wish it were true."

Mark patted the young man on the back. "Solana is a strong girl. She will be fine until you get back to La Rosa. Once you get away from General Vargas, the two of you can be married."

Emilio nodded, but the concern didn't fade. He gave Mark a funny look, as though he were trying to gauge him. "One of Señor Salazar's men reserved rooms for us at this more modest hotel." He pointed at a dilapidated building to their left. "We're in rooms 13 and 15. Call if you need us."

Mark waved and started across the street. "See you tomorrow."

Emilio did his best to smile as he returned their wave. "Enjoy your time together," he advised with wisdom older than his years. "Monday will be here soon enough."

* * *

The Charleston Cartagena, formerly the Santa Teresa Monastery, was incredible beyond anything Kate had imagined. Marble floors and high ceilings interspersed with stone archways and painted wood and gilt mirrors combined to give the old monastery a luxurious feel. Mark led her straight to the elevators. Kate knew he was trying to avoid the interest or attention of any of the hotel staff, but she felt like a wayward teenager sneaking off to spend unsupervised time with a disreputable boyfriend.

The elevator dispensed them on the fifth floor, and they followed the thickly carpeted hallway to room 502. Mark opened the door, and they slipped inside. The interior of the room was dark and cool. Kate walked over to a lamp, twisted the switch and flooded the sitting area with soft light.

"It's gorgeous," she whispered. "I'm almost afraid to move for fear I'll break something we can't afford to replace."

Mark smiled. "The FBI is paying for this little holiday—damages and all." He pointed at the balcony. "Look at the view."

She crossed the room to the glass doors that faced the ocean. "Can we go outside?"

"We'd better not," he replied. "But we can open the doors."

Once the ocean breeze was blowing into the room, they stood arm in arm and stared at the waves crashing onto the beach in the distance. "Does this remind you of that night in Miami at Mr. Morris's house?" she asked him, referring to the night Tony had been killed for the second time.

He considered this. "Well, the architectural style of Mr. Morris's house was similar to this hotel. Our room there had a balcony, and both places had armed guards roaming around. I guess I don't mind the comparison as long as there isn't a shootout during dinner . . . and as long as there's no Tony."

She smiled and turned in his arms so that her face was against his chest. "Are you hungry? We could order room service."

"I'm not hungry. Who has the kids?"

"They're at the Gambles' house with Miss Eugenia and Miracle and a couple sets of FBI agents."

"I thought the Gambles were in Atlanta."

"They came home because Jack felt like I might need him with you gone," Kate explained. "When he found out I was coming to visit you, he insisted that Emily and Charles stay at his fortress until I get back."

"Jack's a good friend," Mark said, his chest shuddering a little with emotion.

"Yes," Kate agreed. Then she reached up and rubbed his chin. "When did you decide to grow this?"

"I thought it went well with my bandit persona."

"It's kind of scary but cute," she decided.

"It's not as easy to maintain as you might think," he told her. "You still have to shave every day—you just can't cut off too much."

She laughed. "Poor Mark. I know how you hate to waste time primping."

"For the past few days, I've had plenty of extra time."

Kate's fingers strayed to his lips. "I'm here now."

"Yes, you're here." He closed his eyes and held her close.

* * *

On Sunday morning when Mark awakened, he kept his eyes closed and whispered, "Kate?"

"Hmmm," she murmured, obviously still half asleep.

He reached out and pulled her to him. "I was so afraid that it was all a dream."

She laughed as she nuzzled his neck. "It would have been a very good dream."

"I'll take even a grim reality to a good dream anytime."

She pulled back with a frown. "Did you just call me a grim reality?"

"Of course not. I was waxing philosophical."

Kate pushed herself into a sitting position. "I think you might be going crazy. We'd better call room service and get you something to eat."

Mark raised his hands over his head in a satisfying stretch. "I won't argue with you on either point." He looked across the bed and met her eyes. "The craziness or the idea about ordering breakfast."

She walked over to the desk in the sitting room, and after a brief perusal of the menu said, "Uh oh."

"Is the menu in Spanish?" he asked.

She returned and handed the menu to him. "It's got English translations, but I still don't know what most of it means. So you can order."

"Are you a little hungry or a lot?"

She smiled. "A lot." Then she moved toward the bathroom. "I think I'll try out that tub that's the size of Rhode Island while we wait for our breakfast to arrive."

* * *

Mark had time to check in with Perez and Emilio before Kate walked out of the bathroom dressed in one of the hotel's thick velour robes. She was towel-drying her long hair and looked better than he could ever remember.

"Have I told you lately that you are the most beautiful woman in the world?"

She wrapped her arms around his neck. "Maybe I could get used to this state of craziness you're in."

There was a knock on the door, and Mark opened it to admit the room service waiter. Then they ate in front of the open balcony doors with the air conditioner working as hard as possible to counteract the influx of hot air. When they were both full, they leaned back on the overstuffed couch and stared at the sea.

"So, tell me more about the kids," Mark said. "Miss Eugenia and Miracle are keeping them at the Gambles' house."

"After intense negotiations, we had decided to take the kids to Annabelle and Derrick's house in Albany and let Miss Eugenia and Miracle watch them there. But then Jack arrived and insisted that we bring the kids to his house. Unfortunately for him, that meant he got Miss Eugenia and Miracle and the others too."

Mark smiled. "Jack can handle them."

"He said to remind you that he has the best security system in Dougherty County. And after all those rumors we heard about the fence around his property being electrified, I didn't dare argue with him. Besides Jack, you've got two sets of FBI agents from Atlanta taking shifts outside the gates, Miracle and Miss Eugenia inside the house, and Winston stopping by on a regular basis. The children are well protected."

"That's a relief."

"Oh, and I completely forgot." Kate jumped up and hurried over to her purse. "Jack said to give you this." She extracted a small envelope and handed it to him. "He said it was very important."

Mark tore open the envelope and read the short note.

I finally got the memo you sent me. It was delivered by mistake to another senator's office, so I got it a day late. I think it will keep you out of jail, and I know I can keep your kids safe. You concentrate on getting back on American soil, and we'll take it from there.

Jack

Mark silently apologized to Britta Andersen for the unkind thoughts he'd had about her integrity. If Jack had the memo, there was hope.

* * *

Solana stood at the window of the sitting room in her suite and looked down on the front of the house. Since yesterday afternoon she had stayed in her suite, feigning illness to evade General Vargas. She was thankful to have been spared his evil leers, but there had been a price to be paid. By avoiding General Vargas, she had also sacrificed precious time with her father. The light was still on in his office, and finally she decided to brave an encounter with the general in order to see her father.

Surprisingly, when she reached his office, she found her father alone. "Where's General Vargas?" she asked, trying to keep the dread from her voice.

"He's in the barracks, preparing for the big trip tomorrow," her father replied. "Are you feeling better?"

She nodded. "A little."

"Maybe you would like something to eat?"

She was starving but felt that it would be suspicious to display much of an appetite immediately after an illness. So she shook her head. "No."

He laughed. "Well, I am hungry. Will you keep me company in the kitchen?"

She had to smile. "I wouldn't want you to be lonely."

They made omelets. Her father was surprisingly at home in the kitchen, and it was a pleasure to watch him work. She couldn't help imagining him in her mother's small house in Stockholm—cooking omelets for the three of them.

"Is something the matter?" he asked as he placed a generous piece of the omelet on a plate in front of her. "For a moment you looked so sad."

"I was thinking of my mother," she told him honestly. "Did you ever cook for her?"

He nodded. "Many times. We were young then—not so many servants." He leaned closer. "No terrible chefs who have been trained in fancy culinary schools but know nothing!"

This brought a smile back to her face. She ate some of her omelet and then said, "Thank you for all you have done for me—and especially what you did for Emilio."

"I appreciate the sacrifice you made in coming to La Rosa." He toyed with the food on his plate. "I have enjoyed getting to know you and regret now that I was not a part of your childhood."

"I wish Mother would come here. I think she would like it."

"Perhaps that is why she doesn't come," he said. "Maybe she doesn't wish to enjoy a life that she feels is wrong." He stood and scraped his omelet into the garbage. "All those years ago, when your mother told me that we were going to have a child, I didn't think that I had a choice. I thought I had been born to this life. But now I wonder . . . What if I had turned my back on my father and the business and married your mother—moved to Stockholm."

"Maybe it is not too late. Maybe instead of waiting for my mother to join you—you should join her."

He seemed to be considering it for a few seconds, then he shook his head. "It *is* too late—I am wanted in every country."

"You could make a deal." Solana didn't look at him and tried to choose her words very carefully. "If you told certain people things they would want to know, and if you stopped your . . . business, maybe they would let you live in peace."

"I don't know. Maybe." He put his arms around her, and she savored the rare moment of closeness. Too soon he pulled back and cupped her face in his hands. "While I am gone, you must be cautious. Don't go anywhere without Lucien. You may visit Emilio at Mr. Iverson's house, but there's no need to mention this to General Vargas before we leave."

Solana nodded. The last thing she wanted to do was cause a confrontation with El Diablo.

"But other than visits to Mr. Iverson's house—which is also guarded by my men—you are not to go anywhere. No trips to La Rosa for shopping, no movies, no visits to the daughters of Cristobal Morales. I know that you do not understand the restrictions of the life I must lead, and so I try to be lenient, but it is very important that you follow these instructions until I return."

Solana looked at the ground, so he wouldn't be able to see her eyes when she lied. "Okay."

He pressed a kiss to her forehead. "Good girl. Now go to bed, and hopefully you will be fully recovered from your illness by tomorrow."

* * *

Mark and Kate watched the sunset from the safety of the couch in the sitting room of their hotel suite. But once a cloak of darkness had fallen on the city, Mark felt it was safe to sit on the balcony. When the room service waiter delivered their dinner, they carried it outside and ate under the stars.

After the food was gone, he forced himself to bring up the subject he'd been avoiding ever since they'd met in the marketplace in El Centro. "Now why don't you tell me about Tony?"

He heard her sharp intake of breath, but she didn't protest or claim ignorance. "I think he's alive," she said slowly. "But I don't believe he means us any harm."

Mark wasn't convinced of that but decided not to voice his concerns. "He's been living in Las Vegas?"

"Apparently. When all this is over, I guess we'll have to talk to Mr. Evans and find out if there is anything we need to do legally . . . about my marriage to Tony and to you."

"If Tony is still alive, I'm sure the FBI had your marriage to him ended legally. They wouldn't let you be a bigamist. That would leave them open for all kinds of lawsuits."

"That is what I think too," she said. "Not because I trust the FBI so much, but during all this time together and in the temple on our wedding day, if we weren't really married, it seems like we would have felt that something was *wrong.*"

"We're married," he said firmly, as if he could make the words true through emphasis alone. He stroked her hair for a few minutes before adding, "I wonder why he waited so long to come to Haggerty?"

"We don't know that he didn't come to Haggerty before. He may have come many times over the past four years. This may just be the first time that I noticed him."

Mark couldn't really argue with that logic. Since he didn't want to tell her about the possibility that Tony was trying to destroy him when he was helpless, he let it go. "How do you feel about having Tony as a part of your life again?"

She curled into the crook of his arm. "You're my husband. No one can change the way I feel about you—not even Tony. But if he's alive, I'm glad. And if he wants to have a role in Emily's life, then I think we can work that out." She looked up at him. "How do you feel about it?"

He pressed his lips against her forehead. "I don't want to share you or Emily," he told her honestly.

"It's not something we have to figure out now," Kate assured him. "We'll have plenty of time to decide things when you get home."

He hoped that was true.

"I wish we could go to church," she murmured.

"It would be nice."

"We could sit by each other for a change. It's been years since we've been able to do that."

Mark thought that soon this would no longer be an issue since it was very likely that he would be released from his calling as bishop when, or if, he was able to return to the United States. There was also a good chance that he would lose his job with the FBI. His arm tightened around Kate, and he said a silent prayer. *Dear Lord, I'm willing to accept Thy will in all things, but if I can just keep my family. Please . . .*

* * *

On Monday Kate and Mark woke up early. They took turns in the shower, and then he ordered room service while she dried her hair. She waited until after they were finished eating breakfast before she explained about the arrest attempt during the trip to Medellin. Mark was pale when she handed him the gum and explained its purpose.

"One hour and eighteen minutes after you leave La Rosa, you chew the piece of gum," she told him. "Then you'll be very sick. Hopefully Mr. Salazar will have someone bring you here, but wherever you end up, you'll have to find your way to the airport here in Cartagena. I'll be waiting for you, and we'll fly home."

She put the prescription packet of gum into his hand, and he stared at it, making no comment.

"Mark, do you understand what I'm telling you? It's very important."

"You're asking me to betray a friend," he said finally.

This annoyed her. "All I'm asking you to do is chew a piece of gum," she snapped more harshly than she intended. She took a deep breath and continued. "You don't make policy decisions, Mark. Officials in the U.S. government do that, and your superiors give you orders based on those decisions. You're an agent for the FBI. You're a husband and a father." She resisted the urge to grab the fabric of his Colombian cotton shirt and shake him until his teeth rattled. "You *will* do this, Mark."

He nodded slowly. "I know. I'm just surprised and disappointed. In the meetings I went to before I came, they didn't mention anything about trying to arrest Salazar." Mark rubbed his temples. "I was warned not to like him, but I can't help it. I do."

"I'm sorry," Kate said. "But your feelings for Salazar don't change anything."

"I'm not even sure that taking Salazar out of the power position down here is the right thing to do," Mark continued. "I wish I could talk to them and tell them what I've learned, what I know."

Kate grasped his hands in hers. "But you can't. You've been given an assignment. You'll chew the gum one hour and eighteen minutes after you leave La Rosa."

Mark looked like he wanted to argue, but finally he nodded. "I'll chew the gum."

"Then you will get very sick. It might be a good idea to mention not feeling well a little before that—maybe you could blame it on something you ate this morning. If you have anything to say about where they take you—suggest Cartagena. Once you get to a hospital, you'll have to lose your escort, grab a taxi, and get to the airport. I'll be watching for you there."

"I understand." He seemed distant and distracted, which concerned her.

"Mark." She claimed his full attention. "I can't leave the airport. I don't speak Spanish, I don't know the area, and I would be defenseless wandering around Cartagena. You *have* to come to me."

"I will," he promised.

"And I really am sorry about your friend," she said softly.

He touched her cheek. "I know."

She stood up and drew a deep breath. "Okay, it's time for me to finish packing and head to the airport. Then you can call Emilio to pick you up for the trip back to La Rosa."

* * *

As Mark watched Kate drive away in the taxi, he felt confused and conflicted. For the past week the FBI had misled him on almost every point of his mission. On the other hand, Rodrigo Salazar had shown him nothing but kindness and generosity. In spite of this, he was going to fulfill his obligations to the FBI and turn his back on Rodrigo Salazar.

Rationally he knew that Salazar was a criminal, a drug lord responsible at least indirectly for many deaths. But personally he seemed so different. Mark closed his eyes, realizing that the only place he could put his trust was in the Lord. He whispered a quick prayer and felt immediately calmer. Then he used his cell phone to call Emilio. They agreed to walk down to the conference center on the corner and have Salazar's men pick them up there.

When the men sent from La Rosa arrived, they reported that Mark's Jeep and Salazar's truck left in the public lot Saturday were being watched by several different parties, including the Colombian military and the Cartagena police. So they were all to return home in the trucks that had been driven up that day and let the lawyers handle retrieving the other vehicles.

The trip home was quicker and less eventful than the one to Cartagena on Saturday. Mark kept thinking about Kate sitting in the airport, hoping she was safe. Unconsciously he reached into the pocket of his pants and fingered the gum package. Since it was supposed to be several weeks old, it would probably be good if it showed a little wear. Then he realized he was touching his method of betrayal and let go of the package.

For a few minutes he wondered how Salazar would fare within the American legal system. Salazar would probably do as well as anyone could. He had plenty of money and could hire the best lawyers. Even though he would most likely spend the rest of his life in prison, he might be able to arrange to live in a relatively comfortable one. And hopefully he could continue his relationship with Solana and possibly even Britta.

Mark smiled bitterly. He knew he was just looking for a way to ease his conscience. The fact was that he was going to break a trust—return evil for good—and the thought made him sick. He sighed. Even that was something of an advantage since he was supposed to start exhibiting signs of ill health soon.

When the trucks pulled to a stop in front of Mark's house, Emilio talked to the guards posted on the road and determined that everything was secure. Then all of Salazar's men climbed into one truck and left the other for Emilio and Mark to drive to the compound when Mark was ready to leave for Medellin.

After waving good-bye to their escorts, Mark led the way to the front door of the house. He pressed his palm on the screen and entered the code into the keypad. The lock clicked, and the door swung open.

Emilio stepped inside first and looked around. "Everything seems fine," he reported.

Mark nodded. "I need to make a couple of phone calls. Then I'll be ready to go on to Mr. Salazar's compound." He knew the young man was anxious to see Solana and expected no argument.

"I think I'll check the refrigerator and see if there's anything to eat," Emilio said.

Mark carried his suitcase upstairs and threw it on the bed. He was starting to get some shirts out of his closet when Emilio called to him. It wasn't exactly a scream, but Mark could tell by the timbre of the young man's voice that he was under extreme stress. Fearing that Vargas had broken in again, Mark pulled his gun from his shoulder holster and hurried back down the stairs.

But when he reached the kitchen, there were no armed guards, no Hector Vargas—only a very frightened Emilio. And Pilar's body lay dead on the floor. Mark checked the condition of the corpse and guessed that she had been dead for several hours. Near the lifeless fingers of Pilar's left hand was a postcard addressed to Britta Andersen requesting that she come to her daughter immediately.

Emilio's breathing was ragged, and while Mark felt sorry for the young man, he knew he couldn't treat him gently. "She was stabbed."

"Yes," the young man gasped.

"At home under circumstances like this, I would call the police," he said in a matter-of-fact tone. "How are such things handled in La Rosa?"

Emilio made a noise that Mark could only describe as a contemptuous sob. "Here the police are a joke."

"So what do we do?"

Emilio rubbed his sleeve across his eyes. "First I will get a blanket to cover her."

While Emilio was gone, Mark picked up the postcard and put it in his pocket.

So all this time Pilar had been Solana's contact with Britta. Anger welled inside him. Anger at Perez and the FBI for insisting on excessive secrecy. Anger against Salazar for employing an animal like

Hector Vargas—who was certainly responsible for this latest atrocity. Anger at himself for failing to protect Pilar. And then finally things came into focus for Mark. He had a purpose for being in La Rosa, and his actions could not be governed by friendship. This was war— good against evil—and the lines were more clearly drawn than he had realized.

Emilio returned with the blanket and spread it over Pilar's lifeless form.

"Now what?" Mark asked.

"We should call Señor Morales," Emilio said.

Mark nodded. "If you'll take care of that, I'm going to make my own calls. Then we'll go on to Mr. Salazar's compound."

Emilio reached for the phone, shaken but functioning.

Feeling suddenly very tired, Mark walked back upstairs and signed onto his PDA. He typed:

Returned from Cartagena to find my housekeeper murdered— presumably by Hector Vargas. She had a postcard addressed to Britta Andersen. Hope you have plans to get Solana and Emilio out of here fast. The danger is increasing by the minute.

While waiting for Perez to write back, Mark called Kate.

"Are you okay?" he asked when he heard her voice.

"Yes, but my flight has been delayed," she said for the benefit of anyone who might be listening in. "Be careful," she begged.

"I will."

He disconnected the call as a message appeared on the PDA screen.

Solana and Emilio will be removed soon—details are not need- to-know for you.

Mark thought if it wasn't so absurd, it would be funny. He was the one standing in a house in Colombia with a dead woman a few feet away, but the FBI was still keeping simple information from him. Running his fingers through his hair in frustration he took a deep, calming breath. This was the most poorly run operation he'd ever been a part of, and he couldn't wait to get home. He signed off the PDA, grabbed his overnight bag, and hurried downstairs.

Emilio was waiting for him in the salon. "Señor Morales is sending someone for Pilar."

Mark nodded. Then with one last glance toward the kitchen he said, "Let's go."

* * *

Mark and Emilio were stopped by guards when they arrived at the outer walls of Rodrigo Salazar's compound. The facility was even more imposing from the ground than it had been from the aerial photographs Mark had seen in Atlanta. The walls seemed higher, and the guards more numerous. The guards waved them through the metal gate, and they moved on to the next checkpoint.

Finally they arrived at Salazar's residence, where twelve vehicles were lined up two abreast in preparation for their journey. Emilio parked the truck behind the procession as Salazar came out of the house to greet them. Hector Vargas was at his side.

"Welcome!" Salazar said with a cheerful smile. "It looks as though we have a fine day for our travels."

Without speaking, Mark climbed the few steps that separated them and placed the bloodstained postcard in Salazar's hand. The smile disappeared from Salazar's face. "What is this?" he demanded.

"When I returned from Cartagena this morning, I found Pilar dead," Mark informed him bluntly. "Stabbed." He glanced back at Vargas. "It felt *personal*."

"That is a terrible shame," Salazar said softly. "She was a very good cook. I had hoped to convince her to come and work for me when you no longer required her services."

Mark stared at Salazar for a few seconds. Then he asked, "Is that all you have to say? She was obviously killed for trying to mail this postcard!"

Salazar shook his head. "She was obviously killed by local bandits." Salazar spoke over his shoulder, addressing the general. "Hector, we must figure a way to do something about the lawlessness in La Rosa. I am trying to convince Mr. Iverson to bring his family here permanently, and incidents like this do not help my cause."

Vargas nodded. "I will do what I can."

Mark stood there astonished. He couldn't believe that Salazar was going to brush off the murder of a young woman so casually.

"Well," Salazar said. "It is time to load up. Come on, Mark. We have a long drive ahead of us." Salazar moved down the stairs.

With a smirk in Mark's direction, Hector Vargas did the same.

* * *

Solana had been watching for Emilio and Mr. Iverson to arrive, and as soon as she saw them, she hurried down to meet them. The minute she descended the stairs, she could feel the tension. She wanted badly to run to Emilio and throw her arms around his neck, but she satisfied herself with a quick visual reconnaissance. He seemed pale but otherwise okay, so she moved over beside her father.

"What is wrong?" she asked.

"I'm afraid I have some bad news," he told her. "Pilar was killed by local bandits."

"Pilar?" Solana repeated stupidly. "She's *dead?*"

Her father nodded. "I know it is a terrible shock. I try to warn you often about the dangers of traveling alone in La Rosa. That is why I insist that you always have Lucien with you. Unfortunately, Pilar didn't have a father to look after her."

Tears spilled over onto Solana's cheeks. "Poor Pilar." She turned to Mr. Iverson. He was regarding them both with a strange, hard look. In fact, everyone looked uncomfortable except General Vargas. "There's something you're not telling me."

"Solana," her father began in a soothing voice.

"She died in my kitchen with a postcard in her hand," Mr. Iverson said. "It was addressed to your mother asking that she come here immediately."

Solana heard her father curse softly under his breath, and her heart began to pound. "Pilar was killed for trying to mail my postcard?"

"Pilar was killed by bandits who prey on helpless women," her father insisted firmly. "The fact that she had a postcard addressed to your mother was incidental."

Solana knew this was a lie and pressed a hand to her trembling lips. She had to think quickly or all was lost. "I told Pilar how much I miss my mother and that I wish she would just come and talk to you." She turned her tortured eyes to her father. "I love you both."

He nodded. "I know."

"I told Pilar that I agreed to come here, hoping that my mother would join us and that the two of you would get back together. But it has been two months, and she is not here. I asked Pilar to send a postcard to convince Mother to come." Solana batted at the tears that continued to fall. "I gave her Mother's address in Stockholm and suggested that she make the situation sound urgent so Mother would hurry."

She threw her arms around her father. "I never meant to get her in trouble." That at least was true. "And I can't believe she was killed because . . ."

"Solana," her father interrupted. "I told you that Pilar's death was random—completely unrelated to the postcard. I have asked General Vargas to take measures to increase security in the area so nothing like this happens again."

Solana looked over at the general and read the truth in his eyes. He had killed Pilar and wanted Solana to know that he had. She turned away from him.

"Don't be afraid," her father whispered. "If you do as I ask, you will be safe."

She hugged her arms to her chest and nodded.

Salazar raised his voice and addressed the others. "Let's go. Everyone get into your assigned vehicles. Mark—you ride with me."

"My Jeep hasn't made it back from Cartagena yet," Mr. Iverson said. "Can Emilio continue to borrow your truck until it does?"

"That is fine," Salazar agreed easily, but General Vargas blocked the young man's path as he attempted to return to the truck.

"We need Emilio to come with us to Medellin," the general said.

For a few seconds there was total silence. Finally Mr. Iverson stepped up beside his bodyguard. "I need Emilio to stay here. My housekeeper has just been killed so things are a little unsettled at my house. Emilio will keep an eye on things until I get back."

Vargas raised an eyebrow in obvious challenge. "Since your house-keeper is now dead, I don't see what's left to be guarded," he countered. "And until we can do something about these lawless local bandits roaming the woods, it would be much safer for Emilio to be with us than alone in that house."

"Emilio can take care of himself," Mr. Iverson replied with growing annoyance.

"I'm sure that is true," Vargas said with a derisive look that expressed just the opposite. "But since we have two men in Cartagena trying to retrieve your Jeep, we are shorthanded. Surely, after all that Señor Salazar has done, you won't mind contributing one man to help protect the convoy on the way to Medellin."

Solana watched the drama unfolding before her with a combination of horror and fascination. Vargas had killed Pilar. He had taunted Mr. Iverson, and now he had maneuvered them all into this awkward standoff. Either he knew that she and Emilio had plans to escape while they were gone to Medellin, or he was just taking measures to make sure they didn't try. If she didn't hate the man so much, she could almost admire his evil genius.

Finally her father shrugged and addressed Mr. Iverson. "If Hector says that we need Emilio, can you spare him?"

So General Vargas had won again. Solana saw the look of satisfaction on his face and wished she had the power to wipe it off.

Mr. Iverson couldn't really refuse. "I suppose."

Emilio risked a quick glance in her direction. His desolation was apparent. This meant that their escape plans were ruined. She and Emilio would not be in Stockholm by that time tomorrow as they had hoped.

"Emilio can ride in the truck with me," General Vargas said.

"Emilio rides with me," Mr. Iverson corrected firmly. "He is my bodyguard, after all."

"It is true," Salazar said, clapping the general on the back in a friendly manner. "Emilio rides in the SUV with Mr. Iverson. Now, everyone in your vehicles. We have wasted too much time already and will be very late reaching Medellin."

He started toward the black Pathfinder parked in the driveway. Then he turned and came back to kiss Solana's forehead. "If you need me, call my cell phone," he said. Then he hurried over to the SUV, swung inside, and they were gone.

CHAPTER 11

After three hours at the airport in Cartagena, Kate was starting to get bored. She knew she wasn't supposed to use her cell phone unless there was an emergency, so she walked over to the bank of pay phones and inserted a handful of coins. A few minutes later she was speaking to Beth Gamble.

"I can't thank you enough for all you're doing for us," Kate said.

"We're glad to help," Beth replied. "And honestly, I don't know when I've had so much fun. Miss Eugenia is like a one-woman variety show."

This remark was a little scary, but Kate decided she really didn't want to know what Miss Eugenia was up to. She had enough to worry about. "Tell Emily and Charles I said hi and that I'll see them tonight," Kate requested, then walked up and down the terminal several times, checking the available flights and times.

She knew it would be foolish to buy their one-way return tickets too soon—since that would alert anyone watching for them. And there wasn't any rush since it didn't really matter where they went as long as it was out of Colombia. There were plenty of flights leaving Cartagena that afternoon and evening. They could go to Los Angeles or Las Vegas or even somewhere distant like Munich, Germany. Then once they were out of Colombia, they could get a flight to Atlanta. But she would feel better once she had her reservations in hand.

With a sigh, she found an inconspicuous spot and sat down to wait some more.

* * *

Solana watched until the convoy was completely out of sight. Then she surveyed the compound. There was still at least one guard in each of the towers. There were also men walking along the walls. She was sure there were guards at the checkpoints and probably some in the hills outside the walls as well. There would be another shift in the barracks, resting or sleeping, and a few others roaming the compound—but there were far fewer men around than usual, and there was no Vargas. It was the perfect time to escape. Unfortunately, this couldn't be used to her advantage since there was also no Emilio.

Frustrated by the way Vargas had managed to ruin her plans and feeling sad and guilty over Pilar's death, Solana walked back into the house. Her footsteps echoed in the empty salon as she passed through to the large kitchen. She didn't see any other servants, but she couldn't be sure there wasn't one lurking somewhere. She found the chef in the walk-in freezer.

"I am looking for something to prepare for dinner," he said when he saw her.

"I missed breakfast and was hoping you wouldn't mind if I fixed myself some toast," Solana said as an excuse for being there.

"Help yourself," he invited with a little more volume than necessary.

She rubbed her arms against the cold and stepped closer. "Emilio was forced to go with my father to Medellin," she whispered. "You need to call off the helicopter for this afternoon."

"We have a nice leg of lamb that I could fix with mint sauce," the chef said. "Or perhaps you would prefer chicken." He pulled a frozen carcass from a shelf and held it up for her inspection "I can't cancel the helicopter," he hissed. "You will meet it as planned, and we'll arrange another one to come back and get Emilio later."

She shook her head. "No!" She gave him an apologetic smile. "I do not care for chicken." As he replaced the frozen fryer on the shelf she continued. "I will not leave without Emilio."

The chef extracted a large beef roast. "This looks good," he said for the benefit of anyone listening. For her ears only, he added, "I still can't cancel the helicopter, and I've been ordered to leave with it. I don't know when we'll be able to get someone else inside the compound or arrange another rescue attempt."

Solana closed her eyes briefly. Then she nodded that she understood the risks associated with her decision to stay in La Rosa. "Thank you for your help and good luck."

He looked unhappy. "I'll hold the helicopter as long as I can this afternoon, just in case you change your mind."

* * *

For the ride to Medellin, Salazar handled the seating arrangements in the black Pathfinder. He and Mark were seated in the middle section with Emilio in front beside the driver and two additional men in the far back. Mark didn't feel much like talking, which wasn't a problem since Salazar spent the first hour on his cell phone.

Mark watched the almost familiar terrain pass by and thought about Kate and Pilar and the acting job that would soon be required of him.

"Are you okay?" Salazar startled him by demanding. "You haven't said two words since we left La Rosa."

Mark rubbed his stomach. "I don't feel very well." This was not completely untrue. "Maybe it was something I ate, or maybe my stomach objects to so much riding in the car over the last few days."

Salazar leaned forward and instructed his driver to turn up the air conditioner. "Sometimes that helps," he told Mark.

"Or it could be that I'm just missing my wife." Mark was careful to keep his gaze averted, afraid that Salazar might be able to read the guilt in his eyes. "It was wonderful to see her but so hard to say goodbye."

"I understand," Salazar commiserated. "But you will be reunited with her again soon."

"And the business with Pilar was very upsetting as well."

Salazar glanced at the back of the driver's head to indicate that this was a discussion that could not be held in front of the men. "Yes. Of course."

Mark kept his watch positioned so that he could check the time without being obvious about it. Finally the moment came. He offered a silent prayer for strength and wisdom. Then he reached into his pocket and withdrew the packet Kate had brought him in Cartagena. He popped the gum into his mouth and chewed a few times quickly.

"Something to settle your stomach?" Salazar asked.

Mark extended the prescription wrapper for Salazar to see. "It's just gum—a special kind the doctor prescribed that's supposed to keep from damaging my dental work. But I'm feeling worse, and I'm hoping that the gum . . ." He never completed the sentence. The nausea overtook him so quickly and so completely that the next thing he remembered was lying on the ground outside the Pathfinder with Emilio kneeling beside him.

"I feel terrible," he muttered.

"You are very sick," Emilio agreed gravely.

"Tell me I didn't vomit on Señor Salazar."

"No, but you barely missed." Salazar stepped into view behind Emilio.

Mark used a shaking hand to shade his eyes and looked at Salazar. "I'm so sorry."

"No apology is necessary," Salazar said with a shrug. "My men will have it cleaned up soon. The question is what to do with you."

Before Mark could answer, another spasm of nausea overtook him, and Emilio helped him turn onto his side so that he could empty his stomach contents onto the warm earth. "Maybe it's food poisoning," Mark gasped when the vomiting stopped, "or a stomach virus."

This comment had the desired effect. He saw Salazar step back. "Either way, my friend, I don't believe you can continue with us to Medellin."

Mark tried to sit up. "If you'll give me just a few minutes." He began to wretch again.

When he was able to control his stomach, he heard Salazar talking to Emilio. "Take him to the hospital in Cartagena. If it is food poisoning, he may become dehydrated. Once they're sure he's recovered, you can contact me at this number. I will arrange for someone to meet you and bring you to Medellin."

He heard Hector Vargas suggest that they send one of their own men instead of Emilio.

"No," Salazar said, sounding unusually firm. "Mr. Iverson will be more comfortable with his own bodyguard. Besides the drive to Medellin is a dangerous one. I want to keep all our men with us."

"But Rodrigo," Vargas tried again.

"Hector, I have spoken."

Mark glanced at the general. Vargas was obviously very unhappy about Salazar's decision, but for once, he was powerless to change it.

Mark lifted his head and managed to say, "What?" Then his head lolled back down, drool dripping from his slack lips.

"I am leaving a truck with Emilio," Salazar told him from a safe distance. "He is going to use it to take you to Cartagena. It is only about an hour away. Once you receive medical care, I will have you brought to Medellin."

"Sorry," Mark said to the ground.

Salazar patted him briefly on the back. "It couldn't be helped." Then he stepped away and called to the rest of his party to return to their vehicles.

"Some of Señor Salazar's men are going to lift you now," Emilio warned him, and Mark felt hands at his shoulders and feet.

His stomach muscles continued to contract as the men carried him to a truck at the back of the convoy and dumped him into the front seat. Mark was so weak that he could barely hold himself upright. He clung to the open window, hoping that if there were any future episodes of vomiting, he could at least protect the truck's interior. Emilio started the truck and turned the vehicle around. Mark was vaguely aware of the convoy heading the other way as they bounced down the road toward Cartagena and Kate.

* * *

Mark stopped vomiting a few minutes after they left Salazar's convoy, and by the time they reached the outskirts of Cartagena, he was able to sit upright. At the first shopping area where taxis were available, Mark asked Emilio to pull over.

"I've got to tell you some important things," he said. "And I don't have much time, so listen closely." The young man nodded. "I don't have food poisoning or a virus. I got sick because I chewed some gum that my wife brought me during her visit to Cartagena. In fact, that was the entire reason she came."

Emilio blinked but didn't comment.

"I had to get away from the convoy so that I could join my wife at the airport in Cartagena and leave the country. I don't know the details, but I'm aware that a rescue attempt for Solana has been scheduled. I also know Solana well enough to realize that she won't leave La Rosa without you. It was very fortunate that Salazar assigned you to bring me to Cartagena. Now you need to get back to La Rosa and meet that helicopter—if it's not too late already."

Emilio shook his head. "It is not too late. It is coming this afternoon."

Mark was relieved. "I'm sure that Vargas has called the compound and told his men that we left the convoy, and he might have even arranged for someone to come looking for us. But one thing is for sure—you can't just go driving back up to the compound. You will have to go straight to the location where the helicopter is scheduled to land."

"But as you said, Solana won't be planning to meet the helicopter since she thinks I am on my way to Medellin. How will we let her know to come?"

Mark rubbed his temples, trying to ignore the lingering nausea and debilitating weakness. "The FBI has an agent actually inside Salazar's compound." Mark ground his teeth in frustration. "Of course I don't know who and have no way to contact him directly since 'lack of communication' defines this entire operation."

He saw the blank look on Emilio's face and waved his complaints aside.

"Anyway, I can use my PDA to contact Perez. Then Perez can notify the agent inside the compound that you're going to be at the meeting point, and the agent can get word to Solana. It's awkward and circuitous, but it's the best we can do."

"I understand," Emilio said.

"When I send the message to Perez on my PDA, I'm going to have to word it carefully, because there are some aspects of my mission that he doesn't understand—things that could compromise my wife's safety."

Emilio nodded again.

Mark pulled the PDA from his suitcase and signed on, quickly typing in a message.

Got sick on the way to Medellin and had to leave convoy. On way to hospital in Cartagena. Solana thinks that Emilio is going to Medellin with me, and so she is not planning to leave with the helicopter. Need to let her know that he is on his way back to La Rosa and will be at the pickup point.

"Solana may think this message is a trick to get her out of her father's compound," Emilio said as he read the words on the PDA screen over Mark's shoulder. "Could you add a personal message from me so that she will know it is the truth?"

"That's a good idea," Mark agreed.

"Please say that I swear by all that is holy that I will be at the meeting point and that we will spend our honeymoon in Stockholm."

Mark didn't ask for explanations. He just typed in the additional message and pushed *send*. Without waiting for Perez to reply, he signed off the PDA and put it back in his suitcase. Then he opened the door of the truck. "You must hurry back to La Rosa. Avoid contact with others as much as possible. As I said, they might be looking for you."

"What about you, señor?" Emilio asked.

"I'll take a taxi to the airport, where my wife is waiting, and we'll fly back home."

Mark had expected the young man to be thrilled that he was being given the chance to return to Solana and to leave Colombia. But Emilio seemed hesitant.

Mark pushed himself into a standing position and fought the dizziness that threatened to overwhelm him. "What's wrong?"

"You are sick," Emilio replied. "I'm not sure you can make it to the airport alone. I should go with you."

"If you go with me, you might miss the helicopter. And if you're not there, Solana won't get out of La Rosa. You have to go."

"But I am your bodyguard," Emilio argued. "I am responsible for your safety."

Mark looked across the truck at the young man. "We are both many things, but right now the safety of the women we love is our most important responsibility. Go to Solana."

Emilio nodded but still looked worried.

Finally Mark smiled. "And just to make sure you don't have any second thoughts—you're fired."

Emilio looked startled. "Señor?"

"You are no longer my bodyguard. Now get out of here."

Mark slammed the truck door shut and moved as quickly as possible to the first available taxi. He slipped into the backseat and said, "Rafael Nunez International Airport." Once the taxi started moving, he rested his head against the seat and closed his eyes.

* * *

Solana was in the salon, staring morosely at the chess board, when the chef found her.

"Excuse me!" he boomed from halfway across the large room. "This afternoon I must go into La Rosa to purchase some vegetables. Since your father is away and has instructed you that you cannot travel alone, I thought I would invite you to accompany me." He drew closer, and she waited expectantly.

"How kind of you to ask," she said as he placed a small scrap of paper on the chess board. She read the message twice, and then tears blurred her vision. Emilio had left the convoy and was on his way to the spot where the helicopter would pick them up. They were leaving La Rosa this evening as planned. "I do need to pick up a few things," she managed. "What time will you leave?"

"I will go at three o'clock so I will have time to prepare dinner when I return," the chef said. Then he retrieved the small piece of paper and slipped it into the pocket of his pants.

She nodded ever so slightly. They would leave at three o'clock in order to make sure that they arrived well before the helicopter did.

"Meet me at the truck parked by the service entrance at three o'clock," he said.

"Lucien?" she whispered.

"Don't worry. I'll take care of him." Then the chef walked off toward the kitchen.

* * *

Kate looked up from the salad she had been picking at for over an hour and stared out the restaurant's window at the airport entrance. She wasn't really hungry but had started to feel conspicuous, so she'd come into the restaurant and ordered a seafood salad. The waiter had come by several times asking if she needed anything else. As much as she dreaded the thought of returning to the terminal, where she had already spent the better part of the day, she was more afraid of becoming a curiosity in the restaurant.

She raised her hand and motioned for the check. Just as she put the appropriate amount of money on the ticket, she saw Mark walk in the terminal entrance. His appearance was, once again, greatly altered from the husband she knew. He was very pale and was almost staggering.

Throwing caution to the wind, she rushed out of the restaurant and greeted him.

"Mark!" she called, slipping an arm around his waist in what she hoped would look to casual observers like a hug. Really it was intended to provide him with some much-needed support. "The gum must have made you very sick."

"Pretty bad," he acknowledged. "But I'll be okay. Let's just get our tickets. Once we're on a plane I can sleep it off."

Kate led him to the airline counter. "Call me superstitious," she told him, "but this just feels lucky."

He gave her a wan smile. "Let's take the flight that leaves in an hour for Los Angeles if they have any seats available."

The ticket agent listened politely to Kate's request and asked to see their passports. After entering an incredible amount of information into the computer, she was pleased to inform them that there were seats available on the flight. Then she requested a form of payment. Kate fumbled in her wallet for a credit card while trying to keep one eye on Mark, who looked ready to faint at any moment.

Finally, after giving Mark a long look, the ticket agent handed them their boarding passes. Then she pointed the way to the security area and gates. Kate took Mark's suitcase from him and held them both in her right hand while wrapping her left arm back around his waist.

"This way," she encouraged him. "It won't be long now."

"I'm just so tired," he whispered.

As Kate dragged both Mark and their luggage to the security screening area, she wondered what had been in the gum. Either the drug was more potent than Mr. Evans had realized, or the fact that Mark rarely took any medication had caused the drug to affect Mark for longer than anticipated.

The lines at the security area weren't long, but they didn't seem to be moving. Kate put the suitcases on the floor so she could hold on to Mark. He rested his head on her shoulder, and in a few seconds she heard him snoring. He was asleep on his feet.

* * *

Mark startled awake and found himself standing in line at an airport, holding onto Kate. He blinked, trying to remember where he was and what he was doing.

"We're in Cartagena," she whispered. "We're going to get on a plane headed to Los Angeles if we can ever make it through security."

He nodded as it all came back to him. La Rosa, Salazar, Pilar, Solana, Emilio, Vargas.

"Are you feeling better?"

"A little," he gave her the closest thing to a smile that he could muster. Then he lifted one hand off her shoulder and pointed at the metal detectors. "What's taking so long?"

"I don't know," she replied. "They seem to have plenty of employees, but they aren't letting anyone through."

"My friend Emilio says that *slow* is an integral part of the Colombian disposition." Mark paused to yawn. "But this is worse than slow." His eyes narrowed at the security personnel who were milling around the X-ray machines and conveyor belts, and suddenly he realized what would have been obvious sooner if he wasn't so groggy. "They're stalling."

Kate's eyes widened with concern. "What?"

"I don't know why, but for some reason they're just holding everyone here."

Kate glanced over at the idle workers. "Do you think it has anything to do with us?"

He swallowed hard. Apparently, the arrest attempt on Salazar had already happened and whatever the results—Vargas was coming for him. "I'm afraid it probably does." Following a brief moment of indecision, Mark said, "We've got to get out of here—*now!*"

The concerned look in Kate's eyes changed to complete panic. "But where will we go?"

"Anywhere is safer than here. Vargas could arrive any minute." He leaned down close to her ear and whispered, "I'm going to pretend that I need to go to the bathroom. Play along." Then he raised his voice and said, "I need to go to the bathroom, but I don't think I can make it alone. You'll have to help me."

Kate picked up the suitcases and wrapped her other arm firmly around his waist. "I told him not to drink the water," she said to the couple behind them. "He's been sick all morning—throwing up."

They gave her a sympathetic smile before moving aside to let them pass.

"We'll make a quick stop by the bathroom in case anyone is watching us," he told her once they were free of the line. She walked with him to the men's room and paused by the door. He walked in but stopped just inside.

"Now what?" she asked, facing the hallway.

"Go down to those phones and pretend to be making a call. Then move around the corner and wait for me."

She did as she was told, and a few minutes later he was beside her. He took her hand and pulled her toward a side exit. Moving as quickly as possible without attracting too much attention, they hurried to the front of the airport. Mark signaled for a taxi and opened the door when one pulled up in front of them. He let Kate slide in first and had just ducked inside when he saw Salazar's familiar green trucks race around the corner and screech to a stop near the airport's main entrance. Several armed men jumped out and ran into the building. The only one Mark recognized was Hector Vargas.

"Museo de Arte Moderno," Mark said to the driver. Then he slid down in the seat as far as he could without being too obvious and took out his PDA.

"The Museum of Modern Art?" Kate guessed. "That's where we're going?"

He nodded. "We need some place to mix in with crowds, and I don't want to go back to El Centro since that's probably where they'll look first." He signed on to the PDA.

"You're calling for help, I hope?"

He nodded. "There's a U.S. helicopter coming to La Rosa today," he said softly. "But I don't think I could get a taxi to take us that far so I'm going to contact the agent in charge of my operation and see what assistance he can give us."

While they drove through the streets of old Cartagena, Mark typed on the small keyboard of the PDA. He explained their situation to Perez succinctly, and after a few minutes Perez replied:

Cristobal Morales is in Cartagena picking up the Jeep you abandoned there. He can take you back to La Rosa.

This was better than Mark had dared hope for.

Can he meet us at the Museo de Arte Moderno *as quickly as possible?*

Perez answered:

He will be there in fifteen minutes. Then he will take you to meet the helicopter.

Mark was overwhelmed with relief. After all the confusion and misinformation and danger—finally everything was going to be okay. The FBI had not abandoned him after all. They were going to get him and Kate out of Colombia. Solana and Emilio were going to be rescued. He leaned his head back against the seat. Kate reached out and squeezed his hand, indicating that she had read the messages.

He wanted to leave it at that, to be happy that they were going to get out alive. But he couldn't. With fingers that trembled slightly, he typed one more word.

Salazar?

The response came quickly.

Dead.

Mark couldn't stand to see the word staring out at him like an accusation, so he signed off and closed the PDA. Kate rested her head on his shoulder, offering what comfort she could. Without conscious thought, he slipped his hand into the pocket of his khaki pants, and he closed his fingers around the small package that had once contained a single piece of chewing gum.

* * *

Beth Gamble walked into the playroom and found Miracle and Annabelle watching the children. "Where's Miss Eugenia?"

"I'm not sure," Miracle replied.

"Well, she just got a call from Miss George Ann reminding her that the Haggerty Bell Choir has a practice on Sunday afternoon at two o'clock," Beth told them. "If I don't deliver that message, I'll be on Miss George Ann's bad side, and that's a place where no one wants to be."

Annabelle raised both eyebrows. "Eugenia's going to be in the Haggerty Bell Choir?"

"Is that one of those groups that shakes bells to the tune of songs?" Miracle asked.

"Yes, and our Haggerty group is particularly bad," Annabelle acknowledged with a frown. "Eugenia always said the Statue of Liberty would jump off her pedestal and swim back to France before she'd be a part of that choir."

"And now she's practicing with them at two o'clock on Sunday," Miracle said. "Somebody better check and see if the Statue of Liberty is still in New York Harbor."

Beth laughed, but Annabelle didn't even smile. "It seems like Eugenia's been doing several things lately that she said she'd never do."

Miracle nodded. "Now that you mention it, that's true. At the bridge club meeting, she missed an opportunity to make fun of Miss George Ann for bragging about her daddy donating the land the church was built on. She agreed to help fold napkins in the shape of baby diapers for Miss George Ann's neighbor, and now she's joined the bell choir."

"Maybe it's stress from all this with Kate and Mark that's affecting her personality," Beth suggested.

"Or maybe George Ann is blackmailing her over that bridge club hosting," Annabelle proposed.

Miracle's eyes narrowed. "Surely even Miss George Ann wouldn't be so low."

"Have you *met* George Ann?" Annabelle demanded.

"You've got a point there," Miracle said.

* * *

When they reached the art museum, Mark paid the taxi driver and led Kate up the stairs and into the building. He took a position near a window, where he could lean against the wall and watch for the man with the Jeep. A guide walked up and asked if they would like to sign up for the next tour. Mark shook his head and said something in Spanish. The guide nodded politely and moved away.

"What did you say?" Kate was becoming increasingly frustrated with her inability to understand most of what was said around her.

"I told her that we were waiting for a friend to join us," Mark replied absently, his eyes searching the street outside. He checked his watch. "Eight more minutes."

Kate studied Mark and was thankful that he looked much better than he had in the airport—still not robust by any means, but well enough to stand without the constant risk of collapse. She had the chance to look at just a few of the exhibits nearby before Mark called to her. "Cristobal is here," he said.

They walked out into the warm Colombian sunshine and climbed into the battered Jeep parked by the curb. The man behind the wheel looked to be in his mid-forties, and Mark introduced him as Cristobal Morales.

"Cristobal has been very helpful to me during my stay in La Rosa," Mark told her after the formalities were out of the way. "He rented a house for me and purchased this fine Jeep."

"Thank you for taking care of my husband," Kate said to the lawyer. "And thank you for giving us a ride to La Rosa."

"It is my privilege," he replied courteously. "And I apologize in advance for the necessity to rush out of town. But I guess you heard about the attack on Señor Salazar's convoy?"

Mark nodded. "We heard."

"I know you were his friend," Cristobal said. "And because of that I offer you my condolences. As a result of the attack, there has been talk of declaring martial law—which might be for the best. Lawlessness seems to breed lawlessness, especially here in Colombia."

"You think Salazar's men will retaliate?"

Cristobal shrugged. "They might. Others will take the opportunity to settle old scores, and soon bullets will be flying everywhere. It seems that you have chosen a good time to leave La Rosa."

"If we can get to the helicopter in time," Mark replied.

"Yes," Cristobal agreed. "That is the big question."

The trip to La Rosa was hot and dusty and stressful. They were stopped several times, Mr. Morales showed the soldiers his paperwork, and they passed through the roadblocks. With the windows down it was too loud for conversation, so Mark dozed against Kate's shoulder in between security checks.

Finally Cristobal slowed the Jeep and turned off the highway onto a gravel back road. "It won't be long now," he said.

Kate took a deep breath and willed herself to relax for the first time since they had left the airport in Cartagena.

* * *

Emilio parked the truck at the base of the hill behind the clearing where the helicopter was scheduled to land in an hour. He quickly checked the area to be sure that no one else was there and then opened his duffel bag and pulled out a PDA identical to the one Mark Iverson had used in Cartagena. He signed on, and after making a report, he waited for a response. Once he had his orders, Emilio signed off and returned the PDA to his duffel bag. Then he hurried up the hill and looked for a good place to hide.

* * *

Solana packed her purse with a few items that she couldn't bear to leave behind and hurried down to the service entrance behind the kitchen. The chef was waiting for her there. He led the way to the truck parked in the driveway used by delivery personnel.

Once they were settled in the cab of the truck, she asked, "Where is Lucien?"

"There is some kind of problem, and all the men have been called to the barracks," the chef told her. "If we leave quickly, we should be gone before he notices, and I won't have to hurt him."

Solana nodded gravely. "I've told several people that I was going shopping with you. Maybe he won't come searching for me if he does notice."

"That was very wise," the chef said as they drove through the first checkpoint. The guard waved them through without interest.

"It must be a very bad problem," Solana remarked. "He barely even looked at us."

"They aren't so concerned about who is leaving the compound," the chef said. "It's people coming in that require more scrutiny."

In Solana's experience, she was watched closely coming and going, but maybe it was the difference that occurred when General Vargas was away. Whatever the reason, she was grateful. They passed through the other two checkpoints with similar ease and turned onto the road leading to La Rosa.

"Well, that was easy," Solana said, her mood improving with each mile they traveled away from the compound. "You must be a lucky man."

The chef smiled. "Yes, today luck has been with us."

At the edge of La Rosa, the chef turned off the main highway onto a gravel road. They followed the road up a hill to a large clearing.

"This is where the helicopter will land," he told her. "Let me notify my contact that we have arrived." He pulled a small PDA from his pocket and signed on. Then he typed in a short message. Solana waited impatiently until he signed off and put the PDA back in his pocket. "Your boyfriend is already here."

"Emilio?" she breathed.

"Yes," the chef confirmed. "Now let's make sure he's alone."

They left the truck and circled around the clearing on foot. They were almost back to their starting point when Emilio came up behind them. Solana embraced him enthusiastically. He held her close for a few seconds before setting her firmly away from him.

"We must concentrate on getting out of here now," he told her with unusual seriousness. "There will be time for celebration later." He turned to the chef. "Agent Esteban?"

"Agent Delgado?"

The men shook hands.

Solana regarded Emilio with a combination of shock and admiration. "Agent?"

"I'm sorry I couldn't tell you sooner," Emilio said. "But you weren't need-to-know."

"You are an agent—for the Americans?"

"I *am* an American," Emilio admitted. "And an FBI agent. I'm just not very funny or very fast."

She shook her head. "I can't believe it."

"You'll have time to get used to the idea later," the chef said. "Right now I suggest that we separate and take up positions on opposite sides of the clearing."

Emilio nodded and checked his watch. "The helicopter is scheduled to arrive in five minutes. Mr. Iverson and his wife should get here about the same time."

"*They* are going with us?" Solana asked.

Emilio's expression was tense. "If they can make it before the helicopter leaves."

She frowned. "The helicopter won't wait for them?"

Emilio shook his head. "Everyone for miles will see it land, so it will be able to stay only for a few minutes."

"What will Mr. Iverson and his wife do if they don't make it in time?" Solana asked.

The agent Solana had known as her father's chef shrugged. "They will find another way out of Colombia."

"Don't worry," Emilio told her. "They will make it."

The chef pointed to the far end of the clearing. "I'll go over there. Delgado, you stay here with Solana."

Once the chef was gone, Emilio pulled Solana into the trees and put a finger to his lips. She nodded that she understood. They must be silent. Now there was nothing to do but wait.

* * *

Mark heard the sound of the helicopter's rotor in the distance as Cristobal parked the Jeep beside a green truck that Mark recognized as one from Rodrigo Salazar's fleet of military vehicles. Hopefully it was the one Emilio had driven from Cartagena.

"Come, we must hurry," Cristobal urged as they climbed from the Jeep and walked toward the clearing.

Mark shaded his eyes and saw the Blackhawk helicopter descending. Emilio and Solana emerged from trees, and the two groups greeted each other with a quick wave. Then they all moved toward the helicopter.

CHAPTER 12

After several hours of being bossed around by Miss Eugenia, Miracle told Annabelle, "She's just about to make me sorry I helped her."

Annabelle stopped and regarded Miracle. "You helped Eugenia?"

"I sure did," Miracle replied proudly. "You know how that hateful Miss George Ann made Miss Eugenia be her partner in bridge and join the embarrassing bell choir?"

Annabelle nodded. "Yes."

"Well, a little while ago, she called to remind Miss Eugenia about that baby diaper napkin folding meeting. I told her I thought Miss Eugenia was too busy pre-tilling her garden to come to the phone."

"Pre-what?"

"Pre-tilling," Miracle repeated. "It's just something Miss Eugenia made up to keep Kate and the kids busy. But I told that mean woman that I'd heard it was the secret to Miss Eugenia's success with gardening."

Annabelle's eyes got wide. "And what does this 'pre-tilling' involve?"

"You have to spend hours and hours in your garden with a rake turning over the top few inches of dirt right after you turn under your old garden but before the first frost."

"We may not have a frost until January," Annabelle pointed out.

"But you can't be sure. So I suggested that Miss George Ann had better get herself out in her garden and start raking if she wanted to have nice vegetables next summer."

Annabelle threw back her head and laughed. "Miracle, you're a genius!"

The agent smiled. "You got that right, too."

* * *

Emilio and Solana stood just in front of Kate and Mark in the clearing as they all watched the helicopter make its final approach. Cristobal was behind Mark, and everyone was braced against the wind created by the rotor.

"You should go with us," Mark yelled over his shoulder to the lawyer.

Cristobal shook his head. "No. My future is in La Rosa."

The helicopter touched down, and after a brief pause the pilot opened the side door. "We need to load quickly," he informed them. "The sooner we get out of here, the better." Then he returned to his seat.

Emilio helped Solana up into the helicopter and stepped back for Mark to do the same with Kate. Once the women were inside, the men threw their bags in. Then Mark waved toward the open door. "You next," he told Emilio. But before the young man could comply, shots rang out.

Startled, Mark turned to see General Vargas and a couple of Salazar's soldiers emerge from behind the helicopter. Apparently, they had been waiting in the woods on the far side of the clearing and had used the helicopter to shield their approach.

"Stay away from this door," Mark called to Kate and Solana. Then he stepped forward and pulled his gun. Emilio did the same.

Vargas and his men were arranged in a neat little arc, effectively pinning Mark and Emilio against the helicopter. Getting the advantage had been child's play for Vargas, and once again Mark was forcefully reminded of Bowen's dire predictions regarding his abilities to survive a real field operation.

"Well," Vargas favored Mark with an evil grin, "you thought you could come to our little town, ingratiate yourself to Rodrigo Salazar, do your foul deeds, and then turn tail and run. I'm sorry to disappoint you, but I really have to deny your fairy tale a happy ending."

He waved toward the helicopter with his gun. "At the very least, I think I deserve to get the girl."

"Why you . . ." Emilio snarled and ran toward the older man.

One of the soldiers with Vargas raised his weapon, and the general yelled, "Do not fire! I will handle him."

Instead of shooting Emilio as logic demanded, Vargas braced himself for the impact. The two men collided violently and struggled upright briefly before Vargas swept Emilio's feet, and they fell to the ground. Mark was trying to think of a way to either help Emilio or use the distraction caused by the fight to disarm one of the soldiers. But before he could formulate a plan, a bullet whizzed past Mark's face, and the soldier in front of him collapsed with a neat hole in the center of his head.

Then Mark watched in fascination as a man dressed in a chef's uniform dove from behind the helicopter and tackled the other soldier. Mark rushed to help the chef, and in minutes they had the second soldier subdued and tied up with duct tape that the chef produced from his pocket.

"I never leave home without it," the chef said. Then he held out his hand and introduced himself. "Agent Esteban. You're Iverson?"

Mark nodded. "You're leaving with us?"

"Yes," Esteban confirmed. "But my assignment was to stay back until the last minute in case of trouble." He glanced down at the men grappling on the ground. "I decided this qualified as trouble."

Once again, Mark felt inadequate. He should have been watching for trouble himself—then Vargas and his men wouldn't have found it so easy to sneak up on them. "Is there anything we can do to help him?" he asked, pointing at Emilio and Vargas, who were locked in a mutual death grip.

The chef shook his head. "I don't dare take a shot for fear I'll hit Delgado."

Mark glanced through the open door of the helicopter and saw that Kate and Solana were watching. He motioned for them to stay low. Then he circled the fighting men, determined to be prepared if Vargas gained the upper hand. Finally, after several tense minutes, youth triumphed over age, and Emilio rolled on top of the general. The young man took the opportunity to slam his fist into the general's face. Panting, he said, "That is for putting your filthy hands on my wife."

"Your wife?" Vargas gasped through his bleeding lips.

Emilio smiled, but there was no humor in his expression. "That day we had the flat tire—when Solana should have been in the theater and you assumed I was taking advantage of her. That missing hour was actually spent standing before a priest."

"You presumptuous little . . ." Instead of finishing his insult, Vargas whipped his right hand up and buried a small knife in Emilio's chest. "That is for taking what was rightfully mine," the general hissed.

Shock and pain registered on Emilio's face as he collapsed backward off of Vargas.

Solana screamed, "Emilio!" Then she leaped from the helicopter and ran toward the prone figure on the ground.

"Stay back!" Vargas commanded, but she ignored him.

Throwing herself on top of her husband, Solana grabbed Emilio's gun and pointed it at Vargas. "If you come closer, I'll shoot you!" she promised.

"Don't be ridiculous, Solana," Vargas said, his voice taking on a wheedling quality. "You don't even know how to fire a gun."

She proved him wrong by squeezing off a shot that missed his head by inches. As Vargas ducked, Mark and the chef both stepped forward. The chef grabbed Vargas by the arms, and Mark covered the general with his gun.

"It's over," Mark said. Then he turned to the chef. "We're going to need a little more of that duct tape."

The chef pulled the roll out of his pocket and tore off a long piece.

"Once you get the general tied up, we'll take him with us on the helicopter," Mark said.

"I'm afraid I can't let you do that." The voice was soft and apologetic, and for a minute Mark couldn't remember whom it belonged to. Then he turned his head slightly to see Cristobal Morales standing a few feet away. He had a revolver in his hand pointing right at them. "Drop the gun," he instructed Mark. "You too, Solana."

"Cristobal?" Mark tried to force his tired brain to think clearly. "What are you doing?" he demanded.

"I'm sorry," the lawyer said, and he really did seem to be. "Now put down your gun."

"But you work for the FBI," Mark reminded the man. "You work for *me!*"

Cristobal gave Mark the typical Colombian shrug. "I work for many people. Working for you has been pleasant, but you have no money. The FBI pays me well, but General Vargas has threatened to kill my daughters if I don't cooperate with him. I didn't think he would really go that far, but after Pilar . . ." Cristobal shook his head as if to clear it. "Drop the gun, Mark. I don't want to shoot you in front of your wife, but to save my daughters—I will. I have no choice. I'm sure you understand."

And of course, Mark did understand. He dropped his gun, and Solana tossed Emilio's down beside it.

"Now you," Cristobal motioned to the chef. "You let go of the general."

The chef gave Mark an irritated look and then released Vargas's arms.

The general leaned down and retrieved both the guns. "Now, where were we?" He glanced around. "Oh, yes. Solana, stand up before I shoot you."

Whether to save her own life or to prevent a bullet from hitting Emilio by mistake, Solana obeyed.

"And Cristobal, you help the chef put Emilio's body into the helicopter. Then they can be on their way. Only Mr. Iverson and the beautiful Solana will be staying with me." The general turned his malevolent smile back to Mark. "As you said earlier, with the two of you, it is *personal.*"

Mark gave the chef a slight nod. Then he stood back and watched as Emilio was unceremoniously dumped into the helicopter. However, when the chef climbed in and tried to close the door, Kate stopped him. "Mark!" she called.

He looked across the space that separated them. He'd always thought that when the end came, it would be important to him that they at least have the chance to say good-bye, but as the reality of the situation sank in, he realized that no amount of time would have seemed sufficient. They'd had a great weekend in Cartagena, and they had the promise of eternity. It would have to be enough. He smiled and gave her a little wave of farewell.

Solana was younger, less mature, and had not reached the same understanding. "We have to do something!" she cried desperately.

"Anything we do might keep the helicopter from leaving," Mark pointed out. "And I want my wife to get away safely." He looked at Solana. "If Emilio is still alive, he'll need medical attention soon to stay that way."

Tears coursed down Solana's face, but she nodded. The helicopter must leave.

The pilot revved the motor in preparation for departure, and Mark felt a mixture of relief and panic. Kate would be safe. Kate would be gone. He ignored Vargas, who was approaching them slowly, and Solana, who was crying pitifully. Mark knew he was going to have to figure out some way to protect Solana from Vargas, but that could wait until he was sure that Kate was safely on her way. Then an explosion rent the afternoon air.

His first thought was that Vargas had blown up the helicopter, and he forced himself to look that direction, but the helicopter was still hovering a few feet above the ground. Mark turned to the spot where seconds ago Hector Vargas had been and saw only fire. Then a lone figure came running toward them from the woods.

"Perez," Mark whispered.

"Did you think I would leave you to handle this yourself?" the other agent asked.

That was exactly what Mark had thought, but he'd never been so glad to see anyone in his life. Well, almost never.

Perez waved to the helicopter, and it circled around and lowered to the ground. "Hurry and get inside," he instructed Mark and Solana. "I just blew Vargas up with a flare. Anyone who didn't already know we were in these hills does now."

As the door of the helicopter opened, Mark searched for Kate. She was strapped into a seat near a window and looked terrified but otherwise okay. He and Perez assisted Solana into the helicopter then jumped in themselves. As they left the ground, Mark saw Cristobal standing by the edge of the clearing, the gun hanging at his side. He could have made an attempt to stop them, but he didn't.

"Help me get this door shut!" Perez called to Mark over the roar of the engine and the rotor.

Mark put his shoulder against the open door, and together they slammed it closed. Then he leaned over and wrapped an arm around Kate's shoulders. "Are you okay?" he whispered.

"I think so," she replied weakly.

Mark studied Emilio, who was stretched out on the floor of the helicopter. Perez, Solana, and the chef were all clustered around him.

"He's alive," Perez reported when he glanced up and saw Mark watching them. "We're going to an aircraft carrier where he can get basic medical attention. Then they'll fly him to a mainland hospital."

"What about us?" Mark asked, hoping he didn't sound selfish. "We have children we need to see about."

Perez nodded. "Don't worry. We will get you home."

Mark sat down and pulled Kate close beside him. Once Perez had done what he could for Emilio, he joined them.

"So, Emilio was the second agent inside Salazar's compound?" Mark said.

"Yes," Perez confirmed. "Until you removed him."

Mark frowned. "If you hadn't been so secretive about this operation . . ."

Perez held up a hand to forestall further comments on the subject. "You saved his life, and I'm not complaining. But it did reduce my workforce. Fortunately the chef, Esteban, was in a good position to relay information."

"And they didn't know about each other?" Mark asked.

Perez shook his head. "That would have been too dangerous. Vargas had a tendency to torture people if he thought they had a secret. It was best to keep everyone in the dark."

"Well, if that was your goal, you were successful," Mark said, a little less resentful of the secrecy now that he understood the purpose behind it. "When we found Pilar dead, I assumed she was one of your people."

"No," Perez replied. "She was just a nice person trying to help a frightened girl."

Mark put a hand to his temple and rubbed. "So much killing."

"You have no idea," Perez answered. "The casualties on this mission have been minimal." He glanced over at Emilio. "I hope we can save him. He was a great recruit. Both his parents are naturalized American citizens. Emilio himself was born in the U.S., but his grandmother lived in Bogotá until her death a year ago. Once he was recruited and trained, we placed him back there, living with his grandmother and mingling with college students. He was able to get a great deal of information that way. Then when his grandmother died, he applied for employment in Salazar's army without causing any suspicion."

"What was his role in the operation?"

"He didn't have one," Perez surprised him by saying. "We got Delgado in months ago and intended for him to be a long-term plant, almost a sleeper. He fed us information occasionally, but mostly he was just there if we ever needed him. I didn't anticipate his assignment as Solana's bodyguard, and I sure didn't expect them to fall in love. Once he got on Vargas's bad side, I knew I was going to have to get him out. But I'll find another spot for him."

Mark looked back over at Emilio. "He's been through a hard time," Mark said. "He may want a desk job for a while."

This thought seemed unfathomable to Perez. "Not too long, I hope. He's got the potential to be a great undercover agent."

Mark watched Solana stroking the young man's cheek and smiled. "Don't get your hopes up," he told Perez.

* * *

When they landed on the aircraft carrier, Mark watched as the side doors of the helicopter were flung open and Emilio was taken off by medics. Solana paused to give Mark a quick hug before she hurried after the stretcher that held her husband. A man wearing a jumpsuit and headphones indicated for Kate and Mark and Esteban to follow him.

"You're not going with us?" Mark asked Perez.

"No, I've got to go back to La Rosa. There are a few loose ends still to be tied up there."

"Does Solana know about her father?"

Perez shook his head. "She has enough to deal with right now. Her mother can tell her later."

Mark extended his hand. "Thanks for your help."

Perez clasped his hand briefly. "Good luck." He waved to Kate and Esteban. Then he pushed the doors closed, and the helicopter lifted off from the deck of the ship and lumbered back toward the Colombian shore.

Once the combined noise of the rotor and the engine faded, their escort pulled off his headphones and smiled at Mark and Kate. "I hear you folks have a plane to catch."

* * *

Kate, Mark, and Esteban were taken to a small lobby to wait for their respective planes. When Mark went to the restroom and saw himself in the mirror, he was shocked by his appearance.

"Remind me to thank Mr. Mitchell for that gum," he told Kate when he returned to the lobby. "That stuff nearly killed me."

Kate bit her lower lip. "You might not want to mention the gum to Mr. Mitchell."

Mark frowned. "Why not?"

"Because he doesn't know anything about it."

"Then who gave it to you?"

Kate was staring at her hands. "I'll tell you after this is all over, after you've answered all the questions you're going to be asked when you get back to Atlanta. But not now."

"Kate," he began.

"Please, Mark," she interrupted firmly. "You're just going to have to trust me on this."

He considered for a few seconds and decided that other than for curiosity's sake, he really didn't need to know where she got the gum. He put an arm around her shoulders and pressed a kiss to her cheek. "I trust you."

Esteban returned from the restroom and took a seat across from them. He picked up a magazine, leafed through it briefly, then tossed it back down. "Man," he said. "Am I glad that assignment is over! It is a wonder Salazar didn't kill me!"

Mark thought of his dead friend. "You're lucky Salazar was so patient."

"I guess I can't be too mad at Perez, though, since he saved our bacon in the end," Esteban continued.

Mark nodded.

"He took his sweet time though," Esteban added.

"Yes," Mark agreed, wishing the other man would be quiet.

"I kept wondering when he was finally going to come help you."

Mark felt the beginnings of a headache and didn't know if it was the residual effects of the gum or Esteban's incessant talking. "What do you mean?"

"I saw Perez get there about the same time as Vargas and his goons, but he didn't approach. I guess he was doing reconnaissance, or maybe he was waiting for the right time or something. I was afraid he was going to wait too long—until Vargas shot you."

"Perez has had a lot of experience in situations like that."

"Yeah, I guess," Esteban replied.

The door of the lobby opened, and a crewman stuck his head inside. "The plane for Albany leaves in ten minutes."

Mark stood and pulled Kate to her feet. "That's us," he said.

* * *

Miss Eugenia hung up the phone and called the room to attention. "Kate and Mark are on their way home. They should be here in a couple of hours."

"So, what are the plans?" Miracle asked.

"Plans?" Miss Eugenia seemed stumped by the question.

"Aren't we having a welcome home party?" Miracle elaborated.

"With the marine band playing 'When Johnny Comes Marching Home'?" Annabelle joined in.

Miracle was enjoying herself now. "And the Mormon Tabernacle Choir singing 'God Bless America'?"

"I'll bet Jack could get the president of the United States to come and give Kate and Mark some kind of medal for bravery," Annabelle suggested.

"Maybe we could make some signs that say 'Welcome Home Y'all'!" Miracle contributed.

Miss Eugenia shook her head. "You two need to go take a nap. You've obviously gone crazy."

The smile left Annabelle's face as she met Miracle's eyes. "Shoot," Miracle said.

Annabelle shrugged. "She always wins."

* * *

It was almost eight o'clock on Monday night when Kate and Mark drove into Haggerty. They pulled up in front of their house on Maple Street, where all was quiet.

"I was hoping that Miss Eugenia and the kids would be home," Mark said as they sat in front of their dark house. "But I guess that would have been too good to be true."

"We didn't tell her to move the children, and their safety has been an issue," Kate said in defense of their friend and neighbor.

Mark sighed. "You're right." He eased the van away from the curb, turned around in their driveway, and headed for the Gambles' house.

Based on the number of cars parked along Highway 11 by the sign that welcomed visitors to the Crossroads subdivision, Mark could tell that all was not quiet at the Gambles' home. Television vans with satellite equipment on top were gathered on the playground, countless cars lined the curbs, and crowds of people were gathered in the street.

"That's Winston's squad car." Kate pointed through the windshield. "That's Miracle's FBI car, and the other one belongs to the agents from Atlanta. I think that's Miss Polly's old Pontiac parked right beside it."

"I didn't think Miss Polly drove anymore," Mark said as he pulled to a stop beside a heap of bicycles.

"She rarely does," Kate confirmed. "I guess she didn't want to be left out of the fun."

Mark surveyed the bedlam before him. The flashing lights, the camera crews—there was even a little platform erected in the park across from the Gambles' house. The mayor was standing on the platform tapping a microphone repeatedly and saying, "Testing . . . testing."

"Apparently Miss Eugenia plans to welcome us home in style," Kate said.

Finally Mark sighed. "You're going to think I'm a coward."

She smiled across at him. "I doubt that."

"I know Miss Eugenia means well, but I just can't face this. Not tonight."

"I understand," she said. "But how can we avoid it and still reclaim our children?"

He considered the question for a few minutes and then pulled his cell phone from his pocket. He checked the previously dialed numbers and picked one. A few seconds later Jack Gamble answered. "Mark!"

"Hey, Jack," Mark responded. "We're here in Haggerty. In fact, we're parked a little ways from your house behind a few hundred vehicles and a thousand spectators."

Jack laughed. "Miss Eugenia just wanted to make sure you knew we missed you."

"We appreciate the thought," Mark assured him. "But we're exhausted. Is there any way we can slip the kids out and deal with all this tomorrow?"

"Just a minute and let me check with the boss," Jack requested.

Mark covered the receiver and told Kate, "He's asking Miss Eugenia."

She nodded.

A couple of minutes later Jack was back on the line. "Miss Eugenia has an idea, and I think it's a good one, but before we decide to go with it, I should warn you that it might lose you some points with the press. If you ever get into a fight with the FBI and need the media's help, you may regret dodging them tonight."

"I think I'm okay with the FBI," Mark told him. "Once I make a couple of money transfers tomorrow and fill out some expense reports, all the money I took should be accounted for."

"Okay then," Jack replied. "Here's the plan."

After ending his call with Jack, Mark turned to Kate. "Jack is going to tell the news crews that we were transported from an aircraft carrier to Albany."

Kate frowned. "That's true."

"What he's not going to tell them is that it happened an hour ago and that we're already in Haggerty. He'll lead them to believe that he's taking Emily and Charles to Albany to meet our plane."

"Then they'll follow him?" Kate guessed.

"That's the plan."

"And once they're all gone?"

"Whit Owens will drive Miss Eugenia and the kids to our house."

Kate sighed. "Sounds perfect to me."

Mark put the van into reverse and looked over his shoulder. "The hard part is going to be backing out of this mess."

* * *

Kate was standing at the living room window of her house thirty minutes later when Whit's Lexus drove quietly down Maple Street and turned into their driveway.

"Mark!" she called. "They're here!"

Mark rushed down the stairs wearing sweat pants and his favorite T-shirt. His long hair was still wet from his shower, but the scruffy beard was gone.

"You shaved," she said as they walked together toward the kitchen. "And just when I was getting used to that look."

"I'll never get used to it," he assured her. "And if I knew a barber who made house calls, I'd have a haircut before the night was over."

Kate was laughing when the back door swung open and their children rushed inside.

Several hours later, after Miss Eugenia and Whit and Miracle and Annabelle and Derrick and the Gambles and Miss Polly and Winston had all left, Kate climbed the stairs for the final time. When she reached the landing, she looked down the dark hallway and remembered about Tony and the fact that the situation with him had not yet been resolved.

"Kate," Mark called from their bedroom.

"Coming," she replied.

Then she hurried in to join him and tried not to worry anymore that night.

CHAPTER 13

On Tuesday morning, Kate and Mark tried to sleep in, but the children woke them up at seven. They tucked Emily and Charles in between them and listened to a detailed description of all that had happened during their stay at the Gambles' house. They were just getting to the good part when they heard someone knocking on the back door.

"That will be Miss Eugenia and Lady," Kate predicted.

"Can we go let them in?" Emily asked.

"Do we have to?" Mark muttered.

"Daddy means yes," Kate said with a stern look at her husband.

A few minutes later, Emily ran back into the bedroom. "It *is* Miss Eugenia and Lady," she confirmed. "They brought Annabelle, Miss Polly, and Miracle too!"

"And doughnuts!" Charles added as he rounded the corner behind his sister.

"Miss Polly brought sausage balls," Emily added.

Mark covered his head with a pillow. "And I thought getting shot at in La Rosa was the worst thing that could happen to me."

Kate put a hand over her mouth to hide a smile. "Tell the ladies we'll be down in just a minute," she instructed her children. She waited until the sound of little feet had faded down the stairs before pulling the pillow away from Mark. "Come on. You can take a little Southern hospitality."

Before Mark could answer, the phone rang. He smiled. "Saved by the bell."

She checked the caller ID and handed him the phone. "If you consider Dan Davis good luck."

Mark sighed. "I don't." Then he pushed the talk button and said, "Iverson."

* * *

When Mark walked into the kitchen a little while later, his family and their uninvited guests were all sitting around the table.

"We have pastries from Marsh's Bakery," Miss Eugenia announced.

"And a hundred sausage balls." Miracle held up a crystal punch-bowl brimming with Mark's favorite appetizers.

Miss Polly blushed with embarrassment. "I forgot that the FBI men were gone until I'd already made two batches."

Mark popped one in his mouth. "Their loss is our gain." He sat down beside Kate.

She frowned at the suit he was wearing. "You have to go to work today?"

He nodded as he searched the bakery sack to see what was left. "I've got to fill out some paperwork and handle a few financial things. Then this afternoon we're having an 'end of the operation' meeting. I hope Mr. Mitchell wants to go over everything that went wrong because I have quite a list."

"Mr. Mitchell?" Kate repeated, her displeasure obvious. "You're going to *Atlanta?*"

Mark looked up from the doughnut he'd just chosen. "I'm sorry. I thought when Dan Davis called earlier, you'd realize I'd be going into the field office there."

She shook her head. "No, I thought you could handle the paper-work and whatever else from Albany."

"It shouldn't take more than a day or two," Mark tried to be reas-suring.

"A day or *two!*" Now Kate looked close to tears. "The children haven't seen you in a week and . . ."

"Why don't you and the children go with Mark to Atlanta?" Annabelle suggested. "Derrick has some coupons for a free night's stay at the Peachtree Marriott that I'm sure he'd be glad to give you. That way while Mark is taking care of his paperwork and attending meetings, you and the kids can be relaxing in a luxury hotel."

Kate smiled at Annabelle. "Thanks. That sounds like a very good idea."

"If you've got more of those hotel coupons, I might take one," Miracle said. "My plane leaves early tomorrow morning, and I'd rather drive up to Atlanta today and spend the night."

"We've got several coupons, and you're welcome to one," Annabelle said generously.

"I think I'll go too," Miss Eugenia said. "That is if I can get Whit to keep Lady for me. I'll stay in the hotel room with Miracle and be nearby in case Kate needs help with the children while Mark's working in Atlanta. Then whenever he's finished, I'll ride home with them."

"Eugenia!" Annabelle cried. "You just shamelessly invited yourself along on their trip!"

"Not until after Miracle did first," Miss Eugenia pointed out. "And I only suggested it because I didn't want Kate to be alone with the children."

Annabelle was unconvinced. "Can't you leave these poor people alone for just a few hours?" she demanded.

"Of course I can, and I wouldn't dream of imposing!" Miss Eugenia replied.

"Miss Eugenia would be a big help," Kate said in a conciliatory tone.

Miss Eugenia gave her sister a haughty look. "In that case, I'll go and pack my bags."

* * *

Mark pulled the Iversons' van to a stop in front of the FBI field office in Atlanta. Miracle, who was driving the car the FBI had loaned to her, parked behind them. Mark climbed out, and Kate got behind the wheel.

"How long do you think this will take?" she asked.

"I'll hurry," he promised.

"And you're sure your FBI car is here?"

He nodded. "I'm sure. I'll meet you at the hotel as soon as possible."

Kate nodded. Then she followed the directions Miracle had gotten off the Internet to the Peachtree Marriott.

Miss Eugenia presented their coupons at the registration desk, and a valet led them up to their lovely, adjoining rooms. By the time Kate had paid the valet and closed the door, the children had jumped on all four of the beds and had turned on the big screen television.

"Can we watch a movie?" Emily asked.

"I think that sounds like a fine idea," Miss Eugenia said, referring to the *TV Guide* for an appropriate choice. "*Finding Nemo* is on pay-per-view."

"We like that one," Emily said with approval. Then she settled on the middle of a small couch centered in front of the television and gestured for Charles to join her.

Miss Eugenia moved toward the little kitchenette. "I'll get you some snacks out of this teensy refrigerator while Miracle figures out how to start the movie."

Once the movie was playing and the children were happily watching while eating M&Ms, Miracle and Miss Eugenia sat down by the window and started talking about chicken casserole recipes. The stress of the past few days had finally caught up with Kate, and she felt drained. She excused herself and walked into the adjoining suite. There she stretched out on one of the queen-sized beds. She closed her eyes and, without intending to, fell into a deep sleep.

She dreamed that she was at home, climbing the stairs. When she reached the landing, she looked down the hall and saw Tony standing at the far end—beckoning to her. She took several steps down the hall toward him. He spoke, and this time she was able to make out the words. *Mark is in danger. Go to him.*

Kate startled awake, and slowly the hotel room came into focus. She could hear the television and an occasional giggle from her children. From across the room came the muffled sounds of Miss Eugenia and Miracle still discussing recipes. *It was just a dream,* she told herself. But it had seemed so real that a lingering sense of disquiet remained.

Mark is in danger. Go to him. She shook her head, trying to shake free of the dream's grip. Mark wasn't in Colombia anymore. He was in Atlanta filling out paperwork at the FBI's field office. *Mark is in danger. Go to him.* She shuddered, unable to dismiss the persistent thought from her mind.

"Are you cold, Kate?" Miss Eugenia asked. Kate looked up to see the older woman standing in the doorway, watching her. "You keep shivering."

"I'm not cold," Kate replied. "But I had the dream again."

Miss Eugenia crossed the room and perched herself on the edge of Kate's bed. "The dream about Tony?"

Kate nodded. "Only this time I was able to understand what he was saying to me."

Miracle joined them and shifted smoothly into FBI agent interrogation mode. "What did he say?"

Kate hated to speak the words aloud, but she had come too far to back down now. "He said, 'Mark is in danger. Go to him.'"

The other two women regarded her for a few seconds. Then Miracle asked, "Where's your cell phone?"

Kate reached down to the side of the bed and pulled the phone out of her purse.

Miracle pointed at the cell phone in Kate's hand. "Call Mark now."

"You think he's really in trouble?" Kate asked as she pushed 1 on her speed dial.

"I think it's crazy for us to sit here and wonder," Miracle returned logically.

"I got the answering machine," Kate told them when she heard Mark's voice requesting that she leave a message.

"Try again."

Kate dialed again with the same result.

"Okay," Miracle said. "Now let's call Dan Davis. You got a speaker feature on that cell phone?"

Kate nodded.

"Good, use it so we can hear what he has to say."

Kate searched the phonebook on her cell phone and found Dan's number. She pressed *send* and *speaker*. His secretary answered and put Kate on hold. She drummed her fingers restlessly until Dan's voice came on the line.

"Mrs. Iverson!" he sounded friendly and anxious to help her. "What can I do for you?"

"I've been trying to reach Mark, but he's not answering his cell phone," she told him. "Do you know how I can get in touch with him?"

"I can't imagine why he wouldn't be answering his cell phone," Dan sounded honestly confused. "I spoke to him about an hour ago. He was leaving the bank and was headed to the dentist to have a special tracking device removed. Then he was supposed to stop by the warehouse on Market Street where we arrested all those pornography people last week. We found out this morning that there were some additional papers there that needed his signature. After that, he'll be coming back here for a meeting with Mr. Mitchell, and I can have him call you."

Kate frowned. "Why did Mark have to go to the warehouse to sign the papers? Couldn't they have been brought to the field office?"

They heard Dan sigh. "Look, Mrs. Iverson, I'm not sure about the details, but I was told that Mark would be here after he made a stop at the warehouse."

"I have a bad feeling about that." Kate didn't add, "My first husband came to me in a dream and told me Mark is in danger," deciding this admission would not strengthen her position. "Miracle Moore, the agent from Chicago, is here with me. I think the two of us will drive to that warehouse and check on Mark. Give me the address please."

There was a short pause, and then Dan said, "You don't want to go there, Mrs. Iverson." He sounded positive. "It's not in a good part of town, and the stuff lying around that warehouse was, well, pretty raunchy."

"You're right," she began. "I don't *want* to go there, but I feel I *need* to." Kate pulled a sheet of Marriott Hotel stationery and a pen from the nightstand drawer. "The address, please."

Dan recited the address with obvious reluctance. Then he said, "If you're worried about Mark, I'll be glad to call the Atlanta PD and ask them to send a car over to the warehouse—just to check things out."

"The police car is a good idea," Kate responded. "Thank you for your help." Then she disconnected the call and stood up. "Can you watch the kids for me, Miss Eugenia?"

"Don't I always?" the elderly woman replied.

Kate looked at Miracle. "Then let's go."

* * *

As Mark drove from the dentist's office toward the warehouse on Market Street, he reached for his cell phone to call Kate and was surprised to find it missing. He double-checked, but it wasn't in any of his pockets. It wasn't like him to misplace things, and the missing cell phone bothered him. But he knew that worrying about it was pointless. He just had one more stop to make, and then he could go back to the field office for the meeting with Mr. Mitchell. He was anxious to go over the entire operation and find out exactly what had been planned and what had been accomplished. Surely now that it was all over, the need-to-know policy would be moot.

He turned onto Market Street and started watching for the warehouse. This street was lined with buildings in similar states of disrepair, so it wasn't as easy to locate the warehouse he needed without police cars surrounding it. Finally he found the address and pulled his car to a stop at the curb.

The place looked deserted. Annoyed that Agent Faust was apparently going to be late—and even more annoyed that he had no cell phone to call him with—Mark climbed out of his car. He walked up to the front entrance, where a bored-looking security guard was standing.

"Excuse me," Mark said.

"You Iverson?" the man asked, pushing away from the wall and flicking a cigarette to the already littered ground.

"Yes," Mark confirmed. "I'm supposed to meet Agent Faust here."

"He told me to bring you back." The man fished in his uniform pocket and came up with a key that he inserted into the lock. The warehouse door swung open with a squeal of protest, and they entered the dark interior of the building. "This way," the guard said. Then he continued forward, weaving around deserted movie sets and stacks of chemical barrels.

With each step they took, Mark's uneasiness grew, and finally his hand moved to his service revolver. "Where is Faust?" Mark asked as he eased the gun from its holster.

"Watch your step," the guard warned, skirting a puddle of something in the floor. "Faust is in that little back office."

When they rounded a corner made mostly of old cardboard boxes, the small room where he and Dan had picked up the suitcases the previous week came into view. The light was on in the office, but there was no sign of Agent Faust. Mark was just about to ask the security guard if he could use a phone to call Dan Davis, when the other man turned suddenly.

Mark wasn't completely surprised to see a gun in the man's hand, but the phony security guard seemed stunned to find that Mark was ready for him.

* * *

Kate and Miracle arrived at the address Dan Davis had given them and saw Mark's FBI car parked in front. "If Mark was meeting an agent here, I wonder why there's not another car parked by his," Kate said as they climbed out of the car. "And what is that racket?"

Miracle led the way across the street to the warehouse. "Freight train," she said absently. "It must be close."

"It must be," Kate shouted back.

"The front door is standing open," Miracle pointed out when they reached the entrance. She pulled her gun and released the safety. "I'm going in to see what's happening. Stay right here."

Kate watched Miracle slip into the warehouse. She glanced around and decided she wasn't any safer on the street than she would be inside. Ducking into the old building, she hurried to catch up with Miracle. She found the agent working her way through a maze made of movie sets.

"I thought I told you to stay outside," the agent whispered loud enough to be heard over the train.

"Shhh!" Kate hissed. "Don't you know anything about sneaking up on people?"

Miracle rolled her eyes, and they proceeded forward silently and cautiously. When they reached a stack of chemical barrels near the rear of the building, Miracle threw out an arm to stop Kate. Then they peeked around the barrels and saw Mark and a security guard standing a few feet apart, pointing guns at each other. Kate's heart skipped a beat as Miracle put a finger to her lips in a completely unnecessary gesture.

Kate moved back and motioned for Miracle to do the same. Once they were a safe distance away, Kate whispered, "We've got to do something!"

"What?" Miracle demanded. "Mark's between us and that other guy, so if I try to shoot him, I might hit Mark instead. And anything we do will distract Mark and possibly get him killed. All we can do for now is stand quietly and watch. But if I see an opportunity to help Mark, you can be sure I'll take it."

Kate wanted to scream with frustration, but she knew Miracle was right. So she clenched her fists and nodded. "Okay."

* * *

"Why are you doing this?" Mark asked the other man. "I don't have any money with me. I've already given it all back to the FBI."

"I'll get paid," the man assured him. "Don't you worry about that."

"What are you getting paid for?" Mark asked. Then a terrible possibility occurred to him. "Did someone pay you to *kill* me?"

The man shook his head. "No, I'm just supposed to hold you until another guy gets here. But if you cause trouble, I have permission to wound you. So be still."

"I've got a gun too," Mark pointed out.

The other man shrugged. "So I guess whoever gets off the first shot wins."

"Or whoever aims best," Mark countered.

The other man shifted his weight from one foot to the other. "You got a point."

"How much longer do we have to wait until your boss gets here?" Mark asked, hoping the man would glance at his watch. Just a moment of distraction might be enough for Mark to rush him.

The man smiled but kept his eyes firmly on Mark. "Nice try. Don't worry, he'll be here soon."

Mark hoped that was true. The gun was heavy, and he wasn't fully recovered from the events in La Rosa. He wasn't sure how long he could hold it up and steady.

* * *

Kate looked between Mark and the fake security guard like a spectator at a ping pong match. She kept hoping to see the opportunity to help Mark that Miracle had mentioned. And finally she did see something. In the shadows behind the fake security guard, she saw a slight movement.

Squinting, she concentrated on the row of chemical barrels stacked along the far wall. There it was again—just a flicker that she wouldn't have noticed if she hadn't been specifically watching for it. Kate wanted to alert Miracle, but she was afraid if she took her eyes off the spot where she'd seen the movement, she'd never be able to find it again.

And then a face became visible around the edge of a barrel. Tony's face. His eyes met hers, and he nodded in silent communication. Unlike Miracle, he was in position to take down the security guard without risking Mark's safety. She nodded back. It felt good to be working with Tony again, especially to help Mark.

For a few seconds, her attention was torn between the armed standoff in front of her and Tony's maneuvering in the shadows. Then another voice spoke from the small office.

"Mark." Agent Perez, the man who had saved them in La Rosa, stepped into view. He was holding a gun and had it pointed at the man dressed as a security guard. "I have him. You can lower your gun."

Mark's shoulders slumped with relief as the hand that held the gun dropped to his side. "You keep turning up just in time to save the day," Mark said with a smile.

Tony stepped out from his hiding spot and crouched instantly into a shooting stance. In horror, her eyes followed the direction of his aim. His gun was pointed at Mark. She opened her mouth to scream a warning, but the sound was swallowed up by the explosion of gunfire.

Kate was turning toward Mark when Miracle tackled her to the ground. She was forcefully reminded of those awful seconds four years before, lying under the table at Mr. Morris's house in Miami. Guns were firing, people were dying, and she had been helpless to stop it then just as she was now. "Tony," she whispered. "Mark."

The gunshots stopped, but the feeling of déjà vu continued as Miracle rolled off Kate and several Atlanta police personnel rushed into the room, followed closely by Dan Davis. Kate pushed up to her knees and surveyed the room.

Mark was standing a few feet away and seemed to be unharmed. Tony, too, appeared okay. He was still crouched near the chemical barrels, several of which had been hit by stray bullets and were now spewing their contents onto the warehouse floor. Both Agent Perez and the man wearing the security guard uniform were lying in pools of their own blood.

"Grab him!" Mark directed the policemen to Tony. "He just killed an FBI agent!"

The policemen surrounded Tony and subdued him with more force than necessary.

Kate stood and ran across the few feet that separated her from Mark. "You're okay?" they asked each other simultaneously.

A quick hug reassured them both.

Then Mark turned and knelt beside Perez. Based on the size of the hole in his chest and the amount of blood he had already lost, Kate knew that his chances of survival were minimal.

Dan bent down on the opposite side of the fallen agent. "The other guy's dead," he told Mark. "I've called an ambulance for you, Perez. Try and hang in there for a few more minutes."

Perez laughed softly. Then he winced in pain. "I was told years ago that the best strategy can be destroyed by the smallest detail," he whispered. "And I guess that is true. I thought you were a brilliant choice," he told Mark. "Perfect for my plan, but in the end you proved to be my fatal mistake."

Mark frowned. "What are you talking about?"

By this time, Miracle had made it to her feet and had joined the group circling Agent Perez. She pointed at the wounded man and gasped. "He was going to shoot Mark."

"Perez?" Mark asked incredulously. "You mean *Tony* was going to shoot me."

Miracle shook her head. "No." She sounded positive. "Tony shot Perez to keep him from killing you!"

"He's not Tony," Kate corrected, looking at the man who stood across the room watching with his hands held behind his back by a police officer. The resemblance to Tony was very strong, but now she could see that the man was not her first husband.

Kate's comment didn't seem to register with Mark, however, since all his attention was directed at the FBI agent bleeding to death on the dirty warehouse floor. He grasped Perez by the now blood-soaked shirt and demanded, "*You* came here to *kill* me?"

Perez flinched. "Yes."

"You were the one who hired the phony security guard?" Mark's voice had lost the confused tone and now rose with anger. "We were waiting for *you!*"

"Yes, yes," Perez admitted wearily.

Clearly Mark still couldn't accept what he was hearing. "But I thought you were in La Rosa tying up loose ends."

Perez laughed again, but he was weaker now, and the sound was more like a moan. "I was headed there when I heard you and Esteban talking about me watching your confrontation with Vargas. I knew it was just a matter of time before you realized that I arrived with Vargas."

The look of shock on Mark's face deepened. "You *heard* me talking to Esteban? That's impossible. You were in the helicopter."

"The crown on your tooth provided me with audio whenever I wanted to listen in on your conversations."

Mark's teeth were clenched with fury as he demanded, "But why would you want to kill me—" Suddenly, understanding seemed to dawn on Mark's face. "You were working *with* Vargas?"

Perez shook his head. "Vargas worked for me." His voice was barely a whisper now. "Once I eliminated Salazar, I was going to take over his drug empire. I told you I have been studying the Colombian drug trade for years. I finally came to the conclusion that stopping the flood of illegal drugs that come into this country is impossible. Controlling production and distribution is the key. Salazar had the right idea, but he was too soft. I would have been different."

"I don't understand why you went to all the trouble to involve me," Mark said, his frustration obvious. "What was my purpose in the operation?"

Perez did his best to shrug under his dire circumstances. "I wanted something or someone to distract Mitchell and Bowen in Atlanta and Salazar in La Rosa. This element of my plan wasn't essential—but I felt it would give me extra room to maneuver. I looked through the files of almost a hundred Spanish-speaking agents, but I always kept coming back to you. Somehow I knew Salazar wouldn't be able to resist you, and I was right." Perez grimaced. "What I didn't know is that your incredible luck would bring down the whole operation."

Mark looked ill as he asked, "I guess you always planned to kill Vargas—you didn't do that just to save us."

"I knew from the beginning that at some point Hector Vargas would have to die," Perez rasped. "The man was too volatile. After Salazar and Vargas were out of the picture, I intended to have Cristobal Morales represent me with the other Colombian drug lords. I would use my position as an agent for the FBI to significantly reduce the competition. By the time I assumed my position as Salazar's successor openly, I would be in total control. However, I couldn't risk you making the connection between me and Vargas before I was ready. And so I decided you must die. But I hoped I could make your death look like it was connected to the porn bust . . ."

"It might have worked," Dan told Mark, "if your wife hadn't gotten worried about you."

"And if that man hadn't been following me." Kate pointed across the room to where Tony's look-alike stood listening to them.

They heard sirens in the distance.

"Too late," Perez whispered. And then he closed his eyes for the last time.

* * *

They all stood aside as the ambulance attendants rushed in and went to work on Perez. Kate watched them attach tubes and give injections, but it was useless. The man was dead.

Tears were leaking from her eyes, and she started to tremble. Mark removed his suit coat and draped it over her shoulders. Then he put an arm around her, trying to provide warmth and comfort. They watched silently as the ambulance attendants strapped Perez and the security guard onto stretchers and rolled them out of the warehouse. Once they were gone, Mark told the policemen to release the man who had saved his life, who looked so much like Tony.

Rubbing his wrists, the man approached them. When he stopped in front of Kate, she held out her hand and said, "I don't believe we've met. I'm Kate Iverson."

He took her hand in his. "I've had so many aliases over the years that I'm not sure who I really am, but the name I'm currently using is Terrance Sprayberry."

"Frisky?" Miracle asked.

The man nodded.

"Frisky?" Kate repeated. "The exotic dancer who's been renting a house from Miss Agnes Halstead?"

Frisky nodded again. "That's me."

"You also have an apartment in Las Vegas rented in the name of Troy Sorenson," Kate continued.

"I've lived in the Vegas area most of my life."

"And you look enough like my first husband to be his twin."

Frisky sighed. "That's how we met. They needed a couple of agents who could substitute for each other without the suspect noticing. So I was temporarily transferred to Chicago, and we were paired because of our resemblance."

"You're still buying his soap?" Miracle interrupted.

"Yes." Frisky didn't try to deny this either. "He got me hooked on that stuff."

"Why didn't you change the order out of his name after his death?" Miracle asked.

"It's his special scent," Frisky admitted. "I wasn't sure they'd sell it to me if I told them I wasn't Tony."

"And why do you have Tony's softball and a snapshot of the two of us on your mantel?" Kate persisted.

"He left them behind in the hotel room we shared during the case we were working. I took them with me, meaning to mail them to him in Chicago, but then I heard he'd been killed. I called and asked Mr. Evans what I should do with them, and he said since they didn't have any monetary value, I might as well just keep them."

Kate nodded. "That explains why they were in your possession. But I still don't understand—why did you have them prominently displayed in your apartment?"

For the first time, Frisky looked a little uncomfortable. "The ball and picture have been in a box with a bunch of other junk for years.

But a few days ago, Mr. Evans called and asked me if I still had them."

"Mr. Evans?" Mark repeated in confusion.

Kate was less surprised. "He told you to get them out of the box and put them on your mantel?" she guessed.

Frisky nodded. "And to lighten my hair and have it cut the way Tony used to wear his."

"Then to get on a plane for Albany?" Kate continued, feeling like a fool. She swung her head around and gave Miracle a suspicious look.

The other agent lifted her hands in a gesture of surrender. "I didn't know, I swear."

Kate returned her attention to Frisky. "Mr. Evans asked you to come to Haggerty and follow me?"

"It was more than that," Frisky replied. "He told me to be subtle, but he wanted you to think . . ."

"That Tony was still alive," Mark finished the sentence, his tone grim.

"Yeah. I only went into your house that one time so you'd smell the soap. The other times I just drove past or walked by."

"Why would Mr. Evans do that to me?" Kate whispered, hurt and angry at the same time.

Frisky shrugged. "I don't know."

"And why were you still following me?" Kate demanded. "The operation in Colombia is over."

"Actually, I was following Perez," Frisky admitted. "Mr. Evans released me from my assignment this morning and told me to catch a military transport back to Las Vegas. When I got to the base, I saw Perez and wondered what he was doing there when he was still supposed to be in La Rosa."

"How do you know Perez and where he's supposed to be?" Mark asked.

"As a security precaution, I've been monitoring all your phone calls for over a week," Frisky told them. "The more I learned about the operation in Colombia, the more concerned I got. It's very unusual for an agent to be running the show while keeping his SAC in the dark. I asked Mr. Evans to e-mail me everything he could find about the operation and the people involved. I smelled a rat before I saw Perez at the base, but his presence there confirmed it for me. So I followed him here."

"And it's a good thing you did," Miracle interjected. "Otherwise Mark might be dead right now."

"I appreciate your help," Mark said grudgingly. "But I'm not happy about the total invasion of our privacy, and I have a lot of questions about the whole operation."

Dan Davis clapped his hands together and said, "That's certainly understandable. Why don't we head down to the field office? Mr. Mitchell can probably answer most of your questions, and I'm sure he'd be glad to call Mr. Evans if necessary."

Mark gave his supervisor a bland look. "I don't know how glad Mr. Mitchell is going to be to see us, but I agree that we need to get to his office right away."

"I'm not really all that curious," Frisky told them. "So I think I'll head on back to Vegas." He gave Kate a little salute. "You've got my address if you need to contact me."

She nodded. "Thanks," she glanced up at Mark, "for everything."

He waved in acknowledgment and headed for the front entrance. Once he was gone, Dan stepped around a puddle and motioned for the others to follow. He led the way out of the warehouse to the government vehicles parked on the street.

By the time they got to the cars, Kate was crying again.

"I'm sorry you had to see all that," Dan Davis apologized, as if it had been his fault.

"You might be in the early stages of shock," Miracle added in concern. "Hold that coat tight around you."

Kate didn't argue, but she knew that it wasn't shock that was making her cry. For the past few days, she'd gotten used to the idea that Tony was alive. She didn't want him to be her husband, but she liked the idea that he was out there somewhere. Now she had to accept that Tony was really gone. After four years, it still hurt.

* * *

Mark opened the passenger door of his car. Once Kate was seated, he walked around and slid in behind the steering wheel. When he saw that Kate was crying and shivering, he turned on the heat, although it wasn't really cold in the car.

"Are you all right?" he asked.

She nodded. "Could you call Miss Eugenia and let her know we're okay?"

"I'll have to use your cell phone. Mine has disappeared." He frowned. "I guess Perez arranged that too."

Kate fished in her purse and pulled out her phone. Mark dialed Miss Eugenia's cell number and had a brief conversation with her. "She said the kids are fine. I told her we'd be back to the hotel as soon as we can." He handed Kate the cell phone. "Would you like me to take you to the hotel before I go to the meeting?"

Kate shook her head. "No, I've got some questions for Mr. Mitchell myself." She wiped at the tears on her face. "And Mr. Evans."

* * *

When they arrived at the field office, Dan pulled up beside Mark's car and told him to park in the visitor spaces near the front entrance. Then, after a brief stop at the security desk, Dan led them up to Mr. Mitchell's office. As Mark stepped over the threshold, he felt a familiar sinking feeling. It seemed that coming here was never a good thing.

Howard Bowen was sitting in the large leather chair behind Mr. Mitchell's desk. Dan walked over and stood behind the assistant SAC—whether in a supportive or protective position Mark couldn't tell. Britta Andersen was seated in one of the chairs in front of the desk, looking lovely and composed—and a little sad.

"How is Emilio?" Mark asked as he and Kate took the two seats beside her.

"He is doing well," she replied. "He had surgery last night, and the doctors are very hopeful. I will be going to Miami to join them as soon as we conclude our business here." Britta leaned a little closer. "Solana told me some of what you did for them. I cannot thank you enough."

"She's a fine girl," Mark replied softly. "Very brave. You should be proud."

Britta nodded. "I am."

"And Emilio is completely devoted to her. I think they will be very happy together."

Britta smiled. "I hope so."

"I'm sorry about Salazar."

The Swedish woman lowered her eyes. "Thank you."

Miracle dragged a chair over and placed it beside Kate. Introductions were made, and Mr. Bowen said, "I'm not sure exactly where to begin. Some of what needs to be said will have to wait until we excuse Ms. Andersen and Mrs. Iverson."

"Ms. Andersen and my wife already know a great deal about this operation," Mark pointed out. "And since they are under no obligation to keep silent, it seems wise to encourage their cooperation rather than to insult them."

With a long-suffering sigh, Mr. Bowen nodded. "Very well. Ladies, I request that you keep anything you hear in this room today confidential."

Both women nodded in acceptance.

Mr. Bowen looked relieved. "Thank you."

"Where is Mr. Mitchell?" Mark asked.

Mr. Bowen cleared his throat. "He is on a jet headed to Washington."

"About Perez?" Mark guessed.

Mr. Bowen nodded. "Total disaster was averted by the death of Agent Perez, but if he had been successful in his attempt to install himself as head of the Colombian drug cartels . . ." Mr. Bowen shuddered.

"It would have been a terrible humiliation for the Bureau," Dan said, completing the thought for his boss.

"You got that right," Miracle concurred.

Mr. Bowen glanced briefly at Miracle before he turned to Mark and said, "Dan has been fully briefed on the operation, and before he left, Mr. Mitchell authorized us both to answer any questions you have."

"Maybe you could start by telling us what the actual operation was," Mark suggested with barely concealed hostility. "Since the story I was given to start with was pure fiction."

"What you were told was basically accurate," Mr. Bowen corrected. "You just weren't given the whole truth. That's standard procedure for covert operations—which we wouldn't expect you to understand since you have no training in that area."

"Don't expect me to believe that the FBI handles other covert operations the way this one was run," Mark countered. "Otherwise the United States wouldn't be a superpower."

Neither Mr. Bowen nor Dan seemed to have a response, so Mark pressed on.

"You told me I was being sent into La Rosa to befriend Rodrigo Salazar, to distract him so his daughter could be rescued. Actually I was being sent to help you kill him."

"Agent Perez created and ran the operation," Mr. Bowen said. "He deceived us all."

"Are you saying that you and Mr. Mitchell didn't know he planned to kill Salazar?"

"We knew that there was a chance Salazar would die," Mr. Bowen admitted. "But *murder* was not the stated goal of the operation, and Salazar has been on the FBI Most Wanted List for years. His death is not something I'm willing to apologize for. I do apologize that I failed to see that Perez had gone over the edge. He was my right-hand man. I worked closely with him and should have noticed."

Mark agreed but decided that he would accomplish nothing by saying so. Suddenly he felt extremely tired. He hoped he never had another covert assignment. He just wanted to go home—back to Albany and the quiet resident agency there. "What will happen now—in Colombia?"

"Someone else will take over for Salazar," Mr. Bowen said. "Maybe it will be a moderate with a sense for business like Salazar. Or maybe it will be a bloodthirsty psychopath like Hector Vargas. But either way, the war will go on. We will continue to fight, and someday we'll win."

Mark nodded. "I hope so."

Kate cleared her throat, directing everyone's attention toward her. "Excuse me, Mr. Bowen, but I have a question."

"Go ahead, Mrs. Iverson," the assistant SAC invited.

"I'd like to know why Mr. Evans asked my first husband's former partner to impersonate him and make me think that he was still alive." Kate's eyes filled up with tears. "Do you have any idea how much pain that has caused us?"

Mr. Bowen glanced at Dan and sighed. "I guess we owe you an apology for that, too, Mrs. Iverson."

Dan leaned forward. "I know it's hard to understand, but running an operation is kind of like orchestrating a little war. Sometimes you have to make difficult choices. You posed a threat to the operation in general and to Mark specifically. So Mr. Mitchell had to distract you."

"We called Evans in Chicago." Mr. Bowen took over the explanation. "He offered to loan us Agent Moore and to arrange for your first husband's look-alike to come in from Las Vegas. They were to provide additional protection as well as the needed distraction."

"And I might point out that they were both very useful," Dan reminded her.

Kate looked over at Miracle and nodded. "That's certainly true. Thank you for telling me the reasons behind your decision."

Mr. Bowen stood. "Well, if that's all your questions, I have a lot of damage control to do."

"So this is over?" Mark asked. "I can go back to Albany and resume my normal life?"

"Actually," Mr. Bowen said, "when Washington called to request a meeting with Mr. Mitchell, they felt that it would be best if you were inaccessible to the press for a couple of weeks. Also, they want to be sure that no one from Colombia still has any ill will against you."

"Vargas and Perez are both dead," Mark pointed out.

"True," Dan agreed. "But they just want to be sure."

"So you're going to be on vacation for a while," Mr. Bowen informed him.

"How long?"

"At least the next fourteen days, and that might have to be extended depending on intelligence and press reports," Dan answered.

Mr. Bowen looked at Kate. "Of course, what we're proposing is a fully sanctioned, paid vacation."

Kate smiled. "I expected no less." Then she turned to Mark. "Your parents have been upset by all this. It would very reassuring for them to be able to have a nice long visit with you."

Mark didn't have any objection to taking a few days off work, but what he really wanted was for things just to be normal again. However, it sounded like he didn't have any choice in the matter. "Okay."

Miracle leaned forward. "Now you just got to figure out how to keep Miss Eugenia from tagging along on your vacation."

Kate laughed. "She does think she's a part of the family."

Miracle nodded. "That's what I'm talking about."

"She's pretty attached to Miracle, too," Mark said thoughtfully. "I'll bet I could arrange a trip to Chicago that she'd enjoy."

That wiped the smile off Miracle's face. "I'll be kind of busy for the next couple of weeks—no time for visitors."

Mr. Bowen took a step toward the door. "If you'll excuse us . . . Dan, would you step out into the hall?"

Once they were gone, Mark said, "I think Mr. Bowen is trying to give us a few minutes alone to say good-bye."

Britta smiled. "That is remarkably sensitive of him."

Mark smiled back. "This must be very difficult for you."

"Yes."

Mark cleared his throat. "I didn't want to betray his friendship . . ."

Britta held up a hand. "I understand, and Rodrigo did too. In those last seconds before he died, I'm sure he did not blame you. He knew the dangers of the life he had chosen."

She reached out and pressed something into Mark's hand. He looked down and saw that it was a snapshot taken of Salazar many years before. The boy in the picture was smiling at the camera, confident of his future and unencumbered by mistakes from the past.

"This is Rodrigo when I first knew him," Britta said. "This is how I will remember him."

Mark stared at the picture, afraid he might not be able to control his emotions. "This is how I will remember him, too." He cleared his throat before asking, "Does Solana know yet?"

Britta shook her head. "No, I will tell her tonight."

"They had gotten as close as the peculiar circumstances would allow," Mark told her.

Britta acknowledged this with an inclination of her head. "She always wanted to know him, and I'm glad she got her chance. My only regret is that now Solana will have to grieve for him as well."

"In the end, after the pain has faded, I think she'll feel that knowing him was worth the pain of losing him," Mark said. He hoped that eventually he would feel the same.

He took Kate's hand in his. "I wish you and Miracle could have known him."

Kate smiled, but Miracle shook her head. "Don't ask me to have any sympathy for Salazar."

"Miracle," he tried to stop her, but she wouldn't be deterred.

"I can't feel sorry for a man living in a multimillion dollar compound with servants and a private army when there's babies starving in the streets of Chicago because their mama is too strung out on drugs to feed them—not that she has anything to feed them with anyway, because she spent all her money, sold everything she had, including her own body, to pay for drugs. In fact, half the time she doesn't remember they even exist. Drugs steal everything from a person—their dignity, their sense of responsibility, their soul."

"You didn't know him," Mark tried.

"It doesn't matter," Miracle reiterated. "So he was a charming guy. So he was your friend. He was a drug importer, Mark. That one bad thing cancels out all the good."

Britta nodded. "What she says is true. I told you—Rodrigo's danger came from his ability to erase the lines between right and wrong. That is why I couldn't go back to him. I knew I wouldn't be able to resist him."

Mark sighed. "You're right, Miracle. There can be no compromise where drugs are concerned. But in spite of everything, he was my friend, and I'll miss him." He stood and pulled Kate gently to her feet. "Now let's go. I've had enough of this place to last me for a long time."

* * *

Solana was hovering over Emilio's hospital bed when he finally opened his eyes.

"You're awake," she whispered.

"Are we in Stockholm?" he wanted to know.

She laughed. "No, we're in Miami, and you've just had surgery to repair the hole Vargas cut in your chest."

The arm that didn't have an IV tube strapped to it came up and caught her around the waist. He pressed her to him in an amazingly strong embrace for a man who was just coming out of general anesthesia. "Where is Vargas?"

"Dead," she assured him. "We're safe. My mother is flying down tonight, and we'll go to Sweden as soon as you're well enough to travel."

He closed his eyes and smiled. "For our honeymoon."

She snuggled against him, careful not to disturb any of the bandaging that covered his wound. "Yes, but in the meantime there is something I need you to teach me."

Emilio lifted his eyelids. "This time I will be teaching you?"

"Yes," she acknowledged. "It is about prayer. I am willing to accept the possibility that there is a God and that he does listen to those who pray. I have felt that over the past few days. But I'm not sure how to pray. And if I am going to pray, I want to do it right."

He smiled. "So you want prayer lessons?"

"Yes. By the time you leave this hospital, I plan to be an expert prayer giver."

His hand reached up and stroked her hair. "I have a feeling you're going to be a natural."

* * *

That night after a nice dinner in the hotel restaurant, Kate and Mark put their children to bed. Then Mark suggested that they go down to the indoor pool.

Kate shook her head. "I didn't bring a swimsuit."

He smiled. "I don't want to go swimming. I just thought it would be nice to sit by the pool for a while and visit."

"Okay." She stood and crossed to the door that connected their room with the one that Miss Eugenia and Miracle were sharing. "Let me see if we can round up some babysitters."

Miss Eugenia and Miracle were both talking to their gentleman friends, but both agreed to keep an ear out for the children. Mark opened the door and led the way down the hall and into the elevator. He took Kate's hand and pressed her fingers gently.

Once they were settled beside the empty pool, Kate said, "So, what was it you wanted to talk about without the risk that the kids might overhear?"

"You know me too well."

She nodded. "I do."

"I guess I just wanted to be sure you were okay about Tony."

She considered this for a few seconds. "I'm sad," she admitted. "It was kind of nice thinking that he was around for those few days. Not that I'd rather have him than you," she was quick to assure him, and Mark gave her a grateful smile. "But I was looking forward to the chance to talk to him and tell him all about Emily. I think he would be really proud of her."

"Anyone would be proud of Emily."

Kate raised Mark's fingers to her lips. "True. Do you think my dreams were really visits from Tony?"

She watched as Mark thought about this for a few seconds. Then he said, "In the scriptures, dreams are used sometimes to get messages from one side of the veil to the other."

"Is that a yes?"

He nodded. "It's a definite maybe. I'm sure Tony still cares about you and Emily. I believe that he is mindful of you and would help you if he could. I guess what I find interesting, and even kind of touching, about your dream is that it indicates that Tony may care about me as well."

"I hadn't thought of it that way," she whispered.

"Maybe he's only concerned about me because I'm the guardian of the women he loves." Mark smiled at her. "But for whatever reason, I appreciate the help."

Kate wiped at the tears that slipped onto her cheeks. "Me too."

They sat in silence for a few minutes. Then she asked, "So, how do you feel about this vacation the FBI is forcing us to go on?"

He tucked her fingers around his hand and pressed it against his chin. "Basically good. It will be nice to spend some time with the kids and to see my parents."

"And if the FBI does extend the length of time you have to be off, I figure we can go on up to Utah and visit my mother and sisters for a while. It would be nice to spend Thanksgiving with them. Maybe it will even snow." Kate's face glowed with excitement. "The kids would love that."

"You'd better not share those plans with Miss Eugenia," Mark warned. "If she finds out there's even a chance we'll be gone during a major holiday, she'll stow away in the back of the van."

* * *

Early the next morning, the Iversons and Eugenia said good-bye to Miracle and returned to Haggerty. A few tenacious news reporters were camped out on the Iversons' lawn when they arrived, and Eugenia offered to keep them busy while Kate and Mark went inside to prepare for their trip to Texas.

Whit's Lexus pulled up just as the Iversons were climbing into their fully loaded van an hour later. He stood on the edge of the driveway and held Lady so that Eugenia would have both hands free to hug and kiss the children. Once all the good-byes had been said, she joined him and reclaimed her dog. She waved bravely until the van was out of sight. Then she allowed the tears to fall.

Lady whimpered and licked at Eugenia's cheeks. "It's okay, girl," she told the little dog. "I'm just an old sissy."

"How long are they going to be gone?" Whit asked.

"Supposedly a couple of weeks," Eugenia told him. "But I heard Emily say that after they got through visiting their grandparents in Texas, they might go to Utah for Thanksgiving. So they could be gone long enough to learn to do without me or even to forget me entirely."

"No one who's known you could ever completely forget you," Whit said gallantly.

Eugenia wiped at the tears that just wouldn't stop falling. "They might even like it out West and decide to move there permanently," she voiced as her worst fear. "Mark's not very happy at work, and it probably wouldn't take much to convince him to relocate."

Apparently Whit couldn't think of an encouraging comment on the topic because he remained silent.

"I thought my heart had broken when Charles died, but now I realize that there are still plenty of soft spots left."

"They'll come back, Eugenia."

She sniffled. "I hope so."

"What are your plans for the evening?"

"Oh, I thought I would get out the picture album Kate gave me for my birthday. It's full of photographs of Emily and Charles. I'll look at them and remember all the good times we've had together and cry until I dehydrate."

Whit chuckled. Then he asked, "Would you like me to look at the pictures with you?"

Eugenia nuzzled Lady's wiry coat. "I can't promise that I'll be very good company."

"You're good company under any circumstances, and you'll need someone to hand you fresh tissues."

Eugenia laughed. "Well, in that case, you're more than welcome."

EPILOGUE

Solana was sitting on the couch in front of the fireplace, staring at the flames, when Emilio found her.

"Well," he said as he sat down beside her. "We have been in Stockholm for a month, and I am basically healed up. I know the FBI said for us to take our time, but soon I need to contact them and find out what my options are for a new assignment."

"We will have to go to America?"

He pushed the silky hair from her face. "There may be some European assignments available. That is what I've got to find out."

"And must you continue to be an FBI agent?"

"I've signed a contract with them," he said gently. "So for a few more years, yes. But after that, if you are unhappy, I will look at other jobs."

"It doesn't really matter where we live, as long as we are together," she said. "I would like to finish my education, but I can do that anywhere."

"A girl as smart as you, we will have to search the world over to find a university that has something to teach you."

She laughed. "That is true."

He patted her cheek. "You're still grieving for your father."

She turned slightly and pressed her lips into his palm. "Yes. I can't believe that he is really gone—that I will never see his face again."

"I'm sorry."

"What haunts me most is something my mother said when she told me he had died. She said that my father made wrong choices and that nothing good can come from something bad." Solana looked up at him, tears glittering in her eyes. "But I am going to prove that something good *can* come from my father." She took Emilio's hand and pressed it to her heart. "I am going to be that something good."

He smiled at her. "You already are."

HAGGERTY HOSPITALITY

CHICKEN ENCHILADAS

10 flour tortillas
16 oz. sour cream
1/2 teaspoon chili powder
1 can diced green chilies
2 cans cream of chicken soup
2 chicken breasts (boiled and shredded)
2 cups cheddar cheese (shredded)

Preheat oven to 300°F. Lightly grease a casserole dish. Mix half the sour cream, 1 can of soup, chilies, chili powder, and chicken in a bowl. Divide chicken mixture between the flour tortillas; roll and put them in the casserole dish. Mix remaining sour cream with other can of soup and pour over enchiladas. Top with cheese. Cover with foil. Bake for 30 minutes.

BEEF ENCHILADAS

10 flour tortillas
2 lbs. lean ground beef, cooked and drained
1 package taco seasoning
1 small container of salsa or picante sauce
1 large can of enchilada sauce
1 can refried beans
2 cups cheddar cheese (shredded)
1 cup sour cream for garnish (optional)

Preheat oven to 300ºF. Lightly grease a casserole dish. Mix ground beef with taco seasoning and salsa. Spread a thin layer of refried beans on each flour tortilla. Divide beef mixture between the tortillas and roll. Place rolled tortillas in the casserole dish and cover with enchilada sauce and cheese. Cover with foil and bake for 30 minutes.

LAYERED MEXICAN DIP

Large bag of tortilla chips
16-oz. carton of sour cream
1 package of taco seasoning
Small container of picante sauce
Refried beans
Medium pitted black olives
2 cups cheddar cheese (shredded)

Use a large, round plate. Spread refried beans on the plate as the bottom layer. Mix taco seasoning into the sour cream and spread this as the second layer. Use the picante sauce as the third layer. The cheese is the next layer. Slice the olives and sprinkle for the final layer. Serve immediately with tortilla chips.

BEEFY NACHOS

2 lbs. Velveeta cheese
1 lb. lean ground beef, cooked and drained (rinsed)
2 cans diced Ro-Tel tomatoes/chilies
2 Tbsp Worcestershire sauce
1–2 tsp chili powder (depending on how hot you like it)
Large bag of tortilla chips

Combine cooked meat, Ro-Tel tomatoes/chilies, Worcestershire sauce, and chili powder in a large skillet over low to medium heat. Add cubed Velveeta and stir until melted. Serve immediately.

HIPOLITA'S CHICKEN CASSEROLE

1 box Rice-a-Roni Spanish rice (prepared according to package directions, excluding can of tomatoes)
4 chicken breasts, boiled and chopped
1 can cream of chicken soup
1 can Ro-Tel tomatoes
1 can cream of mushroom soup
8 oz. carton of sour cream
2 cups cheddar cheese (grated)
2 cups Nacho Cheese Doritos (crushed)

Lightly grease casserole dish. Prepare rice according to package directions (excluding can of tomatoes). Put rice in the bottom of casserole dish. Heat soups and Ro-Tel tomatoes in a medium-sized saucepan. Sprinkle a layer of crushed Doritos on top of rice. Spread chicken out on top of Doritos. Put remaining Doritos on top of chicken. Pour soup mixture over chicken and Doritos. Top with cheese and cover with foil. Refrigerate for 2 hours. Bake at 350°F for 30 minutes (or until warmed all the way through).

MISS POLLY'S BREAKFAST SAUSAGE BALLS

1 1/2 cups grated cheddar cheese
1 pound Jimmy Dean regular sausage (mild)
2 cups Bisquick
1/8 tsp chili powder
Dash of garlic salt

Bring all ingredients to room temperature. Preheat oven to 350°F. Combine ingredients and shape into 1-inch-round balls. Place on a cookie sheet and bake for 18 minutes. Can be frozen before or after baking. (If you prefer things spicy, you can change to sharp cheddar and hot sausage).

PECAN PIE

3 eggs, slightly beaten
1 cup sugar
1 cup Karo Light corn syrup
2 Tbsp butter, melted
1 tsp vanilla
1 1/4 cups pecan halves
1 (9-inch) unbaked or frozen deep-dish pie crust
Pinch of salt

Preheat oven to 350°F. In medium bowl, beat eggs slightly with fork. Add sugar, Karo syrup, butter, vanilla, and salt; stir until blended. Stir in pecans. Pour into pie crust. Bake for 50 minutes. Cool completely before serving.

ABOUT THE AUTHOR

BETSY BRANNON GREEN currently lives in Bessemer, Alabama, which is a suburb of Birmingham. She has been married to her husband, Butch, for twenty-five years, and they have eight children. She loves to read—when she can find the time—and watch sporting events—if they involve her children. She is the Young Women president in the Bessemer Ward. Although born in Salt Lake City, Betsy has spent most of her life in the South, and her writing has been strongly influenced by the Southern hospitality she has experienced there. Her first book, *Hearts in Hiding,* was published in 2001, followed by *Never Look Back* (2002), *Until Proven Guilty* (2002), *Don't Close Your Eyes* (2003), *Above Suspicion* (2003), *Foul Play* (2004), *Silenced* (2004), *Copycat* (2005), *Poison* (2005).

If you would like to be updated on Betsy's newest releases or correspond with her, please send an e-mail to info@covenant-lds.com, or visit her website at http://betsybrannongreen.net. You may also write to her in care of Covenant Communications, P.O. Box 416, American Fork, UT 84003-0416.